Cassandra
NYWENING

Hidden Grace Trilogy - Book Three

THE
MIRROR
A Novel

THE MIRROR
Copyright © 2014 by Cassandra Nywening

All rights reserved. Neither this publication nor any part of this publication may be reproduced or transmitted in any form or by any means, electronic or mechanical, including photocopying, recording or any information storage and retrieval system, without permission in writing from the author.

This is a work of fiction. Names, characters, places and incidents either are the product of the author's imagination or are used fictitiously, and any resemblance to actual persons, living or dead, businesses, companies, events, or locales is entirely coincidental.

Scripture taken from the HOLY BIBLE, NEW INTERNATIONAL VERSION®. Copyright © 1973, 1978, 1984 International Bible Society. Used by permission of Zondervan. All rights reserved.

Printed in Canada

ISBN: 978-1-4866-0186-8

Word Alive Press
131 Cordite Road, Winnipeg, MB R3W 1S1
www.wordalivepress.ca

WORD ALIVE PRESS

FSC MIX Paper from responsible sources FSC® C016245

Library and Archives Canada Cataloguing in Publication

Nywening, Cassandra, author
    The mirror / Cassandra Nywening.

(Hidden grace)
Issued in print and electronic formats.
ISBN 978-1-4866-0186-8 (pbk.).--ISBN 978-1-4866-0187-5 (pdf).--
ISBN 978-1-4866-0188-2 (html).--ISBN 978-1-4866-0189-9 (epub)

    I. Title. II. Series: Nywening, Cassandra. Hidden grace trilogy.

PS8627.Y93M57 2014   C813'.6   C2014-900010-3
    C2014-900011-1

This book is dedicated in memory of Anna Roffel (2011-2012) whose life was lived in testimony to God's ability to heal the most broken heart.

> He heals the brokenhearted
> and binds up their wounds.
> Psalm 147:3

ACKNOWLEDGEMENTS

It has been a long journey from The Mask to The Mirror, and I would like to take some time to thank all those who have helped me along the way. First of all I would like to thank Jake Hogeterp, who has done endless amounts of editing to help make all three books into the works they are today. I would also like to thanks my parents who have provided both financial and moral support along with my wonderful husband Nathan, who has been a constant support and encourager through the entire writing and publishing process. The Mirror would not be here today were it not for the entire team at Word Alive Press, who have so expertly guided me through the publishing process and I would like to thank them for all the hard work they have done. Finally, to everyone who has helped and encouraged me over the past few years, thank you. I could never have done it without all your love and support.

PROLOGUE

THE LAST SWALLOW OF WHISKEY burned a warm path down to Caman's toes as he threw away the empty bottle and looked around the deserted street. She was late, and there was nothing Caman hated more than waiting for a woman to show up. With a small grunt of frustration he began to pace, debating whether he should leave, but the sweet temptation of a night lost in the arms of a woman kept him there, waiting, tapping his foot impatiently.

He had almost turned around when a slight form stepped out into the streets, and a smile once more lighted upon his lips. "My lady," he murmured as the woman drew closer. He could not recall her name.

She smiled tentatively at him. It was obvious this was her first time breaking the rules, and she wasn't sure yet if she wanted to.

Leaning forward, Caman whispered a few sweet nothings in her ear that ended in a long, lingering kiss.

She giggled as she pulled away. "Oh, it's so cold."

Caman pulled her close once more, denying her the chance to think of what she was about to do. "I know a place where we'll be nice and warm," he said as he gently pulled her behind him into the next street. Kissing her brazenly once more under the moonlight, he suddenly stopped.

Deep-seated anger roiled in his belly as another woman stepped out into the street in front of him. Rose Wooden, dressed only in a pair of unmentionables with a sword at her hip, glowered at him with as much hatred as he felt for her, but this time there was no James Hyden to protect her.

Caman's lady friend suddenly gasped and tried to hide behind him when she realized who stood before them, but Caman was not so easily dissuaded.

"Rose! How nice of you to join us. I see you are dressed appropriately for the occasion. Would you like me to take you for a dally in the woods?" He let his eyes rove over her. If she hadn't had such a haughty air, she would have been quite attractive. He could understand why Mr. Hyden was so possessive of her.

"Go home, Miss Cummings"—ah yes, that was the young lady's name—"while you still have the chance to keep your virtue. I tell you, this man does not have good intentions. You will only find yourself hurt."

Caman smirked. So Miss Wooden wished to save the virtue of Miss Cummings. How ironic considering the rumours that were so rampant about Miss Wooden's virtue, or rather, the lack of it.

"I will not go. You must go. I am going to spend the night with my love." Miss Cummings stroked Caman's cheek as she stood up to Miss

The Mirror

Wooden. Caman smiled sickly and wished very much that his night had not been so rudely interrupted.

Rose drew her sword, and Caman had to fight back the laugh that arose at the ridiculousness of the night's events. What was Miss Wooden doing with a sword, and did she really think it would protect her against a trained soldier like himself?

"Did you not hear your lover's words? Go. Leave us before it is too late for you. If you do not leave, you will force me to talk to the curate about your nightly excursions, and he will not be as forgiving as I."

Miss Wooden's words seemed to hit their mark as a look of horror crossed Miss Cumming's face and she scurried away into the night.

"That was a nice touch with the sword," said Caman as he watched Miss Cummings disappear. "Do you always carry it around on late night excursions? I must admit, it did a very good job of scaring off the competition."

With a startled flinch, Caman stepped back when Rose's blade rested on his throat.

"This is not a play toy, Mr. Caman. You are a military man and known to carry a weapon. I suggest you draw it now to fight for your honour, or I will cut you down where you stand."

Anger, like a steel fist squeezing his heart, caused him to retaliate in a way he thought would cause the most pain. "Come, Rose. Do you always make men go through this process before they can sleep with you?"

With a fury that put Caman on guard, Rose attacked. If Caman had not been trained, she would have ended his life right then and there, but he dodged her sword and was able to unsheathe his own weapon before she backed off.

"Are you ready to fight now, Caman, or do you wish to make more remarks that will only serve to sign your death warrant?"

Ready to do away with the pest that Rose Wooden had become to him, Caman took the ready pose and prepared to fight.

He had thought to disarm her quickly and send her on her way into her lover James Hyden's arms. But Rose was no fool with a blade, and Caman found himself trying desperately to keep his sword in hand and his feet under him. But, too late. His sword flew from him, and he found himself on the cold packed dirt of the street, Rose's weapon at his throat.

"Give me one reason not to kill you, and maybe I'll spare your life," Rose snarled.

For a moment, Caman thought this was the end. Rose would kill him, and the inhabitants of Emriville would find his body in the streets in the morning. Perhaps Miss Cummings would cry for him. Perhaps she would even get up the nerve to tell someone who had killed him. And, suddenly the solution to Caman's predicament came to him. "Is that all you can do? Then do your worst. Take my life if you wish, but remember yours also will be forfeit to a hangman's noose."

He watched his words hit their mark, saw the look of frustration, the options whirling through Rose's mind. Then, the hint of an idea lit her face, and her sword traveled from his neck to a very important area of his midsection.

"You may not value your life, but there is one other thing I could take from you that is sure to be missed."

The Mirror

Caman gulped at the triumphant gleam in her eyes. There was no way out of this one, none whatsoever. "What do you want from me?" he pleaded.

"I would have you leave town and never return. I wish never to lay eyes on you again, or hear the gossip of your ill deeds. I wish to never see a woman mistreated by you ever again."

He wished to call her all sorts of names, to tell her she was being unreasonable, but instead he said, "Am I to be a bandit, then? Am I never to have a home, for fear that you will come to town, and I will again be forced to leave? Am I never to see my family here again?"

She seemed to consider his words. "I will allow you to come back on one condition. You must first prove yourself worthy. If you ever present to me a wife that you love and cherish and who loves and cherishes you, I will lift this ban from you, and I will no longer terrorize you if you come into my presence. Do you understand these terms?"

Caman let out a heavy groan. This woman did not know what she asked. She did not know the terrors or the heartache of his past. She could not understand that she was demanding the impossible.

"Yes, I do understand these terms," Caman replied when Rose seemed to be growing impatient. "But I fear that they damn me to life as a nomad, for what you demand is impossible."

"If you believe thus, then you are damned, and I wish you good luck. But if you change your ways, perhaps there is still a chance for you, nomad or not."

Caman scrambled to his feet and sheathed his sword.

"Now go. I give you till morning to be gone from this place."

Staring at Rose, Caman couldn't decide if his feelings toward her were more akin to anger or respect. Bowing, he made up his mind. "My lady," he said, then disappeared into the night.

ONE

Rose sighed as the carriage pulled up to the palace. It had been a long journey. She had heard that travelling with children was difficult, but travelling with two infants was nearly impossible. Her husband Henry helped her down from the carriage, and Elizabeth, her current nursery maid, handed down the twins.

Taking a deep breath, Rose grasped her children and allowed her husband to direct her up the steps. Servants lined the hall, many trying to stand at strict attention while also trying to catch a glimpse of the young royalty. Only one was brave enough to step forward.

"Your highnesses," murmured the man as he came out of a deep bow.

"Good to see you, Samuel. I am sure that things are as well as they were when we last corresponded?" the king asked the willowy butler.

Samuel let his strict composure diminish ever so slightly with a disgruntled little huff. "As well as can be expected, though Mrs. Penling is in a fit again about the state of her kitchen. She is certain that someone is purposefully rearranging her stores, but perhaps it is just Leah again misplacing the salt. I am sure it is nothing to worry about, but I will be sure to properly look into it."

"Yes," said Rose as Elizabeth stepped forward to help her with the twins. "Mrs. Penling and Leah do seem to have their disagreements. Let me know if things start to get out of hand. It may be time for us to hire another kitchen maid."

"Is that all then, Samuel?" Henry asked.

"Yes, Your Highness, everything else is as it should be."

"Very well. Thank you for your diligence, Samuel. I am sure you and the rest of the staff have much to do, so please carry on."

The servants swiftly departed to go about their tasks as the Queen Mother and King Father glided into the large entrance hall.

"Where are my darling angels?" demanded the lady.

"Mother, Rose and I are a little old to be called darling angels, don't you think?" Henry teased.

"You were never an angel, dear boy, though Rose has always been one. Now, where are my grandchildren?"

Rose beckoned Elizabeth forward. "Let me introduce you to Rosalie and James, as well as Elizabeth. She is Shoals' daughter and a marvellous help."

Picking up her young grandson, the Queen Mother sighed contentedly. "It is a pleasure to meet you, Elizabeth. If I hadn't already been told that you are Shoals' daughter, I would have guessed it. You look very much like him."

The Mirror

Elizabeth shied away from the older woman and held out Rosalie to the Queen Mother, who happily took her granddaughter. "If you don't mind, Your Highness, my father would like to show me my new home, and John has asked that I allow him to show me around Silidon."

"That would be wonderful, Elizabeth," Rose said. "If you will come back in the morning, I will show you around the palace. Don't feel rushed, though. Take your time to adjust."

"Thank you, Your Highness." Elizabeth curtsied and, taking her father's arm, they left together.

"Was that John Borden she mentioned?" asked the Queen Mother.

Rose smirked at the woman's insinuation, but didn't respond to it. "Let's get the men, and then you can show me to the nursery. I don't know how long we will be delayed if they get onto matters of state."

Taking the lead, the Queen Mother took her husband's arm with her free hand and began to pull him away from his conversation with their son. Rose smiled at Henry and took his arm. They turned to walk down the hall toward the nursery.

They had just about left the room when the front entrance burst open. Rose gasped as Henry quickly pulled her behind him and drew his sword.

A man stood before them, hair tangled and clothes muddied. His eyes had a wild, desperate look. Rose hardly had time to acknowledge this as two guards jumped through the door and tackled him before he could take another step.

"Your Majesties," gasped the one guard as the two of them struggled to restrain the man. "Terribly sorry. He managed to charge through the gate. But we've got him. It won't happen again."

Henry stepped forward and placed his sword at the man's throat, and he immediately quit his struggling. "Many men have tried to harm me and my family. All have been caught, and all have been severely punished. Did you think your brazen attempt would work?"

The man knelt cowering beneath Henry's sword point. "I meant no harm. I only wished to speak to the queen." The small crowd watching gasped at the man's words.

"You should have come to court with your petition, and waited with everyone else. As it is, you will now wait in prison. Take him away, gentlemen. Tell me when you discover more about this man."

"Wait, wait!" cried the man as the guards began to pull him away. "James Hyden…James Hyden once told me that if I knew who he was I would regret my actions. Well I do, I do regret my actions. Please. Please. I need your help."

"Stop," Henry called, and the guards obeyed, warily holding the man back.

"What is your name?" queried the king.

"Jeremy Caman, sir. I was in the army, and I returned to Emriville when you were there as James Hyden. Please, I need your help."

Rose stepped forward and stretched out a trembling hand to her husband. "I remember him," she told him softly. "I remember his name, and I remember his face."

"Very well," Henry said as he looked at his wife's pale expression. "Take him to the prison to wait while I make my decision."

The Mirror

Caman paced around the small confines of his prison cell. He wondered if the king had made his decision. He wondered if he would be left to rot in this prison until he died. Such hopeless thoughts had been haunting him all day and had kept him awake the past night as he lay on the thin sheet offered to him by the prison guard.

"What were you thinking, Caman, what were you thinking," he muttered to himself. "Did you really think you could save Sarah by charging into the royal palace and demanding they help you? You fool, you were better off waiting to see the king like every other person does."

His guard appeared and slid a bowl of stew through a small opening in the bars. Caman looked at the meagre contents of the bowl and sighed. Army rations were better than what they afforded you in prison. He pictured all the wonderful meals Sarah had made for him as he wondered how long he could survive on these scanty dinners.

His stomach groaned with hunger, and Caman hastily finished his stew before it became indelibly cold. Laying aside the bowl, he sat on his blanket, and he waited.

───※───

"I don't like this, Rose," said Henry, breaking the silence in the parlour. "Caman never was any good. And we can't be sure that he has changed."

"Neither can we be sure that he hasn't changed," Rose replied as she set down her tea. The debate had been going on all day. What was to be done with the infamous Jeremy Caman?

"But why would he need to speak to you? Why to you and not to me? I would have an easier time with this if he had asked to speak with me alone. I could hear him out and then send him on his way, resting in the knowledge that I had at least given him the chance of an audience."

"But he didn't ask to speak to you, Henry. He asked to speak with me. Likely because of the time we duelled and I sent him from Emriville."

"I remember him from Emriville. I remember how he hurt you with his remarks at the ball," Henry said, a frown creasing his brow. "What if he only seeks to hurt you again?"

"What if he really does need our help?" It was the looming question that made the situation seem so impossible.

"Yes, what if he really needs our help?"

There was silence as both Henry and Rose sipped their tea. "Fine," Henry said as he placed his cup down a little more forcefully than necessary, "he can have an audience, but I want Shoals and Jasper present. And, I want you to be carrying a weapon. Something small, that can be concealed but easily managed if you need to defend yourself."

"Very well, love." Rose got to her feet and crossed the room to where her husband sat. Leaning forward, she placed a kiss on his brow. "I will arrange everything. Will this evening work well for you?"

"I will make it work," Henry replied, his eyes closed, as he leaned against the back of his chair. "The sooner this problem with Caman is dealt with the happier I'll be."

The small parlour bristled with tension as Caman was led by his guard to speak before the queen. Bowing low before his monarchs, he dared not rise until the queen spoke, for fear he would lose his opportunity if he in any way offended her.

The Mirror

"Please sit, Caman," Queen Rose stated, her voice fraught with anger Caman supposed he deserved.

Rising slowly to his feet, Caman fumbled his way toward the nearest seat, keeping his head bowed.

"Jeremy Caman, in a rash act, you have endangered the life of the queen, the prince, and the princess." Caman listened as the king spoke to him, wondering what punishment he was about to receive. "Such crimes are treated with the utmost severity and often punishable by hanging. As it is, the queen has persuaded me to be merciful. You are therefore given this opportunity to speak before the queen as you requested. But be warned, one false move and your life will be forfeit."

"Yes, Your Highness," Caman replied. "I understand."

"Good, now how about you tell us what is so urgent that you could not wait to gain an audience with the queen through the court."

Caman felt stunned, and the words he longed to speak seemed to abandon him. He looked up at the king, his mouth opening and closing wordlessly.

"Well," stated the queen, tapping her toe slightly impatiently.

"I—I have come from Owzan," Caman began. "I have been there close to a year now, living with the curate. And I fell in love with a woman, but she ran away."

"I am not here to help you with your love life, Mr. Caman," stated the queen sharply. "If I recall correctly, you never seemed to need any help in that area before."

"You don't understand. Sarah ran away to Croden, to her home town, but I believe she is in great danger there because everyone in Croden believes her dead."

There was a pause as if the king and queen were not sure what to say. Caman was not sure how to take their silence, so he continued to explain. "Sarah ran away to Owzan twelve years ago after she was brutally attacked by a member of her community. She's been working at the inn the entire time, but she decided to go back to Croden to see if she could make her peace with…with—well, with everyone, I guess. But Stuart Morgan—that's the curate of Owzan—he has records from Croden showing that a Sarah Livton died there a little over twelve years ago."

Again there was silence and again Caman filled it with more words. "I can't help but feel that when Sarah shows up in Croden, the people will not take too kindly to the fact that she is not dead, and I think she may be in very real danger."

"Very well," said the king in a very near whisper. He cleared his throat before he continued. "Colonel Jasper here will accompany you back to your cell, where you will wait until further notice."

Caman bowed to his monarchs as Colonel Jasper came up beside him, and turned to leave, his hopes trailing behind him.

"One more question before you go," the queen called out.

"Yes, Your Highness?"

"Do you happen to know the name of Miss Livton's alleged attacker?"

"Seth Hepton, Your Highness, and a more evil man I've not heard of."

The Mirror

"Is it possible? Could Sarah be alive, Henry?" the queen asked after Caman had left the room.

"If she ran away, I guess there is that possibility." Henry stared darkly at the door. "Seth never saw her die. He left her on the doorstep near death, which means she may have survived."

"But why would the people of Croden believe her dead? Is Caman making this up to cause trouble?"

Henry rubbed a hand roughly across his face. "I would like to think it is a lie, but I can think of no rational reason why Caman would lie about something like this. I don't even think he knows who Seth Hepton is. He was long away from Emriville before the truth came out, and who would have said that Seth Hepton and Caleb Taylor were the same person?"

"So what do we do?" Rose asked.

"Shoals," Henry called, and the knight stepped out of the shadows where he had been waiting patiently for his king's command. "I want you to go to the record keeper. Find out whatever you can about Sarah Livton of Croden. Then look up the same name in reference to Owzan. Look for any deaths about twelve years ago. If you find anything, even the slightest hint that this story might be true, ride immediately to Croden along with two or three of your men. Send a page to keep me informed."

Shoals left the room to go about his task.

"And what are we to do about Caman in the meanwhile?" Rose asked.

"We let him wait. I have Shoals looking into what he has told us, and I see no need to change his accommodations until I am certain he has no nefarious motives."

"And what if we can find nothing to verify his story?"

"He will be punished. Severely."

TWO

CAMAN SAT QUIETLY IN HIS PRISON CELL, watching the guard pace back and forth. "Do you really have nothing better to do than to walk in front of my cell?" Caman asked as the guard passed him by for the sixth time in what seemed like a matter of seconds.

The guard gave him a sideways look and continued his pacing.

Back and forth, back and forth, Caman watched him until he thought he might be sick. Lying back on his small cot, he closed his eyes, but the slight squeak the guard's boots made every time he turned worked like a steady drip of water on Caman's mind until he finally exclaimed, "Oh come now, you must have someone other than me to watch."

The guard stopped his pacing and looked into the cell. Caman could tell that he was young, maybe twenty, but his stance bespoke much military training. Caman waited for the guard to speak, but the boy only looked at him sullenly before he turned away.

"Bother, are you forbidden to speak?"

"No."

Caman, not expecting to get a response, jumped at the voice. Recovering quickly, he responded. "Then tell me, how long do you think I should expect to stay in this prison?"

The guard shrugged. "Two days, a week. Depends on how long it takes the king to make his decision."

"And what will happen to me once the king makes up his mind?"

"Who knows? Most people in this prison end up in the tower or the gallows. It really isn't a true prison. More a holding cell for known criminals. Like last week, we had a man who was caught attempting to murder his wife. He was only in for a day before he was hanged."

"But I've done nothing wrong. I can't be sent to the tower if I've done no wrong."

"People always say that, and it always makes me wonder, if they've done no wrong, how did they end up in here?"

"And I wonder why it's only the prigs and the pretty boys who volunteer for guard duty." The guard's face turned scarlet, and he resumed his pacing.

"Wait," Caman called after his retreating back, but the guard ignored him. "Come back. I'm sorry. I didn't mean what I said." The guard ignored him. With a scowl of frustration, Caman flopped back onto his cot and was once more tormented by the squeaking of the guard's shoes.

Much to his surprise, it was moments later when the guard was standing at his cell once more. Caman jumped to his feet, but his face fell when he saw what the guard held in his hand.

"They gave me your saddlebag and told me to discover what I could about you. Shall we begin to discover?" There was meanness in the guard's eyes that had not been there before. Caman clenched his jaw as the man began to ruffle through his personal items.

"Your clothes are covered in filth," he said as he pulled out a spare shirt. "Didn't your mother ever teach you to wash? Or perhaps she was a piece of dirty scum like you." Caman turned his back on the guard, trying to ignore the sneering words.

"Let's see what else. A journal."

"Don't." Too late, the guard was already flipping through the pages.

"It's empty."

Caman relaxed once more. "May I have that? My curate gave me that journal. He said I should start writing in it. He said it might help me."

The guard looked at Caman suspiciously. Laying the journal down, he said, "If you can reach it, you can have it."

Caman pushed his arm through the bars and reached as far as he could, but the book was just beyond his grasp. The guard laughed as he struggled and continued to rummage through the saddlebag. "Well look here, another journal."

Caman stopped his struggling and watched with horror as the guard opened the journal to the first page. "And this one isn't empty," he said as he began to read aloud the first page. "'I hate you! I hate you! Oh dear God, I hate you! How many will you take? How many of my children must slip from my womb and into your care before you will allow me to cherish one at my bosom? I don't understand.'"

He stopped reading, a perplexing thought furrowing his brow. "I think I will keep this book for now," he said, shifting uncomfortably on the spot. Turning, he haphazardly kicked the empty journal on the floor toward Caman. "Oops. I guess you get your journal after all. Clumsy of me. Though everybody does say I am rather careless. Look, I've just dropped my pencil, and it has rolled right into your cell."

Caman watched the guard, unsure at the change in him. "What's your name?" Caman asked as he collected the pencil and the journal.

"Gustave de Giarden, and I expect no trouble from you."

"But your name," Caman gasped.

Gustave shook his head. "I told you, Jeremy Caman. No trouble." Without any further words, Gustave walked away, the second journal tucked securely under his arm.

Caman stared blankly at the white pages of his own journal. "Well Stuart," he murmured, "you told me to write, so here it is. I will write."

Caman tapped the blank page a few times with his pencil, then began to write.

I guess you could say it started on the night I duelled with Rose Wooden, and she sent me running from the only home town I had ever known...

―※―

I was angry, and I stormed around the house until I woke my mother. She watched me as I packed everything I owned. She didn't ask any questions—just watched. Finally I asked her what she wanted. "Doesn't a mother have a right to know what her son is doing so early in the morning?"

"Isn't it obvious?" I replied. "I'm leaving." She didn't respond. She allowed me to continue to force my clothes into the confines of my rucksack. When I finished, I asked, "Aren't you going to ask why I'm leaving?"

The Mirror

"I have my own guesses. The top one being that you were finally caught by some poor girl's father and now you're running from the matrimonial knot."

"Not exactly," I muttered. "They were a little more persuasive than an angry father."

"How long are you planning on being away?"

"Count on forever."

I walked out the door and didn't turn back. It wouldn't have mattered. My mother wasn't crying. She must have been rejoicing, for I hadn't ever done anything for her but cause trouble. My leaving would bring her peace.

I spent the early morning dragging my sack of possessions down the road out of Emriville. As the sun rose higher in the sky, my anger dissipated and was replaced with shame. I was not ashamed of my treatment of the young lady. My shame was that I was running scared from a little girl. What kind of man runs from a girl? So I turned once more toward Emriville.

My mother was still at the door. She smirked when she saw me. Taking my bag from me, she took it into my room and began to unpack it. I sat in the kitchen eating while she worked.

It wasn't much later when she came into the kitchen with a much smaller sack that I could easily carry over my shoulder. Tossing it at me, she laughed. "You always wanted to take too much with you. This should suit you much better."

"What do you mean?" I asked.

"Well, you said you were going to be gone forever. So I'm just helping you along your way."

I stared at her. My own mother was asking me to leave—forever? "But, what will you do without me?"

She laughed at me again. "Boy, I have been doing just fine without you for most of my life. In fact, you are so much like your father that I do better when you're not around." She patted my cheek. "Now, go out into that great big world and do something worthwhile with your life. I don't want to see you until you've straightened yourself out."

Doubly banished, I picked up the much lighter sack and walked out the door. This time I looked back. My mother waved at me. I didn't wave back. I was angry again.

Life was not easy. All I had ever known was the army and women. Now, I drifted about aimlessly from town to town. I worked enough to provide myself with liquor, women, and food. Two years passed in such a manner, and by the end of that time I had built a reputation for myself in more than a couple of towns as a scallywag and a drunk.

It wasn't until February of this year that anything changed. I had just entered a new town. Owzan. It was cold outside, and I was looking for a place to stay the night. I had very little money left, and I wasn't sure I could afford lodging. But the cold drove me to seek a place of refuge despite my lack of funds.

I entered the inn, which had a blazing fire and was far too crowded for my liking. I sat at the bar where a woman was working, and waited to be served. The woman was less than welcoming in appearance. She had a large scar down her right cheek, and hair pulled back in a severe bun. Her nose was slightly crooked as if it had been broken before, and when she walked, she had a slight limp.

The Mirror

When she finally came toward me, I asked her for a room and a pint. Neither seemed to please her, but she did as I bid her. Taking my money, she placed the beer in front of me and said a man named Billy would show me to my room later. I nodded and began to slurp at my frothing drink.

As the night progressed, she served me more and more of the drink. With each cup she would ask if I wanted a meal, but I always replied in the negative. It had been my habit recently to leave out the meal entirely and just drink. This only gained me her disapproval.

When I had drunk far too much, I asked for another, and she denied me. "You can't do that!" I slurred. "I pay for a drink, and I deserve to get one."

"I have every right to prevent you from getting so intoxicated that you are a nuisance to fellow guests. If you want more to drink, you can spend your time at the saloon two streets over. Besides, I already need to charge you more if you're to cover the cost of your room for the night."

I ignored her comment about money, hoping she wouldn't mention it again until the morning, as I had no more coins. Instead I deferred to her other comments about drinking. "Who am I disturbing?" I looked around drunkenly. "I only see men here, and they all seem to be familiar with drinking."

"They may be, but as a woman, I am quite unfamiliar with it. I therefore cannot permit you to drink anymore under this roof."

I swore and she cringed. "A right ugly woman like you has to be familiar with drinking. Now, give me another beer."

Even though I was drunk, I can still remember the silence that resulted from that last comment. My host went ramrod straight, and in a crisp, forced voice she called for Billy. A burly man came out of the back room where he must have been working in the kitchen. "What is it, Sweet Pea?" he asked.

"Our guest, Mr. Caman, has asked to be escorted to his room. Unfortunately, I think the only space we have free is above the stable." Billy nodded in a manner that did not bode well for me. Taking hold of my arm, he dragged me from the room and up a stairwell. I fought, but the man was strong as an ox and didn't let go.

Finally we arrived at what was to be my room. It smelled of horses and cow manure, and it was bitter cold. There was no bed, only a pile of straw with a couple of blankets. The ceiling was peaked and low. Billy dragged me into the room and I knocked my head on a lower beam.

Billy grunted. "That may hurt come morning." He pushed back his thinning hair and looked at my scrawny figure. "I suppose your head is going to be aching in the morning anyway. Oh well, that was your own darn fault." He pushed back his hair once more. "Don't cause me no more trouble," he said as he left. "Just to be sure, I'll lock the door. Sam will be by in the morning to let you out."

Then he was gone.

I didn't know what to do with myself. My things were still sitting by the bar, if no one had snatched them, and there was no way I was getting out of my new abode. The door was locked, and there were no windows. I wondered if anyone would bother with rescuing me if there was a fire. It wasn't like I would be missed.

Deciding it wasn't worth thinking too much about, I grabbed what few blankets I had and tried to get comfortable on the pile of straw. It wasn't easy. Straw poked into my clothes, and if I moved wrong, it

The Mirror

would cut my skin. But if I didn't move at all, pain would seep into my joints from the cold and the hard floor.

That night was the coldest, longest night I have ever experienced. The temperature dropped drastically, and I shivered trying to keep warm. When morning finally came, I hardly felt alive. My head pounded and my body ached. I shivered spastically. No one came to my aid.

I heard a clock strike far off. It must have come from the lobby where I had drunk that night. At last the door creaked open, and I groaned as the squeal echoed in my head. A little girl peeked her head in and giggled. I groaned and she gasped.

She disappeared again behind the door, which shut with a bang. I reached for a pillow to throw at the wooden monstrosity, but my hand only grasped at straw. The door again opened, and the girl reappeared with a steaming tray.

"Are you alive?" she asked.

My voice was thick and slow to come. "No, I'm dead, and unless you leave me alone now, my ghost will haunt you for the rest of your life."

She giggled again. "I'm more scared of Mom than any ghost. She'd have my hide if I went downstairs without delivering your porridge. She says you may be an unwelcome guest, but a guest nonetheless, and all guests must be fed. Seeing as you were locked in here, I supposed you had an excuse for missing breakfast when it was served."

"Can you quit talking?"

She bit her lip and looked at the porridge bowl. "You must have really angered someone to have gotten this room," she whispered. Apparently the task of not talking was too much of a chore. I took the porridge and didn't respond.

"No one gets this room unless we're packed and it's the middle of the summer. Of course, every now and then Billy puts a drunk man up here. Mom says he should just turn them out, but Billy is too kindhearted. He couldn't turn out the meanest, drunkest man."

"Do you ever quit talking?"

She shook her head. "Mom says I could out talk a chatting chipmunk if ever one existed. I'm not sure exactly what that is supposed to mean. I suppose it means that I shouldn't talk so much, but there is so much to say."

I finished the last of the porridge and, tossing aside the bowl, I fell back on the straw. "Well, you can go back to your mom and tell her you've done your duty. And leave the door unlocked. I need to be finding work today, as I'm broke, but I'm going to let this headache pass first."

The little girl picked up the bowl and stood with her head down. Long blonde braids hung around her face, but she didn't move or speak. "Is there a problem?"

She bit her lip again. "Well, I was supposed to tell you that you must leave once you are done your porridge." She gave me a quick look then rushed on. "You hardly paid for one night, and Billy had to persuade my mom to include your breakfast in that cost, but he also says with the way you behaved last night, it would be better if you found another room two streets over." She went back to looking at the floor.

"Well, you can go tell Billy that if he wants me to leave, he can come and get me. I have more time than that to get out of this room which he never uses anyway, and I am going to get rid of this headache before I leave," I growled. The young girl jumped and turned to run out

The Mirror

of the room. "Tell Billy that I also want my things back if they haven't already been stolen!"

I didn't know if she heard me. My head screamed at me, and I fell onto the straw to get some more of the sleep that I was lacking. I must have been more tired than I thought, because I soon lost consciousness and did not wake until later that night when I was shaken by the same small girl as before.

"What do you want?" I moaned.

"You don't look too good."

I wasn't feeling too well, either. My head still ached, which was odd, for normally the alcohol's effects wore off by evening. I sat up and the room began to spin. "What time is it?"

"Supper time. Since you insisted on staying, Billy said you could have supper downstairs with us, and because it is Sunday, Billy says he will let you have the food out of good Christian charity. I think he is feeling kind of bad for letting you sleep up in this room all night. Especially when rumour has it that last night was the coldest Owzan has seen in nigh on forty years. He says you can have this room as long as you would like because of that, and he will even give you an extra blanket and a pillow."

"How kind of him."

"Mom wanted to throw you out on your ear this morning, but when you were already sleeping when we got back, Billy won the argument."

"What does your father have to say about all this?"

The girl bit her lip. "He doesn't say too much about anything." She was silent. I rubbed my ears to make sure I wasn't going deaf. She laughed at me, and I winced.

"You look like old man Brunus when you do that. He's got so much ear hair that he has to push it out of the way to hear."

I admit that I laughed at the picture created by her words. It is not every day that someone so vividly describes ear hair. "What's your name?"

"Samantha Joy. Sam for short. What's your name?"

"Caman. My name is Mr. Jeremy Caman."

"Are you going to come down for supper, Mr. Caman? It's going to be really good. I made it myself."

I sighed. I really didn't feel like eating, but to say no would insult the girl, and I was beginning to find her presence entertaining. "What are we having?"

"Beef stew except with pork instead of beef because Billy didn't want to kill the cow this year. He said that the pig got to live last year, so the cow gets to live this year. Mom thinks he's a bit loony keeping a cow sitting around like that when it really would make some really good beef. But Billy is too soft and can't stand to kill any of his animals."

"How about you go tell your mom that I will be down for supper, and then I can clean up a little bit before. How does that sound?"

She nodded and sauntered over to the door. "By the way, your sack is over in the corner there, and you might want to wash at the basin I put over beside it. You kind of smell like the cow." She wrinkled her nose at me and left.

I stood up and the entire room went momentarily black. When my head cleared up a bit, I moved toward my sack on unsteady legs. Pulling out a fresh pair of trousers and a shirt, I changed, then turned toward the basin of lukewarm water. It felt good to wash, but still my head throbbed.

I carefully made my way out of the room, aware that if I stood in the wrong places I would knock my head against the low ceiling. I was not exactly sure where I was going, but there weren't many options. I found the stairs down. This led me to a room just outside the dining room.

I again took a seat at the bar, but instead of the ugly woman of the night before, a matronly woman was there to serve me.

"So, little Sam persuaded you to come down for dinner, did she?" the woman asked.

"I suppose you could say that."

"Well, good thing she did. You're too thin and sickly. If you want to pass your days up in that cold attic, then we're going to have to put some meat on your bones."

She placed a bowl of stew in front of me.

"Where's the woman from yesterday?"

"Miss Livton?" her face soured at the name. "She's in the kitchen tonight. She wanted to make sure Sam wasn't going to poison anyone."

I nodded and took a bite of the stew. It had a unique flavour, but was, surprisingly, not bad. Even my stomach, which was tossing and turning, didn't object to it. "This is good."

"I told you it would be," said a voice by my elbow.

"Hello, Sam," I said.

"Hello Mr. Caman. I'm glad you like the stew even though it's made with pork instead of beef. My mom said it wouldn't taste right, but I think it tastes spectacular. Mom always says food that leaves the kitchen always has to be good enough to feed thirty-five hungry men, and if it's not that good then it wasn't worth making."

"Why thirty-five?"

"Because we have around that many hungry men to feed every night. They come out every night. Old man Brunus sits in the corner. Mr. Wyatt sits by the window. Mr. Ryker and Mr. Stimons sit at the bar and argue over their meal. Mr. Lamin sits all by himself in the middle of the room and doesn't talk to anyone. Mr.—"

"Do you know all thirty-five men?" I cut in. She nodded. "Why do they all come here?"

"Because they can't cook for themselves of course, and the preacher would have their hide if they went to the saloon for supper. Most of them are good men, but Billy sometimes sends them home early because they've had too much."

"Don't any women come?"

"What would a woman be doing at an inn for supper? Every woman I know knows how to cook for herself."

"I suppose." I sighed and turned back to the stew.

"Do you want any more of that?"

"No, I don't think so, but I would like you to point out old man Brunus to me. I want to see all this ear hair."

Sam giggled. "Old man Brunus won't be here tonight. It's Sunday, and the preacher says only guests are allowed to have meals at the inn on Sunday, because otherwise we would never get a break. That's why I get to make supper on Sunday nights."

The Mirror

"I think I would like to meet this preacher that seems to dictate what the men of this town do," I muttered, but Sam's quick ears didn't miss it.

"Don't worry, he'll stop by tomorrow. He always visits with the visitors. Especially the ones who get stone drunk and then dare to stay a few days. He'll probably sermonize to you about the evils of drinking and then suggest you get a good job right here in Owzan."

"He sounds like an interesting character. Why doesn't he send the drunkards on their way? And, how do you know so much about drinking when you're only eight years old?"

Sam scrunched up her face and stomped a foot on the ground. "I am eleven, nearly twelve, and I have seen enough drunken men in my lifetime to know all about it. It's not like it's that hard to figure out. Besides, the preacher talks about it an awful lot, and Mom says he has no couth about what he says. I asked Billy what that was supposed to mean, and he says that means the preacher is blunt and doesn't beat around the bush."

"Well, I suppose I better get some sleep if I'm to meet such a man in the morning." I stood to go.

"I'll get your extra blanket and pillow. Do you want me to wake you when the preacher gets here?"

I gave Sam a non-committal nod and headed back toward my room.

THREE

I WOKE TO MUTED THUDDING on my attic room door. Before I could garble a response, the door sprang open and Sam careened into the room. "Hello, Mr. Caman," she said. "The preacher is here, and so I came to wake you."

I groaned and rolled over. "What time is it?"

"Nearly six o'clock," Sam chirped.

I chortled, thinking she must be joking. "No sane person is as happy as you are before six in the morning." My comment met only silence. Turning to see what the matter was, I found the little pixie making a face at me. "What?" I asked.

She shrugged. "I'm up at five every morning with Mom to make breakfast. The preacher comes at five-thirty and after he eats he asks to see the town drunks. He says any drunk will be brought to his senses at six in the morning when his head is still paining him and he has no sense but to listen." Again Sam shrugged. "You aren't drunk, but I figured you would suffice. After all, you were drunk once."

She grabbed my hand and pulled me to my feet. Small in stature though she was, she was also mighty. "Let me get cleaned up before you drag me to the preacher."

Sam nodded. "I'll wait outside the door."

As I washed my face and changed my clothes, I heard her pacing back and forth. Now and then I heard the thumps of her shoes as if she were dancing a bit of a jig or doing a couple of small hop-steps. When I opened the door, she was twirling in a circle, the skirt of her dress swirling around with her. She blushed when she realized I had caught her, but nothing could stop her for long. Taking my hand, she pulled me down the stairs, stopping only once we reached the door leading into the dining room. She peered in, and we both listened.

"Sarah," a strong male voice said, "you should come to church. You don't need to keep hiding in this inn. No one from our community would judge you. Half the church is made up of former drunks. Most whom you have served here."

"There's more to it than that, Stuart, and you know it. There is no need to hash out old history. Besides, I gave up on God a long time ago. If he exists, he obviously doesn't want anything to do with me. If he did, life would be a lot different for me now," replied a soft female alto.

"Come, Sarah, you know the Lord hasn't given up on you, and neither will I. I know you know about God's love. I've heard you reciting scripture like it was engraved on your heart..."

"Don't go there, Stuart," Sarah cut in. "I've decided already. I will live with that decision."

Stuart sighed heavily. "I'll be praying for you." There was a long pause which Sam decided was the perfect time to barge in. Taking my hand once more, she slammed unnecessarily hard into the door so that it banged sharply against the wall. Sarah and Stuart both jumped to see who had intruded.

"Hello, Sam. Who is this that you have brought me?" Stuart asked.

"Hi, Stuart Morgan," Sam chirped. She tugged once more on my hand so that I stepped forward. "Stuart Morgan, this is Mr. Caman. Mr. Caman, this is Mr. Stuart John Morgan, the preacher." I reached out my hand to shake the preacher's. He responded in kind.

Turning toward Sam, Stuart laughed. "Sam, I thought you were bringing me a fierce drunk who needed God's redeeming fire to scour him clean." He looked me over thoroughly, and I began to squirm under his intense stare. "Mr. Caman here looks like he has already been touched by the Almighty's hand."

Sam turned her own critical eyes to me, and like an expert seamstress began to walk around me, measuring me up. "You may be right, but he still needs some work. I would suggest a gentle rebuke and a dose of everyday cleansing. After all, he does have a tendency to drink."

Sarah snorted from where she stood behind the bar. I turned and finally took note of her. She was the woman from my first night at the inn. She looked just as treacherous as on that night, but now I was sober enough to note a hardened look in her eyes and the set of her jaw.

"Sam, go start dishing out porridge for the men. Some of them will be arriving soon. We don't want to keep them waiting," Sarah said.

"Yes, ma'am." Sam disappeared into the kitchen.

"Preacher," Sarah said, "I couldn't care less about the spiritual wellbeing of this man, but if he doesn't start paying for food, I will have to force Billy to send him out. So, if you don't mind, try finding him a job before you save his soul." With her message duly delivered, Sarah left the lounge to follow Sam into the kitchen.

"She's a tough case," I muttered to the preacher.

"But she is loved by God."

I stared mutely at the preacher, uncertain what he meant. I tried to formulate a response, but Stuart spoke first.

"What is your opinion of God, Mr. Caman?"

I shrugged. "I suppose he's out there, but I can't see him being too interested in what I'm doing anymore." I paused a moment, and the preacher waited as if anticipating my next words, egging me on with a severe gaze. "Look, I'll go to church, and I'll stop drinking, and I'll even find decent work while I'm here. What more does God want of me?"

The preacher stared at me, and I began to squirm under his gaze. "Sam was right," he muttered to himself, "a dose of everyday cleaning should do the trick." I cleared my throat to get his attention again. He smiled. "The Lord wants much more than what you suggest, Mr. Caman, but I will accept that for now. As for a job, I have one in mind, but I need to speak with a couple of people. Enjoy your breakfast, and I'll be back later with something confirmed."

I nodded, and the preacher turned and left.

How we had come to the conclusion that we did, I wasn't completely sure. All I knew was that there was no way I was staying long in Owzan. Alcohol was a necessity and if I couldn't drink, I would not survive.

The preacher wasn't lying when he said he had a job for me. I was just finishing my breakfast when he came back into the dining room and beckoned me. I sauntered over to see what he had to say.

"I have a job," he said. "There is only one hitch." He rocked back and forth on his feet, and I wondered what the hitch was that could make him so nervous.

"What is it?" I finally asked when he didn't supply the answer.

"Well, the pay isn't exactly amazing." He hesitated before he continued. "Actually, there is no pay at all, just room and board, but I'm sure you'll be happy to start in about five minutes. I mean, you don't have anything else to do. Now, you go and finish your breakfast, and your boss will show up and tell you what to do."

Stuart Morgan's last words slid from his mouth like a prepared litany, and he was gone before I could object to his plan. I mulled over who my boss could be, and I cringed when Sarah's face came to mind. It wasn't that she was so horrendously ugly, but her cold demeanour was enough to put a damper on anyone's day. Not to mention she had every right to hate me for insulting her so thoroughly in my drunken state.

I took a swig from my mug and about spewed it out when a small hand tugged on my jacket. Swallowing quickly, I turned to find Sam staring up at me. She crossed her arms and tapped her foot. "You're late for work." With her message delivered, she turned and walked away.

The Mirror

I pushed away from the bar and chased after her. She led me to the kitchen. Billy was standing by a large wood stove stoking the fire within. When he was satisfied that the blaze was good and strong, he disappeared outside with a tin pail in hand. Sam turned and rolled her eyes at me. "Are you coming, or do I have to wait all day for you?"

I smirked at her. Falling into a familiar soldier's stance, I saluted her and marched to where she now stood beside a large bucket of sudsy water. "At ease soldier," she said. I slumped my shoulders, and she grinned at my evident willingness to obey.

"Are you my new boss?" I asked.

Sam scowled at me. "Do I look old enough to be your boss? You're practically old enough to be my father!"

I feigned insult. "Who, me? You, my dear, are greatly mistaken. I will have you know that I am still very young. So young, in fact, that I don't plan on becoming a father for at least another three years."

Sam scrunched her nose as if deciding whether to ask a question. Her mind made up, she spoke. "How do you know that you don't have any kids?" I gaped at her, not sure if I should answer that question.

"Um, well Sam, I'm not married, so how can I have a child?" I hoped this answer would suffice, but she didn't seem appeased.

"Mom says that not all kids know their dads and that not all dads know that they have kids. How do you know that you don't have kids? You could, couldn't you?"

"I suppose I could," I answered, the truth of the statement making me uncomfortable. "But, that is something you'll understand better when you're older. So what am I supposed to be doing?"

Sam grabbed my hand and turned me toward the tub of water. "You are washing the dishes." I looked at the stack and cringed. Many of the men had come and left behind their dirty bowls and utensils. There was also a large stack of kitchen implements that needed to be cleaned. "When you're done that," continued Sam, "you can help me in the kitchen for the lunch meal."

"Isn't this the kitchen?"

Sam shook her head. "This is the old kitchen. We built a new kitchen when the men started coming in and Stuart Morgan started getting them to stay. This kitchen wasn't big enough. Billy built it. He does all the fixing around here."

I nodded, wondering how recent the addition was. "Well, I better get going," sighed Sam. "Those noodles aren't going to get in the pan by themselves, and I have to churn more butter. We've almost run out."

She slipped out a side door into what I assumed was the new kitchen. Turning to the stack of dishes, I began to wash. It wasn't long before the water had become tepid and filled with soggy oats. With a frustrated sigh, I dumped the water outside the door and looked around for something to refill the tub. There was a pot of water boiling on the stove. I reached to grab the pot's handle and cursed when it burned my hand.

Slowly the angry red line across my palm blistered and swelled. Clenching my teeth, I grabbed a towel from a rack by the stove and carefully picked up the pot. It only filled the washtub up halfway. I searched for more water but could not find any sitting in the kitchen. With a groan I picked up the dratted pot and went out to find a pump.

The wind blew bitterly and I wished I had grabbed my jacket. Instead of turning back for one, I decided to tough it out. If I could survive

The Mirror

the army, there was no reason I couldn't survive a couple minutes out in the cold searching for a pump.

I caught sight of the spigot sticking out from a snow bank. Icicles dangled from its mouth, and I knew there was no use trying to get water from it. I gave the useless pump a disgusted look and trudged back toward the inn. As I stepped up to the door, I slipped on the sheet of ice which had formed from the dishwater. Cursing again, I wondered why I was going through this torment just for room and board.

Sam had the solution for the water problem. When I finally came limping back into the old kitchen, she was sitting by the washtub, up to her elbows in suds. "Where did you get the water from?" She nodded toward the new kitchen. "You have water in there?" I asked.

She rolled her eyes. "There isn't a river close enough to get water in winter time. We use the snow. Billy gets a couple pails three times a day so that we have enough for dishes and meals."

I felt myself cringing at my own stupidity. In Emriville, it had hardly ever been cold enough to freeze the pumps so thoroughly. Owzan had a much colder climate, and it would only be logical for them to use the snow as a resource for water in the winter.

"I thought I was supposed to meet you in the other kitchen when I finished," I said, avoiding the topic that would only prove my ignorance of basic facts.

"Mom sent me back here, 'cause she says dishes are more important to get done than peeling potatoes because potatoes are for supper, and the dishes are needed for lunch." Sam sighed dramatically. "I said I would help with making lunch, but she said she could handle the soup and that I should just make sure the dishes were done."

Rolling up my sleeves, I bumped her gently aside with my hip and dunked my hands into the hot water. I cringed when the burn on my palm contacted the heat, but I was determined to ignore it. "I'll wash. You dry. The work will get done faster that way."

Sam grinned at me and, grabbing a towel, she began to dry. Slowly, the stacks of dirty dishes were replaced with rows of clean mugs and piles of sparkling bowls. We had just finished the last bowl when Billy bustled in.

He carried a pail of steaming milk and had a pleasant smile on his face. "Hey Billy," Sam chimed. "Do you think I can take care of the milk? I promise I will only drink one cup." She looked at him hopefully. He nodded, and with a whoop of delight, Sam carefully lifted the pail and carried it into the new kitchen.

Slowly Billy removed his coat and hung it from the hook by the door. "She sure is a charmer," he said, his eyes sparkling with evident love. I nodded, understanding the effects the young girl could have on a person.

"She yours?" I asked.

Billy shook his head. "Naw. Martha and I weren't so blessed. We never had one of our own." He sighed. "God blessed us with that little angel, though. I guess he knew we'd be just the place for her." Billy moved to the stove and held his hands up to the heat. With a rumble of contentment, he began to hum.

I looked around trying to find something to do with myself.

"I know you aren't getting paid for your work, but I was hoping you wouldn't mind helping out while you stay in town. We'll pay you what we can when we can, but winter's always a tough time for all the men, and well, that makes it a tough time for all of us." Billy looked at me with apologetic eyes. "I know it ain't normal to go without pay, but we really do need the help, and Martha and I are less of that as we get up in our years."

"What about Sam's mother? Doesn't she help?"

Billy gave me an odd look. "Of course she helps."

"And Sam's father?" I asked.

Billy shook his head with a sad smile. "That man hasn't been in the picture for a while."

"Did he die or something?"

"Something like that." The room fell silent. I waited for clarification, but it seemed Billy wasn't prone to gossip. I don't think he thought it was his place to provide such personal information.

The door from the new kitchen burst open, and I turned to see Sarah trotting into the room. When her eyes fell on me, she stopped and glared. "First you give him a room and now you let him into the kitchen. Billy, what are you thinking? Guests are to stay out of my kitchen. Especially the unwelcome ones."

I expected Billy to blush or at least to cringe at Sarah's harsh words, but he remained unmoved. "Mr. Caman is going to help in the kitchen in order to pay for his room and board. If you have a problem with that, I will see what chores I can find for him outside."

Sarah bristled, but she seemed to know a lost battle when she saw one. "Just make sure he stays out of my way." She left just as briskly as she had come.

To my surprise, Billy cringed as she left. "She really isn't as tough as she makes herself out to be. Underneath she has a heart of gold. Honest truth."

I couldn't make myself believe Billy. There was just no way someone that harsh could have a heart of gold. "Why is she so angry, anyway?"

I had offended Billy with my question. I could tell by the scowl that appeared on his face. He chose not to answer me.

The door peeped open and Sam looked in. "I need the bowls," she whispered. I picked up a stack and thrust them toward her. My good cheer had left, and my headache had returned. Sam looked up at me with wide eyes, and I felt like a cad for being so rough, but I couldn't force myself to apologize. Taking the stack, she scurried back into the kitchen.

"What do you want of me now?" I grumbled.

Billy shrugged. "I suppose you could start cleaning out the rooms."

I wasn't quite sure if I heard him right. Why in the world would I be cleaning the rooms? What rooms would I be cleaning? "Follow me," he said.

We walked out of the old kitchen into the dining room and down a hall. Billy began to whistle a tune. Finally we came to a room, as Billy called it. There were six bunks, two hanging off each wall excepting the wall with the door. There were four drawers under each bottom bunk, and a table with six chairs stood in the middle of the room.

"There are four rooms identical to this," Billy said. "This is where the men board until they move on or until they can build a house for themselves. We clean them because most of them wouldn't know how to. In summer, these rooms are full. Usually by winter they clear out a bit."

The Mirror

I gulped, looking at the room. Blankets hung off the bunks, drawers bulged open. Dust covered the tabletop, and the sheets looked like they hadn't been cleaned in quite some time. "We try to clean everything once a week, but it gets harder in the winter because water is harder to come by." I nodded, not quite comprehending what he was saying.

"Well, if you could just gather the sheets from the four rooms, Sam will show you how to wash them, and then once that is done, she'll help you make the beds up again. Tomorrow you can work on wiping everything down. Sarah will appreciate that. She doesn't like spending much time in the men's rooms. She doesn't trust them."

Billy left me standing there gaping at the room. I took a step into the room and began to strip the first bed of its linens. Oh the many things I had taken for granted when I lived at home. Never again would I look at a clean bed the same way.

That night I lay awake. Sarah had refused to serve me alcohol, citing my promise to Stuart Morgan. Neither did I have money to buy any. I rolled on my side trying to ignore the craving, but it tickled the back of my mind with tantalizing thoughts of a good beer in the belly. Slipping on a pair of shoes and my coat, I left the inn and walked down the street. The saloon was still open. Warm light beckoned from inside, and I was drawn to it. I stepped inside and was embraced by the smell of stale beer and a harlot's perfume.

A group of girls were giggling in the corner, but I knew I wouldn't have any luck with a prostitute. I scouted out the area until I found a girl who just might be desperate enough to fill my need. She was a waitress of sorts. Her dress cut low, and her eyes told the sad tale of a young woman in need of sweet-talking. I sauntered on over. It didn't take long to have her soaking in my compliments and willing to do anything I bid.

In the morning I woke up, and she was gone from my side. Sam's words came back to haunt me. How did I know that I didn't have any kids out there?

FOUR

"YOU'RE LATE!" SAM BELLOWED when I finally entered the inn later that day. I groaned. My head was pounding, and I did not want to be at work, especially if my chores were the same as the day before.

"Sorry," I mumbled to Sam, who was waiting for my response.

"You weren't in your room, and Billy said he didn't know where you were."

I didn't know what she was getting at. Did I have to tell Billy every time I went out?

"I had things to do last night. I ended up staying at another place." Sam gave me a stern look. "It was because I didn't want to wake anyone here," I lied. She scowled.

I grabbed a dish and shoved it into the water. "I don't have to prove myself to you," I muttered under my breath. "You're just a little kid. You don't know what I've been through."

Sam wasn't as chatty that day. She didn't smile, and if I tried to start a conversation she would just shrug. Finally I gave up. It was her fault if we didn't talk. It wasn't like I hadn't tried.

Sam disappeared from my side as soon as possible, but Billy found me not long after. With a look of chagrin, he handed me two baskets of laundry and asked if I could possibly finish them by the evening. Apparently his Martha was ill, and could not finish the wash for the men as she normally did. I cursed at my bad luck. I had done many things in my life, but I had never been so disgraced as to become the "washer woman."

I wondered what Sarah was doing. She was probably laughing at me as she enjoyed herself in the new kitchen. Most likely she was sampling the evening dessert and puttering around doing whatever she pleased. She now had my back to whip. Why not use me until I had the sense to move on, or until she killed me.

I let the fire go out, but I didn't notice until the kitchen was cold. Sarah scolded me when she came in and could see her breath. I'd had enough.

"If you think I am so useless, why don't you do it yourself?" I tossed the shirt I was scrubbing back into the tub of water. "After all, I've been slaving in here all day doing women's work, and what have you been doing? Enjoying yourself, laughing at me?" I sounded like a spoiled selfish brat, but I didn't care.

I expected Sarah to respond in anger, but instead she laughed. The nerve of the woman. "Mr. Caman, you must be the most egotistic male I have ever met." She laughed at me again. "You came here with no money, but acting as if the world owed you everything. You cuss, you whine, and you have no respect whatsoever for women. Yet because of Billy and Sam, I let you stay here. Now, you have the audacity to think I laze around all day." She had a look of bemused humour. "You astound me."

My mouth gaped open and my words spluttered forth. "I will not spend my days washing laundry. I cannot—I will not—degrade myself in such a manner."

"And what, may I ask, is so degrading about washing laundry? Is it because it is dirty? You have washed dishes. Is it because you are not getting paid? You're given room and board. Or, is it because you know of no other man who has washed laundry before?" Her face was fierce. The scar that slashed her cheek was red with rage, and her eyes flared with a brightness that proved she was used to getting her way.

"Women wash the laundry," I said through clenched teeth. "It's the way it always has been and always will be. I will not do it again."

"Very well, I will have Billy do it. He seems less concerned about what others think of him. Funny, you would think he would be more concerned about image seeing as he has an image to maintain. You, on the other hand, I don't think you could have any less self-respect after spending a night in the saloon."

She left me blowing clouds in the cold room. I kicked at the wash bucket but only managed to bruise my foot. I cussed and, leaving the room, slammed the door behind me.

I attempted to leave that night. I was out the door with my bag across my shoulders. The wind was blowing, and snow swirled about my feet as I stepped out onto the road.

"Where are you going?" a quiet voice asked from behind.

I spun to see who had snuck up on me. "What are you doing out here, Sam? It's cold. You should go back in before you get sick."

She nodded as if she understood something more than what I was saying. "It's a mighty cold night. Someone could nigh on freeze to death in this weather. I was just getting back from bringing food over to Mr. Morrison. Mom says he is too old and too sick to be wandering out into this weather. He told me this is the coldest weather Owzan has ever seen, and I believe him. He also says that nobody should be leaving Owzan for the next little while. The closest town being twenty miles away, a feller might freeze as he walks. Unless you've got a horse to take you, you might as well just stay inside."

I smiled at Sam, and hurried her into the inn. Once more I attempted to leave, but her ominous words haunted me. It was bitterly cold, and the next town was a long way. I considered the road ahead of me, and with a sigh of defeat, I headed two streets over to the saloon and the comforting arms of a lonely barmaid.

The week passed, and then it was Sunday. Billy brought me to church, though my head was still banging from the previous night's festivities. I really didn't have the money to drink, but the way my week had been going, there was no way I could survive without a drink. Billy had paid me a little, and now the money was all gone. I would have to stay in Owzan for another week.

The sermon dragged on. I didn't hear much of it, though everyone else seemed fairly attentive. I tried my best not to fall asleep, but it was one of the most difficult things I had ever done.

The Mirror

After the service, Billy abandoned me. I looked around the small meeting room to see if I could leave without him, but his back was turned, and he didn't seem in any rush to tell me what to do. I sighed and slouched toward the door. Billy could find his own way back.

I was almost out the door when a hand on my shoulder stopped me. "I would like to talk with you, Mr. Caman, if you don't mind."

Preacher Morgan.

Remembering my promise, I plastered on a smile. "How are you, Mr. Morgan? Great sermon this morning. It certainly was a crowd-pleaser."

The preacher frowned. "I wouldn't call a sermon on hell a crowd-pleaser, but to each our own, I suppose."

I cringed. "I was referring to people's attentiveness. But you said you needed to talk to me about something?"

Preacher Morgan sighed heavily. "Perhaps you should come to my place for lunch. I think it will be best if we talk about things there."

"What about Billy?" I asked, not wanting to be stranded at the preacher's house for the entire afternoon.

"*What* about Billy?"

"Well, I came with him, don't you think I should return with him? Besides, I am probably needed at the inn. I mean, Martha and Sam and Sarah, they couldn't even come this morning because they were busy. Well, Martha is sick, but still Sarah and Sam are one hand short. I should go back and help them." My rambling wasn't getting me anywhere.

"Sarah and Sam will be just fine. I think it's best that you come over for lunch."

I sighed and consented.

Because he was the preacher, Mr. Morgan could not leave immediately after the service. Instead, he made his rounds from person to person, listening to their joys and concerns. I sat in a corner trying to ignore the odd stares and the occasional cold look. Mothers hugged their daughters when they passed me, and fathers glared as if I had come straight out of the preacher's hell.

I sighed. It wasn't like these churchgoers were any better than me: they had their own sins. I just wasn't so discrete about mine. In fact, I think I even saw one of those men who guarded his wife so thoroughly at church throw himself at a prostitute the night before. So what did it matter if they knew I was a sinner. At least I admitted it. They were just hypocrites.

Finally the preacher beckoned that it was time to go. I put my hat on my head and followed him out of the door. We didn't walk far before we came to a small house. It was slightly dilapidated, the white clapboards muddied from years of wear and lack of fresh paint. Smoke billowed from the chimney, and I couldn't wait to enter into the warmth.

We were met at the door by a tiny woman who must have been Mr. Morgan's wife. She had a mousy face, and was incredibly shy. She took our coats without speaking a word, then disappeared. The preacher led me to a small room that acted as his study, and I took a seat.

"You have to leave the inn," Mr. Morgan said as he sat.

I laughed. "What, this town's kicking me out and I haven't even been here over a month? That was quick. What did I do? Drink too much? Forget to pay a bill? What was it?"

Mr. Morgan cringed. "You didn't do anything, but your reputation precedes you. The town's people are worried about your...philandering."

The Mirror

"So they're kicking me out before I can even prove myself. That's very Christian and hypocritical of them. I guess they're only doing what's best for their families." I stood to leave. "I guess I'd better go pack."

"Sit back down," the preacher demanded. I obeyed. I had been in the army long enough to know a voice that commanded obedience. "I never said the town kicked you out. I just said you had to leave the inn. Meaning you must move out of the inn. There are some general concerns about you living there."

"There are over a dozen other single men at the inn right now. Why isn't the town concerned about them?" I was angry. It wasn't like I was stupid enough to do something to mess up my only living accommodations.

"Yes, but you are the only one who also works there. That, as well as your reputation as a seducer, increases the likelihood of something unsavoury occurring."

"Who could they possibly think I would seduce?" These men just wanted me out of their town. They wanted things to be normal. I represented a threat, and they would not tolerate me. Well, I wasn't leaving.

"They are very concerned for Miss Livton..."

"Miss Livton? They honestly think I would seduce Miss Livton? Well, you can let them know that Miss Livton is unseducable. Even if she weren't, I wouldn't try."

I had done it again. This time the preacher was angry with me. "If you wish to stay in town, you will have to begin to treat women with respect. You may not think much of them now, but maybe if you showed them an ounce of decency you would realize they are more than just washer women and prostitutes."

My face heated at the scolding. "I'm sorry."

The preacher sighed. "No you're not, but that will have to do for now." He pulled some papers from his drawer and began to flip through them. "I am giving a sermon on heaven tonight. It is man's permanent home. Now, I can't promise you that permanency, but if you would like to stay in Owzan, I can allow you to stay with my wife and me. We have a spare bedroom, and the town will stop their talking if you are under my roof."

I cringed at the thought of spending my days in the tiny house with the preacher so near, but I saw no way around it. I had not determined to stay, but I refused to be pushed out by a bunch of hypocritical pew warmers who didn't even know my name.

"If you are going to stay," continued the preacher, "you will have to follow certain rules. After all, you are in the curate's house, and this house is provided by the church." I nodded. "First of all, you will not go back to the saloon. I know you promised that before, but you haven't been very faithful to that promise. You will not seduce any women, and you will remain in the house unless you are at the inn or have told me where you are. Finally, you will attend services every Sunday. Do you agree?"

"Do I have any freedom?" I asked. "I am a grown man after all."

The preacher looked me up and down. "You may be a grown man in stature, but your attitude has been that of a child. When I believe you trustworthy, I will not be so pernickety about your whereabouts."

"Oh boy, I can tell we're going to have lots of fun."

Stuart Morgan roared with laughter. "You may be surprised, but I am sure we will. Yes, I do believe we will."

The Mirror

When I returned to the inn, I found Sam waiting for me in the dining room. She sat with her legs crossed to the side, and her hands folded neatly in her lap. Her age showed more clearly when she sat so demurely. It would only be a few more years, four at the most, before she would be ready to go to her first ball.

She didn't smile when she saw me, but neither did she run away like she had gotten in the habit of doing. "I've decided I am going to talk to you," she said.

"That is nice to know. What made you stop talking to me before?"

She didn't reply.

"Did you decide to stop talking to me again?"

She giggled. "No." Biting her lip, she looked at me as if slightly uncertain of what to say next. "Do you want to help me make the soup for supper?"

I was taken aback. She wanted *me* to help with supper. The most I had cooked was the occasional egg or army ration. To help make soup would imply that I needed to know something about cooking.

Sam rolled her eyes at my blank expression. "It really isn't all that hard. Basically all you have to do is add stuff to a boiling pot of water." I was still hesitant.

Taking my hand, Sam led me to the new kitchen, rambling about her favourite types of soup, and what type of soup we would make that night.

After dinner, I needed to pack. Sam didn't understand, and she followed me up to my room to inquire about my decision.

"Why do you have to pack? Are you leaving us?" She scowled at me.

"I'm going to live over at Curate Morgan's place."

"Why? Don't you want to stay with us at the inn?"

"I do," I said, trying to calm her. She was getting to be hysterical. "I'll be back to work, but the curate thought it would be easier on everyone if I didn't live at the inn."

She calmed. "I guess that will be alright, but you better not be late in the morning." She jumped down from her stool and left the room without another word.

With a sigh, I picked up my sack of clothes. Taking one last look around from the door, I realized what a mess I had left. My blankets were sprawled out across the straw. The pillow that had been given to me was lumped in a ball in the corner. And, what used to be a neat pile of straw was now strewn across the floor.

With a grumble, I walked back and began to clean my mess. When everything was tidied, I retrieved my sack and left without looking back.

Stuart was waiting for me when I finally arrived at the parsonage. He led me to the guest room, then left me to settle in. Looking around, I congratulated myself on the upgrade. Instead of a pile of straw, I was given an actual bed. Instead of two simple sheets and a pillow, I was given a hand-made quilt, multiple sheets, and a feather pillow. Instead of thin walls with cracks that let the wind through, I was enclosed by solid whitewashed walls and a window with curtains. Perhaps it wouldn't be so bad living at the parsonage.

Falling back onto the bed, I delighted in the comfort of such a luxury. It had been some time since I had been able to sleep on a bed. Crawling under the covers and closing my eyes, I decided to take every benefit it had to offer before I had to leave for work in the morning.

FIVE

TWO WEEKS PASSED IN A HAZE of work and sermonizing from Stuart Morgan. So it was with a heavy sigh that I left for work on a Monday morning. Sam greeted me at the inn's front door with a near hysterical hello. I asked her what the fuss was, but she didn't respond. Instead, she pulled me from the dining room down the hall and into the old kitchen. She was so out of breath I had to wait moments longer while she calmed herself before she could tell me her news.

Taking one last deep breath, she was finally able to speak. "We're hosting the town meeting tonight, and that means we have a lot of work to do. Mom says there's probably going to be around seventy people here. Can you believe that? That is more than double the usual, and the boarders aren't even included in that number."

"What do we all need to do?" I asked.

"Everything! We have to make sure everything is in top shape. Mom says the dining room will have to be dusted, the tables rearranged, the fireplace cleaned and the woodpile stocked, the dinner made, the dishes washed, the drinks ready—" I held up my hand to still her tongue.

"Where do we start?"

Sam pointed to a stack of dishes, and I groaned.

"Mom always says, 'You got to do the first things first, Samantha.'" Sam shook her finger in an imitation of her mother, earning a laugh from me. She smirked back.

"Where is your mother? I don't think I have ever met her."

"She's in the kitchen," Sam replied, "but she'll be hoppin' mad if she comes out here and finds the dishes untouched, so we better get going." With one last heavy sigh, I turned toward the dish piles and, with Sam's help, got started.

The day flew by with Sam and me working side by side. We completed everything on her list and more. Lunch passed without us marking it with a meal, and before long it was time for dinner. A slow stream of people began to meander into the dining room. Men with their wives sat at dinner tables while single men took to the bar. It did not take long for the room to be bustling, but still a few last stragglers tottered in and found a corner to stand in.

"Get to work!" someone snapped at me from behind. I turned to find Miss Livton all in a fluster. Her face was tinged red, and a trickle of perspiration ran down her brow. Her blond hair was mussed and some of it hung loose at her shoulders.

Out of all my limited time working at the inn, I had never seen Sarah so flustered. She glared at me when I smirked. As a sign of truce, I asked her what she would have me do.

The Mirror

"I need you to clear tables. Sam has been keeping up fairly well, but there are way too many people here for her to continue so. I don't know what that Mayor was thinking. And to tell me just the day before. Honestly, sometimes I think that man is dense." With a shake of her head, she disappeared back into the kitchen.

I grimaced at her retreat, but soon turned to clear the tables. I saw Sam and noticed her shoulders drooping from fatigue. Picking up my pace, I stepped up to the first table and began to pick up the dirty dishes.

For the most part, people just ignored me, and I overheard their conversation.

"It is necessary," one young mother said. "We cannot expect to raise civilized children without the help of a school and teacher."

"Bah!" grunted a stern old man. "Anything a man needs to know he can learn from his father, and a girl can learn well enough to cook and clean by the example of her mother. Schools are for those blue bloods who can't bother getting their hands dirty. Real men work by the sweat of their brow for a living."

"But what about bankers and store clerks? A town needs such as these in order to prosper. Owzan will die out unless we train our children beyond our own knowledge."

"Perhaps, that is so, but what about the expense? Can Owzan really afford to pay for a teacher and a school building? Just think of how much that will cost. Perhaps we should wait until later. Maybe in a couple of years."

On and on the conversations went. Every person had an opinion about the children's education, even though some did not even have children of their own. I wondered what sort of debate would follow.

A couple of hours passed before the dinner was officially completed, and the mayor was ready to begin the meeting. Lumbering up to the front of the dining room, he stepped up onto a hastily made platform and cleared his throat, gaining everyone's attention. With a quick nod as if in approval of everyone's silence, he began. "Ladies and gentlemen, as many of you know, we are here to discuss whether Owzan is to have a schoolhouse." On this note, the building filled with boos and cheers, and the mayor scowled at the interruption. When the room quieted, the mayor continued, but I did not hear what he said.

Sarah came up behind me and touched me on the elbow. "Once you have these tables cleared," she whispered, "you can go back to the kitchen and help Sam wash dishes. I'll make sure things go smoothly out here."

I wanted to object. The debate had stirred my curiosity, and I wanted to see the outcome. But Sarah had more right than I to be present for the town meeting, and I had no fuel for my argument to stay and watch other than curiosity. Picking up the last of the dishes, I headed to the back.

I found Sam up to her elbows in suds. Nudging her to the side, I handed her a towel to start drying. I could wash faster, and if the dishes dried a little on their own, nobody would be any the wiser. She smiled up at me, and I saw the bags forming under her eyes. I wondered what she thought about the idea of a school.

"Hey Sam," I began. "What do you think of all this? Do you think Owzan should have a school?"

The Mirror

She shrugged. "It doesn't really matter all that much to me. I mean, I guess it would be good if all the kids could go to school, but I don't think I would ever go."

"Why wouldn't you go to school? If there is a school built this spring, you could go in the fall. You aren't too old yet."

She shrugged again. I waited for an actual response.

"Mom needs me at the inn. I wouldn't have time to go to school."

"I'm sure your mom would want you to learn to read and write. Don't you think she would like you to know all that stuff?"

She made a face at me. "I'm not five. I already know how to read and write. And I know how to do my times tables and division and all that. Mom said I needed to know those things if I were to run an inn of my own someday."

"So, your mom has taught you everything already, has she?"

"Yup," Sam replied with all the assurance a child has in their parent.

"Has she taught you geography?"

Sam wavered a bit. "A little. I know all the provinces and lakes in Samaya. I know the major oceans, and I can name all the towns in three counties."

I nodded in approval. "What about history?"

Sam rolled her eyes. "That is way too easy. I can name all the kings and queens of Samaya all the way up to the present King Henry and Queen Rose!" I heard the excitement building in her voice. She no longer worked slowly. There was a new bit of gusto about her.

"Did you know," she continued, "that the new queen was once a commoner? In fact, she was an orphan from Golan, and she met the prince when he was in Emriville. They say she was there visiting with her cousin's cousin or some other odd sort of arrangement."

I dropped the mug I was holding into the dish tub. "W–What?"

Sam laughed at my reaction. "It's the truth. Billy told me yesterday. He said that no one really knew the queen's history, as it was all kept sort of hushed up, but word was getting out now because the queen and king were going to go visit Emriville again."

My mind cleared and I regained control of my appendages. A small smile curved my lips. "Did you know," I said to Sam, "that I met Queen Rose before she was the queen?"

Sam looked at me in disbelief, then started to laugh. She dropped the mug she had been drying and grabbed at her sides in order to hold them in place as tears of mirth rolled down her cheeks.

"What is so funny?" I asked.

"Y-y-you," she finally made out as she wiped away her tears of laughter. "You got to be joking that you met the queen before she was the queen."

"Believe what you want, but I could tell you some stories."

Sam just kept laughing, and a roar of anger erupted from the next room. With a startled yelp, Sam jumped off the ground and wrapped her arms around my waist. Her grip didn't loosen until the voices in the next room over died down.

"What was that all about?" I wondered aloud.

"Men," Sam muttered in a voice that sounded almost exactly like that of a grown woman. "Mom says that once they make their minds up about something they bicker and fuss over it, until someone gets

The Mirror

hurt. Then they finally decide to make a decision." She shook her head and her shoulders drooped once more as she picked up her dish towel.

"Sam," I asked, "Why were you so scared when they started yelling out there?" She ignored me. "Sam?"

She sighed dramatically. "The last time there was a town meeting, the men got into a fight, and my friend Zach got beat up pretty bad. The doctor took him away and worked on him for two weeks. Mom says Zach just wasn't strong enough to hold on once the fever set in. Billy and the doctor carried his body back to his family in the next county. The authorities couldn't do anything 'cause everyone says it was a fair fight. Besides, no one knows who really killed him 'cause everyone was fighting."

I wasn't sure what to say. I decided to try to avoid the topic of Zach. "Do you know what they were fighting about?" Sam nodded. "What was it?"

Sam turned her face away and danced uncomfortably on her feet. "I need to go to the privy," she finally said and raced out of the room.

The kitchen fell silent except for the quiet rumble of a solitary voice from the room over, indicating someone had finally gained enough attention from the crowd to voice an opinion. I wondered if Sarah was worried at all about the townspeople breaking out in anger. I felt myself cringe every time voices were raised, but they always died down without incident. Sam came back and helped me with dishes, but after an hour I told her to take a break while I changed the water. When I came back, she had fallen asleep in the corner.

Sarah came in and out carrying mugs to be washed and mugs full of refreshing drinks. Apparently such debate left people thirsty, but I began to wonder when she started carrying out plates of pastries and baked goods. She smiled at my inquiring look. "Food always keeps men in a good mood." I couldn't be sure, but I thought that maybe I heard an undertone of fear in her voice. If I had been paying more attention, I would have realized she was terrified.

It wasn't until around midnight that people started to head home, and it was nearing two in the morning before the inn was finally quiet. Sarah came into the old kitchen exhausted. "What was the final decision?" I asked quietly. Sam was still sleeping on a heap of blankets near the stove.

Sarah groaned. "They didn't reach one. They've decided they'll have another meeting in June when it will make more sense to start the building process. I think the mayor is hoping someone will change their mind and that the town won't be in such a tizzy about the entire issue."

She looked at my remaining stack of dishes. "At least I will have a little more warning next time they decide to have a meeting," she murmured as she picked up the dishcloth Sam had abandoned long before.

"Why can't they decide about a school?" I asked. "Wouldn't it be better if the town had a school? I mean, the more educated a town is, the better the commerce."

"Who needs a school to teach about commerce? Women teach the basics, and a boy can learn whatever trade he wants through an apprenticeship. The only ones who need schools are those who want to become preachers and teachers, and there are schools in the city for that."

The Mirror

"So you would deny kids the chance to learn because they don't live in a city?" I felt my voice rising. I didn't like what Sarah was saying.

"Now, Mr. Caman, you understand why people get all worked up about whether the town should have a school. Imagine seventy opinionated persons in a room all wanting to have their say, and then you get a town meeting. It just doesn't work."

I felt my cheeks redden when I realized how worked up I had gotten over an issue that I needn't even deal with. "What happened at the last town meeting?"

Sarah stiffened. "Who told you that there was anything to be said about it?"

I held my hands up defensively. "Sam was scared, and she told me about her friend Zach. Who was Zach, anyway?"

"Zach," Sarah sighed, "was a traveler who was in the wrong town at the wrong time. He got involved in the town meeting, and when he spoke up, people got mad. A fight broke out, and when it was done, Zach was bleeding on the ground. Sam came out of the kitchen when the shouting stopped and all she saw was Zach's dilapidated body. She was heartbroken."

"Why weren't charges pressed?"

Sarah threw up her arms. "Who knows? The excuse is that they don't know who killed him, but I think the truth is everyone knows that they are somewhat guilty, and no one can readily charge the man responsible for the death of Zach without first condemning himself." She shook her head. "The town was a mess after that. People walked around with their heads down. It took a long time before people could look each other in the eye again."

"What was the discussion about? Sam wouldn't say."

"Umm," murmured Sarah, "you will have to ask the curate about that. Stuart Morgan will tell you if he thinks you need to know."

I let out a frustrated sigh. Curiosity had a way of niggling at one's mind. The mystery of the deathly discussion had me wondering what type of comment could make a town of civilized people beat a man to death.

Sarah and I finished the dishes in silence, and as I dealt with the dishwater, she put the rest of the mugs in their cupboard. Stepping back into the old kitchen, I stretched my back. It had to be nearing dawn and I was exhausted.

Turning to check the stove one last time, I saw Sam sleeping in the corner. "Where's Sam's mother?" I asked. "Shouldn't she have put Sam to bed, or is she still working in the new kitchen?"

Sarah gave me a strange look and walked over to Sam. She was about to pick up Sam when I stepped in. Sarah was strong, but a twelve-year-old girl with a winter dress on was heavy, and I wasn't going to chance someone dropping her.

"I can handle this, Mr. Caman," Sarah whispered and held her hands out for me to place Sam in her arms.

"Where is Sam's mother?" I asked again.

Sarah stomped her foot on the floor in frustration. "I am Sam's mother, and I would appreciate it if you would let me carry my daughter."

For the second time that night, shock ran through me, but this time I refused to lose control of my appendages. "Well then, *Miss* Livton, you can show me where your daughter's room is." I couldn't help but emphasize her unmarried status. I felt like I had been made a joke of, that I was missing something everybody else knew, but were purposely keeping from me.

Sarah glared at me. "Yes, I am a horrible person because I have had a child out of wedlock." She exited the kitchen, and I followed carefully behind. "At least I own up to it. I wonder how many men have children out of wedlock that they don't even know about. I mean, you must have at least three, but that doesn't matter because you aren't the one who swells up. You—" she turned on the spot and pointed an accusing finger at me, "you can do your damage and then leave in the morning never to be seen again."

I followed as we climbed a flight of stairs to an apartment of sorts in the attic. A small bed sat in the corner, and I laid Sam gently down on top of it. Sarah came up beside me and began to remove Sam's shoes and stockings. "You can leave now," she said.

I bit my lip and stepped back. I felt like a cad, but what could I do about it? This had been the second time in a month that I had been reminded that I might have kids I didn't know about, and the realization stung as new. Turning away from Sarah and Sam, I headed back downstairs. I didn't recall seeing Stuart at the town meeting, and I wondered if he knew where I was.

I cussed lightly under my breath. I was sure to receive a sermon for this. Stuart would probably think that I had got caught up at the saloon and that I was breaking his rules.

I stepped out into the cold February air. I tried to run back to the Stuart's, but the wind made me stumble around like a drunk. I decided it would be better to walk like a sober man than to run as if intoxicated, especially when I was most likely going to face accusations of the like.

The door was unlocked when I reached the house, and everything was quiet. I tried to sneak to my room, but the lack of light prevented me from finding my way in the unfamiliar building. I walked into a chair, and with a soft cuss I pushed it away, but when I stubbed my toe on a door jam, I yelped in pain.

A thud resounded in the next room as if someone had fallen off their chair or out of bed, and it wasn't long before I was standing holding my toe in the flickering glow of candlelight.

Stuart sniffed the air and smirked. "I didn't think you had gone to the saloon." He shook his head and motioned for me to follow him. Candle in hand, he led me toward my room. He ushered me in.

"How did you know I hadn't gone to the saloon?"

"There was a town meeting, was there not?" I nodded. "Yes, the mayor likes to surprise Sarah with town meetings. I expect you must be tired." He handed me the candle. "Get some sleep. I will let you sleep in tomorrow morning. I am sure Sarah will understand if you're late."

I shook my head. "No, I can't be late."

Stuart quirked his brow at me. "Why not?"

Shrugging, I turned toward my bed. "It is my job. It is my responsibility. If Sarah can't sleep in, neither should I."

"I see." Stuart smirked. "Am I right in saying that you have a growing respect for our Miss Livton?"

I shrugged again. "Just wake me up in the morning, will you?" Stuart agreed and left me to return to his bed.

I closed my eyes and tried to sleep, but sleep would not come. I rolled onto my other side, hoping a different position would be more

The Mirror

comfortable and that sleep would sink in. Nothing helped. All I could think about was Sarah and her daughter.

It didn't make sense to me. Who could be Sam's father? Why wasn't he around? Who would leave Sarah with Sam, especially when Sam was...well, Sam?

The sun crept over the horizon, and I let out a sigh of frustration. There was no way I was going to sleep now. Walking over to my dresser, I splashed water from the basin on my face. Pulling on clean clothes, I walked to the kitchen and found a cold breakfast and Mrs. Morgan waiting for me. "Good morning," I mumbled politely.

"Yes," she replied, her voice feathery and soft to go along with her trembling and petite figure. "I suppose it is morning, but I doubt very much that you find it good."

I ripped off a bite of bread and did my best to swallow the dry lump. "You're right. It's not good. I am tired, and it's cold outside."

"Then I shall pray that the good Lord gives you strength and warmth on this day."

"Save your prayers," I muttered as I picked up the remains of my breakfast and headed for the outside door. "Experience has taught me that they are desperate pleas wasted on an unyielding, unforgiving God. I will survive on my own." The door slammed behind me, cutting me off from the warmth of the house and leaving me utterly alone.

SIX

THERE WAS HARDLY A NOISE as I stepped into the inn. Everyone except Sarah was still sleeping soundly. I watched as she cracked eggs into a bowl, preparing breakfast for the men who would no doubt soon arrive. My anger from the night before still simmered in my belly, looking for an opportunity to boil, but common sense told me I was being silly.

"Good morning," I whispered when I thought myself sensible enough not to sound annoyed.

Sarah jumped and whirled on the spot, wielding an egg-smeared spatula in defence against me. The spatula sagged to her side as she realized who had startled her, and her jaw hardened, causing her face to lose the look of peace it had carried for one brief moment.

I had forgotten and forgiven my own anger and rash words from the previous night, but Sarah had not.

The Mirror

"You aren't supposed to be here yet, Mr. Caman," she hissed. "You may as well go back to the curate's house and get some sleep. You aren't expected back until noon. Today will be a slow day after the fiasco yesterday." She turned back to her bowl of eggs and began to stir with a vengeance.

"I have nothing better to do, so I may as well help out. What would you like me to do?" Helpful was not the right attitude to be in at the moment.

The spatula dropped into the bowl, causing some of the egg to spill. Pushing off the counter, Sarah turned and glared at me. "What I would like you to do is to leave. I have no use for you here. You can go find some other hole to hide in, but you leave my daughter and me alone."

"What if I don't want to leave?" I asked as my anger sparked once more. "You have no right to kick me out. I'm not the one who has done anything wrong."

"Not done anything wrong? You came in here drinking and swearing. Acting as if the world owed you everything, yet you still think you are just pearly. Well I hate to bring this to your attention, Mr. Caman, but you are a pig. Worse than a pig. And I don't need you interfering with me and my daughter!" Her hands shook as she picked up the spatula and began stirring again.

Sarah's words stung, but I wasn't ready to give in. "Does Sam want me to leave?" It was the one question I knew would work—the only words sure to have an impact on Sarah's opinion of me. Her gasp affirmed what I already knew.

"Sam is too young to know what is best for her. She doesn't like to see anyone leave. But I, her *mother*, am old enough to realize that you can bring nothing but trouble to the two of us. Now, will you please leave? I don't care if you stay in town. Just stay away from my daughter and me."

"If Sam doesn't want me to leave, then I am staying."

"Why do you have to be so stubborn?"

"Why do you keep acting as if I am the problem and not you?"

"Why do you insist upon displaying the same hypocrisy as the pot calling the kettle black?"

A smile twitched the corners of my lips. With her back to me, Sarah could not see this small hint of humour. Instead, she continued to beat the frothing bowl of eggs.

"Honestly Mr. Caman, ever since you came, you've acted as if your actions are your own affair and that nobody really notices. But people do notice, and those nearest to you are the ones who are going to get hurt."

"So you wish to kick me out in order to protect yourself?"

Sarah shook her head. "I've had enough trouble in my life that I care little about my own person. But you threaten Sam, and that is something I cannot live with. So if you really care about Sam, do what is right, and leave her alone."

"I think I will decide for myself what is best for Sam. Now tell me what I can do to help."

Sarah released a heavy sigh of defeat as she poured the egg concoction into a hot frying pan. "Do you know how to work a churn? The men will be up soon, and they will want fresh butter with their breakfast."

With a smile of victory, I walked over to the churn and began my day's work.

The Mirror

Sam stumbled out of bed around noon. She had a long-sleeved sweater over her dress, but the buttons were not correctly aligned. Rubbing her eyes, she sat down at a bar stool and watched me, her head resting on top her arms.

"What's for breakfast?" Sam finally asked.

I smiled at her innocent question. "Darling, breakfast finished over four hours ago. We are preparing for lunch at the moment."

Sam puckered her lip and rested her head on her fists. "If you would like," I continued, "I can go find you some grub in the kitchen. How does that sound?"

Sam shook her head and hopped down from her seat. "I should be getting to work. The dishes do need washing."

"Hold your horses," I called after her. She turned. Fiddling with the bottom of her sweater, she waited for me to speak.

"The dishes are already washed, and you need to eat something before you go off working. Everything is in good order for lunch, so don't you worry your little self about any of that. You can start working if you want after lunch. Until then, rest, darling girl."

Sam stomped her foot, and it dawned on me just how much she and Sarah were alike. "I am not little, and I'm not darling, and I can work if I want to." She stomped one more time for good measure.

A throat cleared in the corner. "Samantha, is this the way you treat friends?" Sam scowled as Sarah stepped into the dining room. Sarah raised an eyebrow, challenging her to take one more step out of line.

With a heavy sigh, Sam turned toward me. "I am sorry, Mr. Caman. I didn't mean to be ornery." She shrugged, and I let a bit of a smile show.

"You are forgiven," I replied politely.

"Come here, Sam," Sarah beckoned. Sam sauntered over to her mother. Kneeling down, Sarah began to unbutton Sam's sweater. Realigning the holes and buttons, she began buttoning the sweater up correctly.

"Now Sam," she began, "I know that you want to help Billy and me out, but I want to make sure that you are healthy. So, I agree with Mr. Caman. You are going to eat some lunch with us, and after that you can help with some chores. You had a long day yesterday, and it is good for you to sleep in, okay?"

Sam nodded. "Good," said Sarah. "Now, how about you go sit at the counter, and I'll bring you something to eat."

Sam hurried off to do as her mother bid, and I returned to my work. Sam closely observed each move I made as she sat with her head resting on her folded arms waiting for her mom. Her legs kicked back and forth, tapping a steady rhythm against the counter.

"Why do adults always say they're looking out for their children's health when they aren't even taking care of themselves?" she asked me.

I shrugged. "Adults know if they are going to get sick or not, and they can stop then. Kids don't always know when they are doing too much."

"Mom does too much all the time. No one ever tells her to take a break. What happens if she gets really sick? Who tells her to stop then, and why does she get to tell me to stop when I am helping her?"

I sighed, not knowing what to tell Sam. "Sometimes adults are trying to provide everything their kids need, but because of circumstances, they don't have all the money that is necessary. So adults work very hard, even though it might not be good for their health. They do it so that their kids don't have to. It is the parent's job to care for their children even if it means that they get sick."

"Is it easier when there is a dad and a mom?"

"I suppose so. Sometimes even when there is a dad and mom around, it can be really hard."

Sam dropped her head back onto her arms and sighed. Her legs stopped kicking, and soon Sarah came with a bowl of soup. Warning Sam that it was hot, she returned to the kitchen. Hastily gulping back the scalding soup, Sam finished her meal and ran off. When I found her a little later, she was busy peeling potatoes. With a sigh, I left her to her work and wondered which of the two females would succumb to illness first.

I returned to the curate's house in time for dinner. There really wasn't much that needed to be done at the inn. Most of the regulars had decided to avoid their usual eating place, most likely in fear of witnessing something the likes of what they had seen the night before.

"You're home early," greeted Stuart. "Were you that unneeded?"

"Things were quiet. People were scared off by the town meeting. I don't blame them. I've never seen a town get so worked up."

Stuart grimaced. "You have to remember from where this town arose."

"What does that have to do with anything?"

"Most of these men are the rough-and-tumble type. The type not a soul would have touched, but now that they have cleaned up a little, they are a bit more acceptable. Still, sometimes they can't help but revert to their old ways."

I shrugged. "I've known the rough-and-tumble type, but this issue doesn't seem like something that would bother them so much. It is just a school building, after all."

Stuart rubbed his face and pushed out a heavy breath of air. "Don't you see how much this issue does matter to them?" I shook my head, not understanding. "This issue is at their very core."

The curate continued. "Most of these men have never gone to school. They grew up in poor families and learned their trades either as an apprentice or in situations where they must learn or die. Now that they have families of their own, they plan on training their sons and allowing their wives to train their daughters. If they allow a school to be built, they are denying their very way of living. It is almost saying that what they have learned in life is not sufficient, that we must bring in a learned person to train their children because they can't do it for themselves."

All the fuss began to make sense to me. How could the men not be offended by a school, yet how could they not want to better their town and their children's chances at a better life? "So the town is split," I murmured.

"So it is."

Talk of the town meeting brought another question to mind. "Stuart, what was the last town meeting about? I heard that a man was killed. What did he say that made people so angry? I was told I should ask you."

The Mirror

Stuart closed his eyes and his lips moved as if saying a quick silent prayer. I waited, but he did not move, and he remained with his eyes closed. I wondered if he had fallen asleep.

"Stuart," I began again, but he held up a hand. Slowly, he opened his eyes and looked at me.

"I don't think it is time for you to know that yet." I tried to cut in again, but he stopped me with a wave of his hand. "I will tell you someday, but now is not the right time. You will understand, but not now."

I left the curate in the parlour to go to my room. I was angry. What could be so terrible that I couldn't know but a twelve-year-old girl could? I was a grown man, for crying out loud. I was thirty years old, yet they were telling me I had to wait.

I stormed about my room trying to find something to do with myself. I had nothing. There were no books, no chess games, and nothing to do. I replayed in my mind the condescending words of the curate along with his many rules meant to irritate and nag, and I wondered how I could get out of the house without alerting him.

Fie on the curate. Picking up my coin bag, I heard the clink of two small coins and knew it would have to suffice. I slammed the bedroom door behind me and walked toward the front door. Stuart was still sitting in the parlour. He looked up when he heard me clomping through the hallway.

"Where are you going?"

"None of your business," I hollered back at him.

"I beg to differ," he said as he rose from his chair. "Seeing as you are living in my house, you will also abide by my rules. One of those rules is that I know where you are at all times. You didn't seem to have a problem with that rule when you agreed to it. What is bothering you about it now?"

"I am going to the saloon to sate a thirst that has been growing for over two weeks. Are you happy? Now you know, and there is nothing you can do about it." I reached for the door that was so close to me, but a steely gripped hand reached out and stopped me.

"Do you really want to go?" Stuart asked.

"Of course I do, why else would I be going? I'm getting a drink and then I am coming back. Is that okay?"

"What is so appealing about alcohol that you must get some?"

"Why does it matter to you? It's my life. I will do with it as I please. Nothing you say or do is going to stop me."

Stuart released me and sighed. "I suppose you're right. You are free to make your own choices, but I will try to influence them if I can."

I ignored him. Taking hold of the door handle, I disappeared into the night. It wasn't two minutes later when I heard someone walking down the road behind me. I turned, and to my astonishment, I saw Stuart following. The man had to be possessed.

"What do you want?" I called with my back still turned to him.

He didn't even hesitate. "I've decided I would like to go out for a drink. I've heard they have some pretty good concoctions down at the saloon. Is that a problem?" His voice was sugar-sweet, and I was not impressed.

"Shouldn't you be at home with your wife?" I shouted back.

The Mirror

"She understands that I have to make my own choices. After all, I am my own man, and it doesn't matter what she says. She can't stop me."

He was catching up to me. I turned on him. "You are not coming to the saloon. I don't want you there, and you don't need to be there. Go back to your wife and leave me to my peace."

The curate smiled happily at me. "The thing is, you can't stop me. No matter what you say, I can still go to that saloon. It's my decision."

The need for a drink increased and I couldn't bother to stand in the street and bicker with this obstinate man. He could do as he chose. Perhaps it would even be humorous to watch him in a saloon. Turning on the spot, I walked briskly toward my destination. The curate kept in step.

"Are you always this determined?"

He smirked. "Only when it's necessary. It all depends on how stubborn the man that the Lord sends my way is."

Ignoring his last comment, I pushed open the saloon door and approached the counter. The bartender grinned, revealing his two rotten teeth. I was about to give him my order, but he spoke first.

"Now Stuart Morgan, what are you doing in my saloon? Every time you show up I seem to lose a good paying customer."

"Sorry about that, Mick," Stuart replied. "Perhaps buying a drink will make up for it. I'll have a beer, if the stock is worth it."

"Now, are you questioning my stock? Everyone here knows it's the best in this area."

Stuart smirked up at Mick. "That is because it is the only beer in the area, besides the watered down stuff they serve at the inn. Now pour me a pint, will you?"

Mick grinned. "What about this feller? Are you covering his tab or is he on his own?"

"He's his own person, Mick. He can pay for his own and take care of his own. Let him tell you all about it."

"One of those types, is he?"

The urge for a drink was leaving quickly. Not because the alcohol was undesirable, but because the company was. How dare they talk about me as if I weren't even there? There were better ways I could spend my money than handing it over to the likes of Mick.

Turning from the bar, I began to survey the room. The person I was looking for was easy to find. She was flirting with a man in the corner, her low-cut dress tempting him to sample her wares, but he wasn't quite ready to bite.

I was.

I walked toward the woman, took her hand, and emptied my coin sack into it. Placing the coins into a pocket in her dress, she directed me toward the stairs that would lead to her room.

I wasn't the only one who followed her. Stuart fell in step behind me, his beer still sitting on the counter unattended. I cursed, and my partner stopped walking.

"Is there something wrong?" she asked.

"No," I muttered, "just keep walking."

Instead of heeding my words, the girl turned and sashayed up to the curate with a look meant to seduce. "I'm sorry, honey, but I've already been taken for the moment. Perhaps you can wait a little while, or Sandy over there wouldn't mind your company."

The Mirror

Stuart smiled politely. "I have a better idea. How about I pay you double what that man gave you, and you give him his money back?"

The seductive smile turned sour. "I'm sorry, but that isn't allowed."

She took my hand, and we were about to leave the curate behind when he called out, "Don't do this, Caman!"

I grasped the prostitute's hand and attempted to drag her toward the back room.

"Caman, think about what you're doing. Remember those who care about you. Don't do this."

My partner became unyielding. I tried to persuade her to move. I jerked on her arm. She yelped and I released my grasp.

Horror filled me. Images of my father screaming at my mother filled my mind as the terror-stricken girl looked up at me. I turned toward the curate. "Leave me alone."

The girl was grasping at her wallet. She removed the coins and threw them at me.

"Leave me alone!" I shouted at the curate. The saloon was quiet. All the men watched as Stuart and I faced each other. The girl had left my side and I couldn't find her in the crowd.

"Very well," Stuart replied. Tipping his hat at Mick, he took a swallow of his beer and left the room.

Sitting in his place, I finished what remained in his mug and tossed my coins down. "Give me whatever that will buy me." Mick did as he was bid, and slowly the room returned to its normal hum. I ignored the stares and finished two more pints before I walked back out the door and down the street to the curate's house.

Stuart was waiting for me when I returned.

"What was that?" I shouted. "Can't you let a man drink in peace?"

"It was for your own good. What good would it have been if I had let you spend your time with a prostitute? Chances are you would have gotten some horrible disease, but you would be too broke to pay the doctor. What sorry soul wants that?"

"I did! I wanted to get so completely drunk that I'd forget how everyone treats me like a child. Then I would forget everything else that this world deems necessary to throw at me. And, when I woke from my drunken stupor, perhaps after spending the night with her, my head would hurt so bad that I wouldn't have the capacity to think about anything but standing up straight."

"What a life that must be. I can see how you really needed that drink."

"Just because you have a pretty little life here with your wife and your perfect little town doesn't mean everyone else has it as good." I shoved my hands in my pockets and walked toward my room. "I'm going to bed. I have to work in the morning."

"Don't you want your supper?" Stuart shouted at my disappearing back.

"I'm not hungry," I shouted back.

"Sleep well, Caman. I pray your dreams are sweet and you wake refreshed and ready for a new day tomorrow."

The only response I gave him was slamming my bedroom door.

I awoke near the middle of the night with my stomach grumbling. I stumbled toward the kitchen hoping to find something to eat. To my surprise, a plate of cold food awaited me. Beside the plate rested a note.

The Mirror

Jeremy,

When days are long and your thirst is great, do not seek what does not quench. Instead, seek the living water. When your stomach growls and food seems unobtainable, remember that you have been offered the bread of life. For now, there is water in the bucket by the stove, and this plate of food is for you.

I crumpled the note and dug into the food in front of me. Once the plate was empty, I quenched my thirst with the water by the stove. With my stomach full, I walked back to bed and drifted off into deep, dreamless sleep.

SEVEN

THE HEADACHE THAT GREETED ME the following morning was enough to make me long to skip work, but Stuart's pounding on my door prevented me from considering that option for long. Pushing myself off my bed, I walked toward my heap of clothes on the floor and began to dress. Stepping out into the hall, I ran into Mrs. Morgan.

She let out a squeal, and with a horrified look ran back down the hall. I stared after her wondering how I could have startled her so, but with a shake of my head, I continued toward the kitchen. I was hungry, and my bad mood did not improve upon realizing that there was nothing prepared for breakfast. With a frustrated sigh, I decided I would eat when I arrived at the inn. There was sure to be plenty of food there.

It was cold outside, the kind of damp cold that chills you to the bone on an early spring day. As I walked on, I considered turning back

The Mirror

and telling the curate I was sick, but not wanting to be considered petty, I kept walking.

I was late when I finally did arrive at the inn, and there was already a great bustle. All the regulars had returned after their temporary absence, and it seemed they had brought a few others with them.

Sam saw me from across the room and a look of delight spread across her face. Racing to my side, she yanked on my hand. "Isn't it great?" she exclaimed. "So many people liked the food when they came for the town meeting that they have come back for more. Mom says we will probably get at least four more regular customers out of this."

I tried to join in the excitement, but couldn't seem to find joy in the added work. "That's great, Sam," I mumbled.

"Come on," she seemed to scream, and I winced a little. All thoughts of breakfast disappeared as I walked into the old kitchen and saw for myself all that needed to be done.

"Don't worry," said Sam in the same chipper voice as before. "Mom says Martha has been feeling a lot better for the past little while, so she is going to help out in the kitchen today. Also, Billy hasn't got much work to do because he says he's done all he can until the spring thaw comes completely, so I get to work with you today."

She looked up at me cheerfully, and I smiled half-heartedly back. She didn't seem to notice my lack of enthusiasm. "How about I wash while you dry?" she offered.

For the first time that day, a grin split my face. Perhaps working with Sam wouldn't be all that bad. I had no desire to stick my hands into tepid, filthy water, and Sam had given me a way out. I helped Sam fill up the bucket with hot soapy water, picked up a towel, and began to dry the dripping dishes.

My headache didn't fade as the day went on. It grew worse. By the time the dishes were done and the bed sheets washed, even Sam was beginning to notice my dour mood. Her chattering decreased, and her smile dulled. Instead of picking at her chores like she sometimes did, she worked hard beside me all day.

When evening finally came, I was starting to think I might actually be ill. Apparently Sam was thinking the same thing. "Are you feeling alright, Mr. Caman?" she asked quietly. "You look something awful."

I shrugged. "I should be fine, but I think I will go home now. I'll see you in the morning, okay?"

Sam scrunched her nose in thought. "Perhaps you should have something to eat before you go. I could go get you some stew from the kitchen."

I shook my head. I knew how good Sarah's stew was, but my stomach revolted at the thought of eating something so rich. Perhaps I would try some bread when I returned home. My stomach heaved, and I reconsidered the thought of having any food.

"You sure?"

I smiled at her concern. "Yeah, Sam, I am sure. How about you tell your mom that I'm not feeling too good, but I'll be back in the morning."

Sam scrunched her nose again, but she turned to do as I bid her. I trudged my way back to the curate's house. Mrs. Morgan met me at the door, but there was no sign of the terror she had displayed that morning. Instead, she suggested I head to bed, and she would prepare a tray for me. I nodded my thanks and went to find my room.

The Mirror

I must have fallen asleep because when I awoke, the room was dark, and there was a tray on the dresser with some bread and cheese, and a pot of cold tea. Taking a bite of the bread, I tried to swallow. The lump worked its way down my throat and settled like a cold stone in the bottom of my stomach. I shivered and decided to try the tea instead. Too late, I discovered how horrid cold tea tastes. I spit back into my cup, and my stomach heaved. Reaching for my water dish, I emptied the remaining contents of my stomach into the porcelain bowl.

After wiping my mouth, I picked up the dish and made my way out the back door of the house. I fumbled about my task, hoping that someone in the house would awaken and assist me, but no one stirred, and I was too proud to seek the help. Venturing out into the backyard, I went as far as I dared, then dumped the refuse into the snow. The smell of it made my stomach roll once more. Taking snow in my hands, I began to wash out the dish. When the porcelain again sparkled, I began to look for something to dry it.

There was nothing nearby, so I took off my shirt and used it as my towel. With tired steps, I made my way back to the house. The cold seeped into my shoulders and sent a shiver down my back. The house seemed to be getting further away rather than closer. I stumbled and dropped the dish. With a curse, I picked it up and used my shirt once more to dry it. The moon glared down at me, its rays reflecting off the glassy snow. My head ached. My wet shirt clung to me, and sharp tingles ran through my fingers. I longed for something warm to drink or perhaps a shot of whiskey to heat me to the core.

I stumbled into the house and was greeted with a cold, "Where were you?" Stuart's glare was icier than the blasts I had received from my recent, nighttime stroll, but I refused to answer him.

"I'm going to bed," I said, slurring my words and stumbling a bit. He caught my arm to stop me from falling. Sniffing my breath, he began to cough.

His look changed from disgust to concern. "Are you alright? Perhaps I should call Mr. Nelson the apothecary. You aren't looking too well."

I shrugged my way out of his grip. "I'm fine," I mumbled. "It was probably something I ate. I just need some sleep." Walking past Stuart, I found my room and fell onto my bed fully dressed.

I clawed the blankets over myself, trying to capture whatever warmth I could. Stuart knocked on my door, but I ignored him. Eventually his footsteps faded in the direction of his own bedroom. I closed my eyes and tried to sleep, but my mind was a maze of unanswerable questions and unobtainable goals. I tried to run, but I couldn't move my legs...

I awoke with tears of frustration in my eyes. My body was covered in sweat, and my head pounded. I needed to wash myself, but I had emptied my water basin the night before. I stripped off my wet clothes and searched for something else to wear.

The fresh clothes helped, but my body still felt grimy and sweat-covered. I looked to my dresser hoping for water, but both my pitcher and basin were missing. I thought I had only taken the basin the night before, but perhaps I had taken the pitcher as well and left it in the kitchen.

I opened my bedroom door, and there on the floor were my pitcher and basin complete with a clean cloth. Picking up the porcelain items,

The Mirror

I walked to my dresser, closing the door behind me. Stripping down once more, I began to bathe.

The cool water felt refreshing, and the pounding in my head began to lessen as I wiped my brow. By the time that I was fully cleansed, I was certain I would be able to make it through the day working, and that my appetite was surely back in place. To prove my point, I dressed and made my way to the kitchen. Stuart sat across from his wife and a place was set for me at the table.

They did not acknowledge me at first. Rather they remained with their heads bowed holding each other's hand. Finally, Stuart whispered amen and looked up at me. "You are looking a lot better," he said.

I nodded politely, not sure what I should say.

"Have some breakfast. We have some ham and eggs, also some fresh bread. Please, help yourself."

Sitting down, I picked up a slice of ham and placed it on my bread. Taking a bite, I chewed and swallowed. Perhaps it was the food, or perhaps it was my stomach, but I felt as if I were chewing on rotten soldier's rations. Trying to be polite, I continued to eat, but once the slice was complete, I excused myself and hurried off to work. I felt Stuart's eyes watching me as I left.

I made it to the inn in good time. Men were just beginning to sit down for their breakfast, and Sam was still rubbing the sleep out of her eyes. "You look awful," she said.

"Thanks. You look great yourself." She smiled tiredly up at me, and I smiled back.

"We get to work together again today," she said cheerily.

I laughed, truly glad for the chance to spend time with Sam. I was surprised that Sarah allowed, it though. I thought she would try to protect her daughter from my terrible influence.

"What are we going to start with?" I asked.

Sam did a quick survey of the room, then nodded. "We'll have to start with clearing tables. It looks like we're going to have a crowd again today, and we can't be slacking."

I saluted her like I would one of my commanding officers, and with a "Yes, ma'am," I headed off to work.

I went from table to table picking up empty dirty dishes and wiping down the grime left by the tables' previous occupants. Now and then I would see Sam doing the same, but most often I would see her talking with the men at the tables. They would smile at her antics, and sometimes one would reach into his pocket and pull out a penny or a candy. She would smile politely, curtsy, and move on her way.

I laughed under my breath as I watched her. It was no wonder the inn had so many customers when the patrons were treated by such a courteous host. I wondered how many of those men Sam had twisted around her finger. Shaking my head, I went to clear off the next table.

The glare of the man at the table was intimidating. His broad shoulders were hunched, and his bushy brows drew sharp angles inward. Paunchy bags gathered under his eyes, which were red and glassy. His mouth was nothing but a stern gash above his chin.

I considered skipping his table, but thought better of it. Sam worked so hard to keep customers at the inn, I would not deter one by overlooking him. I stepped toward the man, but before I could reach him, Sam stepped past me.

The Mirror

"Mr. Gibbons," she said cheerily. "How are you today?"

A crooked smile appeared on Mr. Gibbons' face, and the looks that were once so ominous became friendly. "Not so bad, little girl," he replied gruffly. It was obvious he was not used to such pleasantries.

"I hope you enjoyed your meal. I know bacon is your favourite."

"Ah, well, your mom always cooks up something good." Mr. Gibbons shrugged his broad shoulders and glared up at me. I realized I was staring and tried to saunter off as if I hadn't been caught.

"Who's that feller?" I heard Mr. Gibbons ask. "He's a mighty strange one if you ask me."

Sam giggled and grabbed my hand. "Don't be silly, Mr. Gibbons. This is Jeremy Caman. He's been here for nearly a month."

"Is that so?" Mr. Gibbon eyed me up and down. "He looks sickly for being here a month. Hasn't your mom fattened him up yet?"

"Mr. Caman was sick yesterday. He'll look better tomorrow. You'll see."

Mr. Gibbon let out a humph and turned back to his bacon.

"Well, I better get back to work," sighed Sam. "There is still lots to do."

"Wait one minute, little lady." Gibbons reached into his pocket and began searching for something. Pulling out a penny, he handed it to her. "You best save that for when you're older. You don't want to be relying on charity, you got that?"

"Yes, sir," replied Sam with a smile. "Thank you very much."

I worked beside Sam for the rest of the day, and by the end my head was pounding, and I was feeling nauseous.

I made it back to the curate's house with the contents of my stomach intact, but by the time I reached my bedroom, I lost it. Once again, my water basin witnessed the remains of what had been my lunch. Fortunately, my pitcher still had water in it, and I could rinse out my mouth. But I was forced to make another long trek to deal with the mess. This time I was smart enough to bring a towel.

When I returned to the house, Mrs. Morgan was standing in the doorway staring at me. I handed her the towel, then walked with the basin to my room. I placed the basin beside my bed and fell fast asleep.

Fits wracked my body. I was falling off the edge of a cliff. I jerked awake. Once more I closed my eyes, hoping I would drift into deep, peaceful sleep. My muscles tensed, and my back ached. I was grasping onto the end of a rope while the wind knocked me back and forth. The rope snapped. I let out a shriek of pain.

Stuart came crashing in the door. I was on the floor rolling in a pile of broken porcelain. A gash was cut along my chest and onto my back. Blood was oozing onto the wooden floor.

"Calm down," soothed the curate. "I'm here now."

I took in deep breaths, trying to stop myself from panicking. With great self-control, I was able to stop. Stuart continued to sooth me until he was certain I wasn't going to move, then he helped me to my feet. Pain seared through my side where I had landed on the porcelain basin, and I almost collapsed from the sheer agony.

"I should get the apothecary," Stuart said as he helped me to the bed. He looked at my tangled sweat-soaked sheets. "You are sick."

"I'm fine," I said through gritted teeth. "I was just having a bad dream, and I fell out of the bed. That's all."

The Mirror

Stuart didn't look convinced. To prove to him that I was alright, I sat up and removed my shirt. I had to clamp my jaw shut in order to keep from shouting in pain, but I was able to make it through.

With a fresh layer of perspiration on my brow, I was able to say, "If you get me something to bandage my side up, I'll be fine in the morning. I just need to get some more sleep."

Stuart still looked doubtful, but he agreed to get me some bandages. He returned shortly with a new washbasin and a couple cloths. Dipping a cloth in the basin, he told me to raise my arm. I did so with gritted teeth, and he began to clean the wound.

It was the most painful thing I had ever experienced. When the blood was washed away, he found a piece of the porcelain stuck in my side. Carefully he worked the sliver out of the wound and dropped it into the basin.

I took short gasping breaths, trying to stay conscious. Stuart left once more and came back with bandaging and fresh bed sheets. He wrapped my entire chest tightly, then told me to go sit in the chair in the corner. He replaced my sweat-soaked sheets, then commanded me to lie down.

I hobbled over to the bed as he began to pick up the pieces of broken porcelain. "Now, I want you to know that there is no shame in being ill. Many men have died because they overworked themselves while they were sick. Worse yet, if you go to the inn while you are sick, you could make someone else sick, and they could die instead of you." The curate stopped his rant to shake his head. "There is no shame in staying in bed for a couple of days if you are ill."

"I am not ill." I was angry with him, and I didn't even know why. "Just let me sleep. I'll be fine in the morning."

"Very well," replied Stuart. "I'll let you sleep."

He turned to leave. I rolled onto my uncut side, but I couldn't sleep. Every time I closed my eyes, my head would start pounding. If I left them open, they would droop and the room would start to spin. I felt like cussing, but it took too much breath, and breathing hurt.

I scowled at the ceiling. I was not going to tolerate this nonsense. Closing my eyes, I commanded myself to sleep. Slowly but surely sleep came, only for it to be rudely disrupted by the pain in my side.

Giving up, I stood and dressed. I had to re-bandage my side, for the blood had soaked through, and by the time I finished with that, the sun was rising, and I decided it was late enough to head over to the inn. Sarah was the only one up. She gave me a look of disgust when I walked in. "Spent your night at the saloon, did you?"

I glared at her. "Do I smell like alcohol? I wish. The good curate wouldn't let me even if I tried."

She waltzed up to me and sniffed my breath. "You look awful," she declared, "but you don't have a hint of alcohol on you. You must be sick. You should get back to bed."

"I am not sick," I shouted as I slammed my hand down. Sarah jumped and the dishes bounced around on the counter.

Turning on me, Sarah stuck her finger in my face. "You will not raise your voice like that at me again, do you understand? I will not have such nonsense in my inn. Now go," she said as she shoved me out of her way, "you can work anywhere but here."

The Mirror

I gasped as her hands made contact with the gash on my side, and I staggered back, trying to keep my balance. "What's the matter with you?" she asked.

"Nothing," I said through gritted teeth. I was not going to be sent home even if it killed me. It would be far worse to spend the day with Stuart Morgan codling me like a child than to be at work and feeling miserable.

She gave me an odd look, but let it be. When I had regained my balance, I went to the lounge to sweep and clean whatever I could find needing it.

I worked slowly the rest of the day. Pain seared my side, and cold sweat ran down my back. By midday, my hands began to tremble. I broke a plate, and nearly dropped a tray of mugs, but I managed to catch myself.

I felt like vomiting, but I refused. I made it home, where Stuart tried to again convince me that I was ill. I refused to listen. I ate supper with him and his wife to prove my point. Later that night after waking from another nightmare, I vomited into the washbasin. This one was new and heavier, but I managed to heft it out to my usual spot to clean it.

Much of the week went by in the same manner. I refused to be ill, but my body would not cooperate. I tried to avoid Stuart and Sarah's persistence that I rest, but it wasn't easy. By Friday, I was so tired I was hardly able to work.

On Saturday, I was so frustrated, I walked to the bar instead of the inn, but when I asked for a drink to settle my stomach Mick denied me. He claimed he did not serve sick patrons and he wanted me out of his bar.

 That night, I did not sleep, and on Sunday morning, I didn't waken.

EIGHT

STUART TOLD ME LATER that he had left me alone to sleep, assuming I had only exhausted myself, but when he came back from the Sunday service, my body was burning with fever. Mrs. Morgan went to get Mr. Nelson while he sat wiping my brow with a cool cloth.

I awoke as Mr. Nelson bustled into my room.

"I thought it was you who was ill," he said to Stuart. "If I knew it was Mr. Caman, I would not have come."

Stuart scowled up at the man. "Don't you think all men deserve care no matter their history? Mr. Caman is ill, and he needs your help. You should at least have the courtesy to help him for my sake."

The apothecary shook his head. "I can't help him even if I wanted to. You see, it's from the alcohol. Surely you have witnessed withdrawal symptoms before."

"Yes, but I don't think these are them," Stuart replied.

"Come Stuart, don't be naive. Everyone knows that Mr. Caman here is a drunk, and that you have been helping him quit the habit. Perhaps he broke into the inn's ale and now he is suffering the effects."

"Mr. Nelson, I trust your judgement, but couldn't you check? What if you are wrong? What if it is not withdrawal?"

"Trust my judgement, Stuart. This will all be over soon."

"What do we do for him now?" Stuart asked, slightly bewildered.

"Treat him as you would any other fever patient. Keep him clean and at a good temperature. It shouldn't last too long. I am told these spells never last no matter how severe the symptoms. At most a couple of hours. And keep him away from the alcohol, Stuart. I am sure neither of us wishes to witness another episode like this one."

The curate nodded and began to wipe my brow with a cool damp cloth. I tried to push his hand away. I felt like a child and it was embarrassing to be treated so in front of another man, but moving took too much energy, and before I could put up too much of a fuss, I had fallen back into a fitful sleep.

Dreams began to haunt my sleep and sometimes lingered when I awoke. Different battle scenes played through my mind, and I began to recognize them as battles I had been a part of during the war against Isbetan. Though they were the same battles, they were far more wretched. The enemy always had more people. They always overpowered us, and I was always left standing in a pool of blood.

Time passed. Most of it I spent in a fitful bout of delirium. When I did wake, it was often to find someone leaning over my bed wiping my arms face and chest with yet another cool cloth. Sometimes I would be screaming, but most of the time my throat was too raw and sore to even whisper.

My chest was no longer wrapped and the gash on the side pussed and oozed no matter how diligent Stuart was at cleaning it. It festered and ached, but bandages only trapped sweat and held it around the cut. So I remained stripped to my waist, feverish and sweating.

Three days passed before the chills and tremors set in. My body was not my own. It jerked and twitched, pulling me to pieces, but I couldn't stop it. The cold was unbearable, worse than the coldest night on the front lines. I begged Stuart to help me, but my cries were lost to the chattering of my teeth.

Mr. Nelson stopped by once more. But he claimed ignorance to the cause and cure of my ailment. He did leave behind a small tonic to clean my wound, which Stuart applied immediately. The pain it caused was terrible. I cried out the vilest words I could think of. I called curses down upon the head of Mr. Nelson, and when I finished my rant, I saw Stuart for the first time with fear in his eyes.

I did not see Stuart for many days after that. Mrs. Morgan tended to me in my pain. She cleaned me and sang to me. She dribbled soup broth down my swollen throat and applied cool, damp cloths to my parched lips when they cracked and bled.

I was angry at Stuart for leaving me in the care of his wife. I longed to speak to him, to speak to anyone, but every time I tried to move, my body rebelled, and Mrs. Morgan would scold me for wasting what little resources I still had.

So I lay in bed, fighting to beat the pain, fighting to destroy the illness, and fighting to stay alive. I did my best, but I was losing the battle. Every hour my health deteriorated, and I gave up a little more of the struggle. By the end of two more days, I was ready for it all to end. Closing my eyes, I prayed for the first time in many years, a true prayer.

"Lord," my heart seemed to cry out. "Lord, look at me. Remember me? How long must I suffer? How long will you leave me here? I can't go on like this. They've won. She has won. Now let me die."

I don't know if God ever heard my desperate prayer, for after the words burst from my heart, I fell into a very deep sleep. I awoke to the sound of raised voices.

"You can't do that, Herman. I won't let you."

"It is the only way, Stuart. If I don't do this, he will die, and you don't want that, do you?"

"Burning flesh is not reasonable or mandatory. You may be the apothecary, and you may be educated, but I will not allow you to do experimental medicine on my charge!"

"Experimental! Bah! You are being ridiculous. The procedure has been done before. It is no longer experimental. The experiment has been done, and it worked. Now if you will let me see my patient, I would like to tend to his wound before it kills him."

"Your patient? Two days ago you hardly acknowledged he was sick."

"Yes, well things have changed."

"I will not have you doing this, Herman. You're being rash."

"You two better leave this room before I thrash you both. Can't you see you are disturbing Mr. Caman's slumber? For a moment there I thought he had woken up. Now get out and solve your disagreements elsewhere."

The Mirror

I dozed peacefully as the voices disappeared. Unfortunately, it wasn't long before they returned.

"We are going to need your help, Mrs. Morgan."

"What do you need me to do?"

"You and Stuart are going to hold him down."

"Surely Stuart will be able to do that on his own. Mr. Caman is weak. He has hardly eaten for over five days."

"Once he feels the pain, he will either thrash about severely or he will pass out completely. I feel more comfortable knowing he will be well secured."

"Do you really need such a big knife, Herman? Surely we could find you something more appropriate in the kitchen."

"Stuart, you agreed that you weren't going to argue."

"Yes, but I didn't realize this would be so brutal."

"Well do your job and keep your eyes closed." Mr. Nelson's words were followed by a grunt, and I felt my arms and legs being grasped in a vice-like grip.

"Okay," Mr. Nelson said in a hushed tone.

My head lolled to the side and I caught sight of a blade the length of a hand before I felt excruciating pain and once more was lost to sleep.

When I awoke, I felt better than I had for a very long time. I did not feel cold or hot, and though my side still hurt, the pain had dimmed to a dull ache rather than a searing or life-threatening throbbing. My stomach growled and I looked about to see if anyone was there to assist me.

Mrs. Morgan sat beside my bed and when she saw me searching, she jumped from her seat and disappeared out my bedroom door. I tried to call after her, but my parched throat only allowed a few raspy syllables to escape. Fortunately, I was not left for long. Stuart strutted into the room and placed himself in the chair his wife had recently vacated.

"How are you feeling, Jeremy? Is there anything I can do for you? Anything you would like?"

I tried to speak once more, but my efforts were again frustrated.

"I'll get you some water," suggested Stuart and once more disappeared.

I leaned back in my bed feeling exhausted by my recent ventures into healthy living, and I considered drifting off back into sleep. Stuart waylaid my plans by once more entering my room, carrying a bowl carefully in his hands.

"Soup," he said. "It will clear your throat and give you some nourishment." He sat and held a spoonful of the broth up to my lips. I tried to grab the spoon from his hands, but the motion caused such a pain that I soon gave up the effort and accepted the inevitable. Stuart helped me finish the broth, and then I was ready for sleep and privacy. Stuart seemed to recognize my needs and left quietly.

Over the next week, I got steadily better and more cantankerous. As I felt better, I longed to do more, but my wound prevented me from moving too much, and my body, easily exhausted, did not endure my obstinacy for long.

So I patiently endured the coddling I received from the Morgans and even, surprisingly, from Mr. Nelson. But never was my patience so sorely tried as when it came time for me to bathe.

Mr. Nelson had assured us that a bath once a day would be good for keeping my wound as well as my body clean and that I should be

The Mirror

allowed to soak in a tub of warm water as long as I liked. Unfortunately, I could not easily get into that tub without help and supervision. How ashamed I felt when they insisted upon the daily dunk, and how stubbornly I tried to avoid it.

On one such day when I'd had enough of their pampering and I was sure I could take care of myself, I refused Stuart's help and told him I could get into the tub myself.

"You aren't strong enough yet. You have only just started to spend more time awake, and if you tax yourself now, you may never heal properly. You will just have to wait another week."

"I'm fine. How taxing can it be to get into a tub of water? I will do it on my own." To prove I was okay, I got up from my bed and stood on my own. I felt dizzy, but I did not let on to Stuart that I was anything but perfectly okay.

He didn't want to, but at my insistence, he left me on my own. With him out of the way, I slowly removed my clothes and made to step into the water. The pain was incredible. I managed to get my second foot in the tub, and I sat down before the pain became too much. But the dizziness would not leave me, and before I could call out for assistance I was overcome and fainted.

When I awoke, I was lying in my bed, and two bright eyes were staring at me. "You don't look too good," the person murmured. "I've seen dead animals look better than you do now. You should probably be doing something about that."

I groaned and turned to hide my smiling face from my harasser. "I'll try, Sam, but I'm not making any promises. The way I feel right now, I might as well be a dead animal."

She giggled. "Mom said that you were really sick and that I couldn't visit you, but Stuart Morgan stopped by today and said you were doing a lot better. I told Mom that if you were doing better, you were probably sick of seeing the big ugly face of the apothecary, and you would probably be real glad to see some new company."

"I bet your mom didn't like that you said the apothecary had an ugly face," I replied. "Did she make you apologize?"

Sam grinned at me slyly. "She tried, but when I told her I was telling the truth and everyone knew it, she was forced to agree." Sam shrugged. "She still made me wash extra dishes, saying I needed to learn to be more polite."

I laughed at her evident dislike for the punishment. My lungs were not ready for the merriment, and I began to cough and wheeze. The motion caused pain, and I winced. When the coughing and wincing stopped, I looked over to find Sam staring at me with fear in her eyes.

"Are you going to die?" she whispered.

"No, Sam, I am not going to die. I just need a little time to heal, okay?"

She nodded, but she didn't look convinced.

I thought for a moment. "How about I show you the cut I have, and you can decide if I am going to die or not. It is really big, but the apothecary has kept it really clean, and it is going to heal."

Sam nodded, and slowly I lifted up the edge of my shirt. I had her remove the bandages and she looked at the gash. "That's awful big." She sighed. "Doesn't it hurt?"

I nodded. "That is why I need a little time to heal before I can come back to work. Is that okay?" She nodded. "Good, now how about you go and tell the curate that I am able to eat something and that I need a little help doing up these bandages. Then you can go back to the inn and tell your mom I will try to be back to work in another week. Also, if she says you can't come back, tell her that I would love to see you any time you can make it. Okay?"

Sam nodded and disappeared through the door. With a sigh of relief, I watched her leave, knowing that both she and I would be happier once I was on my feet again.

I couldn't sleep that night. I tossed about trying to find a comfortable position, but when I found one, the ramblings of my mind brought me back to a place of discomfort. I let out a sigh of frustration and felt my heart beat faster when the door appeared to open in response.

Mrs. Morgan held a candle in front of her as she walked to my bedside. Placing the candle on the side table, she looked at me and smiled. "You couldn't sleep either?" she whispered. I shook my head.

"Well then, we shall just have to keep each other company." With this said, she picked up the Bible that rested next to her candle and began to read.

I sat listening to the soft cadence of her voice. When there was a slight lull as she flipped the page, I decided to ask her about what weighed so heavily on my mind.

"Ma'am," I whispered, "when I was sick—"

"You still are sick, Caman. Let's not kid ourselves."

"Yes, but before when I was sick, there were a couple of days when Stuart didn't come into my room. Where was he?"

"He was praying. The Bible says to pray unceasingly, so he did."

"Did it work?"

"You are alive, are you not?"

"Yes, but how do you know that isn't just the way it was going to be? How do we know that it was because Stuart prayed?"

"Caman, you are alive because God wanted you to live. After Mr. Nelson's second visit, he said he refused to come and care for a filthy drunk. He told Stuart not to bother calling on him again unless he himself was in need. Despite this, two days later, he shows up at our door, demanding to see his patient and tend to him. Perhaps it happened because that is the way it was always going to happen, but I have a feeling there was a lot more going on there than just chance."

I leaned further into my pillow and Mrs. Morgan once more picked up her reading. I was almost asleep once more when another question came to me. "Ma'am," I whispered.

"Yes, Jeremy."

"A while back, I bumped into you as I was coming out of my room. You ran away scared. Why did I scare you so much?"

There was a soft sigh. "Sometimes, Jeremy, the past creeps up on us. You reminded me of something from my past, and I was startled. That is all."

"But what from your past could scare you that much?"

She shut the Bible with a thud. "I think it is time you go to sleep." Setting aside the book and picking up the candle, she turned and walked to the door. Looking once more at me, she smiled and whispered, "Sweet dreams," before she shut the door and I was left once more in the dark.

NINE

CAMAN TUCKED THE PENCIL INSIDE his journal and set it carefully on his cot when Gustave appeared with a bowl of supper. "Whose journal was this?" Gustave asked, holding up the small book he had taken from Caman's saddlebag.

Caman took his supper and answered Gustave between bites. "It belonged to a woman by the name of Martha. She worked at an inn where I have been living for the past half year."

"Is she—that is, is she quite well?"

"I don't want to talk about this. Perhaps you can tell me why you have an Isbetan name."

Gustave ignored Caman's question and took the empty bowl away. "It will be dark soon. Perhaps you should sleep. It may be that the king will have made his decision in the morning."

Gustave walked away, and Caman was left alone with his thoughts. He wondered where Sarah was. He wondered if Sam missed him as much as he missed her company. He wondered if the king had taken any time at all to consider what he had told him. With a heavy sigh, Caman lay on his cot and fell into a restless sleep.

Gustave watched as Caman tossed and turned on his cot. The journal had fallen onto the floor, and curiosity rankled his gut. He could go in and take a peek while Caman was sleeping. Caman would be none the wiser. Perhaps there would be some answers in there about this Martha.

Gustave's mouth went dry when he thought of all he had read in the other journal. Making up his mind, he opened the cell door as quietly as possible and picked up the journal. Scurrying out, he locked the door once more and dragged over a chair and a lantern. Setting them in place, he opened the journal and began to read. If Caman appeared to be waking, he would shove the journal back through the bars.

Caman would be none the wiser, and perhaps Gustave's curiosity would be sated.

The two monarchs sat quietly in the parlour. Rose flipped idly through a book, not taking in a word she read, her thoughts still on the intruder Caman. With a sigh of frustration, she tossed the book aside, considering it a lost cause for the evening. "Henry, dearest," she said when the king looked up from his own book, "have you heard any news from Shoals?"

"No, but I hope to hear soon."

The Mirror

"Well, if you do," Rose said as she stood up, "will you let me know? I'll be in the nursery."

Rose made to leave the room and was about to turn the knob when there was a knock on the door. A young page walked in and bowed when Rose opened the door. Handing a note to the king, he retreated to a corner to await further instructions.

Henry scanned the note and frowned. "You may leave," he said. With another bow, the page left the room.

Rose resumed her seat. "What does Shoals say?" she asked when Henry did not volunteer any information.

"He says he has found Sarah Livton in the Croden records, dead twelve years ago. But he is having difficulty with the Owzan records as they are a mess of errors and corrections that are difficult to decipher."

"So what does that tell us so far?"

"Nothing. We will just have to wait a little while longer."

"Well then, to the nursery I go. If there is any news, please inform me immediately."

Henry smiled at his wife as she disappeared out the door. Rose walked briskly down the hall, her head swimming with uncertainty. Was Caman to be trusted, or was he just as much of a snake as he had been before?

The faint sound of a crying baby greeted her as she turned the corner toward the nursery. Picking up her pace, she entered her children's room to find a very frazzled looking Elizabeth.

"I'm sorry, Elizabeth. I should have been here sooner. I lost all track of time."

"It is alright, ma'am. But I wonder if it might be better for you to get a wet nurse so you will not have to worry about time," replied Elizabeth.

Rose shook her head. "You know better, Elizabeth. I will not have another woman caring for my children. Besides, how would I decide whom to trust? No, I will do this myself." Taking Rosalie from Elizabeth's arms, she sat in a chair and draped a blanket around herself. With Elizabeth's help, she was able to begin nursing the hungry infant.

"That is better," sighed Rose. "They're only hungry."

Elizabeth walked across the nursery to give the queen some privacy. She did not return until she was called. When both children were fed, Elizabeth sat beside her queen and rocked the young Rosalie while Rose rubbed the tiny James' back.

"Have the other serving girls told you about the visitor we had at the palace this morning?" Rose asked quietly.

"No, ma'am. They have hardly spoken a word to me. I am new to them, and they do not trust me yet."

"I see." Rose sighed. "Well, perhaps you remember him from Emriville. His name is Jeremy Caman. Do you recall him?"

Elizabeth nodded, but did not express any of her opinions to the queen. "What did you think of him, then?" Rose asked.

"He was not a man to be trusted. He was cold and cruel. But he may have changed, your majesty."

"Yes," mused Rose. "He may have."

Rose shook her head as if to clear it of muddling thoughts. "Enough of this depressing conversation. You say you haven't spoken to anyone since you have arrived? That is a situation I can remedy."

The Mirror

Elizabeth blushed. "You misunderstand. I–I have talked some with John. He has invited me on a carriage ride and—"

"Did you accept?"

Elizabeth's cheeks tinged an even darker shade of red. "I didn't think it appropriate."

Rose kissed her son's head and gave Elizabeth a mischievous smile. "I think a carriage ride with John would be the most appropriate thing for you to do."

"Have you read your fill?" Caman asked, and was pleased to watch the startled look come across Gustave's face.

"I'm sorry," he said as he handed Caman the journal. "I didn't think you would mind."

"I guess I don't," Caman replied as he flipped through the pages of cramped writing. "Tell me, Gustave, have you ever had a secret that you wished no one would know, but when others found out, you realized you really didn't care all that much?"

Gustave stared at Caman through the bars. "I was born and raised in Isbeta until I was seven. My mother died during a raid in our town. My father was a mean drunk. A Samayan soldier saw me, took pity, and brought me back here to live in Silidon. Yet no matter how much I look or talk like a Samayan, I will always be Isbetan in my blood. I can't change that."

"No you can't, can you?"

"I should be about my work," Gustave said as he picked up his chair and lantern.

"Can you leave the lantern?"

There was a moment's hesitation before Gustave walked away, leaving the lantern on the floor. Flipping to the next blank page in his journal, Caman picked up his pencil and continued to write.

TEN

HEALING DIDN'T GO AS WELL as I had planned. I didn't leave my bed much the first week, and Mr. Nelson came to visit every day to check on me. His visits were routine and quick. He would chat to me while he listened to my heart, checked for any signs of fever, and re-bandaged my wound which he claimed was healing very nicely now. I learned to appreciate his care rather than spite him for initially rejecting me when I was in need.

Sam liked to visit. She often mentioned the dour appearance of my caretaker. I reminded her that though Mr. Nelson may have a grisly face, he had gentle hands. When having a bandage changed, I much preferred his practiced hand to Stuart's clumsy attempts.

Stuart was a near-constant companion. He spent much time at my side entertaining me with conversation or card games. Sometimes he would read scripture to me, but I only tolerated this when I was tired and did not wish to speak. He brought me my meals and changed my bed sheets. He helped me clean myself and so much more.

I owe that man my life for what he tolerated. I make it sound so easy, but I was not a pleasant patient. My need humiliated me, and I often demanded that I should do things on my own. Stuart knew better from the first time he listened to my demands. Now he only allowed me to do the things Mr. Nelson said I was able to do. I would cuss and scream, but he wouldn't listen. Instead, he would grin and help me despite my complaints.

Sam's visits were the highlight to the end of every day. She told me what was happening at the inn, and about the patrons who visited there. She brought me the candies she was given, and we shared the sweets. "What do you do with the coins?" I asked her one day.

She shrugged. "I usually give them to Mom. She uses them to keep up the inn."

"Do you give every single one to your mom?"

Sam shook her head. "Mom won't take them all. She says I should save them. I have a whole jar under my bed. I think someday I'm going to buy a house with them. A nice big house, so me, Mom, Billy, and Martha don't have to live at the inn anymore. I mean, the inn is nice and all, but…"

"But what?"

She bit her lip and shrugged. I wanted to know her answer, but I wasn't sure if I should pry. My mind was soon made up.

"I can keep a secret," I said.

"I want my own room so Mom can get married."

The Mirror

I tried not to laugh, but it was hard. "Darling, what makes you think you need your own room in order for your mom to get married? She could get married while you live at the inn."

Sam shook her head vehemently. "She told me herself. When I asked her if she was ever going to get married, she said that if she got married I wouldn't be able to share a room with her and then where would she and her husband sleep. She said she didn't want to kick me out of my bed, and there are no other rooms available at the inn."

Understanding set in. Sam wanted a father, but Sarah was trying to tell her that was never going to happen. I told Sam to hop up on the bed, and I gave her a one-armed hug. She squeezed me back, doing her best to avoid the bandages. We stayed snuggled close together talking about anything and everything for a couple more hours. Sam only left because Sarah arrived telling her it was bedtime.

Sarah never visited. Perhaps it was my pride speaking, but I felt it was only right Sarah visit me after all I had done at the inn. I wondered if she had the decency to miss the help or if she was just glad to have me out of her hair. Her absence irritated me.

I decided Sam must be company enough for me. She told me about the new calf that had been born. She had named her Lady because she had great big batting eyelashes like a lady must have. I listened to her prattle, and by the end of the week I knew I would not be able to leave Owzan without missing her terribly.

By Sunday, I was well enough to go to church. Halfway through the service I realized just how difficult it was to sit on a wooden bench. Sweat droplets peppered my brow, and pain seared my side. I was glad when Stuart finished speaking so I could stand, but the different position did not alleviate my pain. Fortunately, I was able to leave for home immediately after the service.

The following week I was able to do more and more each day, and the next Sunday I made it through the service without breaking into a sweat. The apothecary saw me after and walked over with a smile that looked like a grimace on his face.

"You are looking good today, Mr. Caman."

"Thank you. I probably owe my health to you. I don't think any other apothecary would have dared cut a man's flesh away."

"It comes with the job. I only wish I had prevented the cut from becoming infected in the first place." I nodded in agreement. "I'll tell you what. I'll come on over after lunch and take one more last look at that cut. If I think it is healed enough, I'll let you go to work tomorrow. Just simple stuff, mind you, but at least you will be able to do something."

"That sounds real good. How about we head over now?"

As I had hoped, I was allowed to do simple work. This meant, according to the apothecary, anything I could do sitting down, including many of my least favourite chores. I didn't care. I was going to be working instead of sitting in a bed. The idea of it was exhilarating. So much so that sleep did not come easily that night. I was restless, and by the time the sun rose, I was ready to be at the inn. Picking myself up off my bed, I dressed and headed down the street to where work waited for me.

Sarah was already in the kitchen. It seemed I could never beat her to work, but she had the advantage of living just upstairs. She hardly looked up at me when I entered. Instead, she sighed as she went back to mixing batter.

The Mirror

"Good morning, Miss Livton," I whispered.

"Good morning." She sighed again. Her shoulders sagged and her stirring slowed. She looked to be asleep on her feet. I cleared my throat and she jumped a little. She shook her head and picked up the pace of her stirring.

"How much sleep have you been getting?" I asked. Sarah just shrugged. "Miss Livton, don't you think you should be sleeping right now instead of working? I mean, you're exhausted."

"I'm fine," she snapped. "If you aren't going to work, you can get out of my kitchen."

I scowled at her back. I was trying to be nice, and this is how she treated me. Finding a knife, I sat down and began to peel the carrots piled on the counter. The silence in the room annoyed me. I had been too much surrounded by silence recently to now enjoy the reprieve it brought.

"How have things been going at the inn? Sam's told me about the patrons, but what about the work? Has it gone well?"

Sarah dropped a dollop of batter into a hot pan. There was a sizzle and hiss before she responded. "If you are looking for a compliment, Mr. Caman, I will give it to you now so that you can quit begging for it. You were missed while you were away simply because Martha was ill again and Billy was busy preparing the garden. We could have used your help."

"That's not what I meant by it!" I raised my hands defensively, completely appalled that she thought I would beg for a compliment. "I was simply trying to make conversation."

Sarah didn't respond. The sizzle and hiss of the pan continued as Sarah added more dollops of batter. The sun began to rise higher in the sky. It felt like only moments had passed when the door to the kitchen burst open and Sam entered.

"The curate is here, Mom, and he says he wants to talk with you. I told him you were busy, but he said that it would only take a moment. He says it's important." Sam wandered over to the stove. Picking up a cake of cooked batter, she ripped off a piece and stuffed it in her mouth. She chewed and swallowed then, looking up at her mom, she said, "He's waiting."

Sarah picked up a towel and wiped her hands on it. "I have three more cakes to make. You finish them, okay Sam?" Sam nodded. "Once you are done that, there are eggs ready to be cooked in the bowls on the table. You can use the same pan, but make sure you have enough butter in the bottom. The meat is staying warm in the stove in the old kitchen."

"I know, Mom. You can go."

Sarah smiled. Taking Sam's cheeks in her hands, she bent and kissed her daughter on the forehead. "Good morning, Sam girl. I love you." She raced out of the kitchen to speak with Stuart.

Sam rolled her eyes as Sarah disappeared. Picking up the ladle her mother had been using, she began dropping batter into the pan. "How are you, Mr. Caman?"

"Very well, Miss Livton. How are you?"

"Oh, okay I guess."

"Just okay?" Sam shrugged. "What's the matter, Sam?"

She refused to respond.

The Mirror

"Come on, Sam. You know you can trust me. I still haven't told anyone what you want to do with the pennies you're saving. Don't you think you can trust me with whatever is on your mind now?"

Sam let out a loud sigh. "Are you going to leave us? I mean, once you are better, are you going to leave us?"

I paused, not knowing what I was going to say. "I don't know when I am going to leave. It might be a long time before I move on."

"But you are going to leave us, aren't you?" Sam's question was accusing, and I felt like a cad. Who was I to come into her life and act like her friend while it was convenient? Once I tired of Owzan, I would leave and Sam would be heartbroken.

"Look, Sam, I don't want to leave, but sometimes a person has no choice. I probably won't be settling down until I get married. Until that day, I'll be wandering from place to place."

Sam sighed and continued working at the stove. She was about to turn to get the eggs when her face lit up. "You could marry Mom," she said cheerily. "Mom needs help around the inn, and she is worried that someday Martha is going to kick the bucket and Billy will be so heartbroke he won't be able to do anything. If you were around, she wouldn't have to worry about that. Besides that, you say you need a wife, and Mom won't admit it, but she needs a husband. It would be perfect."

I gulped, not sure what to say. "Now Sam, there is a little bit more to marriage than what is convenient. I mean, a man and a woman need to be in love if they want to get married. They don't just marry because they need some chores done."

"Stuart Morgan didn't marry for love."

"Is that so?" I asked. "It is Mr. Morgan, Sam, and how do you know he didn't marry for love?"

Sam shrugged and poured the eggs into the hot pan. "Everyone in town knows. It came up at the town meeting. But I guess you wouldn't know that."

"No, I wouldn't." I sighed. "I take it you aren't going to tell me anything more about it."

She shook her head. "Mom says I have to keep my mouth shut about it. After all, it is not my place to spread gossip."

"A smart woman, your mom is."

"Yup, she is. She would be a great wife, too."

"Sam, *that* is enough."

The door slammed open and Sarah walked in. "That man," she muttered under her breath. "Sam, we need a plate. Are the eggs ready?"

"Yes, ma'am." Sam hurried away to get a plate. Sarah took up her position by the stove and began to clean up some of the mess.

"What did Stuart want?" I asked from my position in the corner.

Sarah jumped and blushed at my voice. "Nothing, he is just being his usual self. Telling me I should go to church, and that I would be welcome any time. Things aren't like they used to be. The usual. He's probably telling you the same things."

"No, actually not," I replied, a bit confused. "I have no choice but to go to church. You, on the other hand, have a choice. What I don't understand is why you don't attend."

"Because I don't. Why don't you go help Sam? I can peel those later, and Sam will be too busy if you don't help her."

The Mirror

"I can't. The apothecary says I must stay seated as much as possible, or he will have Stuart bind me to my bed. I won't be able to do anything then."

"Fine." Sarah looked agitated and slightly distracted. Her efforts at cleaning the kitchen were half-hearted, and every time Sam walked in to get another plate of food, she jumped and blushed ever so slightly. I smiled at her jitters. She was acting like a nervous schoolgirl, and it dawned on me that she really wasn't that much older.

As casually as possible, I followed her motion around the room. She was short with long blond hair that curled slightly. Her face was smooth except for some light worry lines at the corners of her eyes. Her mouth was thin and pink, and her eyes deep blue with large black bags hanging under them. A scar bright and vivid drew a line from the corner of her lip to the top of her cheekbone. If it weren't for that scar and the black bags, she would be very beautiful. No older than twenty-five.

"How did you get that scar?" I asked.

She touched her cheek and didn't respond. Instead, she left me to sit by myself in the kitchen. Again I was badgered by silence. Finishing my chore, I wandered into the old kitchen to see if there was anything else I could do.

Sarah was picking up a pan of hot water off the stove when I entered. She poured it into the washtub and looked up. Our eyes locked, and her face turned scarlet. Without saying anything, she placed the pan back on the stove and left the room.

Pondering her retreating back, I looked into the tub to see how full it was and groaned. It still needed at least three more pots of water, and I didn't know how I was going to get them to the tub. Taking a deep breath, I picked up the empty pot and carried it out to the pump.

The snow had all melted while I was incapacitated, and it had left the ground muddy. My boots stuck to the ground as I walked the path, and by the time I reached my destination, they were completely covered in mud and grime. Placing the pot under the spigot, I began to pump. Pain seared up my side, and I groaned in agony.

Knowing a full pot would overexert me, I only filled the pot halfway. Even so, I was sweating profusely by the end. Grabbing the handle with the hand that hung on my good side, I heaved on the pot, and began my journey back to the house. Billy came to my rescue before I even made it to the door.

He scolded me gently. "The curate told me about your side, and I won't be having you getting sick again. You are needed here." I didn't protest too much.

When I reached the door, I looked down at my boots. I knew I should remove them, but I hesitated. It wasn't common for me to remove my footwear in public. Then again, it wasn't likely that I would see anyone but Sam. Slowly I reached down and removed the filthy leather from around my feet. Placing my boots just outside the door, I moved toward my seat by the tub and waited as Billy finished filling it.

"Come and get me when you're ready to switch the water. Don't try changing it yourself or you'll just make yourself sick," Billy said softly as he poured the last pot of water in.

"But I'll be interfering with your work," I said, a little uncomfortable with the fact that I couldn't carry a pot of water.

The Mirror

Billy shrugged. "Sam did all the time before you came. Don't you worry yourself too much about it. You'll be well again soon enough."

"Yes, I suppose," I grumbled as Billy left the room. I sighed as I stuck my hands in the water and began to wash. The door banged open and Sam walked through. She heaved a sigh and placed a stack of dirty bowls down beside me.

"What's the matter?" I asked.

"Mom says I have to wait until everyone is gone before I can go out and play, and there are two visitors that just won't leave. It is the most beautiful day we've had in over three months, and I have to wait around until they're gone."

"That isn't very kind of them. How about you help me with these dishes while you wait? If we get them done quickly, I can help your mom with things in the kitchen, and you can play longer. How does that sound?"

Without hesitation, Sam picked up a towel and began to dry. "I think Mom is really tired today. She's been acting real funny. Ever since she talked with Stuart Morgan, she's been blushing every time I see her. What do you think he said to her?"

"So you noticed that too, did you?" I asked. Sam nodded vigorously. "I don't know if *Mr.* Morgan said anything to her besides what she's used to hearing. She told me he just asked her to come to church again."

Missing my emphasis on the Mr., Sam rolled her eyes and continued. "Stuart Morgan never stops by just to tell Mom to go to church. He must have said something, though."

As if to prove her point, Sarah opened the door let out a little squeak, and disappeared again. "See, she's as jumpy as a grasshopper."

"Maybe. But it's time to change this water. How about you go get Billy? He said he would help us out today."

Sam scurried to the door. Opening it, she shouted out, "Billy! We need you to change the water." I winced as her words reverberated in the room.

"Well, I could have done that," I muttered.

"Of course you could have," said Sam smartly, "but you asked me to get Billy. He always comes running when I shout like that. He says it lets him know he is needed."

"Probably because he thinks the inn has caught on fire and you're trapped inside. I don't think anyone would holler like that unless they were in danger of dying."

Sam scrunched her nose at me and went across the room to peek into the lounge. "They're still there," she whined. "Why would they just sit there like that? Don't they have anything better to do?"

"Let me see," I said and shoved Sam aside. Looking through the crack in the door, I saw the people Sam was talking about. It was a couple. A young woman was sitting elegantly in her chair, and the man next to her leaned over the table so he could hold her hand. She looked at him with complete adoration. When he spoke, she leaned in to hear. She let out a full-throated laugh as if he had said something incredibly funny.

"I want to see," Sam said. She squeezed in under me and peeked a little lower down on the door. "Why's she laughing?"

"Because she is in love, darling. That is what happens when you're in love. You laugh a lot."

Sam shut the door and almost caught my nose in so doing. "I think that's silly," she said as she walked toward the water barrel.

The Mirror

"What's silly?" Billy asked as he stepped in through the back door.

"This girl here," I said, cutting Sam off before she could say anything. "She hollers so loud I think I have gone deaf in one ear."

Billy grinned. "I know what you mean. You should have heard her when she was a wee little one."

"It's a wonder Sarah isn't deaf," I said.

Billy started laughing, and I joined him when I turned to see Sam standing with her hands on her hips. I might have been able to keep a straight face, but when she stomped her foot, I lost it. It wasn't until Sarah came to her daughter's rescue that Billy and I quit laughing.

"Sam told me something today that has been bothering me."

"What is that?" Stuart asked as he flipped a page in his book.

"She said that you had not married for love, and that it had come up at the town meeting."

Stuart paused and looked up at me. With a sigh, he set aside his book and moved his candle so he could look at me better. "I did initially marry for love, but things have changed since then. Why it would have come up at the town meeting just proves the fact that there is not enough gossip to feed the busybodies."

"Do you not love your wife now?"

"I love her immensely. More than when I married her."

"But then Sam's comment..."

"Was a tidbit of information beyond her ken. She will perhaps understand better when she is older."

"Do you think it wise to marry for convenience?"

"Ah, now your true question is revealed."

I squirmed under Stuart's steady gaze, but I did not retract my question.

"Let me put it this way, Caman. There are many reasons why people should get married, but many more why they should not. I would not suggest a marriage of convenience unless the couple is committed enough to remain married when it is inconvenient."

"I guess that makes sense."

"Has someone piqued your interest that you speak of marriage, Caman?"

"What?" I spluttered, taken aback by the question. "Of course not. Marriage and I are not on good terms. In fact, I could live my entire life without marriage."

"What makes you so opposed to the union?"

"History." I pushed back my chair and walked toward the door. "But that is not worth bringing up now. I'm tired. Goodnight, Stuart."

"Goodnight, Caman."

ELEVEN

SARAH'S MOOD CHANGED after that day. She wasn't jumpy or skittish, but neither was she domineering or cold. It wasn't that she had been entirely unwelcoming before. Only in her relations with me had she shown these traits, but now as I worked alongside her in her kitchen, I saw a side of her I hadn't before.

She was kind and warm-hearted. She laughed often and was always gentle with the doddering Martha. We talked a lot. Mostly she talked about Sam, and things she had done while she was growing up. I told her about Emriville and the war and my mother. It was all safe conversation. There were areas that we knew not to venture into. She never once mentioned or alluded to Sam's father, and I never referred to my sordid relationships and heavy alcohol use.

All this time, I slowly healed and began to do more in the kitchen, but it wasn't until the middle of May that I was cleared by Mr. Nelson to go about my normal duties. It was an odd day, that one. I thought to start it in the kitchen, but I knew some things had been lacking since I had fallen ill, so instead I made my way down the hall toward some empty rooms.

Though these rooms normally got cleaned once a week so that they would be serviceable when demanded, there had been no one to take care of them. The room I entered was covered in dust. I went to the old kitchen to boil a pot of water, but to my surprise when I came back to the room, Martha was already dusting off the cupboard. Seeing my hot bucket of water, she took it from me and bustled me out of the room. I had thought Martha too ill to work, but with a shake of my head, I decided to think nothing of it and to find what else needed to be done.

Sam scowled at me when she saw me in the hall. "Mom says you have to help Billy outside rather than help me with the dishes," she said moodily. "It's going to take me ages without your help, and I want to go outside and play this morning but there won't be any time."

"I'm sorry, Sam," I replied as I wiped the sweat from my brow. "Perhaps I will be able to help you tomorrow."

"But tomorrow it might be raining, and I want to go out and play when the sun is shining." She stomped her foot and gave me a dirty look.

"Sam," I said to stop her from walking away. "That's no way to treat a friend. I expect better behaviour from you." Sam bit her lip but didn't say anything. "I'm sure it will be sunny out this afternoon. Perhaps you will have time to play then."

She shook her head. "I have to go to the mercantile then. Mom needs some more salt for tonight's dinner. She says it will taste just awful without it." She sighed and began to walk away again, but I still heard her muttering something about at least the walk being outside.

The Mirror

With a shake of my head, I went to find Billy who was busy pulling weeds in the enormous back garden. "Glad you are here to help," Billy said. "These weeds would take ages for me, working alone. Perhaps we can get through the entire garden today along with some more planting."

Billy and I worked steadily most of the day, and when Billy took a break from the garden later in the afternoon to tend to his animals, I decided to work on the front of the inn. I had noticed a loose storm shutter that needed to be fastened, as well as some large weeds growing up around the door that needed pulling.

With the assistance of Billy's tools, I was working on this when I heard the singsong chanting of a group of boys.

Silly Sammy, she's a baby,
She'll never go to school!
She tries her best to read and write,
But we all know that she's a fool!

I didn't wait to hear the second verse of the song. At the name of Sam, I turned and ran. The gang was just over the hill, their voices raised in song as they each took turns pulling on her braids and pinching her arms.

One of Sam's braids was undone. Her blond locks hung loose at her side, and her ribbon was nowhere to be seen. Her teeth were clenched and her eyes red, but she didn't shed a tear. Instead, she kept walking, holding her basket tightly in her arms. She walked toward the inn without looking back.

My anger flared when I noticed two men watching from the street. Neither of them did anything. They just stood and watched as a young girl was being terrorized.

I ran to Sam and pulled her behind my back to protect her from the gang. "Who are you?" demanded the tallest boy in the pack. His hands were balled into fists ready to fight. His followers did likewise, one even daring to raise his dukes menacingly.

I sneered down at them. "So, you think it's funny to terrorize a helpless girl? You think you're tough because you can pull on braids and sing a song? You are being childish. Now get on home to your daddies and explain to them how you bullied a little girl. I imagine they will be just as disgusted as I am."

"Well at least we have daddies," shouted the boy with his fists raised.

My self-control shattered. I grabbed the boy who spoke by the collar and lifted him into the air. His red curls bounced, and at first, fear filled his eyes. It soon vanished. "You will never speak to me or this young lady like that again," I said through clenched teeth.

The boy smirked, and with a look of disdain, he spat in my face. Turning him about, I kept hold of him as I counted out three quick smacks to his backside. Grabbing his bottom, he looked up at me with terror. I could tell by his quivering chin and watering eyes, that he was fighting tears.

"If this were the army, I would have had you flogged for such behaviour. Now smarten up and head on home."

"You can't do that!" shouted the lead boy. "You can't just go hitting him like that! I'm going to go tell my father, and he'll have you kicked out of town for sure." He raised his fists threateningly. I raised my hand, and he backed away.

"You'll pay for this!" he shouted as he turned and ran. His posse turned and skittered after him. The boy I had hit held his bottom the entire way.

Turning, I saw Sam slumped on the ground. I had forgotten how roughly I had shoved her behind me. Her basket had fallen from her hands, and the salt had spilled onto the ground. Tears welled in her eyes.

"What did you have to do that for?" she shouted angrily. "You—you made me spill the salt," she stuttered around tears.

I picked her up into my arms as the sobs began. Salvaging what salt I could, I also picked up the basket. With my fragile cargo in hand, I made my way back to the inn.

Sarah met me at the door. She must have been wondering what had happened to Sam and me. Horror filled her eyes when she saw us coming up to the door. "Is she alright? Let me see her! I must see her."

As she took Sam from me, the rest of the salt spilled on to the floor, and Sam let out another gut-wrenching sob. Sarah almost shattered. I saw her wobbling. She was trying to be strong, but she was hurting for her child, so I took control of the situation.

Touching Sarah's arm, I got her attention. "Go put water on the stove to make a pot of tea. While you wait, bring a warm damp rag to your room so we can clean Sam's face. I'll clean her face while you braid her hair. By then the water should be boiled, and Sam may be ready to talk."

Nodding slightly, she put her daughter down and went to the kitchen. I looked at Sam who stood solemnly where her mother had left her. I offered her my hand, and she took it. Together we made our way upstairs to her room. She sat down on her bed and grabbed a ragged patchwork doll that rested near her pillow. Holding it close, she stared blankly at the wall.

"Sam," I whispered.

She looked at me with big, sad eyes. "I can read. Honest. I can."

I hugged her close. "I know, darling. I know you can read. Those boys were just being mean. Your mom and I will make sure they leave you alone from now on."

Sam shook her head. "Mom will, but you're going to have to leave town. Devan said he would get his dad to kick you out, and he always gets his way."

"Is that so? Well, we'll have to see if Devan gets his way this time, because I am not leaving my little girl to fend for herself, okay?"

Sam smiled shyly up at me. It was the first smile I had seen since the incident, and it was a relief. She placed her doll back by the bed and got to her feet. "Mom's taking a long time. Do you think she forgot where to find us?"

I laughed at Sam's question, but I was beginning to wonder myself. "How about you stay here and get changed into a clean dress, and I'll go see where she is, okay? Maybe she's having trouble with the pump. Billy said it's been sticking the past few days."

I left Sam to prance about the room deciding what to change into. Entering the dining room, I heard sobs coming from the old kitchen. I quickened my pace.

Sarah was standing by the stove, her eyes blotchy and nose running. The kettle was unfilled, and the rag I had asked her to grab for

The Mirror

her daughter was crumpled in her hand. Taking her into my arms, I soothed her while she cried.

When her tears slowed, she pushed away from me and gave me an embarrassed smile. "When I saw you carrying Sam, all sorts of terrible thoughts raced through my head, and I convinced myself that something dreadful had happened." She wiped at her eyes and sniffed. "I'm sorry. I'm being terribly silly right now."

"Sam's alright, Sarah. She just had the misfortune of meeting up with some bullies. I'm sure they won't bother her anymore."

Sarah nodded. "I suppose you're right." She took a deep, steadying breath and gave me a wobbly smile. "I should go check on Sam."

As she left to tend to her daughter, I filled the kettle at the pump. While I waited for it to boil on the stove, I took out a tray and placed three cups and saucers on it. After preparing the tea, I carried the tray up the stairs along with some warm water and a cloth.

I was about to knock on the door when I heard Sam. "You know, Mom, I forgive them already."

"You do?" asked Sarah calmly. "How can you do that when they haven't apologized?"

"Stuart Morgan says we must always forgive those who hurt us even if they don't ask for forgiveness. I figure there is no use in pushing it off. I mean, if I have to forgive them, I might as well get it done and over with."

"Sam, just because you say you have forgiven them doesn't mean you have forgiven them in your heart. When Stuart Morgan says you need to forgive, he isn't just talking about saying the words. He is talking about forgiving from the inside, too. That means you can't be angry with them anymore. You can't get back at them. It means it is like they never did anything wrong anymore."

"I know," Sam replied, a little less cheery than before. "But, I think Stuart Morgan would understand that I was trying to forgive and that by saying it out loud, it helps me feel it in the heart area too."

There was no response. I figured this was a good time to break in. "Who wants tea?" I said as I opened the door.

"Did you bring the cream and sugar?" Sam asked cheerily.

"Of course. What kind of person would I be if I didn't bring the cream and sugar?"

We enjoyed a few relaxing moments with the steaming beverage before we went back to the bustle of the day and the reality of the ruined salt.

When I returned to the curate's house, Stuart Morgan was not happy. "You spanked a boy?" he shouted. "What came over you that you would do such a thing? I mean, if it had been when you just arrived, maybe I would have expected it, but now? Why, Caman? Why did you have to do this?"

"Who told you this?"

"Mr. Mitchel came by today. He said his son Devan and his friends were out walking the streets playing games and doing what kids do, when you spanked Jace Callaway for stepping on your foot." Stuart shook his head. "For goodness sakes, Caman, Jace Callaway is only thirteen years old. He's still a kid."

The Mirror

My mouth gaped in shock. "So, that is the story, is it? I suppose Mr. Mitchel wanted me out of town. I am a menace who will only harm this community."

"Something along those lines."

"Well, I will have you know, I did not spank Jace Callaway until he spit in my face. That brat, along with Devan Mitchel and his gang were picking on Sam as she walked back from the mercantile. Honestly Stuart, that girl was terrified after they had done what they did to her."

Stuart stood in apparent shock. His mouth opened and closed several times before a muttered "Oh," made it past his lips.

Moments ticked by as I waited for him to say something more. "Is she alright?" he finally asked.

"Yeah, she's doing alright. She lost a ribbon, and has a few small bruises, but other than that she's alright."

Stuart nodded. "There's going to be a town meeting soon. It will be held at the inn again. They are going to discuss whether to throw you out. I will be there to defend you, if that is alright."

I nodded. "The story doesn't hold, though. Why would I spank a boy on the street for something as petty as a bruised toe?"

"It's your word against Mr. Mitchel's," replied the curate, "and Mitchel is likely to convince the town that you have an easy temper. Unless we come up with some compelling evidence, the town is more likely to believe Mr. Mitchel. They trust him. He has been here longer than you, and he is respected in the community. Besides that, most people will side with Mitchel over Sarah. There is too much history for them to be able to trust Sarah."

"I don't get it," I muttered. "There were two witnesses. Two men were standing in their doorways as those boys taunted her. They just watched as Sam was pinched and prodded, and they didn't do anything to help. Why didn't they? Couldn't they see what was going on?"

Stuart shrugged. "I guess we must forgive their ignorance."

"Forgive!" I shouted. The word twisted a sore spot in my heart. "It won't happen. I heard Sam. You want to know what she said? She said she had forgiven those boys just because Stuart Morgan said we are supposed to." I shook my head. "Well, Stuart, I am not that naive. Those two men can rot in hell for all I care. They deserve it after they stood by and watched my Sam hurt and did absolutely nothing."

"Caman." Stuart's voice was firm. "It is not for us to decide who goes to hell. For all we know, those men could have had reasons for not acting as you did. After all, not many adults would get involved in the disputes of children."

"So, you think I was wrong for getting involved?" I shouted. "After all, this was just a child's dispute. I should have just kept out of it and let them harass Sam."

"That is not what I said, Caman." Stuart was getting frustrated. "I just don't think we can condemn the men for not getting involved."

"I'm sorry, Stuart, but I do condemn them. They should have done something, and because they didn't Sam got hurt."

"I understand that, but—"

"There are no buts!" I shouted at him. "You don't understand. Sam was hurt. She shouldn't have to deal with that, and she did. I don't care who did the hurting, but if someone could have stopped it, they are just as much to blame as the one who did the deed."

The Mirror

Stuart held up his hands in defeat. "I don't agree with you, Caman. But I don't think that I am going to convince you tonight. Maybe someday you will be able to forgive those men."

Ignoring Stuart, I stormed out of the parlour and into my bedroom. Slamming the door, I flopped down onto my bed and closed my eyes. I didn't want to think. I didn't want to move. I was angry. I should have done something. I should have protected Sam better. I should have been there for her, and none of this would have happened.

I looked around my room for something to do, but the only thing that wasn't furniture or clothes was a Bible. I was not desperate enough to pick it up. Instead, I rolled onto my side and tried to sleep.

A couple hours later, there was a knock on my door. "I don't want to talk, Stuart," I shouted. There was a pause and then the knock sounded again. "Honestly, Stuart, I am still angry, and I don't want to talk about it."

There was another pause. "May I come in?" It was a soft, feminine voice.

I wasn't sure what to say. The door creaked open a crack. "Did you hear me?" the lady asked.

"Yeah," I stuttered. "Yeah, you may come in."

The door opened fully and Mrs. Morgan walked in. She was carrying a tray with some tea and a piece of cake. She placed it by my bed and took a seat in the chair by the nightstand. I sat up, feeling just slightly uncomfortable that Mrs. Morgan was in my room.

"Eat up," she said. "I made it just this afternoon. You should like it."

I bit into the cake. It was moist and sweet. Taking a gulp of tea, I burnt my tongue and nearly cursed. The presence of Mrs. Morgan stopped me. When I was finally done eating, I sat and waited for her to say something.

"There were once two women," she began. "Both of them were beautiful and respected by the town. They had good husbands and happy homes. One day, the first woman's husband came home and found her talking with another man. He was angry because he was afraid that his wife did not love him anymore. The woman apologized, and the man forgave his wife.

"On another day, the second man came home to find his wife in his bed with another man. The town soon discovered the truth about this woman's affairs, and they mocked her and her husband. Despite this, the man forgave his wife for her disloyalty, and together they rebuilt their life.

"Of these two women, which do you think loved her husband more? Was it the one who was forgiven for speaking with a neighbour without her husband's knowledge? Or, was it the one who publicly disgraced her husband but was still forgiven?"

Mrs. Morgan waited for me to answer. "I don't know," I finally said. "I suppose the one who was forgiven for sleeping with another man. At least her husband loved her more. That is certain."

Mrs. Morgan nodded. Picking up the tray with the empty dishes, she turned to leave. "Wait," I called. "I don't get it. What do those two women have to do with anything?"

Mrs. Morgan smiled. "Many times we are hurt by those God calls us to love. Sometimes the hurt is worse than other times. Despite what someone did, we need to forgive them so that we show them God's love, and they in turn will show us God's love back. Forgive much, Mr.

The Mirror

Caman, and you will soon learn that you have been forgiven much. Seek revenge, and you to will find yourself in a grave next to your enemy."

She turned and walked out of my room.

TWELVE

I HELPED SAM WITH HER WORK the next morning. She was quieter than usual, but by the time we were done, she was ready to go outside and play. I was nervous. What if the boys returned? What if this time they seriously hurt Sam? But my fears couldn't hold her back.

Sam trekked out into the yard and began swinging on the swing that hung there. I watched for a while as she played, to make sure all was well, then turned back to work. Sarah must have been nervous about her daughter as well, because halfway through cleaning the men's rooms, she barged in on me.

I looked up, startled. "You have to watch Sam," she said.

"What do you mean, I have to watch Sam?"

Sarah fidgeted, indecision evident on her face. "I have to go to town to pick up salt. Everything that Sam brought back yesterday was ruined. I need you to make sure Sam is okay while I'm gone."

The Mirror

"I can do that," I replied.

A small smile crept to the corner of Sarah's mouth. I smiled back, and she blushed. "Thank you," she murmured. Then she left.

Deciding it would be wise to see what Sam was up to, I went to check on her. She was twirling happily in the yard enjoying the spring sunshine. When she looked up, she saw me and waved. I waved back and returned to my work.

It wasn't ten minutes later when Sarah returned. I heard her bustling through the inn, and I expected her to go to the kitchen, but she didn't. Instead, she stormed into the room where I was working. I was on my hands and knees examining a rickety bedpost when she started shouting.

"Who do you think you are?" she said pointing a shaking finger at me. Her face was red with the exertion of walking and her fury at me. "I went to town, and the first thing I hear is 'Did you hear about that Caman man? He went and spanked Jace Callaway the other day.' And, if that weren't enough, I ran into Mr. Mitchel, who is determined to throw you out of town and kindly reminded me that there would be a town meeting this Friday to discuss the matter."

I cringed. Perhaps I should have told her, but I hadn't expected her to hear about it so soon.

"Honestly Mr. Caman, what were you thinking?"

I got up from my position on the ground, and Sarah had to go from staring down at me to glaring up at me. Either way she was rather menacing. She crossed her arms and started to tap her toe, waiting for me to begin. I cleared my throat.

"First of all, I think you have the wrong story—"

"So you didn't spank Jace Callaway, and there isn't going to be a town meeting on Friday?"

"No, no. Those parts are quite accurate. Just my reason for hitting Jace is a little different than what you probably heard."

"Is that so? Well, I'm so glad that there was a reason for your mad act. Pray tell me, what was this purpose?"

"To protect your daughter."

Sarah didn't believe me. I could tell by the look in her eye. She thought I was bluffing, and she wasn't going to be taken in.

"Honestly! Jace was one of the boys picking on Sam. When I suggested they leave, he made another rude comment. Then he spit in my face. That boy deserved far worse than a spanking."

"I don't care, Caman," Sarah said as she shook her head in her hands. It was not lost on me that this was the first time she had used my given name. "Because of what you did, you are most likely going to be kicked out of town. Not only will I lose a good worker, but Sam will be heartbroken. It will be just like when Zach left, only worse, because Zach was dead, but you, you're just leaving her."

"Sarah," I said, reaching my hand out to her.

"No, don't touch me." I pulled my hand back. "I have work to do," she said softly. "After all, the entire town is going to be here in two days."

The next two days passed by excruciatingly slowly. Sarah seemed to want to protect Sam from me, and I was refused access to her. First I tried to help her with the dishes, but Sarah said I needed to fix the bedpost. By the time I had finished that, Sam was out playing, and Sarah had written out a list of things she wanted me to do. The list was long enough to last me a week, and all the jobs required me to work by

The Mirror

myself. By the time Friday night came, I was sure that I was no longer welcome, and I wasn't certain if I even wanted to stay.

I was cleaning windows as townspeople began to enter the inn. Some glared at me while others chose to ignore me. Finally the room became too crowded for me to continue, so I began to help Sam clear tables.

That was a very poor idea. As I walked from table to table, I was called names like child beater, drunken louse, and useless cur. Perhaps I deserved some of what they said, but their words wore on me, and by the time the meeting was ready to begin, I was ready for a fight.

"Ladies and gentlemen," Mr. Mitchel said as he strode to the front. "We have within our midst this night a stranger. A man who came into this town without a soul knowing his name. Despite us not knowing who he was, we showed him hospitality and kindness, and what did he do in return? He beat our children and blemished this town with his drunkenness and philandering."

A loud booing rose from the crowd. I stood to my feet, rage pouring through my veins rattling in my ears like the constant boom of a drum. So this is what they thought of me. Me, the one who hadn't touched a drink in over two months. Me, the one who had only gone to the saloon a few times since I had arrived while others made it a weekly habit. Me, the one who was working at the inn for free while they all took advantage.

If there was any reason for them to kick me out of town it was for spanking the child, but if that was their reason, they should have left the rest of that rubbish out of their speech. The booing had stopped when I stood. The crowd turned to look at me. They were waiting for me to speak. I looked around to see if I could find Stuart. He was nowhere to be seen. "So much for your support," I muttered.

"Is there something you would like to say, Mr. Caman?" spat Mr. Mitchel. There was no pity in his tone. He looked down on me with a sneer on his lips and condescension in his eyes.

"Yeah. I was hoping you could name this person you accuse, for I can't think of who you could possibly be speaking of." There was a sharp intake of breath from the women in the crowd. They started chatting together animatedly, but all of this was covered by the roar of anger from the men.

"Quiet!" shouted Mr. Mitchel over the noise. Slowly, people returned to their hushed voices and gossiping whispers. "Now, Mr. Caman, do you not know that we refer to you?"

The crowd applauded Mr. Mitchel, and I cringed. This was going to be a long night. "When you came into this town," Mr. Mitchel shouted, "you couldn't even walk straight for the alcohol in your blood. You hadn't even been with us a day when you went to visit the saloon." I raised my hand to object. "Don't try to deny it, Mr. Caman. I was talking to Mick, and he recalls quite clearly the day when you first walked in."

"You know Mick?" I asked. "That must mean you have done your fair share of drinking and philandering, because I don't think any man would know his name unless they spent some time in his establishment." It was probably the wrong thing to say. The room fell completely silent. Some men stood with their fists raised, and I wondered if one of them happened to be the father of Jace Callaway.

"You see, ladies and gentlemen? Is this not the very best example of this man's vulgarity that he would accuse a married and well-respected

The Mirror

man like myself of cheating on my wife and drinking excessively? Such despicable behaviour, and from a stranger at that."

"Let's throw him out of town!" shouted a voice from the crowd.

"Better yet," cried another, "let's flog him and leave him bloodied and bruised like he did our children before we kick him out of town." Cheers of ascent filled the building.

"I think it is time to hold a vote!" shouted Mr. Mitchel above the noise. "All in favour—"

He never finished his sentence. The door slammed open, and the entire town turned to see who had just entered. "Curate," Mr. Mitchel said in a sugary voice. "How nice to see you. You're just in time to vote on the matter at hand."

"Vote," said Stuart, a look of bewilderment on his face. He looked down at his pocket watch. "The meeting has hardly started. How can you be voting on the issue if it isn't even eight o'clock?"

Mr. Mitchel's face reddened. "It does not take long when Mr. Caman here has been accused of drunkenness, philandering, and beating children. Not many people would object to throwing him out of town based on those charges."

"Hmm," muttered Stuart. "Those are quite curious charges, considering Mr. Caman has not committed any of them. Or at least he has not committed any of them recently."

"He's a drunk!" someone shouted, to loud murmurs of agreement.

"It is awfully funny you should say that, considering Mr. Caman has not had a drink for over two months. Besides that, I have talked with the apothecary, Mr. Nelson. He says that if Mr. Caman does decide to have another drink, he will become terribly ill. It seems rather pointless then to accuse him of such activity."

"What about his philandering?" accused yet another man from the crowd. His wife sat beside him with a pretentious look on her face. It was very obviously her question that she dared not ask.

"From my knowledge," replied Curate Morgan, "it is not a crime for a man to visit with the women at Mick's saloon. If it were, why does such an establishment exist? But if you must insist upon accusing Mr. Caman, you must be aware that Mick has not allowed him on his property for over three months. Again your accusations come too late and are no longer valid."

"What about his child beating?" this time it was a woman who spoke. Unshed tears glistened in her eyes. "I can stand a drunk and a man who visits that place, but I cannot and will not tolerate a child-beater."

"What child has he harmed?" asked Stuart. "Please, step forward if he has harmed your child. Step forward if he has left one mark on your babe."

"He may not have left one mark on my son, but my boy was there when Mr. Caman spanked Jace Callaway. He saw the entire thing. Poor Jace couldn't sit down for two entire days. Such treatment cannot be tolerated." Mr. Mitchel's face was covered in red blotches. His argument was falling apart, and he was determined not to lose. A roar from the crowd followed his words and Stuart had to wait until the noise died down before he spoke.

"Where is Jace? Where is Mr. Callaway? Where is Mrs. Callaway? If they are the ones harmed by Mr. Caman, why are they not here to have their accusations heard?" Mutters flowed through the crowd. No one had taken time to notice the absent family.

"Just because they are too afraid to stand and protect this town from people like Mr. Caman, it doesn't mean we should not hold him responsible for what he did." Mr. Mitchel's words brought a half-hearted cheer from the crowd. "Unless you can prove that Mr. Caman has not laid a hand on Jace Callaway, we must expel him from our town."

Stuart thought for a moment. "Does anyone know why Mr. Caman spanked Jace Callaway?" The room remained silent. "Perhaps it was because Jace was in the way, but who ever heard of such a poor excuse for hitting a boy? The truth is that Jace Callaway along with Devan Mitchel and a group of other boys were picking on a girl who is dear to many people in this room."

There was a pause as the effect of the curate's words began to take hold of the crowd. Stuart went on. "Jace Callaway was not spanked until he had cruelly insulted Samantha Livton and then spat in the face of Jeremy Caman, Sam's protector. Many of you would agree that such despicable behaviour should be treated with the severest punishment."

"How dare you insult my son like that!" shouted Mr. Mitchel. "My son is not so plebeian that he would be caught teasing a little girl. How dare you make such accusations based on the words of one man?"

"I did not know it was plebeian to insult a little girl," said Stuart with a note of curiosity. "I only thought it was human. But if your son is so saintly that he does not dwell amongst the ranks of us humans, perhaps he should tell us the story of what really happened when Jace received the blow."

Raucous laughter followed the curate's speech, and I smiled. There was no possible way Mr. Mitchel was going to have his way this evening.

"You always do side with the sinner, don't you, Curate?" spat Mr. Mitchel. "Well, we have had enough of your contriving. We will vote now. If you wish to side with the child-beater and the friend of the sinners, then allow this man to stay in our town, but if you have higher sights for this town, expel this man from our presence and let peace and order be brought to our land!"

Men and women alike jumped to their feet and began shouting at each other. Fingers were pointed, fists were raised, and spittle flew. I tried to creep away, but it wasn't easy. I felt a hand in mine and a gentle tug on my arm. "Come with me," mouthed Sarah. I did as she bid. She pulled me to a back corner and told me to stay there.

It was dark where I stood. The candlelight didn't quite reach the corner, which had fallen into shadows. Despite my dark vicinity, I could still see what was going on.

Stuart was trying to calm Mr. Mitchel, but Mr. Mitchel just kept screaming at him. His face was purple and the veins on his throat stuck out, making him look deranged. The entire time, Stuart stood there speaking softly if he even spoke at all.

In other areas, the shrill voices of angry women were raised as they accused each other of not caring for their children as they should. The men were no better than their wives. They stood with angry faces, some feeling accused for their acts of drinking and philandering, the others offended only by the apparent act of child abuse.

The Mirror

The yelling and screaming continued until the door to the outside closed with a loud bang. Everyone looked on in shock as Jace Callaway with wide eyes and shaking knees stood before the crowd.

"Is—is Mr. Caman here?"

Eyes and heads turned to look for me. I decided no more damage could be done than what had already been said, so I stepped forward. The room was silent as Jace looked up at me. Fear and embarrassment were evident on his face.

"I want to apologize, sir," he started, "for my impertinence. I should never have spit in your face. I was very wrong. Will you forgive me?"

He had memorized what he had to say. His words could not have been more scripted if he had read them off of a sheet. "Do you know why I gave you that spanking?" I asked him.

"Because I spat in your face," replied Jace with his head turned down.

"Because you insulted a little girl when she had done you no harm." He shrunk away from my words. "Do you know how much you hurt Sam by what you said and did?" For a moment I thought Jace was about to cry. "No one deserves that kind of treatment."

"And that is why he is going to make a second apology tonight." The voice came from the doorway. Mr. Callaway was a big man. His swarthy arms hung from his broad shoulders, and hairs stuck up from the neck of his shirt where the expanse of his chest had popped one button.

"Go on, son. You've done your duty by Mr. Caman. Now, go ask Samantha for forgiveness."

Jace looked around. I think he was hoping that Sam wasn't present, but such was not his luck. As soon as Mr. Callaway had started speaking, Sarah had disappeared and returned with Sam. When Jace saw her, his face blushed scarlet.

Getting up his nerve, he stepped toward Sam. The entire audience watched. "Hey Sammy," he began.

"Her name is Samantha, son," Mr. Callaway said.

Jace gulped. "Right," he muttered. "Um, I was wondering, Samantha..." he paused, not sure what to say. "I was wondering if you would forgive me for pulling on your braids and saying what I did about your dad. I know it wasn't kind, and I was hoping you would accept this as an apology." He held up two new ribbons.

Sam bit her lip and looked back at her mom. "Mom," she whispered as softly as she could while still being heard. Unfortunately the quiet of the room meant everyone else could hear her as well. "Can I still accept the ribbons if I forgave him before he asked?"

Sarah gave a quick nod as soft chuckles filled the room. "I accept your apology," stated Sam in a very formal voice.

"Do you want the ribbons?" Jace asked. He must have been getting uncomfortable holding up such a girly article while the entire town stared on.

"Very much," replied Sam with a nod. Jace handed her the ribbons, and Sam placed them reverently in her pocket.

"Thank you," she said as a grin broke onto her face. The two children stood uncomfortably in the middle of the crowd as the adults looked on. Sam looked around and let out a big sigh.

The Mirror

"Do you want to go to the kitchen with me? I don't think the adults are going to finish their arguing while we stand around, and there's cake in the back. I could cut you a slice if you'd like."

Jace's eyes lit up at the mention of cake, but he knew better than to just run off. He looked back at his father who nodded approvingly. Sam didn't miss the look. Taking Jace's hand, she pulled him along toward the kitchen where the cake was waiting. Jace, who at first gaped with shock at having Sam's hand in his, soon followed along with a smile on his face.

As soon as the children disappeared, the atmosphere changed. There was tension as everyone waited for someone to speak first. Mr. Mitchel took the opportunity.

"Just because that boy has been beaten into submission, it doesn't mean that we all should let this by. You saw the way Jace walked. He might never walk straight again. We can't allow someone like Caman to run our streets doing that to our children." There was little support for Mr. Mitchel's campaign.

"So now I am a child beater as well?" boomed Mr. Callaway.

"That is not what I said."

"But of course you did," replied Callaway. "You said my Jace has been beaten into submission. That sounds to me like you think I have hit him to make him say what he has said." There was a muttering throughout the crowd. "I'll have you know, Mitchel, just because your sniveling boy can't take it when he is bullied back, I will not send a man out of town. Mr. Caman has only treated my son as I would have had he said and done the same things in front of me."

Mothers around the room glared at Mr. Callaway. "Now, I am not condoning child beating, but I do understand the need to protect a child we love from those who would harm them. Perhaps Mr. Caman went a little far, but I will not accuse him. I doubt he will ever hit a child again in this town, and I doubt that he ever has before unless he was equally provoked."

"How dare you?" yelped Mr. Mitchel. "You insult my son, and you agree with the man who beat your child." The crowd had stopped listening to Mitchel, so I did likewise. He continued to yip on, but others had moved on in their conversation.

"I guess it's time to go home," said one woman to her husband. "There's no use staying now that there's no issue to deal with."

"We might as well stay and have a little desert before we leave. I haven't had a chance to talk with Mr. Newgate over there since the last town meeting, and that was nearly two months ago," replied her husband.

Other couples followed their example while some young men drifted out of the building. A chess tournament was started in the corner, and many onlookers went to watch.

I looked on in amazement. Only moments before I thought I would be leaving Owzan. Now I was left standing watching as the town that only moments before had accused me, turned and asked me if I would be so kind as to get them a piece of cake.

Realizing the meeting was over and that there was still work to do, I went to the kitchen and started cutting cake. It wasn't until later that night, when the crowd was gone and Sarah and I were finishing up, that the full realization of what had occurred, hit me.

THIRTEEN

BY SATURDAY MORNING, I hadn't quite finished the work Sarah had listed for me. So, first thing in the morning, I trotted to the dining room to find the rocking table that Sarah mentioned. I had just found it when the door to the old kitchen opened.

"Hey," Sam called, "aren't you going to help me with the dishes?"

I waved her off. "Your mom has a list of things for me to do. You're on your own today, kid."

Sam would not be turned down. "Mom says none of that has to be done. She says you can throw out the list if you want. There are more important things that need to be done."

"Is that so? You seem to have been doing fine since Thursday without me. What changed your mind?"

"Martha's sick again. I told Mom that Martha is always sick, but Mom says it's just because she is getting older. Besides that, Mom says Martha is our benefactor, and we must be grateful."

I left the table and went to join Sam. "How is Martha your benefactor?" I asked.

Sam shrugged. "Mom said it's cause Martha owns the inn, and we are just workers here. She says we really don't belong, but Martha was kind enough to take us on." Sam handed me a dish, and I began to dry it.

"It is always a kind thing to take someone in. How long ago did Martha and Billy allow you two to come live here?"

Sam shrugged. "It was before I was born. I don't know. Mom doesn't talk too much about those times. She says it ain't fitting for me to know about them, at least, not yet."

"*Is not*, Sam. I know you have better language skills than to use such terms as ain't." Sam scowled at me, and I grabbed the soaking dish from her hand before I continued. "You must like Martha very much, then. She must be like a grandmother to you."

Sam bit her lip and hesitated in replying. Finally, she spoke. "Mom says I shouldn't say such things, but I don't think Martha likes me or Mom very much."

I lifted my eyebrows. "What makes you think that?"

"She's always talking to herself and giving me strange looks. She doesn't work much anymore, and she stays in her room a lot. Billy says she means well and doesn't mind us all that much, but I saw him sleeping above the stables the other night. He said it was to give her some peace and quiet because she wasn't feeling well again, but I heard her hollering at him and it wasn't just about married stuff as Mom says. Martha was right mad at Billy and she mentioned both Mom and me."

"When I've talked with her, she has seemed pleasant, and I can't say there would be any reason for her to dislike you."

The Mirror

Sam shrugged. "Yeah, she's nice sometimes, but other times she is kind of not so nice."

"Perhaps we shouldn't talk so much about Martha," I said, feeling a little uncomfortable with the topic. "Besides, if there is a lot to do, we should be working much more quickly on the dishes, don't you think?"

"Okay," sighed Sam. "Oh, I almost forgot. Mom says she wants you to help in the kitchen on Saturdays from now on. She says Billy has everything outside in good order, and she says if you take care of the rooms during the week, it shouldn't be any problem." Sam turned happily to washing the dishes as I dried and stacked them in the cupboards. With the two of us working, it did not take long for our chore to be done, for Sam to run off outside to play, and for me to go to the new kitchen.

Sarah stood by the counter pouring a creamy white batter from a bowl into a shallow pan. "What are you making?" I asked.

She smiled over at me. "It's a surprise," she said as she continued to pour the batter.

"A surprise? Since when do we have surprises? Is there going to be enough surprise for all forty men?"

Sarah shook her head. "Perhaps the surprise is just for a few people later on tonight. After the dishes are cleaned up, of course."

"So the surprise is a sort of celebration?" I teased. "What are we celebrating?"

"The fact that we did not lose a valuable employee at the hand of Mr. Mitchel." She blushed as she said it, but the fact that Sarah valued my work was a compliment far beyond my imagining.

Trying to save her from any further embarrassment, I responded, "You don't think Mr. Mitchel could get rid of the likes of me. Even though," I paused and lifted my head, and with a small sniff of my nose added a little whine to my voice, "he always gets his way."

Sarah chuckled and I couldn't resist. With the same whining voice, I continued on my rampage. "Don't laugh at me." I stomped my foot. "We shall vote on this. Vote now, woman. We cannot tolerate this laughing in the new kitchen."

By the time I was finished my spiel, Sarah was holding her sides from the laughter that rippled through her. The bowl on the counter was forgotten as the two of us joined together in laughing at the previous evening's occurrences. It felt good to laugh at what just the day before seemed like the end of my life in Owzan, and I realized this was the first time I had heard Sarah laugh.

I worked the rest of the day in the kitchen with Sarah. I did whatever she bid, and she continued to bake, cook, and clean. We chatted amiably the entire time. Now and then I was able to make Sarah laugh, and I enjoyed the sound of it. At one time Sam peeked her head into the room, but when she saw it was her mother laughing, she grinned and left.

Later that night Sam, Billy, and I waited in anticipation of Sarah's dessert. Martha had decided to stay in her room. Sarah entered with some flourish, presenting her cream cake. We attacked the treat like ravenous beasts, each of us asking for seconds, and me for thirds until the dessert was gone and my stomach bulged slightly over my belt.

A month passed in that manner. It was one of the happiest months I spent in Owzan. Sarah worked in the kitchen while I cleaned the

The Mirror

place. Sometimes Sam would help me, but she went out to play as often as possible with the weather as nice as it was. There were times when I would look out the window to check on her and I would see that she was not alone but playing with Jace Callaway. One time when I looked out, he was pushing her on the swing. Another time he had brought over his marble set and was showing her how to flick the tiny balls across a ring they had made on the ground. I smiled when I saw the two, realizing that Jace was most likely Sam's only friend.

Some days, when Martha was about, I would watch her. I thought about what Sam had said about the lady. She had seemed pleasant enough to me, but now that I watched her, I began to notice things Sam had mentioned. Many times, I caught Martha mumbling harsh words under her breath as she left the kitchen. Other times she would scowl at Sam as she played in the back yard. Once, I caught her peeking into the room I was working in. When I looked up, she disappeared. Despite her odd behaviour, I could not say for certain as Sam did that she disliked Sarah and Sam. Perhaps it was only age that made her do such things.

At the end of the month, I spent more of my time in the kitchen. The strawberries from the garden were ready, and Sarah needed help making preserves. At first I was shocked when she trusted me with boiling, mashing, and preserving strawberries, but I soon got the hang of it, so much so that Sarah could leave the kitchen for a time while I continued to work.

Yes, it was a good time at the inn, but problems began to appear in July. They started when Sarah got a fright one night. She had woken because of a noise, or at least that was what she thought. She said she had just calmed herself when it sounded like pots and pans had gone crashing to the floor in the kitchen.

When she made it down the stairs to see what was going on, there was no one there. Four pans and six large spoons were set in a neat pile in the middle of the room. When she investigated further, she discovered that an entire bag of flour was missing from her pantry.

The next morning when I came into work, she told me about what she had seen. I could tell that she was scared. There was a tremor in her voice when she spoke, and she fidgeted with her hands. I suggested she have Billy sleep downstairs the next evening, but she would not impose upon Billy, so I volunteered to come early the next morning to check on her.

The next morning was a Sunday. When I awoke, Stuart was already up pacing the kitchen, going over his sermon. I nodded at him, and before he could object I stepped out of the door. A candle was lit already when I made it to the inn. Sarah sat straight and stiff by the flickering light with a serious look on her face.

She ran to me when I entered, and I caught her as she flew into my arms. "I didn't hear them," she murmured, "but they were here."

"Shh. Hush now, you're alright. No one was hurt. You're okay." I rubbed large circles on her back and she slowly calmed herself, though she couldn't stop shaking.

"I got up early this morning and went to see if anything had been moved in the kitchen. Everything was fine until I looked in the pantry. I'm missing three pounds of sugar. It makes no sense. Who would take flour and sugar? Can there be any reason for them coming to the inn to take these things?"

The Mirror

"I don't know. Maybe someone is desperate. We'll have to see if they come back. Just promise me that if you hear someone in the kitchen again, you won't confront them. They could be dangerous, and I don't want you or Sam to get hurt."

Sarah nodded against my chest. I continued to rub her back gently until I realized what I was doing. Sarah must have realized it as well, for she suddenly stiffened. Clearing her throat, she backed out of my arms and turned her face away. Despite her best efforts, I could still see the red glow on her cheeks in the candlelight.

"Well," she said, slightly breathless. "I should start getting breakfast ready. It won't be long until the others are up. You may leave if you wish, Mr. Caman. I'm sure you are lacking sleep because of my nerves."

I shrugged. "I'm up now. What can I do to help?"

"Um, well, perhaps you could start cooking the ham."

"Okay." I worked with Sarah until the others woke up. Sam stepped into the kitchen, sleep still in her eyes. Yawning, she stretched her arms and looked around. Her eyes alighted on me.

"What are you doing here?" she asked.

Sarah gave me a look of warning. "I decided to come visit with you this morning. Is that alright?" She grinned at me.

We were partway through our breakfast when there was a knock on the front door. I saw Sarah raise her brows in a look of confusion. I got up and opened the door.

Jace Callaway stood with his hair slicked back and dressed in his Sunday best. His hat was in his hand, and he stood with his feet slightly apart and his chest puffed out as if trying to look just a little older.

"I was wondering if I could have permission to take Samantha with me to church this morning," he said in his most formal tone.

Sam jumped from her seat and raced over to the door. "Hey Jace," she chirped. "What are you doing all dressed up?"

He smiled at her. "Hey Sammy. I'm going to church this morning. You want to come?"

Sam's eyes lit up. "Sure thing," she replied and was about to race off to get ready when I caught the scruff of her dress. "Hey," she shouted in surprise. "What did you do that for?"

"No running off so fast. You'll have to ask your mother if it is okay for you to go. I don't know if she'll be too pleased about this." Letting go of Sam, I sent her to her mother and I turned to Jace.

"How about you come in for a moment, Jace," I said. He looked up at me with large round eyes. I wondered if he thought I was going to hit him again. "Don't worry, I won't touch you." He gulped and did as I bid. Sitting down, we waited for Sam to come back.

Jace fidgeted uncomfortably in his seat. He scratched his head, then flattened the hair that had been misplaced. I cleared my throat and he jumped.

"So, why are you inviting Sam to church?"

Jace squirmed even more. "Well, my dad said it would be a good idea because Sam has never come to church. Dad said she might enjoy it."

"So you're just inviting her because your father suggested it?"

"Well, no. I mean, I am inviting her because Dad said I should, but she is my friend, too. That's alright, right?" His voice squeaked as he finished his sentence, and I had to concentrate in order to keep my stern gaze in place.

The Mirror

"Of course it is okay if you are friends, as long as you are just friends. I mean, Samantha is only eleven."

Jace blushed scarlet. "How old are you, Jace?"

"Thirteen," he squeaked.

"Do you have any plans for the future? Are you going to be taking up your father's business or is there another career ahead?"

"I can shoe a horse. And, I've been helping my dad around the shop. He's a cooper."

"So you want to become a cooper?"

Sam bounded into the room, cutting my interrogation short.

"Mom says I can go as long as Mr. Caman comes with us. She says I have to be back in time for lunch, though."

Jace gulped as he looked up at me. Trying to ignore my presence, he turned to Sam. "That's great. I told Dad we would meet him at the church before nine. Do you think you can be ready by then?"

Sam nodded. "If I go right now, I'll be ready in time." Without another word, she raced off to get changed, leaving Jace once more sitting alone with me.

"So, Jace." He let out a slight whimper. "Have you had any breakfast?" A look of relief crossed his face as he shook his head. "Come on," I said. "I think Miss Livton might be able to put together a plate for you."

"Thank you, sir. I really do appreciate it."

I gave him a small smile. He would have to put up with a lot more if he ever tried something on my Sam, but for now he would suffice. He was, after all, Sam's friend, and I couldn't think of anyone else who filled the position.

After breakfast, I walked with Sam and Jace to the church. Sam wore the hair ribbons Jace had given her and her best dress. Her boots looked like they had received a quick polish, and as she walked beside me, I thought she looked like one of those little porcelain dolls sold at the mercantile.

Jace and Sam kept up a running dialogue the entire way, but when we reached the church, Sam quieted. She looked around with big round eyes as the building filled up with worshipers. When the music began she let out a gasp and ogled at the piano player. She listened to the words of the songs, never once joining in. When Stuart got up to give his message, she watched him intently.

By the end of the service, I thought for sure that Sam's eyes would forever be bulging out of her face in amazement. We filed out of the building, and Sam said a quick goodbye to Jace who promised to come over to play some time that week. I walked beside a soundless Sam on the way home.

When we reached the inn, she stormed into the kitchen where Sarah was enjoying a cup of tea. "Why didn't you tell me that church was so wonderful?" Sam shouted. "I would have gone every day of my life if I knew it was that much fun."

Sarah looked up in mute shock. Sam stood with tears of fury glistening in her eyes. "They played the piano and everybody sang and it sounded like angels. All the ladies dressed so pretty, and their perfume made the entire building smell like flowers. Then, Stuart Morgan got up and spoke, and everyone listened like he was someone real important and even though I could hardly understand what he was saying I

The Mirror

knew he was saying something special because of the way the other folks acted."

"So, you had a good time," said Sarah.

Sam stomped her foot. "You should have told me about church, Mom. I want to know more about church."

Sarah's face turned red. "Well, I can't tell you more about church. You will have to ask Mr. Caman. He attends, so he will be able to answer your questions." Picking up her teacup, Sarah moved toward the stove and began to busy herself. "You will have to talk with him somewhere else. I have to prepare our lunch." Her dismissal was clear. I took Sam's hand and we walked out into the backyard.

Sitting down on the swing, Sam kicked at the ground. "I don't get it," she huffed. "Why did Mom not let me go to church before? She's gone. She knows how wonderful it is. Why didn't she bring me sometime?"

I thought for a moment. "Do you remember the bean dish your mom tried last week?"

"Yeah," Sam replied with a smile. "It tasted like swamp weed. I gagged because it was so bad."

I laughed at her expression. "Do you remember what I thought about that dish?"

Sam shrugged. "You said you liked it. You said it reminded you of something your mom used to make."

"I did, didn't I?"

Sam nodded and kicked at the ground again.

"Sam, church is kind of like the bean dish. Some people like it, and some people really don't."

"But, why? Why doesn't she like it? She used to go. I know she did. She told me about it once when I heard Stuart Morgan talking about Jesus. She told me that some people believe he is God and can save us. So, if she used to go, why doesn't she go now?"

I shrugged. "I don't know, Sam. Maybe she has a bad memory related to church. Like when you eat too much candy and you get sick. You never eat too much candy again, do you?"

"I don't get it," sighed Sam. "How can church make you sick?"

I smiled down at her. "Darling, church didn't make her sick. Church just has bad memories for your mom, so if she went back to it, she wouldn't see all the nice things that you see there."

"But, maybe if she gave it another try she wouldn't hate it so much. Maybe if she went with me, I could show her all the beautiful things that I see. I could show her the dresses and let her smell the perfume. She could hear the piano, and she could understand Stuart Morgan." Sam looked up at me with pleading eyes. "It could work, couldn't it?"

"I don't think so, darling," I said sadly. "Remember when I told you how good the bean dish tasted?" She nodded. "No matter how often I told you about what I tasted, you still tasted the same swamp weed, didn't you?" She nodded again. "No matter what you tell your mom, she is still going to see the same things at church. Even if you see all those wonderful things."

Sam sighed. "Do you think she'll let me go again?"

"I don't know, Sam. You'll have to ask her."

Sam winced. "I wasn't very nice to her when I got home, was I?" I shook my head. "Stuart Morgan says we should always be good to our parents, and she is the only one I got. Do you think she will forgive me?"

The Mirror

"What do you think?"

Sam shrugged. "Maybe I should wait until later." I gave her a stern look, and she jumped down from her swing. "Okay, I'll go now." She stopped halfway to the door. "If I die," she said solemnly, "it's all your fault."

Laughter was the only sympathy she received.

"Bean soup, huh?" Sarah had found me in the yard swinging on the seat Sam had abandoned. "I don't think I would have ever compared church to bean soup, but I guess it works."

"Yeah I guess it's what Sam needed to hear."

"Bad memories are a nasty thing, aren't they? It is amazing how often they come around to try and bite you again."

"Hmm," I muttered.

"What bad memories do you have?"

"Ones bad enough to make your hair curl. Ones that sent me to the army. Ones that kept me from church nigh on ten years."

"It has been twelve years since I've gone to church. I'm sure whatever your memories are, they can't top my past."

"Wanna bet?"

"I don't know if I want to tell you my history. I mean, I haven't even told Billy all of it. How do I know I can trust you?"

I scooted over on the swing and patted the space beside me. Sarah hesitated but then hopped up, and we began to swing. "I'll start. When I was about fifteen, I was a responsible boy. I took care of my mother and my siblings because my father had deemed it necessary to abandon us the previous year. I went to church, and I spoke with the curate often about going to school to enter into the ministry. The problems started when I was eighteen, and I met a girl."

"A girl, really? You met a girl and that is where your problems start? Isn't that where the problems usually start for the female sex? I mean, men are generally more problematic and uncontrollable. Females have class, manners, and don't like to get into trouble."

"Hush, you. This is my story, not yours. You can negate it later."

Sarah rolled her eyes and gave the ground another kick to keep us swinging.

"I met Isabel when I was eighteen. Oh, she was classy alright. Her manners were impeccable, but boy did she have a knack for getting into trouble. At least that's what I thought all the times I caught her with boys that she shouldn't have been with in situations that were less than seemly.

"She always played me off as her hero. I liked that a lot. So much so that I started courting her. But then I found out who she was. I never attempted anything with her, honest truth. But she came to me one time crying, and I knew I couldn't say no to whatever she asked. So I took her for a walk, and one thing led to another, and, well as you said, men are uncontrollable. Even less so when they are being so strongly encouraged by a willing female.

"I tried to do the right thing and marry her, especially after I found out she was pregnant with what I believed to be my child. But on the day that was supposed to be our wedding day, the true father of the child stepped forward and claimed her hand, and I was left standing at the altar with everyone to know my shame and no wife to attest to my integrity."

"That's all?" Sarah asked.

"What do you mean, that's all?" I spluttered. "My dreams were shot. There was no way I was allowed to enter the ministry. Not a single female longed to be wed to me, and to top things off, the only career choice I had left was the army."

"So what? I mean you act as if you are the victim, but come on, you made choices. You practically threw your virginity at a girl who didn't deserve it, and then instead of rectifying things, you proved you were an idiot by destroying whatever integrity you had left."

"The army is no place to rebuild integrity," I argued.

"Sure it is. It is a place of strict rules and honest living. It is the best place to build integrity."

"Well what about you? If I'm victimizing myself, what are you doing? I at least am now making my way back to church. You, you've wasted twelve years of your life."

"The difference was that I was actually a victim."

"Oh really, were you forcefully put into a situation where Sam was produced? What man would actually do something like that without provocation?"

"One man, and I hope he burns in hell for it!" Jumping down from the swing, she ran into the kitchen as I gaped after her.

FOURTEEN

"WHY DON'T YOU GO TO CHURCH?" I asked Sarah as I sat peeling potatoes. The week had passed with an odd amount of silence between us. Neither of us wished to speak about the conversation on the swing, but what we had learned about each other still loomed about like a restless monster.

"I am sure I intimated enough to you for you to draw your own accurate conclusions."

"Let's pretend we never had that conversation."

"Very well, then to your question, I am never going to answer you in that regard."

The sass displayed in her answer reminded me of Sam, and I laughed. Sarah smiled slightly, then with a heavy sigh she turned back to her work. "You know, you are as bad as Stuart Morgan for bringing up my need to go to church. But it doesn't matter, I will never return there. Not once will I step across the threshold again."

The Mirror

"You're quite adamant."

"Yes. I am certain I will never find the peace and rest that Stuart Morgan claims I will at the building. What he doesn't seem to understand is that church is just not for everyone."

I shrugged. "Maybe you're right. I couldn't say for sure." Dropping the potato into my pan, I picked up another. "On a very different note, why do you and Sam always call the curate Stuart Morgan?"

Sarah smiled. "There used to be two Mr. Morgans in town. There was Stuart as well as a Cleo. Cleo was so particular that he would not tolerate being called anything but Mr. Morgan. So, when he and Stuart were both at the inn, we called Stuart Morgan by his given name. I required Sam to also include his formal name so as not to be disrespectful. Eventually Mr. Morgan moved on, but Stuart Morgan's name was set. We've tried to revert, but both Sam and I slip up. Stuart doesn't mind."

"What do you call his wife?"

Sarah turned and looked me square in the face. "We don't call his wife anything because we don't ever see her. She hasn't been out of the house since the town meeting when Zach died."

"Don't be silly," I chuckled. "Of course she goes out of the house. How else would she survive? Besides, I am sure that Stuart sent her to the apothecary when I was ill."

Sarah gave me a serious look. "Stuart didn't tell you, did he?"

"Tell me what?"

"About the town meeting. About why we had the town meeting. About why Zach died. He didn't tell you anything, did he?" She sounded angry. Her cheeks were tinged red, her jaw clenched.

"I thought you said that it was up to him to tell me."

Sarah turned back to the bread dough. Digging her fingers into its squishy surface, she began to knead. "I guess I just expected him to. I mean, it only makes sense because you are living in his house."

I wiped my brow and looked at Sarah's back. Her shoulders were tense and the bread was getting a good thrashing. "If you haven't noticed, Sarah, I spend more time here than I do at Stuart's house. I mean, the only time I ever eat with them is on Sundays, and that didn't even happen last Sunday."

Sarah started pounding her fists into the dough. "You should ask him again. I think he'll tell you now."

"Why is it so important to you?"

"It's not," she snapped, her work stopping only for a moment. Taking a deep breath, she calmed herself. "I just think you have a right to know. I mean you are living with him and his *wife*."

I began to wonder if I was misunderstanding something. "I'll ask him tonight after work." Sarah turned and smiled at me. It appeared as if her good mood had returned, but I wasn't sure mine was so jovial. Turning to my potato bucket, I realized that it was still half full. I would need to pick up my pace if I was going to help Sarah at all with dinner. With a heavy sigh, I returned to my work.

Later that night when I returned from the inn, I went to search out Stuart. He was nowhere to be found. I checked all the rooms. I shouted his name. I looked in the yard. But all was to no avail. Stuart was not home.

The Mirror

Putting the kettle on the stove to boil, I sat down, deciding that a mug of coffee would be nice. I closed my eyes, resting while I waited. It must have been over an hour later when I awoke and found Mrs. Morgan staring at me.

She pointed at the coffee mug in front of me. "I made you a drink, but it is probably cold now. I could make you another one if you wanted." I gaped at her, but she just kept on staring.

"Umm," I grunted. "That is okay, I'll just head off to bed, if you don't mind. I have an early day tomorrow."

I got up to leave but her voice stopped me. "Stuart won't be home until tomorrow."

I kept my back turned to her. "That's good to know. I'll talk with him tomorrow then. Good night for now." I started to walk again.

"Perhaps I could answer your questions," she stated bluntly.

"What questions? How do you know I have questions?"

"Everyone who wants to speak with Stuart has questions. You were searching for him today. You must have questions." Her voice was so calm and unconcerned that I felt myself relaxing.

Turning, I looked at her. She was wearing a simple brown, cotton dress. Her hair was tied up in a bun at the top of her head, and her eyes were a brown that wasn't happy, but deep and mysterious. I took my seat once more, and she again stared at me.

"Perhaps you *can* answer my questions," I said lightly. I didn't know if I trusted myself to continue. There was something alluring about the woman in front of me. She wasn't beautiful, but there was a mystery to her that drew my attention.

"Are you going to ask?" she pushed.

I nodded. "What happened at the town meeting? The one where Zach was killed."

She let out a soft "Ah," and thought. "There is a lot of history you must know if you want to know the answer to that question. It is a complicated one. Perhaps a story will help you. Would you like me to tell it?"

I nodded. Hadn't I been waiting for this?

She sighed, and her voice hushed into that of a storyteller. She closed her eyes as if to bring herself to the right place, then began.

"Once upon a time in a country very far from here, there lived a man who had two sons. His two sons each had broad shoulders from years of work on their father's farm and, like their father, they both were well respected. In fact, the father's lot in life was coveted by all who knew him. Who else could boast of such a vast farm, and who else could display such sons that would make the farm prosper and grow in the future. Yes, the farmer was envied.

"This all changed when the younger son decided he had had enough of his father's rules and way of life. He began to grumble to his neighbour. 'Why must I put up with his many ways? I am old enough to make my own decisions. He does not rule my life anymore.' The neighbour, eyeing the riches of the father, took this seed of contempt and nurtured it. He coddled the son and played to his fancies. It did not take long for the seed to grow into a weed of hatred and for the son to change his loyalties.

"When the neighbour was sure that his work had been successful, he said to the son, 'Why do you stay under your father's roof when he treats you thus? Go to him curse his name and demand your inheritance. Together we will build a land far grander than the one he

The Mirror

has provided.' The son took the neighbour's words to heart and confronted his father. Cursing his name, he demanded his inheritance and ran off with the neighbour.

"Despite all the promises the neighbour had made, the son found himself disappointed. The money was not used to build a house. Instead, it was squandered on alcohol and prostitutes. When the son tried to speak with the neighbour about his dreams, he was told to be realistic. There was more to life than working. He should enjoy himself and not complain.

"The son did as the neighbour suggested. He partied and drank. He gave himself to every woman who would allow him to touch her, and he wallowed in his misery. Finally, the money ran out. There was no way to buy food, and the neighbour left with his whisky bottle in hand. The son sat on the streets and begged, but none took pity on him.

"It was at that time that the son remembered his life with his father. He remembered toiling hard in the sun yet returning to a good meal and a strong shelter. He remembered taking lessons from his tutors and swimming in the creek. He remembered that even the servants were treated better than he now lived.

"The decision was not easy. The son was too ashamed to face the man he had cursed, but he could not deny the longing in his heart. He would go back, but he would not demand to be an equal. He would only ask to be a slave. Less than a servant, he could survive as long as his shame did not kill him.

"The road was long. He had travelled far, and he was weak with hunger and illness. But he pushed on, knowing a time would come when he would catch a glimpse of the home he loved so dearly. But on the day that he crested the hill that looked over his father's farm, he could not look. How dare he take a glimpse of the things he had so heartily betrayed? So he watched his feet taking him closer and closer to the door he both longed for and dreaded.

"If he had been looking, he might have seen the man running toward him. As it was, he did not see until he was in his father's arms. 'My son,' the father cried, 'long I have waited and long have I searched. You were dead, but now you are alive. You were lost, but now you are found.'

"The son was horrified. 'Father,' he cried, 'I have shamed you and disgraced you. I am unworthy of such treatment. Cast me at the feet of your servants. Make me a slave, but do not call me son, for I am not worthy of such a title.'

"The father could not agree. Instead, he called to his servants to prepare a feast. He dressed his son in the finest clothes and put a family jewel on his finger. Together they ate and rejoiced, but the older son did not come and join him. Instead, his heart was bitter, for his father rejoiced over the son who had cursed his name."

There was a long silence as I waited for Mrs. Morgan to explain. She sat with her eyes closed as if she slept in the chair. "What does this mean?" I finally asked. "Who are these sons? Why did the father welcome the wayward one back?"

Mrs. Morgan opened her eyes and stared at me. "When I was young, I met a man who I fell in love with. He was strong, passionate, and handsome. It was soon evident that he had noticed me, too. Soon after, we married. Stuart was a wonderful husband, and I didn't mind helping him with his ministry, which was his passion, but I soon came to resent it.

The Mirror

"His passion, which I once had loved, I hated. His strength, which I had so admired, now repulsed me. How could it not when all of it was devoted to his ministry, to his work, and none of it to me? At first I tried to do things to gain his attention, but nothing worked.

"Then, one day when I needed a sympathetic ear, the neighbour appeared. He was young and handsome, and he understood what I was going through. Or that is what he said. So, every day when Stuart went out, I would go to the neighbour and confide in him. He was my confidant, my trusted friend. And then he kissed me.

"It was just a simple kiss, but I craved for more of the attention I wasn't getting. So I encouraged him. It wasn't a week later that Stuart came home to find me in the neighbour's arms in our bed. I started shouting at Stuart. I screamed at him and cursed him. Then, grabbing my things, I ran away with that neighbour.

"It didn't take me long to learn that our neighbour had other homes across the country. In fact, he owned many saloons and whore houses across Samaya. When the whisky got to him, and I no longer pleased him, he made me pay for my room and board. Because I had no money, I became one of his prostitutes until his business went under, and I was left without a home."

I couldn't believe her story. It was too horrific. No preacher's wife ever became a prostitute. No prostitute ever became a preacher's wife. It couldn't be true. It just didn't make sense.

"I went out to the streets," she continued, "to beg for food, but most days I went without. As time passed, I remembered my Stuart. I wondered if he would take me back. I knew he had a good heart, and if he did not take me back as wife, perhaps he would help me find a job. So, slowly, I made my way back to him.

"When I was still a long way off, he came to me. He could not have recognized me as I used to be, but he took me in his arms and carried me home. He dressed me in clean clothes that covered my indecency. He put the wedding ring I had thrown at him back on my finger. He fed me the best that he had. But, best of all, he called me his wife."

A tear slipped down her cheek. She was not ashamed of it. "I don't pretend I deserved the treatment he gave me. In fact, I offered to leave. I offered to work as his slave. But he said he forgave me."

"So, so the other story never happened," I said, trying to wrap my mind around what Mrs. Morgan was saying.

"It is an analogy."

"You are the wayward son. You ran away from Stuart who really did love you even though you couldn't understand his love. Just like the son couldn't understand the father's love."

Mrs. Morgan nodded, encouraging me to continue with a small smile.

"What about the other son?" I asked after a moment's pause. "I don't understand how he fits into the analogy or how this all relates to the town meeting."

"The father went out to the son to beg him to join the party, but the son would not. Stuart went to the town, but they would not listen to him. How could they have a curate with a wife who was a prostitute? Stuart tried to get them to celebrate but they wanted me gone."

"What about Zach?"

The Mirror

Mrs. Morgan stared into space with her deep, unfathomable eyes. "Saint Zach. That is what he was called by the townsfolk. He was always kind and considerate. He held the door for every lady he could, and he never once swore or said anything crude. He blew into town on a Wednesday and died just two Fridays later."

"Why did he die? What happened?"

"Because he spoke of forgiveness." She shook her head. "It was one thing for the curate to tell them to forgive, but it was quite another for a stranger to stand up and speak. Who was he to tell them what to do? Who was he that he thought he knew what was best for their town?"

Remembering the two town meetings I'd witnessed, I could imagine the tension. I could hear the grinding teeth, see the clenched fists, and feel the blood pumping through the veins. What must Zach have been thinking?

"Zach stood up and the crowd went silent. 'Who here is without sin?' he shouted. 'Who here has never gone astray? What about you, church elder?' he asked. 'What about you, church deacon?' he demanded. 'Can any of you pretend to be perfect? Yet we all demand forgiveness. How, then, can we not forgive? It is your duty.' That was when the shouting began.

"I do not know who struck first, but it did not stop until there was a scream at the door. Samantha stood horrified. She ran to her friend and put his head in her lap. 'It will be alright, Zach,' she told him. 'I'm sure Mr. Nelson can fix you up. He can fix almost anything.' But the apothecary cannot raise the dead."

"The townspeople scattered after Zach was taken to the apothecary's. Stuart's demand to rejoice was forgotten, and the town's demand that I leave was left alone. Being a prostitute was one thing, and being a murderer was another. Nobody was sure who had cast the deadly blow, but since that day a rift has remained. Stuart has tried to fill it, but I know it will only cause problems if I show up around town. So I stay in the house. I cook and clean and mind myself."

"So they forced you into seclusion?" I said. "What did it matter to them, if Stuart forgave you? It's not like they suffered any from it. They still have their curate and they seemed pleased with him. Why can't they let your sins go?"

She looked at her hands and picked at a nail as if she were bored with the conversation. "Because, Mr. Caman, if they let my sin go, they must admit that they killed a man who was only speaking the truth and that would be a far greater sin than killing a blasphemer."

"What about Sam? How did she make it through all of this?"

"The inn wasn't always as prosperous as it is now. I think the men figured they owed the little girl. The single ones started coming every day for their meals. As the town grew, so did the inn. Eventually the men became so enchanted with the little girl, as they called her, that some of them gave up their homes to live at the inn. It ended up being beneficial. They don't have to clean or cook. They get hearty meals and they are right in town where their work is."

The large number of people at the inn began to make sense to me. Why else would so many men congregate at an inn so consistently? My only wonder was that the inn did not flourish with all the money they must have been bringing in.

"What about you?" I finally asked. "You are satisfied with puttering around the house. You have no problems with being secluded from the rest of the world? Don't you ever wish you could venture into town some time? It must get awful boring staying in one building with no company."

Mrs. Morgan shook her head. "I have seen enough of the world to be satisfied, Mr. Caman. So often Stuart wonders the same thing you do, but I cannot be discontent because I have a God who has forgiven me, and I have my love near me all the time."

She sighed. "Perhaps on days like today it gets lonely, but they only last so long. Besides, I have many things to occupy my time. I can stitch or read. I can play piano or write. Many a time I have written Stuart's sermon for him when he has been too busy. You have seen him rehearsing them, have you not?"

I nodded, digesting what she was saying. Could someone be content secluded like that? I couldn't imagine such a life. "What about the rest of the townsfolk? Do you not hold a grudge against them for their hard-heartedness?"

Mrs. Morgan giggled. "Now, how silly would that sound? How could I be angry at them for their unforgiving hearts? Wouldn't I be committing the same sin as they for such emotions?" She began to laugh in earnest at the thought.

I examined my heart, and knew I would feel resentment. Further examination showed that I already harboured dislike and anger toward many people. I wondered at her words of forgiveness, but I couldn't quite bring my heart to that point. I wasn't ready for it. Why should I forgive? What motivation was there to do such a thing besides someone telling me it was the right thing to do?

I decided to change the topic. "So, you will remain in this house on this property for the rest of your life?"

Mrs. Morgan nodded. "Unless Stuart would like to move towns. It is really up to him. He is the curate after all."

"You could live fifty years behind these walls. Won't you get tired of them?"

"Jeremy," she said softly. I looked into her eyes. "The son was sick when he returned. He lived contentedly for three years with his father and then he died. I too am sick, Jeremy. By the end of the year I will be dead."

FIFTEEN

I WAS ANNOYED WITH SARAH. Why had she pushed me to talk to Stuart? Why had I listened? I ignored her as I picked up Sam on Sunday morning to take her to church. I ignored her when I brought Sam back, even to the point where I refused to have lunch with them. Sam just shrugged and went on her way. I skulked my way home.

Stuart was not at the house because he had been asked to preach at a neighbouring church. It was just Mrs. Morgan and me. Feeling slightly uncomfortable, I decided to head back to the inn. It wasn't like I needed to talk to Sarah. I could play a game with Sam or something like that.

Despite my resolve, I noticed that Sarah was jumpy when I came back. I wondered if she was upset about my shirking her off, but this idea disappeared when I saw her glaring at me. I decided to go find Sam.

"What are you doing?" I asked as I entered the back yard.

Sam looked up from where she was digging in the dirt. "I'm looking for worms. Jace says that if we can find some worms, he'll take me fishing tomorrow. I figured I'd start looking right away."

"Is that so? Did Jace not tell you that the best time to look for worms would be later on at night when it is cool and moist?"

Sam shrugged. "He said the early morning, but I figured I would have things to do in the early morning, so I should look now."

"Do you want some help?" Sam nodded, and I got down on my hands and knees and began digging for worms.

"Samantha, what are you doing?" shouted Sarah from the doorway. Sam gulped and looked up with a worried smile.

"I was looking for worms." Her voice squeaked as she said it.

"Well, you wash up right now. I don't need you digging up my yard with your fingers. If you want some worms, wait until it rains. You know there will be hundreds about, then."

"Y-yes ma'am."

"Mr. Caman," Sarah snapped, "if you have nothing better to do, I could use your help in the kitchen."

I glared back at her. "Fine."

Washing my hands in the old kitchen, I took my time and made sure I dried them extra slowly. By the time I made it to the new kitchen, Sarah was whipping up pancake batter with a vengeance while watching the sausages cooking in the pan and toasting bread in the oven.

I took over the sausage and bread.

With a thud, Sarah dropped the bowl of batter to the counter and heaved a sigh. I turned to see her looking at me. Tears glistened in her eyes, and her entire body shook with fear. My anger dissipated when I saw her terror. "What's the matter, Sarah?" I asked as her tears broke the boundaries of her eyes.

She whimpered as she brushed the tears away. "They came again last night. The person who stole the flour and the sugar." Her hands fluttered about as if they were the only outlet for her nerves. She took in a deep shuddering breath. "This time they took a knife. A big butcher's knife. That thing is dangerous. What could they possibly want it for?"

I pulled her into my arms and tried to shush her. "Why didn't you tell me? I would have been here immediately."

She pushed away from me. "I would have told you this morning, but you ignored me." She was evidently still upset about that.

I shrugged. "I was frustrated this morning. You still should have told me. I wouldn't have been so frustrated then."

"You were frustrated!" She was yelling at me now. "Here I was fearing someone is trying to kill my daughter, and you were frustrated."

"Yes I was frustrated! You made me talk with Stuart about his wife for no reason at all. You know how awful that was to hear. You want to know how terrible I feel now for prying into things I had no business knowing? And for what purpose? None. There is no purpose!" I was shouting back at her. It was too easy to respond in kind.

Sarah smacked her spoon down into the pancake batter, allowing it to spill over the side. "No purpose! What did you want me to do, stand by and watch as she seduced you? Let her do her dirty work so that you would have to leave? Yes, that would be wonderful. Oh, how wonderful it would be as I watch you leave and my daughter crying because yet another man has broken her heart."

"Seduce me!" I yelled as I smacked my spatula into the pan of sausages. Hot grease flew through the air. "I can't believe you said that. Mrs. Morgan isn't like that anymore. Yeah, she used to be, but can't you believe that she has changed?"

"Oh, so poor Mrs. Morgan is changing, is she?" spat Sarah.

"No," I spat back. "She is dying."

Sarah stopped short. She looked at me in shock. Slowly she turned back to her pancake batter and began to stir at a civil pace. "Well," she finally muttered, "she deserves it."

I slammed the spatula down on the counter and cussed. "No one deserves death. No one!" I shouted at Sarah. "Why do you hate her so much? I mean, what has she ever done to you?"

"How many men do you think she slept with?" Sarah asked quietly. "How many marriages did she destroy? How many men did she cause to lust?" Emotion filled her voice. Tears glistened in her eyes. "She had a choice," Sarah said through clenched teeth. "She could have walked away. She could have stayed with her husband. Instead, she gave it up. She had a choice, but instead of doing as she should, she did what she wanted. She had a choice, but I didn't. She was forgiven, but I'm not. She has forgiven those who have wronged her, but I can't. How come she can live so freely when she made the choice, but I am so stuck when I never made any choice?" Sarah shoved her bowl aside and walked toward the door to the back yard.

"Where are you going?" I called after her.

"For a walk," she shouted back.

"What about lunch?"

"Make it yourself. I'm not hungry."

The Mirror

I looked at the pan of sausages and scowled. Dropping my spatula, I went to find something else to do. Sam caught me before I could get too far. "What's for lunch?" she asked.

"No one is hungry. You can make what you want."

Sam scrunched her nose. "It smells like something is burning," she said and pranced off into the kitchen. The next thing I heard was a piercing scream. I raced after Sam to see what the problem was. A small fire licked greedily at the pan of sausage. It was growing rapidly, looking for grease spots to devour.

Grabbing Sam by the waist, I hauled her out of the kitchen. When we made it to the old kitchen, I sent her outside telling her to wait there until I got her. Her knees trembled, but she did as I said. Picking up a towel, I dunked it in the dishwater and ran back into the new kitchen. Smoke was beginning to fill the room.

I beat at the flames that had grown tremendously in size, but I could not defeat them all. I needed help. As if my thoughts had called out, another person appeared amidst the smoke. Together we beat at the flames until they had disappeared.

Grabbing hold of the other flame fighter, I pulled him out of the room to the back yard. Coughing and hacking I fell onto the ground, and he fell beside me. Only, it wasn't a he. It was Sarah.

"Are you mad?" I yelled at her between gasps. She was on her hands and knees coughing as well. "You could have gotten yourself killed."

"And you couldn't have?" she wheezed.

I looked at her dress, which was smoke-stained and grimy but didn't show one singe spot. "You could have run your dress through a flame, and then where would we have been?"

"It is my inn, Mr. Caman," Sarah sighed. "I could not stand by and watch it burn to the ground." She picked herself up and walked toward the pump. She rinsed her hands and face, then took huge gulps of water right out of the spigot. I waited until she was finished before I followed suit.

Taking off my shirt, I noted a singed mark in the back and I cringed. Giving the pump a few good cranks, I washed my entire upper body. It felt good to have the water running over my skin that was hot and tight from the fire. Once I finished washing and drinking, I turned to see Sarah staring at me.

"Did that hurt?" she whispered, pointing to my scar.

I looked at it. It was glaring red and bulging from my side. It must have looked worse because of the heat and exertion from fighting the fire. I shrugged. "Not anymore. It has pretty much healed perfectly." I reached for my shirt. Sarah got to it first. She pulled it to herself.

"It will need mending. I can do that when I mend my own things. In fact, I noticed that a few of your things need mending. Why don't you bring them over tomorrow, and I'll fix them for you."

I nodded. "I'll do that." Sarah nodded back, then turned toward the inn. "Sarah," I called after her. She turned and looked at me. "I'm sorry. The fire was my fault. I shouldn't have left the kitchen with the fire still stoked and grease all over the place. Will you forgive me?"

She gave me a worried look. "Don't blame yourself. I was the one who left first. I should have stayed. That was my responsibility." She didn't give me a chance to argue. Instead, she disappeared into the house, taking my shirt with her.

The Mirror

Suddenly I realized the indecency of my situation. Sarah had just taken off with my shirt, and I had yet to return to Stuart's home. I looked around, bewildered by my predicament and unsure what I should do. I walked back into the new kitchen and began to assess the damage. The whitewashed walls were smoke-stained, and part of the counter was destroyed. The stove had held its own against the fire, and only parts of the cupboards had been seared. I could fix the damage that coming week.

There was a knock on the outside door. When I opened the door, it was to find Sam and Stuart Morgan staring at me. Sam stomped her foot. "I thought you had died," she said angrily. I could tell that she had been crying. "You didn't come to get me."

"Sorry darling," I whispered. My throat hurt too much for me to speak in a normal voice. "Perhaps you should go find your mom right now. I think she might be a little hoarse, so how about you make her a cup of tea in the old kitchen and bring it up to her, okay?"

Sam wrapped her arms around me and gave me a tight squeeze before she ran through the new kitchen to the old one. I looked after her, wishing I had the chance to give her a squeeze back.

"What happened?" Stuart asked.

"It was just a mistake," I replied. "Both Sarah and I were angry, and we left the kitchen unattended with sausages still cooking on the stove." I turned to see what had happened to the sausages. They and the pan were destroyed. "I came back to find the place on fire."

"And your shirt?" he pressed, his voice tight.

I shrugged. "Sarah is fixing it. It has a hole from the fire."

"And what did you plan on doing in the meantime? Were you just going to prance about like it was no concern of yours that you are shirtless? Don't you realize what a compromising situation this is?"

"Yeah, I do," I growled. "Only, I didn't think of it until my shirt had disappeared up the stairs. And, what do you think the more compromising situation is: me downstairs in a burnt kitchen without a shirt, or me upstairs alone with Sarah, half undressed?"

Stuart hefted the case he was carrying onto a piece of unblemished counter. Opening the clasps, he pulled out a shirt and tossed it at me. "Put this on," he muttered. "You can walk home with me and then get changed. As for the kitchen, it will have to wait until tomorrow. While we walk, though, I would like an account on how the elder did with the sermon this morning."

SIXTEEN

CAMAN LAY HIS HEAD DOWN on his hands. Sleep pressed on his eyes, and blearily he looked at all he'd written. It felt like years since he and Sarah had sat in the kitchen together. A slow tear trickled down his cheek as he wondered where Sarah was now. Quickly he wiped it away when Gustave came around the corner.

"Don't you ever sleep, Gustave?" Caman asked as the young guard walked over to his cell door.

"I've had plenty of sleep," he replied as he handed Caman a bowl of porridge. Caman looked at the sickly grey lump with disgust. "It's morning. You don't get anything else to eat for another six hours. I suggest you eat it."

Caman scowled but picked up his spoon.

"Have you written anymore?" Gustave asked.

Caman swallowed a mouthful of lumpy porridge and handed the journal through the bars. "Perhaps you can make some sense of it all," he said as he finished his last mouthful of breakfast. "I'm going to get some sleep." Shoving the bowl back at Gustave, he curled up on his cot and fell fast asleep.

Rose was in the nursery when Henry found her the next morning. "I have another message from Shoals," he told his wife as she sat cradling their daughter. "He says he has found something about a Samantha Livton born in Croden a little less than twelve years ago, but he can't seem to find anything about a Sarah Livton. He's going to start from the beginning of the Owzan records and go through them again, but he is beginning to lose hope."

"What does that mean for Mr. Caman?" Rose asked.

"Nothing good. But I must say I am still puzzled by all this. If Caman was lying, how did he know to mention Seth Hepton, and what did he hope to accomplish by it? But if he is telling the truth, how is it that Sarah is alive when the records say she is dead? I must say I am slightly flummoxed by it all."

Rose laid her sleeping daughter into a cradle and looked at her husband. "I know it doesn't make sense, and a large part of me wishes to toss Caman up in the tower and never think about him again, but I suppose we can't do that, can we?"

"I suppose not. Well, I best be going. I told my father I would meet with him shortly. I'll let you know if I have anymore news, my love."

"What do you think, Elizabeth?" Rose whispered as she stared at her sleeping daughter.

The Mirror

"What do you mean, Your Highness?" Elizabeth asked as she helped Rose settle once more into her chair and begin to sooth the prince.

"You heard what the king said. What do you think we should do about this Caman fellow?"

Elizabeth began to change the sheets in the prince's cradle. "Perhaps, if I may be so bold," she whispered, "I have a thought."

"You may say it. I will not be angry."

Elizabeth looked up, her lips trembling with uncertainty. "Perhaps you could forgive him despite the fact that he could be lying. Perhaps you could trust him, even though he has hurt you in the past. Perhaps, even if he doesn't deserve it, you could show him the love of the Father even if your pride is wounded."

Rose bit her cheek. She had promised not to be angry with Elizabeth, but had not the girl gone too far? Rose allowed herself to scowl, but no words escaped her lips.

"I have displeased you," murmured Elizabeth. "I should not have spoken." She took the prince from the queen when she held him out and placed him in his cradle. Sitting down on a stool, she waited in silence for the queen to speak.

It did not take Rose long to tire of the quiet. "Hang it all. You are forgiven, Elizabeth. You didn't say anything out of sorts. I've just grown a head of pride since I've become queen. I needed to hear that."

Elizabeth looked up hopefully. Rose smiled. "Come, let's go find some breakfast before these children wake and realize that they want some more attention."

Caman woke to find Gustave staring at him. "Did you love her?" he asked.

"Who?"

"Sarah. Did you love her?"

"I do love her. It is not something I did because she is still alive, and I still love her. Now give me my journal, I want to keep writing."

Gustave handed back the journal, but continued to stare at Caman. "I was in the army," he said, "but when they found out I was Isbetan, they kicked me out and put me to work here. They said I wasn't suitable simply because of my heritage. So here I spend my days, in this dank pit because some Samayan soldier killed my mother and another one tried to make me into something I'm not."

Caman opened his journal to where he'd left off. "Mrs. Morgan would want me to ask you if you have forgiven those men, but I think I already know the answer."

"I just don't see how I can."

"No, I don't either," replied Caman as he continued to write.

SEVENTEEN

JACE CALLAWAY CAME the next morning to take Sam fishing, but things didn't go as planned. "Samantha, you are not taking one step off of this property with that boy. Do you hear me? I hardly know him. What if something happened to you, what would I do then? And to think you wanted to go to the river with him. There isn't anyone near by the river. You need to have at least one adult with you."

Sam looked downcast at her mother's words and she dropped the tin of worms she had so carefully collected. Jace was not so easily dissuaded. "But, Miss Livton, my dad is going to come with us. He said he could afford a day off and that he would show me and Sam the best way to fish."

Sarah glared at him, and he shrunk away. "I will have you know, Jace Callaway, I don't know one thing about your father or you. I am not about to entrust my daughter into your hands until I know they are worthy of that trust."

"...Yes, ma'am. I guess I'll see you tomorrow, Sammy," he said as he slunk toward the door.

Sam and her mother were both in a sour mood for the rest of the day. Because of the fire, the old kitchen was used for meals. That was our plan, but we had not realized some of the cooking supplies were ruined. Sarah had to use her entire cooking genius in order to come up with a suitable meal with the remaining supplies.

Not wanting to be in the way of the woman's moods, I stayed in the new kitchen trying to repair what I could. I had not been standing there long when Martha entered and began to look around.

"What a waste," she muttered under her breath. "That girl doesn't know a thing about running an inn, but sure enough, Bill has to give her a chance. Not only a chance! Once he realized that little one was on the way, he practically handed the entire inn over to the two of them. That man!"

I cleared my throat and Martha jumped. "Oh Mr. Caman, I did not see you there."

"That's alright. I was just looking to see what it would take to repair the damage. I think a few boards and a new piece of counter should do the trick. It wasn't that big a fire."

"Easy enough, I suppose. But I don't know where we are going to come up with the money."

I shrugged. "I'm sure it will all be provided for."

Martha sighed and left the kitchen.

Stuart had lumber sent over along with other building supplies, and with the help of Billy, the two of us managed to get all repairs done that day.

The Mirror

I was tired and about to leave when Sarah stopped me. "How much did the repairs cost?" she asked.

I shrugged. "Stuart made sure I had all the supplies I needed. You will have to ask him."

She nodded. "I'm not crazy, am I? For not letting Sam go today? I mean, she is only eleven. She could have been hurt. I don't even know the Callaways that well..."

"Mr. Callaway is a respected man. You probably could have trusted him, but you're Sam's mom. It's up to you." I hoped my words would appease her.

"Just because others trust him doesn't mean I can. He could have any history that I don't know about. He could be a child beater or something worse, and we don't know. It is possible."

I smirked and Sarah scowled at me. "I'm sorry, but those ideas are slightly outlandish. I mean, Mr. Callaway is a firm father; you can see that in the way he made Jace apologize, but he would never beat a child. You have more to fear from me."

Sarah blanked. "I am not making a mistake. I will not make the same mistake as my parents." Colour slowly returned to her cheeks. "That's different, Mr. Caman, you were protecting my daughter, not harming her."

"So you cannot trust another with your daughter because they might not protect her?"

"No, no, that is ludicrous. I could trust Stuart Morgan and Billy, but this is different. I don't know Mr. Callaway."

"Well then, perhaps you should get to know him." The voice came from the door. Sarah looked over and started. The hulking figure of the cooper stood in the doorway. His son was dwarfed at his side. Sarah shrank behind me.

I held out my hand. "Mr. Callaway, it is nice to see you. I never had a chance to thank you for saving me the other night at the town meeting. It was greatly appreciated."

Mr. Callaway shook my hand and nodded to Sarah. "Miss Livton, my wife would be honoured by the presence of you and your daughter at our dinner table tomorrow night. We figure that if you come get to know us, you will not be so frightened of your daughter spending time with our Jace. It will be a hearty meal, and I am sure you will enjoy it."

Sarah shrank further away, but I clasped her arm and pulled her forward. She let out a little whimper as if she feared the man, and I saw her clenched fists quake. "I –" she stuttered. "I–I can't." The words burst from her mouth as she fled the room. I tried to keep hold of her, but in her terror, she broke loose from my hand and dashed up the stairs.

Mr. Callaway looked at me in bewilderment. I shrugged. "I don't know what to say. I have never seen her so distressed before. I will talk with her. Perhaps in the morning she will be in a better mood. It has been a trying day for her."

Mr. Callaway nodded and left with Jace by his side. I turned to find Sarah when I saw Sam in a ball in the corner. "What is the matter Sam, darling?" I asked.

She sniffled. "I ain't ever going to have any friends, and I ain't ever going to get married?"

I sat in a chair and pulled her onto my lap. Wiping her tears, I tried to calm her. "Now, what makes you say you are never going to have any friends?"

The Mirror

Sam shrugged. "Mom keeps saying I can't go out and play either because she needs help around the inn, or because she can't trust Mr. Callaway. I can't do anything because she doesn't like Mr. Callaway."

I pressed a kiss into her hair and smiled. "So you want your mom to let you going fishing with Jace so that you can have a friend?" Sam nodded. "Sam, even if you and Jace don't go fishing together, you can still be friends. Jace can come here and you can do lots of fun stuff at the inn."

"But I don't want to do stuff at the inn. I want to go fishing with Jace and Mr. Callaway. They said I could come, and I want to go."

I bit my lip. "Well, I'll talk to your mom, but for now, you must do as she says because she is only trying to protect you from getting hurt. Now, what is this about never getting married? And I told you to stop using the word ain't."

"Jace says ain't all the time. He says it is only proper."

I laughed. "Well, you tell Jace that a much older and wiser Mr. Caman says what is proper is 'am not' or 'are not.' You only sound uneducated when you say ain't." Sam scrunched her face to show her dislike of the grammar lesson. "Now, tell me why you are never going to get married."

"Because I am never going to find a man to give my veil to."

"I don't understand what you mean, Sam. You're going to have to explain."

She began gently rubbing my back, as if I were an infant. "Mom says that all girls wear a veil that protects them from other people's prying eyes. It is kind of like wearing a dress so no one can see..." she blushed and looked around to see if anyone would over hear. "So no one can see your legs," she said in a whisper. "But, the veil is different from a dress because it covers the inside. Mom says that when you marry a man, the veil comes off, and they know everything about you even when you are angry and when you think mean thoughts and everything. She says it is kind of like you become the exact same person in two people."

I nodded. "So," I said slowly. "You don't think you will find a man who you would want to know you inside out?"

Sam shrugged. "I don't know."

I kissed her forehead. "Sam, darling, you have lots of time to find a man to give your veil to. I don't think you have to worry about getting married for at least another seven years. Who knows? Maybe by then you will have lots of friends, and the boys will be lining up to try and win your veil."

There was a flurry behind the door, and I placed Sam down, knowing that I needed to talk with Sarah. "How about you go see about getting a piece of cake before you go to bed? I'm going to go talk to your mom. Do you think you can give us some time to talk?"

Sam nodded and scurried toward the kitchen. I made my way up the stairs in search of Sarah. She was in her room sitting on her chair stroking a piece of silky white cloth. When I stepped in closer, I realized it was the object of Sam's and my conversation: a bridal veil.

I took a seat on the floor next to Sarah and leaned against the bed. "An interesting analogy," I said, pointing to the veil. "It makes sense. The man lifts the veil at the wedding and then the two are joined as one. I only wonder why you told Sam such a thing."

Sarah continued to stroke the veil. "I didn't think she would remember. I had to tell her something."

"Why did you have to tell her anything?"

The Mirror

She turned and looked me in the eye. "You must answer your daughter when she finds you clutching a veil and crying. It would be unfair to leave her wondering."

"So what did you tell her?"

Sarah sighed. "I told her that once I thought I would have need of this veil." She held up the offensive piece of material. "But, now I know I will never find any man to lift my veil for." A tear slipped down her cheek. "I mean, how could I, when I cannot trust a single one of them?"

"Why can you not trust us?"

She shuddered as she closed her eyes. "Because the last time I trusted a man, he hurt me, and I will not put myself through that again."

I went to wipe her tears, but she pulled away from me. "Was it Sam's father, the man you trusted?" Sarah nodded. "Do you want to tell me about it?" She shook her head vehemently. "You do not trust me, do you?"

"I don't know." Her voice was small, like a scared child's. "I want to. But, what if you leave? What if you hurt me?"

I thought for a moment. "What if I don't?"

"I can't."

"Can't? Or won't?" Before I knew what I was doing, I was moving toward her. Sarah's eyes grew as I moved closer. Her bottom lip began to tremble. My hand caressed her cheek and a shudder ran down her spine. I leaned in closer, intending to press my lips to hers, but my attempt was useless.

She jumped to her feet with a yelp of fear. Her motion was only impeded by my head, which she knocked away with her shoulder. I took the knock on my chin, biting my tongue, which prevented me from cursing. She didn't wait to see why I remained on the floor. Instead, she left the room, tears streaming down her cheeks.

She left her veil behind. Taking it, I ran my fingers through the silky material. With a sigh, I placed it on the bed and left the room. When I exited, Martha was standing there glowering at me. I had never seen such a scowl on her face, but I ignored it.

When I returned to the curate's house, I looked around for a cup and some water and some salt. Mixing the salt and water in the cup, I took a swig of the solution and swished it about my mouth. The pain was awful, but I knew it was necessary.

Stuart found me with salt water in my mouth and a look of pain on my face. "Is this a bad time?" he asked around a chuckle. I glared at him with my cheeks puffed full of the liquid.

Stuart held up his hands in apology. "Who bit you?" he asked sarcastically.

I spit the water back into my cup and glowered at him. "I did," I replied, my tongue thick and swollen.

A grunt of a laugh slipped out of Stuart. He tried to apologize, but it was obvious he found too much humour in the situation. "I'm sorry, Caman, but how did you manage that?"

I let out a snort. "It wasn't my fault." Talking hurt, and my swollen tongue made my words come out in a jumble. "Sarah knocked me upside the chin with her shoulder."

"How would short Sarah knock you upside the chin? Unless..." Stuart's words trailed off.

"I'm going to bed," I grumbled as I left Stuart to his own thoughts.

The Mirror

The next day Mr. Callaway came looking for an answer. I did not have one, so I made it up. "Sarah would rather if you and your family would join us for dinner on Sunday. It is much easier for her than attending another's house."

Mr. Callaway nodded. "I'll make sure my wife and I are present on Sunday. We will bring Jace, but the other six can remain at home with Susannah. She will not mind caring for the babes, and I will not impose all my children on Miss Livton on a Sunday. She already has enough people to attend to."

I agreed and shook his hand. "That sounds swell," I said, and with everything arranged, he left. Jace remained behind, and I decided I'd best tell Sarah about her Sunday dinner guests.

When I looked in the kitchen, Sarah was not there, and neither was she in any of the men's rooms. I returned to the kitchen thinking I must have walked past her accidently. As I had hoped, she was there, but I was not counting on her foul mood.

"That man," she muttered to herself. "To think, the nerve of him. Some days I could wring his neck."

I cleared my throat. Sarah jumped and turned on me. A thick slab of meat hung from her hand and venom was in her eyes. "I don't want to see you right now. You can go dance for the king for all I care, but you are not welcome in my kitchen."

"Come on, Sarah. Is this because I almost kissed you?" She blushed and I regretted my words.

"It has nothing to do with what you did or did not do. I just don't want to see you right now, so go away."

"But—"

"Go!" Bloody meat juices flew from her chosen weapon. Her eyes were pleading.

"Fine," I replied and disappeared out the door. Perhaps I had angered her with my attempted kiss, but there had to be some other reason for her denying me access to her kitchen, and I was determined to figure it out.

"When are you going to marry Mom?"

Sam was sitting in the old kitchen, her arms stuck in a tub of sudsy water.

I shrugged and rolled up my sleeves. Giving Sam a slight shove over, I began washing the dishes as she dried. "I don't know, Sam. I don't know if we will ever marry. I don't know if I want to marry your mom. You see, she isn't letting me get to know her so that I can tell if I want to marry her."

"Duh."

"That wasn't very nice of you," I replied with a pointed look.

"Sorry, but of course you can't know her insides that well when she hasn't given her veil to you. You have to wait until you are married to know that."

I smiled at Sam's understanding of marriage. "So then, how do I know if I should marry your mother?"

Sam scrunched her nose and scrubbed at a dish as if it did not shine as she would like it to. "I guess…you can know if someone is your friend without marrying them, so if Mom is your friend, then you will do just fine once she gives you her veil."

"But what if your mom does not wish to give her veil to me?"

The Mirror

Sam frowned. "Well, that would be her own fault, wouldn't it? I mean, you tried at least, if you ask for it. But if she says no, she's the one who doesn't get to be married."

"I suppose so. Well, Sam, I can't promise that I will be asking your mom. We have to become better friends before I know if I should ask her."

Sam did a giddy little jig with the plate she held in her hand. "If Mom gives her veil to you, does that mean you will be my father? Because Jace says that if Mom marries then her husband is my father. Is that true?"

I gave her a smile. "Jace is right. If your mother marries me, I will be your father." Sam gave another great squeal and wrapped her arms about me. She gave me one tight squeeze, then returned to washing the dishes, leaving me to my thoughts.

When had I decided that I might want to marry Sarah? Was it the day she had cowered in my arms for fear of the thief? Was it when we spent days together in the kitchen preparing meals and canning fruit and preserves? Was it when I heard her laugh for the first time? Was it just because I had not been with a woman for over three months?

My last thought stopped me cold. I had just encouraged Sam in an idea that could have been based on my lust. There was hardly a chance I could propose to Sarah. I wasn't the marrying type. I hadn't been since the night things had gone too far. I had been changed that night, and though I could not feel guilt over what had happened, neither could I forgive the girl for seducing me. Yes I had made a choice, but she had known exactly what she was doing, and I was young.

I shivered remembering that one night so many nights ago. I had been but eighteen. What did I know then of love? How was I to protect myself from the wiles of a woman? If my father had been around, he would have taught me. As it was, my mother did not know I was so vulnerable. Neither did she know the temptations a seventeen-year-old girl could put before a boy.

I grunted, trying to clear my head. There were things not worth dwelling on. That night was one of those things. I should be thinking of Sarah. Could I marry her? Yes, I could. Despite her scar, she was a beautiful woman. Could I be Sam's father? I smiled down at the young girl. Yes. I could be her father in an instant.

Then it was decided. I would seek Sarah's veil. She would become my wife and I her husband. I would be faithful to her. At least I hoped I would.

But the question still remained. Would she have me? And, if she wouldn't, was she really missing out on anything as Sam said? Despite my pride, my stomach tightened with just a little bit of doubt.

EIGHTEEN

BY THE END OF THE WEEK, I had still not spoken to Sarah about her Sunday dinner guests. I stood in the kitchen, knife in hand, cutting onions. My eyes stung, and I knew from experience that they must be red with tears but I refused to let tears actually escape my eyelids. Sarah stood beside me cutting up carrots.

"So," I began. It was awkward. Sarah had avoided talking to me all week. "I've invited the Callaways over for dinner tomorrow. They will be coming to the inn after the church service."

Sarah stopped chopping for a moment, then began again more forcefully. The *shlop, shlop, shlop* of the knife was the only sound in the room. "I suppose you expect me to make a meal for them even though it is my only day of rest."

I shrugged and cut once more into the onion. "They are under the impression that you invited them. I can make the meal with Sam if you want to rest. But they are coming and you will visit with them whether you want to or not."

She turned on me, knife in hand. Instinctively I grabbed the hand with the knife and pinned it behind her back in order to disarm her. Taking the blade from her, I placed it on the counter. She looked at me with some fear in her eyes. "Never wave a knife in a person's face," I whispered hoarsely, trying to justify my actions.

She gulped. "Yes, Mr. Caman. I'm sorry," she whispered. Gingerly she picked up the knife once more and continued to chop her carrots.

"Sarah, I'm sorry. I shouldn't have been so forceful with you. I should have just asked you to put the knife down." I was grasping at straws to find a reason for my actions. "I don't know what I was thinking. I have been in the army too long to not react. I saw the knife, and I didn't think. I just acted."

Sarah nodded. "You are forgiven, Mr. Caman. I understand why you acted that way. I knew better than to wave a knife in your face. I wouldn't have done it to any other person. I just didn't think."

"I'm sorry for inviting the Callaways over without your permission. I thought it would be best if you were able to meet them in your own place. Then I thought that maybe Sam could go fishing with Jace."

Sarah shrugged. "I suppose you're right." She picked up her carrots and brought them to a pot. Dumping them in, she began to stir. I sighed and continued my work.

The Mirror

I was about to leave on Sunday morning to pick up Sam for church when I saw Stuart pacing in the kitchen murmuring to himself. "Did your wife write the sermon today?" I asked.

Stuart smiled and tossed aside the sheets of paper he held in his hands. "My wife has a knack for writing, and sometimes when I am busy I benefit from that knack. She also keeps me from thinking I know everything. She gives me a fresh perspective on things."

"What is the sermon on today?"

"Forgiveness mostly. How we need to forgive each other if we long to live in community with one another. If there is no forgiveness, there is only bitterness, hurt, anger, and the list could go on and on."

"So we need to forgive one another so we all can get along?" I asked just a bit sceptically.

Stuart shook his head. "We forgive because we were first forgiven our treacheries. Community is just the result of forgiveness." Stuart picked up his papers and began to read. When I didn't leave, he stopped his pacing and looked at me. "You should go and pick up your charge. You will learn more in the sermon. It will give you reason to pay attention."

I left the house pondering. What treacheries had I been forgiven? Sure I had done my fair share of philandering and drunk quite a bit, but what treachery was there in that? I was a good person when compared to others. I could think of one person in particular who was far worse than I. It was she who was treacherous, and why should I forgive her? What did it matter if there was bitterness between us? It wasn't like I was going to see her again.

Sam pranced beside me on the way to church. She was excited for the dinner after the service. So much so, she could not sit still in the church pew, and though I had determined to pay attention to the sermon, my mind wandered, and I spent far too much time trying to keep Sam still on the bench.

The lady next to Sam glowered at me when I reproached Sam quietly telling her to sit still. I glowered back. Couldn't she see I was trying to keep the child still? Her husband gave me a knowing look. I determined that was permission enough to ignore his wife.

Finally the service ended, and Sam was free to run loose. She bolted to the front and took hold of Jace's hand. The two took off out of the building in search of things to do. Mr. Callaway was in line with his wife to shake the curate's hand, so I decided I would join the queue.

When I reached Stuart, I shook his hand and he smiled at me. "So what did you think? Does it all make sense now?"

I couldn't bring myself to tell the truth. How could I admit that I had been too distracted to listen? So I told a little fib. "Yeah, it all makes sense now. Thanks. It was a really good sermon." I smiled half-heartedly and Stuart grinned back.

The grins lasted too long. I felt like I was going to suffocate. I pulled my hand away and raced toward the door. I made it outside and took a gasp of air. What was wrong with me? It was just a church. It wasn't going to kill me. But there was something ominous about the building that left my stomach twisting.

I looked around for Sam. "Sam," I shouted when I saw her. "It's time to go. You can talk with Jace later." For a moment I thought she

The Mirror

was going to be rebellious, but with an exaggerated sigh she came to my side. "What was that all about?" I asked.

She shrugged. "I just wanted to stay a bit longer."

I ruffled her hair a bit. "Well, I think we should help your mom out a bit. After all, normally it is her day off, but instead she is making dinner for the Callaways. I think we can help with that, don't you?"

"I guess." She began to skip ahead of me.

Sarah was flustered when we arrived at the inn. The kitchen was filled with scrumptious smells and I saw her favourite dessert sitting out in the corner. "You're not back already?" she wailed when she saw us. "I'm not finished making dinner."

"The Callaways aren't here yet. They won't be here for at least another half hour. What do you need us to do?"

She took a deep breath. "Sam can get the table linen from our room. You can take out the plates that are stored in the old kitchen, and you can set the good table in the dining room." Sarah sniffed the air and raced off. Sam rolled her eyes, and we both headed off to our appointed tasks.

Sarah was just pulling her last dish out of the oven when we returned. She let out a sigh. "We have soup and greens, beef and potatoes and gravy, and vinegar dressing for the greens."

"It smells amazing," I said as my mouth watered at the scent.

"I hope they like it." Sarah wrung her hands and bit her lip.

"Why are you so nervous?" I asked. "It's just the cooper and his family. It isn't like they are going to shun you."

Sarah ignored me. "Let's make sure you set the table properly." She walked into the dining room and looked at the arrangement. "You don't have enough settings."

I counted the number again. "Yes I do. There are five people attending dinner, and there are five place settings."

Sarah shook her head. "There are six people attending dinner, not five."

I shook my head as well. "There are only five. I do not know where you are getting the sixth from."

"There is Mr. and Mrs. Callaway and Jace. That's three people," said Sarah as she worked on proving her point. "Then there is Sam and me and you. That is a total of six."

I kept shaking my head. "That is where you're wrong. I will not be joining you for dinner. They are your guests, and I am sure they have no desire to see me. Besides, you haven't invited Billy or Martha to join you. Why should I be among your guests, then?"

"That is different. Besides, you are the one who put this dinner together. Therefore, you are obliged to be in attendance." She disappeared into the old kitchen and came back with another place setting. She moved to place it on the table, but I blocked her path.

"Let me through."

I crossed my arms. "I can't do that. If I let you through I would have to come to dinner, and I have no intention of doing that."

She tried to step around me, but I again blocked her path. With a frustrated sigh, she made as if I had won, and when I wasn't expecting it, she turned and tried to duck under my arm. With a quick motion, I scooped her up and hung her over my shoulder like a sack of potatoes.

Sarah let out a shriek and began beating on my back. "Let me down," she hollered. "I'm going to drop the plate!"

The Mirror

Sam came into the room and began to laugh. "Sam, come and take the place setting from your mom. She's afraid she's going to break it." Sam did as I bid, but Sarah wasn't about to give up.

"Sam, Mr. Caman has decided that he will join us for lunch. That place setting is for him. You should set it on the table."

"Yes ma'am." Sam went to place it on the table.

"Stop," I shouted. Sam raised her brow at me and put the dishes on the table.

"Victory," hooted Sarah.

"Never! How are you going to make me come to dinner when I am down here, and you are up there?"

Sarah gulped as if realizing the precariousness of her situation. "Um, Mr. Caman, would you perhaps set me down?"

I winked at Sam and, lifting Sarah off my shoulder, I rested her in my arms as if she were an infant. She wrapped her arms around my neck, her eyes wide.

"Is this better, Miss Livton?" Her eyes were beautiful. How had I missed that for so long?

"I–I think I would like to have my feet on the floor." I considered kissing her then, but Sam was watching.

"I don't think I can do that. I mean, that would be a very costly move on my part, and I'm not sure you are willing to pay the price of putting you down."

Sarah pouted up at me. It would have been so easy to kiss her then, but her face soon changed. With a mischievous smile, she moved her hands from my neck to my sides. Squeezing her hands slightly, she made me squirm. I tried to hold still, to keep from laughing, but she was relentless, and if I didn't put her down soon I would drop her.

"I surrender," I gasped. Sarah just laughed. Placing her down gently, I watched as she fixed her hair.

A knock sounded on the door, and Sarah's face blanked. "That must be them," she whispered. I nodded. "What do I do?"

I smiled and whispered back. "You let them in."

Sarah walked to the door and reached out a trembling hand. She opened it. I didn't understand it. Why was she quivering so? She entertained strangers all the time. Why was it now so difficult to be host to three guests?

"Welcome," Sarah said with a forced smile. I could only see Mr. Callaway. His bulk blocked the rest of his family from view. He stepped in and for the first time I caught sight of Mrs. Callaway.

It was easy to see where Jace got most of his looks. Mrs. Callaway had bright red curly hair that she attempted to tame by pulling it back into a tight bun. Her eyes were a pale blue, but their merry sparkle defied their bland colouring. Though her dress was fashionable, it did not hide the girth she had gained from her years of childbearing. She was neither short nor tall, and she was a beauty in her own special way.

"May I introduce my wife to you?" Mr. Callaway was speaking to Sarah. "Miss Livton, this is my wife, Hope Callaway." Sarah curtsied and Mrs. Callaway followed suit.

"My husband is too formal. My name is Hope, and you may call me by that name. I only ask that I may call you by your given name as well."

Sarah blushed. "Yes, that would be quite appreciated."

The Mirror

Hope smiled and turned my way. "Ah, I have seen you before in church. You are living with the curate, are you not?" I nodded. "Forgive me, but I fear I have forgotten your name."

"Jeremy Caman, Madame."

Mrs. Callaway smirked. "Yes. You were in the army, were you not?" Again I nodded. "I thought so. All you army boys came back with a bit of Isbetan language on your tongue and the dust of wanderlust on your boots."

I smiled, understanding what she spoke of. "You are very correct, Mrs. Callaway. I only wonder how you know so much about the men of the army. Owzan is far from being a military town."

Hope smiled. "I grew up in a military town just south of Silidon. I hardly remember a time when there were not soldiers about, and if they weren't just come from fighting Isbetan, it was Englacia or some other foreign country. Isbetan was the most recent country, though I think that we will enter a time of peace with this new king of ours. He does seem like the peace-loving sort."

I had to keep from laughing because I remembered my own encounter with his majesty. I grinned. "Believe me, I think that this king of ours will be the mightiest in battle if need be, but I doubt he seeks confrontation."

Hope sighed. "I hope you are right."

Mr. Callaway cleared his throat. Sarah was standing beside him in the circle, fidgeting with her apron that she had forgotten to remove. Sam and Jace had found a corner in which they were whispering.

"I think," said Sarah, "that it would be a wonderful time to have dinner."

Hope took in deep breath through her nose. "Mmm, it smells delicious in here." Sarah smiled at the compliment.

I helped Sarah bring in the meal as the others took their seats. When the last dish was set in place, I sat down. Sarah was about to begin serving everyone when she caught herself. With a slight blush, she turned to Mr. Callaway. "Excuse me, Mr. Callaway, would you please open this meal with prayer?"

Mr. Callaway nodded and bowed his head. "Dear Father, thank you for the blessing of another meal and time for communion here together. Bless this meal unto those who eat it, and forgive us our treacheries that we have committed against you. In your Son's name we pray. Amen."

My ears perked at the word treacheries, but I could not bring myself to ask about it. Instead I allowed Sarah to stand and serve us.

The meal went by quite quickly. Hope kept up a constant dialogue, which was comforting and helped pull Sarah out of her shell. The kids kept themselves entertained with their own lively conversation, and Mr. Callaway drilled me with questions about the war. I always forgot how little people from non-military towns knew about our country's military excursions.

When everyone was satisfied, Sarah cleared the table, and Sam ran to help her mom with the dessert. Everyone was given a large serving, but not one person took a bite until Sarah had again taken a seat and lifted her fork. She looked around at us nervously. "Is there a problem?"

"None at all," replied Mrs. Callaway. "We just thought we would wait to enjoy our dessert until you could join us."

The Mirror

"Oh," Sarah replied as if she had just remembered some manners long unused. "Thank you."

"This is delicious," said Mrs. Callaway when everyone had tucked in. "I can't say I have had anything like it."

"Thank you. It is my mother's recipe. She taught it to me when I was a child."

Mrs. Callaway smiled. "Your mother must have been a very talented cook. Her daughter definitely is."

Sarah blushed at the comment and continued to eat her cake. The room fell silent as everyone savoured their dessert, and too soon, it was done. Sarah looked around herself as everyone finished. "What are you looking for, Miss Livton?" I asked.

She blushed. "Nothing, Mr. Caman. Mr. Callaway, would you like to close in prayer?"

He nodded and began the prayer. When he had finished, Sarah leapt to her feet and began to gather dishes. "I'll go wash these up," she murmured. "It will only take but a moment."

Her escape wasn't made fast enough. "I'll help you," said Mrs. Callaway. "You have done so much for us already; it's the least I can do."

Again Sarah blushed. I had never seen her turn so red before. I wondered what kept her so on edge. "Thank you. That would be greatly appreciated." The words were in accord, but the grinding of her teeth said otherwise. Mrs. Callaway seemed not to notice.

"Sam," I called to the girl. She looked up at me. "Why don't you and Jace go and play outside for a while." Sam took hold of Jace's hand, and they raced off out of doors. I turned to the one remaining

Callaway. "Would you like something to drink? I can get you some coffee or maybe ale if you would prefer."

Mr. Callaway leaned back and sighed. "Ale would be just the thing to complete the day, if it is not too much to ask." I headed into the new kitchen and came back with a mug for the man, taking a seat across from him.

"Do you not drink?" he asked when I picked up the glass of water I had brought for myself.

I shook my head. "I'd be sick as a dog if I tried a sip of the stuff. Mr. Nelson told me that once I was weaned from the drink, I shouldn't attempt to have it again. He said nothing good could come of it."

Mr. Callaway grunted. "Well the treacheries of the past always seem to have an effect on the present."

I mulled over his word choice before I responded. "Treacheries. That is an interesting word that you use. I'm not sure I understand it."

Mr. Callaway shoved the ale to the side as he sat up a little straighter. Perhaps I was imagining it, but I was sure his eyes had a certain sparkle. "Treachery is just another word for sin. I heard the curate say it once, and I thought it a lot better reminder than sin as to what our mistakes really are."

I raised my brow at him. I still wasn't certain what treacheries had to do with anything. Mr. Callaway read the look on my face. "Every time we do something God doesn't like, it is a treachery, a betrayal or what we often call a sin. It is so easy for us to say we have sinned against God and then be done with it, but when we say we betrayed God, it sinks in how terrible our actions really were."

The Mirror

"So," I began slowly. "Every time I do something God doesn't like, I am betraying him?" Mr. Callaway nodded. "What happens if my betrayals aren't as bad as others'?"

Mr. Callaway thought for a moment. "You are an army man so, tell me: in the army is one sort of treachery worse than another?" I shook my head. In the army, treachery was treachery, and it had the same punishment: death.

Understanding began to sink in. "If I sin, I deserve to die," I muttered.

Mr. Callaway nodded and was about to say something when the door burst open. Sarah and Hope came into the room arm in arm and giggling. I smiled at the change in Sarah, wondering what Hope could have said to cause it.

The conversation turned as the women joined us. We talked of frivolous things and told stories about ourselves our homes before Owzan. By the evening's end, I felt confident that Sarah would allow Sam to go fishing with Jace. But when I asked her after the Callaways had left, she only said, "We'll see."

NINETEEN

THE WEEK PASSED. Sam asked on more than one occasion if she could go fishing, but the answer was always the same. "Not today, Sam. Maybe some other time." Sam was not taking kindly to this answer, and she became moody, stomping her foot and being unnecessarily rough with the dishes. When Sam became a little too reckless and cut her finger on one of the knives, it was time to step in.

"Ow, ow, ow," she cried, tears streaming down her face.

"Let me see," I said even as she shrank away from me. Hesitantly, she held out her hand. The cut was deep but not too severe. Leading her to the water bucket in the kitchen, I wet a cloth and began to clean the wound.

"You need to be careful," I scolded gently as I worked. "If you don't pay attention, you hurt yourself. This is just a scratch, but it could have been worse. Do you understand?" Sam nodded, and I kissed her tear-stained cheek. "Now, let's see about a bandage." I rummaged through

The Mirror

the drawers and came up with an old dishrag. Tearing it into strips, I fashioned a bandage and tied it around Sam's finger. She sniffled a bit, but shed no more tears.

Sitting down, I pulled her into my lap. She snuggled into my shoulder and just sat there. "What's the matter, Sam girl?"

She tried to snuggle in deeper. "I want to go fishing," she said into my shirt. "Mom won't let me go, and you said you would convince her."

I lifted Sam's chin and made her look at me. "I never said I would convince your mom to let you go fishing. I said I would try." Sam scrunched her nose. "Now, I don't want you being angry at your mom just because you aren't allowed to go. Sometimes our parents do things we don't understand, but we have to trust it is for our good. Because they are older they tend to know what is better for us, okay?"

Sam nodded, but she didn't move from my lap. I was content to sit, but I told her I had work to do. "How about you go play outside and let your finger heal for the day. I'll finish the dishes. Tomorrow we'll see what your finger looks like, and if it's looking better, then you can help me."

Sam agreed and ran off to the back yard. I went back to my work. It was Friday, and I still had three more rooms to wash down. If I didn't hurry, I wouldn't be done in time. I entered the first room, and to my surprise, it wasn't empty.

I jumped when there was a motion in the far corner near the dressers. I cleared my throat to announce my presence and the person turned. To my shock, Martha was staring at me. The last I had heard, she was too sick to work. What was she doing in the men's room?

"Um, are you cleaning here?" I asked.

Martha gave me an odd look. I have never quite seen one so strange. Her brow scrunched and her eyes glazed over. But then the look passed and she seemed her normal sweet self. "Yes, yes, I was cleaning, but I am feeling quite ill now. I think I will go to bed. Good day," she murmured as she passed me by and out the door.

I watched her go, then continued with my work. It wasn't until later that I realized what had seemed so odd. Though Martha said she had been cleaning, she had brought no cleaning supplies with her. I shrugged aside the thought. It was probably nothing.

I talked with Sarah on Saturday. "Why aren't you letting Sam go fishing?"

Sarah was stoking the fire and didn't turn. "What reason is there in letting her go? It is unsafe, dirty, and unnecessary. It would be much better if Sam stayed at the inn."

"You let Sam go to town on her own. There are far worse things that can happen in town than at a fishing hole."

Sarah stood and sighed. Moving toward the washbasin, she cleaned her hands, then began pulling ingredients from the pantry. "Town is safer. People are watching in town. If something were to happen, there would be plenty of people to come to the rescue."

"What about the time the boys were teasing Sam? No one came to the rescue then. Two grown men were watching from their shops, but not a thing did they do." I ground my teeth, the memory of that day still irking me.

The blood left Sarah's face, but she did not give up. "Town is safer."

The Mirror

I felt the frustration building inside me, and a long list of curses I longed to say were on the tip of my tongue. "What is so scary about the fishing hole that you can't let your daughter go and spend a day there?" A cuss word left my mouth before I could stop myself. "It's like you have some unnamed fear lurking in your head, and it has you so trapped that you even subject others to that fear."

Her back stiffened and her work stopped. Turning on me, Sarah scowled. "And, what if I do have a fear? Do you not think it is for a rational reason? I was the one who paid for my parents' mistakes, and I will not make my daughter pay the same price I did."

"What price, Sarah? What did you pay? Is this because of Sam's father? Did you trust him too much? Well, the Callaways aren't like that. You can trust them. You don't have to hide yourself from every living soul. We aren't going to pounce on you. Some of us you can trust."

Shouting is never a good idea when there is work to be done, but I had started it, and there was no stopping. "Who do you think I can trust? Should I trust you, Mr. Caman? You said it yourself that you were not to be trusted. Should I trust the Callaways? I've only met them once for crying out loud. I have tried trusting, but ever since..." she halted. "Ever since..." she halted once more. Taking a deep breath, she quit her yelling and looked me in the eye. "There is no one to trust."

"You always have God." Sarah and I jumped. Our arguing had drowned out the sound of the door opening.

"I guess I can always count on you to bring God into the conversation, Stuart Morgan."

The curate smiled, then began looking about the kitchen. "Sam told me that you had another one come in today. I thought I would stop by for a visit. Of course when I heard you arguing, I felt compelled to look in. It is far too amusing when two people argue a moot point." The curate took a slick of pancake batter and stuck it in his mouth. He let out a contented sigh.

"This isn't a moot point," I replied. "As a curate, I would think that you would have a lot to say about trust. I mean, it is important that we trust one another, right?"

"Not at all," replied Stuart. "On the contrary, I believe we should trust no one but God himself."

Sarah looked at me smugly. "But," I gasped, astounded. "But, doesn't the Bible mention trust? It has to. We can't go about keeping to ourselves. Can we?"

"'Trust in the Lord with all your heart and lean not on your own understanding.' 'Do not put your trust in princes, in mortal men, who cannot save.' Two things I gather from this: God wishes us to trust him. God does not wish for us to trust man." Stuart's words were decisive. He began walking around the kitchen looking for things to eat.

"I told you so," Sarah said with only a hint of sass.

"So you are never going to let Sam go fishing?" I asked.

"Why would I when Stuart Morgan just said that we shouldn't put our trust in man."

I groaned, knowing there was nothing I could say.

"Oh dear," murmured Stuart. "I believe I have been terribly mistaken." He shook his head with an air of being slightly bewildered. I had never seen Stuart like this, and it baffled me until I saw his eyes. The merriment there showed it was all an act.

The Mirror

"Trust in man, you must not do, but trust in God is a command. It is obvious that you do not trust in God, Sarah. If you did, you would entrust your daughter to him for a simple fishing trip."

Sarah straightened. "I have never trusted God. He has only disappointed me."

Stuart sighed. "I guess then your only choice is to trust man. Because without God, man is your second best bet."

She crossed her arms. "I trust no one. I will protect my daughter and I will do it on my own. Who could I trust more than myself?"

"God," Stuart said. I snorted a bit, trying to keep in my laughter. "But we have already gone over that option. Let us now examine men as an option. First, you are neither the best trained nor the best prepared for caring for a child. You do not know everything about Sam, and you do not know all her needs and wants. If you did, you would be a perfect mother, which unfortunately no one is.

"Now there is no one who knows more about Sam than Sam herself, and you come a close second, but there are others who could give you advice that would help you in raising Sam if you would trust them enough to take it. Of course, this would be much easier if you would trust God to direct you. Are you following?" Sarah nodded.

"Good. The Callaways are a good family. No, I am not asking you to trust them, but because you have no reason to believe they will do any harm to Sam, I am asking that you believe they will do their best to keep her safe. In this way, Sam will be able to go on her fishing trip."

Sarah had been about to give in. I was sure of that, but something tipped her off. "How did you know the fishing trip was with the Callaways?" Stuart gulped. "I never mentioned it. Neither did Mr. Caman."

"Assumption," replied Stuart quickly. "It only makes sense that Sam would be going with the Callaways. Jace is, after all, her one friend."

Sarah nodded, but narrowed her eyes. "I will think about what you have said, Stuart Morgan. But for now you must shoo. I have lots of cooking to get done, and I am sure the men would like their breakfast very soon."

The curate smiled and slipped out of the door. I turned to Sarah. "So, are you going to let Sam go fishing?"

"I said I would think about it," snapped Sarah. The bacon sizzled and the sausage popped. I waited for her to say more, but she remained silent. With a sigh, I resigned myself to another silent day.

Sunday came with a wave of heat. Church was uncomfortable and sticky. My shirt stuck to my back, which then fastened itself to the pew. The woman next to me had tried to cover her own stench with perfume, and the blended concoction made me nauseous. Even Sam seemed to be miserable in her seat next to me.

The Mitchels were in church again. Their loss at the town meeting had caused them to be absent for quite some time. But Mr. Mitchel was first and foremost a business man. As owner of the copper mine, he commanded respect among the men, but this respect seemed to diminish with his absence from church. So he appeared once more with his family looking miserable beside him.

Stuart's sermon lagged. There were no loud amens to encourage him and all eyes remained dry. Perhaps if the weather were different, it would not have been so dull.

The Mirror

With the last note of the last song, the congregation heaved a collective sigh and headed sluggishly toward the door. Scowls were exchanged along with smart remarks and angry words. When I reached Stuart, he looked worried.

"What's the matter?" I asked.

He shrugged. "I can't say for sure. Perhaps it is just the weather. Maybe it is just me, but I think something just isn't right. Perhaps I'm being silly."

I shrugged. "It is probably just the weather. Everyone is miserable today."

"You're probably right. I just wish I could feel better, but alas, my instinct does not want to listen to my logic."

Just then, a young lady came racing through the front door of the church. "Mr. Morgan," she gasped. "Two boys are fighting in the churchyard and Mama sent me to get you so you could break it up."

Stuart sighed and made his way to the door. I followed close behind.

When I made it outside, I couldn't believe what I was seeing. Jace Callaway and Devan Mitchel were wrestling on the grass. Occasionally one managed to break free enough to land a good punch, but neither of them seemed to be winning the battle. Mr. Mitchel seemed unconcerned about his son's actions until he started to lose. Jace climbed onto the young Devan's stomach and, pinning his arms back, punched him in the face.

Jace's face was red with rage as he swung again. "And that is so not another dirty word ever comes out of your mouth again."

I stood back in shock as Jace picked himself up off the ground, wiped his britches, and held out a hand to Sam who was standing to the side with an undone pigtail and a red line on her cheek. Her arms folded, Sam refused the extended hand and stomped her foot.

"You shouldn't have done it, Jace Callaway," she shouted. "You shouldn't have beat him so bad."

"But Sammy, he threw a dirt clod at you and pulled your braid. I had to make sure he wasn't going to do it again. It's justice."

"I don't see it, Jace. I just don't see it."

"You're a c–coward," stuttered Devan as he got to his feet. He wiped the blood from his lip and shoved his hands into his pockets. "You're a bloody coward."

"And what are you going to do about it, Devan Mitchel?" sassed Sam. "The last I saw he knocked you clean down."

"Shut up, you're just, you're just a–a bastard."

A gasp swept through the crowd of onlookers, and I wondered why Stuart wasn't saying anything. I watched as he finally made to intercede, but he was too slow. Sam pounced on Devan and knocked him to the ground. Swinging wildly, she hit him over and over again.

My mouth gaped as my mind caught up to what I was seeing. Running over to my little girl, I grabbed her around the waist and hauled her away from Devan, who was just beginning to fight back.

Curse words streamed out of the young man's mouth. But I had no opportunity to respond as Sam was still squirming to continue her revenge.

"Go home," I shouted over the chaos. "Go home!"

Mr. Mitchel grabbed his son and began to drag him away from the church. The crowd dissipated, and I was left with a squirming Sam and a bewildered group of Callaways.

The Mirror

"I guess we should all go home as well, shouldn't we?" I muttered.

Mr. Callaway grabbed hold of Jace's shoulder and directed him toward their buggy, and Mrs. Callaway came bustling behind, shooing the rest of her children before her. Sam had quit her squirming, but I could feel the shudder of her sobs against my shoulder as I carried her home.

At the inn I set her down in a chair, and was about to go find Sarah when Sam's words stopped me. "It's not true, is it? That mean word he said? It's not true."

I went to pull Sam into a hug, but she ducked away. "He had no right saying that. I would hit him again if I could. He had no right."

"Samantha! I don't care what Devan Mitchel said about you. You had no right to hit him."

"Yes I did, and I'll do it again the next time I see him."

"No you won't, because you are not a lowly child who doesn't know any better. I know your mother taught you right, and you won't shame her by acting like a scallywag."

"Jace hit him, and you didn't get him in trouble."

"It's not my job to get Jace in trouble. Jace's father will punish him as he sees fit. You on the other hand should learn to look past what Devan says. People like him don't know what they're talking about, but they keep talking because they think it makes them look good."

Sam jumped to her feet and shoved her fists into my stomach. "You don't care! You're just like Stuart Morgan. Well I tried to forgive him. I tried real hard, but I'm not going to do it anymore. I hate Devan Mitchel, and I will for the rest of my life." Sam stormed out of the room and slammed the door to the back kitchen. It did not take long for Sarah to appear with a scowl on her face.

"Don't blame me," I muttered before I explained the day's events. But by the end of my story, I knew she didn't as she sat crying in my arms.

Sam wasn't talking to me. She was still upset about the incident at church. To make matters worse, Jace was banished from the inn until he saw the error of his ways.

The heat remained. It created a hazy atmosphere and wore on everyone's nerves. The men were snarky, and it wasn't uncommon for me to go into the dining room during the meals just to break up a fight. By the end of the week, Sarah had even given permission for Sam to go fishing in order to protect her from the men's tempers. Unfortunately the fishing trip was denied. Jace, it seemed, was still being punished. Sam was furious. She screamed at her mother and blamed her for delaying the trip so long that it was cancelled. This was the first and only time I saw Sarah paddle Sam's bottom. When it was finished and Samantha was in her room, I held Sarah as her tears of frustration and pain overflowed.

The week passed, but the next was not much better. Again Jace did not appear. Sam continued in her sulking, but she did it in solitude as Sarah required my help in the kitchen. It was canning season, and the pears and peaches were ripe for the picking.

There were also raspberries to attend to, and blueberries. The zucchini had to be picked daily and the tomatoes would be ready in another couple of weeks.

The Mirror

With my help in the kitchen, the canning and preserves could be finished, but that left many other things undone. Sam finished whatever she could, but she was too small and too slow to finish all the work. Often Sarah bemoaned the fact that Martha would not help, but Billy assured us that she was really quite ill. So we continued on, working late and starting again early.

So the final weeks of August passed. The heat remained. The people sweated, their attitudes becoming like acid to each other. It was not until the beginning of September that I decided I'd had enough.

I was stumbling into my room after another long day at the inn when Stuart stopped me. "You can't keep going like this."

"I'm going to bed," I muttered as I shoved Stuart's hand off my arm.

"You haven't been to church in weeks. You've hardly been around to share a meal. And, I doubt you have taken a decent bath in over two weeks. Your clothes need washing and mending. Your body needs rest and proper nourishment. Honestly Caman, when are you going to take the time to take care of yourself?"

I shrugged and fumbled with the door handle to my room. Stuart scowled and pushed the door open for me. "You're going to work yourself into an early grave."

"Well what do you want me to do about it?" I shouted, finally annoyed enough with Stuart's nagging to respond.

"I want you to get help. If you just had a few more hands at the inn, you would be able to take some time off. You could rest then."

"That's not an option. The inn doesn't make enough money to support extra help. We'll just have to make do until winter comes and we can have a break."

"I'm not suggesting you hire help. You could always ask for free aid. I'm sure there are many neighbour ladies who would be more than willing to help with the preserves."

"Don't be ridiculous, Stuart. None of the neighbour ladies would be willing to help for free."

"Have you asked?" I shook my head. "Why not?"

"Because I already know the answer. They will all say no."

"You should ask. Some of them might surprise you."

"I'm going to bed, Stuart."

"Goodnight, Caman."

I fell onto my bed and closed my eyes. Sleep evaded me. Stuart's words nagged at the back of my mind, and the truth coalesced. We needed help at the inn. I was tired. Sam was tired. Sarah was exhausted. Something had to be done.

But I couldn't ask just anyone. I went over the many neighbours in my mind, determining which to ask and which to avoid. I hadn't decided on asking anyone when an idea came to my mind.

The next morning I woke up extra early and made my way over to the Callaways'. When I arrived, their yard was very quiet except for the *dring, dring, dring* of a hammer against metal. I walked to the barn hoping to find Mr. Callaway busy at work inside. But it was not Mr. Callaway who greeted me when I opened the door. Rather, Jace dropped his hammer to his side and mumbled, "I'll go get Dad," before he disappeared into the back of the barn.

The Mirror

I had only made the briefest of glances around the great open room before Mr. Callaway entered my line of sight. "Caman! Good to see you. How have you been?"

"Good, good. And yourself, sir?"

"Very well. Busier than blazes, but thankfully I have Jace helping me. I don't know what I would do without him."

My mouth fell into an 'o' as I saw my plan crumble into pieces.

"What was it that you came out this way for?" Mr. Callaway asked.

"I-I..." I stumbled for words. When no excuse came to mind, I decided that honesty was my best way forward. "Look, we are having a little trouble getting all the work done at the inn, what with canning and preserving. Sarah and I are exhausted, and Sam isn't going to hold out much longer either. I was hoping that maybe you would be willing to send Jace over for a couple of days. Just to give us a little help, and it would make Sam feel so much better. She misses him a lot, you know."

Mr. Callaway rubbed his chin as he decided how to answer. I waited as patiently as I could. "Alright, Caman, here is the problem. Have you heard what has been going on with the Mitchel family?"

I shook my head. "Sam's the one hearing the gossip. I've been in the kitchen."

"Well let me fill you in. After the incident at the church, Mitchel decided he wanted revenge, so he cancelled the order the mine had made for more than a hundred barrels. With this lost job, I had to take up an offer from my cousin. I have five hundred barrels that need to be done by the end of the month. The problem is, Mitchel hasn't been able to find anyone to do his barrels, and his wife came back and asked me to make at least thirty for them, but she said I can't let Mitchel know."

"His wife? How does she know anything about this?"

Mr. Callaway waved me off. "Problem was that Mitchel found out. He accused me of improper conduct toward his wife, and now the whole town is talking. Good thing Jace was there to vouch for me, or I swear they would have run me right out of this town."

"That doesn't save your pride."

"Pride! Who needs pride? I could have lost a whole lot more than that. How do you think my wife felt when she heard what Mitchel said? I know Hope to be a strong woman, but no lady likes to hear that her husband may have eyes for another woman. That's as good as torture." Mr. Callaway let out a heavy sigh. "I don't know. Mitchel isn't done yet. He ordered the barrels simply because he needed them, but he is pretty set on getting his revenge."

"So what are you going to do?"

"I don't know just yet." He scratched his chin as if considering something. "But I think I know what will help both of us out. Hope needs to get out of the house, and you need help at the inn. I'm sure that Hope wouldn't mind taking the girls with her for a couple of days to help finish up with the canning. Besides, Grace is about the same age as Sam, and I'm sure they will get along splendidly. All you have to do is talk with Hope. She's up at the house right now."

I considered the direction in which Mr. Callaway pointed before I made my final decision. "Thank you, sir," I said as I shook his hand. "I think I will go and ask. I'm sure Sarah would be mighty pleased with the help, and it would be a good thing for Sam to make more friends."

The Mirror

I heard him laugh as I walked toward the door, but I couldn't understand how such a merry sound could come from someone who had every right to be raving.

TWENTY

"Do you think Miss Samantha will like my doll, Mr. Caman?" I looked down when I heard the sound of my name and the feel of a tug on my arm. One of the Callaway girls held a bedraggled doll up to me. I picked it out of her hands and took my time in inspecting the toy.

"Hmm. You know what, I think Sam will love this doll if you will share with her."

"Uh-huh. I will, I promise."

"Grace!" snapped one of the Callaways behind me. I turned to find Susannah the eldest with a scowl on her face. "Mr. Caman is not interested in your doll. Leave him alone. You should not have even taken her along. We will be working, not idling away the day."

"All is well, Miss Callaway. I have enjoyed your sister's conversation."

The Mirror

"Very well," she replied, but the conversation had ended, and we walked on in silence.

"Where were you?" Sarah shouted as we entered through the back door into the kitchen. "I have been up to my elbows trying to keep the men happy, the dishes washed, and the preserves started. We have twenty quarts of the very last mulberries to preserve and here you come dallying into work at half-past nine as if it were a delightful hour to show up. Have you lost your mind?" There was a pause and then a slight "Oh," from Sarah, as the faces of the Callaway girls began to peek in through the door.

"We've come to work, not idle away the day," piped up Grace who now stood right beside me.

"Grace," hissed Susannah, but the young girl ignored her.

"Um, well, I am glad," replied Sarah, though her face displayed no trace of the gladness she declared. "How—how about you find Sam, while I talk to Mr. Caman. We can get started on the preserves in a bit."

The Callaways needed little prompting. All five of the Miss Callaways trotted into the kitchen and through the door into the dining room. Hope Callaway was close behind, but she took the time to give us a sceptical look before she closed the door.

I did not have long to wait to hear what was on Sarah's mind.

"Are you mad? What could have ever induced you to hire girls to work at the inn before asking me? Do you think we have money to run around willy-nilly spending it all frivolously? I have never been in a more awkward situation. What am I supposed to say to them? Thank you for coming all this way, but you may go home now because we have absolutely no money to pay you? Honestly Jeremy, how could you have been so inconsiderate?"

"It's not that bad," I whispered as the tears rolled down her cheeks and I pulled her into my arms. She snuggled against my shoulder, and a very strange trembling entered my legs. It was as if my knees had lost their strength. I cleared my throat.

"The Callaways have volunteered their service during the rest of the canning season. Just to help us keep up."

Sarah shoved her way out of my arms and glared up at me. "So we are a charity case now, are we? We can't do things on our own. We have to beg our neighbours to help us make ends meet?"

"It's not like that, Sarah. You know that."

"You're cruel, Mr. Caman. That is what I know. You are a cruel, cruel man."

Before I could respond, Sarah had disappeared into the new kitchen, and I was left standing alone in the old kitchen. "Women," I muttered under my breath as I left to find the lot of them that were to be my rescuers.

"Sarah would appreciate if you and the three eldest Miss Callaways would help out with the preserving in the kitchen," I whispered to Hope. She smiled at me and left the table she had been cleaning to beckon her three eldest daughters. I looked at the remaining two and Sam.

"We have a long day ahead of us. Are you ready to work?" I asked.

Sam gave a heavy sigh, and I could tell by the droop in her shoulders and the bags under her eyes that she longed to go back to bed, but

The Mirror

she nodded. Grace nodded much more vigorously, and I hoped that the young girl would be able to transfer some of her energy to Sam.

"Well, let's get started."

The week passed. Sarah seemed to mind less and less that the Callaways were helping out. She appeared more rested and happier. Still, she did not talk to me. She worked in the kitchen with the eldest of the Callaways, and I worked in the rooms and dining areas with the younger girls.

I soon discovered that it wasn't just Sam who could be beguiling. By the end of the week, Grace had won the hearts of many of the men. Still I hesitated in letting the children do the serving. Gossip is a nasty beast, and its power had been unleashed by Mr. Mitchel when he started his rumours. Terrible words were being spoken, and I wasn't so sure that Sam was as immune to it as she appeared.

There was wariness in her eyes as she walked from table to table, and the clenching of her jaw told me things were said that she did not approve of. She was not a little girl anymore, and she understood far too much of what they were saying.

It was all the same rumour. "That man, Mr. Callaway, did you hear he started spending nights at Mick's place?"

"Naw, that's not what I heard. I hear he's got himself a country mistress he likes to visit on them trips he makes."

"Mistress, I hear it's worse than that. You know his boy Jace has been hanging out with Samantha Livton? Well I hear say that the father has a thing for the mother. I wouldn't put it past her, the dirty harlot."

"It's an awful shame, I tell you."

"Him being a church man and all. Spoke the word to me every time I bought a barrel. Bloody hypocrite."

Business at the inn slowed. People did not want to be served by the 'harlot.' Mrs. Callaway lost weight, and Susannah, her eldest daughter, bore most of the burden of caring for the children. When Jace stopped by, his face was sober, lacking that usual joyfulness. But still the rumours grew.

"You know it's not true," I shouted at Stuart Morgan one evening as I paced in the kitchen. "You know he didn't do any of it, and to make matters worse, Mitchel had to drag Sarah into this mess."

"You care about Sarah, don't you?" Stuart replied.

"Yes and no, but I care enough about Sam to realize she understands more than she lets on. No girl should have to listen to people smite her mother like that. It isn't right."

"Well, I am not sure I can help you any." The candle on the table flickered as Stuart pushed to his feet. "I think I will be going to bed now. I am much too tired these days. Do you need this?"

"No," I replied as Stuart blew out the spluttering candle.

The room settled into darkness as I continued my pacing. I dared not go to bed with the dark thoughts of the day still looming in my mind.

"Dreams sometimes bring answers to prayers."

I spun around and glared at Mrs. Morgan. "Yes, but nightmares bring about the work of the devil."

"Is that why you do not sleep?" She set her candle down on the table and took a seat.

"No, my sleep is generally untroubled. I do not sleep because I do not need it."

"Well then, I will leave you to your pacing. Unless you would like to relieve your troubled heart."

"There is no relief."

"There is always relief."

"Believe what you may."

"I will, and I will convince you of its truth."

"Is that so?" I leaned across the table, leaving only enough space for the candle between us. "Darkness comes, and it settles." I blew out the candle. "There is no relief."

"You may blow out the candle in the night, but you cannot defeat the dawn. It will come, but you must be patient."

"I don't have time to be patient. Lives could be ruined today, tomorrow. We spent enough time waiting. It is time things start to change. I won't let him hurt Sarah like that anymore."

"And what do you suggest?"

"Give Mitchel a taste of his own medicine."

"It will not work."

"Why not?"

"Your reputation is already soured. People will believe Mr. Mitchel over you. I have a better idea."

"Is that so?"

"Mmm. I suggest you reveal the truth."

"I've spoken the truth. No one believes me."

"I don't mean the truth about Sarah and Mr. Callaway. Yes, most people already know the truth about them, but they have chosen to ignore it. I suggest you reveal the truth about Mr. Mitchel. If you speak with Mick, you will realize Mr. Mitchel's reputation is not as reputable as he would like you to think."

"What do you mean?"

Mrs. Morgan let out a long yawn. "I think I have quite overexerted myself. I shall go to bed, I believe. Good night, Mr. Caman."

Once more I was left standing in the dark. With a shuddering sigh, I realized how tired I was. With one last yawn, I headed off to bed.

Morning brought with it sense to Mrs. Morgan's words and a plan to go with them. Knowing that Sarah would not like my plan, I avoided the inn and made my way over to Mick's saloon. At the door, I stopped. Sunlight danced in the hazy smoke that crept out around the doorframe. The smell of cheap perfume and alcohol tantalized my senses, and I considered running for fear of what was inside.

With a deep, shuddering gasp, I pushed open the door. The establishment was quite empty. A couple of drunks slouched in their chairs, drool dangling from their dirtied chins, and a young lass, not much older than Sam, walked around picking up chairs and sweeping the floor.

Mick stood at the bar.

My parched lips trembled as I made my way toward him. His glare told me I was not welcome.

"I don't serve the likes of you," the man muttered when I sat on one of the bar stools.

"No," my voice cracked. Clearing my throat, I tried again. "No, you don't serve me, and I don't want any of it."

The Mirror

"Then you can get out of my saloon," Mick growled. He shoved away from the counter and made his way over to the two drunks. Knocking the both of them across the head, he began to shout. "Git, git you two. You have no business here in the mornin' now get your slimy back ends out of my chairs, and don't forget to come back tonight."

"The two men howled in pain and grabbed hold of their ears as they stumbled out onto the street. Keeping my spot, I waited for Mick to turn and see me.

"What are you still doing here? I told you to git with the rest of them."

"I have business with you."

"Well I don't do any business until five in the evening, and Saturday afternoons. So you may as well come back then with the rest of them."

"I'm here on the pastor's business."

Mick paused. "Alright then. Talitha, child, you must leave now. I won't be having you around." The young maiden left her task and disappeared from the room. "Now, what is it that the preacher would be having?"

"I spoke a dishonest word. Stuart Morgan did not send me, but his wife suggested that to solve my problems, I should come visit you."

"A wise woman, that lady, but not much like her to send someone to me. She and I do not exactly see eye to eye always. But as she is the preacher's wife, I can still manage a little business, I suppose."

"I need to know if Mr. Mitchel likes to visit you."

"Ah yes, I understand now." Walking over to the back of the room, he opened a door and hollered, "Scarlet! I need you. Come now."

There was a bustling about before a young lady dressed in a faded cotton dress came stumbling down the back stairs.

"What do you want, Mick," she whined. "I was just starting my breakfast, and if you don't hurry up, it will be stone cold before I get to it. You know how I do hate cold porridge. It's nasty slimy stuff."

"Mr. Caman has a couple'a questions for you. Answer them quick and you can get back to your porridge quick. But you better answer straight or I'll have you in the streets by sunset."

A slight pout turned her pretty lips as she turned to me. I clenched my teeth as the all too familiar longings came rushing to the forefront. Giving my tongue a nasty chomp to return sense to my mind, I tried to ignore the pain as I began to speak.

"I need to know about Mr. Mitchel. Does he come here? What does he do? And I need your help catching him at it."

"Now Mr. Caman, that sounds like a delightful plan, but are you sure that you would not rather experience what Mitchel does rather than just be told?"

The innuendo was alluring, but I ignored it. "Just tell me."

"Well he's a boring man, Mick. And, he's going to lose me business. What you want me to help him for anyhow?"

"You know the way of it, Scarlet. Do as I say and no questions. You don't own the place, and you are two weeks behind on paying your food stub. Now quit your whining and speak."

"Fine." The pretty pout had turned into a scowl that could light coal. "Mr. Mitchel is a very punctual man. He comes every Friday at exactly six o'clock. We do business and then he leaves. If you come

The Mirror

this Friday at quarter past six, I will make sure you find Mr. Mitchel, as they say, caught with his pants down. Now may I leave?"

"Get lost, Scarlet."

"I can't say I will mind losing him. He was a nasty little—"

"Scarlet!"

"Goodbye, Mr. Caman. Come see me again. Perhaps at a better hour."

Scarlet disappeared out the door as I turned to thank Mick for his assistance. An odd look had come over the man's face, distant and cold.

"Why are you helping me?"

The look disappeared when Mick let out a snort and began wiping down his bar with a ragged cloth. "History that ain't worth repeating."

I dared not push my luck, so I went to leave. "Is this self-control I witness, Mr. Caman? You're not asking anymore probing questions as so many others do."

"You have no desire to answer my questions, so I will leave."

"Yes, desires I have, but I will answer your questions even if you do not ask because you should know. Sit back down, Mr. Caman."

I pulled my seat closer to the bar and made myself comfortable. Mick put his cloth aside. "Not long ago, I made a business proposition. It went poorly, and when I could not provide the money I had promised, my business partner took matters into his own hands. He took my daughter, Talitha. He would have made her a harlot were it not for the preacher. The preacher found out about it, and he paid my debt. I got my girl, and he never once mentioned a thing to me about it. So you see, I owe him."

"So I do see. Well Mick, thank you for sharing, and thank you for helping me out. But I better be going. I have a lot of work to be doing and Miss Livton is expecting me yet."

"You treat that woman well, you hear me. She's been hard done by, and she doesn't need the likes of you treating her wrong."

"Of course," I replied as I pushed open the door into the cool fresh air. I gave Mick one last salute, then raced back to the parsonage.

Stuart was sitting in the kitchen drinking a cup of coffee when I arrived. "Aren't you supposed to be at work, Caman?"

I shook my head as I tried to regain my breath. "I need to speak with the elders. If that would at all be possible."

"Of course that would be possible. We have a meeting scheduled tomorrow night. You can't be there of course, but I could set up a time for you if you would like. Perhaps Sunday would be best."

"No, no. Sunday is too late."

"Well I suppose you could just speak with me about the matter and I could bring it up at the meeting. Whatever is the matter, by the way? You have me entirely curious."

"Or perhaps you could write a letter and Stuart could present it at the meeting?" Mrs. Morgan sidled up beside her husband with writing supplies in hand. "Did you ever think, dearest, that perhaps Mr. Caman does not wish to speak to you about the matter?"

"I suppose you are correct. Caman, write away. I will bring your letter to the council, and they can consider it for themselves."

Scribbling down a quick note, I folded it before handing it over to Stuart. "I must be going now. Sarah will be waiting for me."

The Mirror

I scurried out the door, hoping beyond all hopes that the elders of the church would listen to my desperate plea scrawled across a piece of battered stationery.

TWENTY-ONE

THE ANTICIPATION OF WAITING until Friday about drove me mad. The snide remarks continued as I worked at the inn, and it was getting harder to ignore them. I wanted so much to shout out the truth, but I knew things must be done properly.

Finally the day came. I raced through my usual Friday chores, putting Sam in a foul mood with my hurrying. Twice I spilled polishing oil all over the floor and had to clean it up, and once I completely forgot to pick up my swept pile of dust until it had been once more tracked through the entire room.

As five o'clock drew nearer, I ignored Sarah's wishes for me to help with supper and raced over to Mick's. I caught myself short of entering and decided to wait outside. The minutes dragged on and on. I watched to see if I could catch Mitchel entering, but he must have used a back door. Several minutes went by.

The Mirror

I wondered if perhaps the elders had ignored my request. I thought perhaps they wouldn't come. I had almost given up hope when a line of six finely dressed men marched past my hiding spot and into Mick's saloon.

After what felt like an era later, the door opened up and out came two elders dragging a howling Mr. Mitchel. He was still trying to yank up his pants, curses streaming from his mouth. Gentlemen turned to stare at the spectacle, young women turned away with blushes on their cheeks, young boys shouted in laughter, and ladies gossiped in the street.

I looked around triumphantly, but there was no one to share in my joy, so I returned to the inn. Sarah was the first person I saw. I wrapped my arms around her and began to spin. She let out a squeal of fright, but I managed to coax a slight giggle before I set her down.

"What has you so riled, Jeremy?" she said in a slightly breathless voice once she had found her feet.

I grinned. "I have a feeling all our troubles with Mr. Mitchel are going to disappear. And I think we should celebrate. What do you think?"

"I think you've gone loony, that's what I think. Things like this don't just blow over overnight."

"If I were a betting man, I would put a wager on this right now."

"Good thing I'm not a betting woman, or you just might have me convinced to bet against you."

"Perhaps I could still convince you," I called as Sarah began to walk away. "Perhaps we could wager something other than money."

Sarah turned her head, as if interested. "What is there to wager besides money?"

"A kiss?" I suggested hopefully.

Sarah caught her breath, and I thought for a moment she might faint. But she collected herself and shook her head. "You are incorrigible, Mr. Caman. I don't think it's wise to play with emotions like that."

"But you are certain that I'll lose. You could wager something in return. In fact, you could wager that I must do the dishes by myself for a week, or some other bet."

There was a pause as Sarah considered it. "If things have not changed by tomorrow evening, you do the laundry for an entire week. If they have, I will grant you one kiss willingly."

She turned to leave. "We'd better shake on it." I held out my hand, waiting for her to offer hers. She placed her hand in mine, and I grasped it, liking the warmth of it in my own.

Sarah cleared her throat. "Mr. Caman, I need to be going about my chores. There are people waiting for supper."

"How about I help you?" I slipped her hand into the crook of my arm. She blushed, and I liked the look of it on her. But she pulled her hand away and disappeared into the back kitchen. I stood there hoping that just maybe she liked me as much as the churning in my stomach told me I liked her.

The following day, the inn was filled with people wanting to be informed about the latest gossip about Mr. Mitchel. It hadn't taken long for every person to pass the news on to their neighbour: Mr. Mitchel had been caught at Mick's saloon with a prostitute, even after he had so viciously slandered Mr. Callaway for that same act.

The Mirror

When I arrived, Sarah was up to her elbows in bread dough, attempting to make a few more loaves. I rushed over to the stove as the bacon began to smoke, taking it off the heat before I started a second pan for eggs.

"Thank you," gasped Sarah as she raced over to the oven to pull out the loaves made earlier. "I don't know what's going on. It's almost as bad as a town meeting, but without any warning. Sam has been taking orders for breakfast for the past hour. The Callaways haven't arrived yet, and I could sorely use their help. Martha's sick again, and Billy set off for the apothecary before this madness even started. Oh bother."

Sam walked into the kitchen and began dishing out servings of eggs, bacon, potatoes, and bread. When she had filled four plates, she carefully walked out the kitchen door and into the lounge.

The Callaways never showed up. I believed I knew why, but I didn't bother telling Sarah until after lunch, when the last of the ladies had left, having exhausted the most recent gossip. I settled myself into a chair and began some of the prep work for our evening meal.

"I don't know what came over the town today. I have never before seen such a gathering of people without a town meeting having been called."

"Hmm," I replied. "I can't say I know why."

"And to think that of all the people that were there, not a single one of them was a Callaway. I must say, I have grown rather used to having them around."

Again I replied noncommittally.

"Did you hear anything as to why everyone showed up today?"

"Perhaps it had to do with the fact that Mr. Mitchel was caught by the church elders yesterday with a prostitute at Mick's Saloon."

Sarah's mouth puckered into a distinct 'o.' "Does that mean—Are we, I should say—I mean, does that mean everyone believes Mr. Callaway now?"

I nodded, not looking up from my work. A stern look had come across Sarah's face. "I guess that means I owe you a kiss." She had turned pale, and her jaw was set, but she had stopped chopping the onion as if preparing herself for my kiss.

I considered her lips for a moment. They were red, moist, and in every way kissable, but I refrained, not liking to collect when Sarah was so obviously against the kiss. "I think I will wait to gather my wager. If that's alright with you."

Her jaw began to tremble and she turned back toward her onions. I saw a tear streak down her cheek and I went to wipe it away, but she pushed me back. "It is just the onions, Mr. Caman. I'm fine."

I stepped back, not knowing if I believed her. We finished our work in silence, and I decided I should go help Sam. But before I could close the door on my way out, I noticed that Sarah was still crying. She had finished with the onions nearly an hour ago.

The scandal of Friday night was closely followed by what was later called the Sunday chaos. Sarah and I spent a lazy Saturday in the kitchen while Sam played with Jace in the mid-September cool. Nothing was mentioned about the kiss the she owed, and there were no more hints of the tears she had shed the previous day.

The Mirror

Sunday morning, Sam and I went to church and sat in our usual bench with the Callaways. The sermon began and ended as normal. As the last note of the last song struck, the door at the back of the church clattered open.

Mrs. Mitchel walked down the aisle, her head held high, her dress dirtied, and her hair falling out of the bun in thin wisps around her face. She walked all the way up to the pulpit and stood in front of Stuart Morgan with accusing eyes. The congregation remained silent, apparently dumbstruck.

"I would like the right to divorce my husband."

The room was filled with hushed whispers of surprise. Even Stuart seemed uncertain what to say. "Mrs. Mitchel, divorce is nearly impossible in Samaya. You nearly need the king's approval, and I doubt that there is reason enough..."

"I have read and reread the law, Curate Morgan. It states that any spouse—husband or wife—who is shamed to the point of dishonour by the other may make a plea for divorce at the church where they are a member. In this way they may disassociate themselves with the dishonour due their spouse. The list of dishonourable acts is very short but includes marital unfaithfulness, drunkenness, and abuse."

"And in which category do you think you fall, Mrs. Mitchel?"

The lady gasped as if in shock or disbelief that the question had been asked. "Curate Morgan, for the past five years I have watched my husband leave every Friday night, and every time he comes back smelling like another woman. Not only has he been caught with that woman, he has turned to drunkenness as an escape from his shame. I have put up with many things, but I cannot live like this anymore. I must have relief."

The shouting began. Every person wished to speak their own opinion. In all my life I had never once heard of a divorce actually taking place. I had heard of separations and abandonments, but divorce was another thing entirely. I sat in my pew trying to understand what a terrible thing this was that Mrs. Mitchel wanted to do, yet I felt myself wanting to encourage her.

"Quiet!" Stuart shouted above the noise. A hush fell, but mutterings still rippled through the congregation.

"The elders and I must take some time to study the laws regarding divorce and how they must be handled. A town meeting will be held next Saturday where our decision will be announced." Stuart beckoned to his elders as he descended the steps from the pulpit.

Jumping out of my seat, I made my way toward the inn, knowing Sarah would want warning. There was gossip to be had, and the only place to obtain it was at the inn. No meals were served on Sunday, but drinks aplenty would be needed.

I barged into the kitchen and Sarah jumped to her feet. "What is the matter?"

I took a moment to catch my breath. "We need to start making some coffee and tea. If you have any lemons, it would probably be wonderful to get them now and make some lemonade."

"What's going on, Caman?"

"Mrs. Mitchel has just made a plea for divorce, and the entire town is going to come here to gossip about it."

"Oh bother," gasped Sarah as she made her way toward the pantry. I began to boil water on the stove. The crowd was already bustling in.

The Mirror

"Twice in one week. I think I could do with a little less gossip for once," Sarah muttered.

Sunday sped past in a blur of coffee serving and water boiling. The Callaway ladies helped in the kitchen, and we managed to serve baked goods without too much fuss.

By the time I made my way home, I was longing for a nice hot bath and a hefty dinner. Neither was to be found at the curate's house.

Mrs. Morgan's voice carried from their room. "You have to stop it. You can't let this happen!"

"How can you expect me to solve everything?" Stuart's frustration was plain. "It's the law. I can't rewrite it."

"Oh you have to, Stuart. It is all my fault. I can't believe this. I can't believe I did this."

"I can't do anything about this!"

"Oh Stuart, please."

"I can't!"

"Oh, oh." There were heaving gasps and the voices dimmed until they were undecipherable.

I sat in the kitchen not sure what to do. I was about to leave when Stuart came storming in. "What do you want?" he demanded.

"I—nothing."

"Well go to your room. I don't want to see anyone right now."

I went to my room, not sure what had just happened and not sure that I really wanted to know.

Monday dawned in a hush of disbelief. People dared not speak lest the day before was a terrible nightmare, but their fears were laid aside come five o'clock when Mr. Mitchel stumbled drunkenly out of Mick's saloon.

I arrived home after work to find Stuart sulking over a blank piece of paper. "What are you doing?" I asked.

"Writing my sermon."

"What is it about?" I tried to make my voice cheerful. It sounded lacklustre.

"I don't know."

"Umm, how long have you been working on this?"

Stuart rubbed his eyes then laid his head on his arms upon the blank paper. "Leave me alone, Caman," he whispered. I crept away, all the while wondering what had caused Stuart's foul mood.

As I walked past the curate's bedroom on the way to my room, I paused to listen. "Please Lord, look at what I have done." The desperate plea was spoken in an anguished whisper. "No man deserves this. Forgive me for what I have done. Save him. Save him from his folly and mine as well. Oh Lord, please." I hurried past, troubled by the prayer I had eavesdropped on.

The days passed. Each night I returned to a house cloaked in sorrow thick and heavy like a damp winter snowfall. I tried to shake off the feeling, but it clung to me.

On Thursday evening, I sat across from Stuart at a cold dinner table. We each choked down our dry bread and chilled soup. I shoved my bowl aside and leaned back in my seat. Stuart mimicked my actions and stared across the table at me.

The Mirror

"I can't solve everything," he said.

"Of course not."

"I mean, it was Mitchel's own blasted fault that he is in the situation he is in. I can tell my wife it is not her fault. She didn't cause his problems."

"Yes, that is right."

"I mean, how can I stop a divorce? Drunkenness I have dealt with plenty of times. Along with prostitution and the likes. But divorce, how does one stop a divorce?"

"I don't know."

"But there must be a way, right?"

"I am sure there is."

"If only..."

An idea was working in the back of my mind. An outlandish idea, but an idea. Perhaps it was possible to do away with this mood of tragedy. Perhaps if Mitchel could be persuaded to fight for his wife, to defend her honour, there could be hope of reconciliation. I was being ridiculous, though. My idea was silly, and if it didn't work, I would look like the world's biggest git. But I had to try, didn't I?

I looked up at Stuart to try to find an answer. His eyes were blank as if he were drifting off into some idle thought. He did not seem to have a plan, and I was getting desperate.

"I have to go." I pushed back my chair and made my way toward the door. Stuart shouted after me, but I ignored him. There had to be a way to stop this divorce, and I was going to do everything in my power to make it happen.

I made my way all the way across town to the Mitchel's house and knocked on the door. Mrs. Mitchel opened the door. Her hair was down and she looked to be wearing the same dress as Sunday's, but it was even more stained and worse for wear than before.

"Where is your husband?" I asked. She cringed at the word, and pointed back across town.

"Try the saloon. He doesn't seem to leave the building that much anymore." She closed the door on me, and I was left wondering what to do next. Traipsing down the steps, I picked up my pace and once more crossed town to Mick's saloon.

The door was open and that sound of giggling women and drunken men spilled across the street outside. I took a deep breath and entered the building.

Mitchel was sitting at the bar, a small glass of amber liquid before him. I sat down beside him and waved at Mick. He ignored me and continued to wait on his more lucrative customers.

"What you drinking?" I asked. He ignored me. "Have you been having a pleasant day?" Again, no response. I saw the red seeping up his cheeks. I took a deep breath and prepared myself for what was to come. "I saw your wife today. My, is she looking fine. A beautiful woman. Too bad you won't have her for long."

I had struck the right chord.

Mitchel pounced like a fox out of a burning den. His arms were on my shoulders pinning me to the floor that had unexpectedly met my back just seconds before.

"Don't you dare talk about my wife like that," the man growled. I could smell the alcohol on his breath. I waited for his fists to fly, for

The Mirror

him to take out his anger in some other way, but it didn't happen. He got back up to his feet, resumed his seat, and took a swig from his glass.

I pushed my way up off the floor, wishing my idea had been bright enough to avoid the painful side effects, but knowing of no other plan, I stood waiting for the room to be silent enough for my words to be heard. "Fine, have it your way. It's not like anyone is going to want that woman when we know that she's cheap enough for you."

There was murder in his eyes. I ran for the door. Thankfully I had the advantage of soberness. I made it to the streets before I was tackled from behind and plummeted face first into the gravel. I didn't even have time to swear before I was flipped onto my back, and Mitchel was attempting to make my face into something unrecognizable. I tried to defend myself as best as possible. Finally I managed to free one of my hands and bash him across the head. He rolled off of me, and I scrambled to my feet.

Mitchel pulled himself to his feet holding the ear I had pummelled. "I hate you," he said. "You're the one. You're the one who ruined my life. I was doing just fine until you came along and had to start messing with things."

He stumbled toward me, and I knew I would have to speak before he started beating on me again. "What did I ever do to you? Ever since I came here, you've been accusing me of all the worst sorts of things, only to have the truth come out and the whole world see you for who you really are."

My shoulders were once more gripped in Mitchel's vice-like grasp, but it seemed to be more of a balance issue than a menacing gesture. "You took my wife and family from me." He spat in my face.

I wiped away the saliva and stared back at him. "You ruined your life yourself, and only you can do something to get it back."

He was shaking his head. Laughing, as if I had said something hysterical. "You don't know that woman. She's made up her mind. I ain't ever going to see her or that child again. Devan," he finished his sentence with a whisper and a sob caught in his throat. "How dare she take him from me? How dare she leave me like this?"

"How dare you not fight for her?"

"You wouldn't understand," he muttered as he began to ramble away.

"Of course I wouldn't understand," I intoned sarcastically. "Like I said, your wife may be good to look at, but who would want her after you?"

Oops was the last thought that flitted through my head before Mitchel's fist found my cheek and I was lost to consciousness.

TWENTY-TWO

THE EERIE LIGHT of a spluttering candle greeted me when I woke. Hazy shadows flitted along the wall and I tried to find who was making them, but it hurt to move my head. A soft cool cloth brushed across my forehead. I let out a contented sigh.

"Hush now," a voice whispered. "You're alright." I longed to see who my caretaker was, but she had covered my eyes with the same cloth she had used to wipe my brow.

I made to speak, but a shock of pain through my cheek prevented me. I felt a warm trickle down my chin, and I wondered if I had opened a cut. "Look at you." I heard the scowl in her voice, and I knew exactly where I was.

"You are going to wind up dead if you keep up your scallywagging. I know what you said to Mr. Mitchel, and it was very rude indeed. And now you have managed to open your cut which I had so nicely bandaged for you. You should be ashamed of yourself."

I inched my hand along the bed sheets trying to find Sarah, but she swatted at it like a pesky fly, and I heard her stand. "I see you will be fine by the morning. Well then, Mr. Caman. Good night." I heard her chair scrape across the floor and the door click before I was left in silence.

The room was dark, and I felt myself wishing Sarah had not left me. It was lonely without her near my side. I tried to make myself comfortable. The bed was soft and thick, and the quilts were numerous, but still I longed for better comfort than this.

With a sigh, I cushioned my good cheek into the pillow and tried to fall asleep. The land of dreams soon came, where I tried over and over to explain to myself what had so induced me to irritate Mitchel the way I had.

The morning dawned clear and glaringly bright. The cloth had slipped from my eyes, and the sun was using its full glory to awaken me. I tenderly touched my cheek to see if I would be able to speak. I forced a smile to test my face muscles. The pain had lessoned considerably, but my head still felt like it had been smashed repeatedly by a brick. I wondered if Mitchel had ever considered becoming a professional boxer. He definitely had the fists to do the profession justice.

I stumbled down the stairs and into the kitchen. Sam and Jace were sitting in front of the washtub scrubbing dishes when I clattered through the door. Sam let out a startled squeal and I covered my ears to lessen the pain in my head.

"No loud noises," I muttered to Sam, but she was ignoring me. Yanking on my arm, she pulled me over to a chair and had me sit down. I felt her gentle fingers prodding at my face and watched as she peered earnestly at my cut and bruises.

The Mirror

"You need another bandage," she finally said, and pranced out of the room.

I scowled at Jace. "What are you looking at?" He turned away and stared at the sudsy water in front of him.

Sam came back with her bandage, and began to apply it to my cheek. "That should hold," she said, and made her way back to her work. I wanted to rip the bandage from my face, but I dared not with Sam looking on disapprovingly.

Shrugging my sore shoulders, I left to find Sarah in the new kitchen. She scowled at me. "You look ridiculous."

"Thank you," I murmured as I took a seat by the counter. "Do we have any coffee?"

"No, the pot was finished, and we need to go to the mercantile to get more."

I laid my head on the counter and tried to ignore the pounding in my ears. It was time for a holiday, I thought. It would be so nice to have just Sarah and Sam with me relaxing in some parlour somewhere, not thinking about whether the floor had been swept. I closed my eyes and imagined myself there.

I woke with a start. "You're drooling on my counter." Sarah was scowling at me with a rag in one hand and the other resting on her hip. "If you can't do anything useful, get out of my kitchen."

I wiped my mouth and began looking for a knife to begin helping out with lunch. My eyes felt tired and bleary. I considered leaving and going to bed, but I couldn't leave Sarah with all the work. So I trudged on through the headache and the fatigue.

After we had worked for some time, Sarah finally spoke. "Why'd you do it? Why'd you have to go and rub it in his face? I mean, it's one thing to do it defensively, but to kick him when he's down like that... That was just mean, don't you think?"

"I don't know. I guess I just wanted to get a point across."

"Well don't!" She slammed her ladle onto the counter, and it skidded to where I caught it before it could clatter to the floor.

"Easy there. It's alright now, isn't it?"

"Alright? Alright? Do you know how ashamed I was when I had to drag you out of that crowd unconscious? Everyone was looking at me like I was some desperate sot who can't help but cling to any man who may enter her life even if he is a shiftless lout. My goodness, Caman, have you no shame?"

"Shame? Do you think I just went about this little escapade to taunt Mitchel? I may be shallow, but I would never stoop to that."

"Well then, what were you doing, Caman? To everyone else it looked like and sounded like you had it in for Mitchel. I don't know what else you could have been intending, but if you thought you would accomplish anything good by it, you were vastly mistaken."

"I—I," I tried to think what I had been trying to accomplish. I had wanted Mitchel to fight for his wife, to maybe make a difference by standing up for her. Had I so badly misjudged the man that I had only accomplished making a fool of myself?

"I'm sorry," I finally whispered. "I must not have been thinking right."

"That doesn't cut it, Mr. Caman. I expect better behaviour from someone who works for me."

The Mirror

Words of retaliation were on my lips, but Sarah didn't give me a chance. "Watch the soup," she said as she walked out the door.

I muttered words of vehemence the entire time I worked on finishing the soup. Sarah reappeared just in time to prevent me from spoiling the pot and to start serving out hearty portions. The smell of the thick broth made my stomach ache with hunger, and I decided to help myself.

I let out a cuss after my first swallow. The burning liquid had scorched my throat and seared my tongue. A soft tsking came from the door.

"Mother always warns me not to gulp the first spoonful of soup. You always end up burning your tongue," Sam said as she came toward me. She tapped my chin. "Open up." I did as commanded.

"Well, there is only one thing for this."

"What is that?" I asked.

"A glass of cold milk. I'll be right back." It wasn't long before Sam came back and handed me the milk. I took a sip and then set it down.

"Is this actually supposed to help?"

Sam shrugged. "I don't know, but it tastes good." She lifted my glass from the counter and took a large swallow. I laughed at the moustache that tipped the corners of her lips.

"It's rude to laugh," she said as she wiped the corners of her mouth.

"Who said?"

"Me."

"Then I am terribly sorry, my dear."

"Uh huh." She rolled her eyes and continued to take sips of milk. The silence stretched.

"Why'd you do it?" Sam asked once her milk had disappeared.

I sighed and considered what I could tell her. Sam was a young lady, and she understood much of what was going on, but should I really explain what I was hoping to accomplish? "I don't know, Sam. I guess I thought things might get better if Mr. Mitchel realized that his wife was worth fighting for."

"I wouldn't have bothered. If Mom and I can survive without Dad around, why couldn't Mrs. Mitchel and Devan? If I were Mrs. Mitchel, I would have left that man a long time ago."

Sam's age was showing in her words. "No you wouldn't have, little girl. Come here." I held out my arms to her. She hesitated but then came to snuggle. "Sometimes people do bad things, terrible things that hurt us really badly, but it is never right to forget about them, leave them behind, and move on with your life."

"But why not?" Sam pushed away from me. "My dad left. He was never around. He didn't even stay so that I would remember him. I don't even know what he looks like, or his name, or anything. And I'm just fine, so why not? Why can't Mrs. Mitchel just leave?"

"Sam." I tried to think of words to say. What could she understand? What would make her see the hurt that Mrs. Mitchel was causing? She was waiting for me to answer. "I—I..."

"Samantha, come here." Sarah was standing in the doorway. There was a diminutive frown on her lips. Sam raced over to her mother and wrapped her arms around her waist. "Let's go have a talk. There are some things you need to know."

The two left me sitting in the kitchen with a cold bowl of soup and a pounding head. I sighed and looked around. I had lost my appetite.

The Mirror

Pushing the bowl aside, I left to start gathering bed sheets. It had been nearly two weeks since they had been washed.

———⚬———

Stuart was in a chipper mood when I arrived at home bleary-eyed and exhausted. "I don't think I could have had a better day," he nattered on as I slumped over my pile of mashed potatoes. "I mean tomorrow being Saturday, I thought it would be a miserable day and all, but everyone seems fairly happy with how things are going. Even Mrs. Mitchel is content that we are doing our very best. I never would have thought this possible. I only wonder what brought on this change. Do you have any idea, Caman? Someone said you had an altercation with Mr. Mitchel, but I hardly think that being knocked senseless could change anything. What do you think?"

He waited patiently for me to reply. "I haven't a clue what you are talking about, Stuart," I muttered. "I need to go to bed." I took one last bite of potatoes and dropped my spoon onto my plate.

"Have a good night!" Stuart called as I stumbled down the hall.

Saturday dawned much too brightly for my bleary eyes. I pulled my pillow over my head trying to block out the cheery autumn sun. "Go away, go away, go away," I chanted. When I lifted the pillow from my head, I was disappointed to find my wishing had failed. With a scowl of disapproval, I pulled on a clean pair of trousers and a shirt and walked down the street to the inn.

It was a relief upon entering the inn to find someone in a similar mood as I.

"Ridiculous, completely ridiculous," muttered Sarah as she wiped tables and noisily relocated chairs. "Of all the things to have a town meeting over. When will the curate learn that I will not use my inn as the local town hall? 'Oh its nothing,' he says. 'Just a few people will show up. Not a problem. I am sure they will all be civilized.' Civilized? My—" Her ramblings cut off when she saw me standing in the door. "What do you want?"

"Coffee," I replied.

"Well, we're out."

"Out! Sarah, I just picked up five pounds of the stuff from the mercantile. How can we be out?"

"Well maybe if you didn't drink so much." She tossed her rag at me.

"I drink too much?" I began to scrub the table with a fury. "I'm not the one who can hardly function without a cup of the brew nearby."

Sarah's jaw dropped. "Well at least I have bought it with my own money."

"You mean the money you haven't paid me for my work here?"

"Well I—I... If you want money, I will pay you at the end of the workday. Meanwhile, why don't you go to the mercantile and pick up more coffee, and get a blasted shirt while you are at it. You look horrendous in grey."

"Should I buy ten pounds?" I hollered at her disappearing back.

"Five, Mr. Caman. We only need five pounds. It has always been enough, and it will be enough now. Someone just needs to stop drinking so much coffee."

I made a face in her direction.

The Mirror

"That woman is going to put us out of business." I about crawled out of my skin with the nearness of the voice.

"Martha, it's good to see you out of bed."

She raised her eyebrows as if unimpressed with my cordial salutation. "Five pounds of coffee missing? First it was the sugar. Then it was the flour. Now the coffee. What will she run amuck with next? You know the inn cannot afford such waste. I would hate for her and Samantha to have to leave."

The chill in her voice sent shivers down my back. I wondered what she meant by the sugar and the flour. Had Sarah been lying to me about the thief? Had something happened that I was not aware of? My stomach turned with unease as I watched Martha disappear to her small apartment above the kitchen.

Bottling up my thoughts, I stuck them in the corner of my mind to deal with later. Walking to the mercantile, I picked out a shirt and a five-pound bag of coffee. Mrs. Wiston, the store clerk, smiled. "You must drink a lot of the stuff." I smiled back at her and left the store.

The day was busy. I had donned my new yellow shirt when I had entered the inn, but after wiping tables, cleaning pots, polishing silverware, and baking cakes, it was beginning to look a little dingy.

Jace had come over to play with Sam, but she had turned down his offer, saying she needed to work. I tried to persuade her to go have some fun, but she rolled her eyes at me, and gave me a look so much like her mother's I gave up before I had made it through many of my arguments.

Finally, it was time for the town meeting. The crowd had reached a phenomenal size and by the time Stuart Morgan came to the stage, everything was a mess of noise and food stains. A hush fell when the curate cleared his throat, and I raced around trying to wipe the tables while everyone's attention was elsewhere.

"As you all know, we are gathered here tonight to decide whether it is right or acceptable for Mrs. Willa Mitchel to divorce in this public manner, her husband, Mr. Ryan Mitchel."

There was uproar. Boy, was I ready to do away with these passionate, loud people. Couldn't they discuss anything with even a pretence of civilization?

The mayor let out a loud whistle and the crowd silenced. Their attention was once more riveted on the curate. "Well as I was saying," he looked about happily as if the inn were an overzealous congregation, "this meeting will no longer be necessary, as Mrs. Mitchel has revoked her claim in light of present circumstances."

Silence, utter silence. I wiggled my fingers in my ears to make sure the sudden uproar that should have happened had not made me deaf, but no, I could hear Sam singing as she worked.

"Well, enjoy your evening," Stuart said as he left the stage.

The murmurs began. What could have happened? Was this all some joke? Had Mitchel had some mysterious conversion? I felt myself asking the same questions as the crowd, but I could not find any answers, so I continued about my work, enjoying the much happier note that this evening had somehow lighted upon.

Sarah hassled me with questions when I entered the kitchen, but I found I could not present an explanation for the crowd's quiet whispers. "I'm baffled," I told her. "I don't know what could have changed Mitchel's mind."

The Mirror

"Don't be so dense," she replied with a giddy smile on her face. "It was you, and you know it was you. I heard what you said to Sam. You suggested Mitchel fight for his wife, and he did. What else could have made this happen?" Sarah kissed me on the cheek and swept past me to Sam and hugged her.

I touched the spot on my cheek, finding I liked that kiss a lot. I wondered what it would take to get another. My thoughts were cut off when Sarah returned to me with another stack of plates.

Sarah set them in front of me. "Come trials or happy endings, people always bring an appetite when they show up."

"Good thing we have lots of coffee."

Sarah paled at my comment, and my questions about the return of the thief seemed to be answered. I was about to pursue a more complete answer, but Sarah had already walked away leaving me wondering if she and Sam were all that safe by themselves.

The evening rushed by in a flurry of potatoes, ham, and coffee. Dessert was served at nine and by eleven the place was just beginning to empty. At twelve, I was wiping my last table as Sam made her way upstairs to her bed, and Sarah put away the rest of the dishes.

In the kitchen, I tossed aside my rag and watched as Sarah stood on tiptoes to place a final dish in the cupboard. "I should make you a stool," I said when she turned to look my way. She raised her brow in question. "It would be safer for you than having to reach all that way. I'll bet it's easy breaking dishes that way as well."

"I've managed."

"The same way you have managed with the disappearing sugar, flour, and coffee."

"Who told you about that?" I didn't respond. Rather, I waited for her to give a fuller answer.

"I was careless. I misplaced the items, and I found them again later, after I had bought some more supplies. We now have ten pounds of coffee."

"Don't be silly, Sarah. I have worked with you enough to know that there is a place for everything. You are too organized to misplace such large quantities of things."

Sarah picked up my rag and began to scrub the counter. Wisps of her blond hair fell from her chignon and danced around her cheek. I stood and took the rag from her. Brushing back the stray hairs, I waited for her to tell me the truth. She pushed my hand away and began to rinse the rag in the bucket.

"There is nothing to tell, really. Things disappear and then they show up a day or two later. Usually they are spoiled in some way. The flour had maggots, the sugar had been wetted. I suppose whoever is doing this could not think of a way to spoil the coffee for it seems harmless, but I didn't dare use it tonight, just in case, you know."

"Have you told Billy?"

"What should I tell him?" The rag dropped into the bucket, and water sloshed over the sides. "I can't prove anything. For all I know I am just beginning to go crazy. I mean, why not? Who says I didn't leave the flour out and the maggots got in then? Perhaps I did leave the sugar by an open window when it rained last week? As far as I can tell, there is no proof that any crime has been committed."

"You've thought about this, I see."

The Mirror

"Of course, Caman. It has been all I can think about. Am I losing my mind, or is someone creeping about the inn at night? Neither thought is comforting, if you ask me."

"You're not losing your mind, so be comforted on that front."

"Prove it." She crossed her arms, waiting for my evidence that she was completely sane.

I wracked my brain trying to think of proof. "Well, no one has noticed anything different about you. If you were losing your mind, there would be changes. Neither Sam nor I have noticed a difference, and we are around you nearly all the time."

Sarah shook her head. "That is hardly proof. I'm not convinced."

"You don't eat raw chicken and pull out your hair?" I waited. She hesitated, but then the smile bloomed across her face, and a giggle escaped her lips.

"Okay, I am not losing my mind."

"Glad we established that."

"So what do I do about the things that go missing?"

"Well..." I considered all the terrible things that could happen to Sam and Sarah with no one there to protect them. "You need to protect Sam."

"Agreed, but how do I do that?"

I considered the possibilities. "Well you could marry me, for one thing." Before I even realized I had voiced the thought aloud, Sarah had fled the room.

TWENTY-THREE

SLAMMING MY FIST on the counter, I slouched onto the potato sack. "Come on, Caman," I muttered to myself. "What kind of lout proposes like that? Man, you thought you had botched other relationships. Well, you destroyed this one. Just wait, you'll be on the streets by sundown. Oh you big oaf. Why can't you learn to keep your mouth shut?"

I considered my options. Should I chase after her, or should I continue home and act as if nothing had happened? I was still pondering my conundrum when Sarah re-entered the room.

"I want to apologize," she rasped. "I shouldn't have left. You just took me by surprise."

I nodded, unsure where this conversation was going. Sarah looked at me as if waiting for me to speak. I kept my silence.

The Mirror

"Jeremy, I can't marry you. It would be all wrong. I would feel so terrible, like I had forced you into something. And I know you would do it for Sam. But, I just... I just can't."

"Who says you would be forcing me into anything? What happens if I really, really want to marry you? What if I want to marry you, not because of Sam, but because of who you are?"

"Don't be ridiculous. Everyone knows we don't get along. You hardly tolerate me."

"Hardly tolerate you? Blast it, Sarah. For the past month I couldn't decide whether I was going crazy or just terribly in love with you."

"Well, you haven't started eating raw chicken and pulling out your hair."

"See, I love you. Marry me, Sarah."

I grabbed her arm before she could once more walk away from me. "I can't," she whispered, her eyes pleading with me to understand.

"Do you not love me?"

"Yes—no—I don't know, Jeremy."

"Why can't you marry me, Sarah? Please, just give me an answer."

She didn't look at me. Her eyes were on her feet, and her shoulders were slumped. It was so quiet I could almost hear the tears roll down her face when she answered me. "Because I don't trust you."

It was a deathblow, meant to send me staggering out of her life, but I only managed to make it as far as the Morgans' house before I collapsed.

Stuart and his wife were still awake when I dropped into the chair by their kitchen table. I stared vacantly into space. Mrs. Morgan must have made a pot of coffee, because after some time I felt something warm placed between my hands. I was aware of Stuart sitting across from me, but he didn't say anything.

"Don't trust me," I muttered to myself. "How could she not trust me? I have been the perfect model of trust ever since I arrived. Of course, in the past I haven't been the most reputable person, but surely she must know I have changed. I help with Sam and the inn. If she can let me help with those, why can't she marry me? Ours would be a spectacular union. I could be a spectacular father. I could be. I would never leave her of course. Not like… not like…"

I felt the past creeping up on me. Its dark tentacles wrapped around my heart, squeezing. I felt the corners of my eyes prickling with unshed tears.

I looked at Stuart, acknowledging him for the first time. "Do you think that I can win her?"

"I am sure you could."

"She says she doesn't trust me."

"She doesn't trust many people."

I took a sip of my coffee. I spit it back into the cup with a scowl. "Do you have any sugar?" Stuart pointed at a bowl in front of me. I took two heaping scoops and began to stir.

"I think if she understood why I made the choices I have. Maybe then she could trust me."

"Perhaps, but I think a better method would be to earn her trust."

"How do I do that?"

"Oh, many ways. Don't lie or cheat. Always be very honest with her and don't keep any secrets. You know, the usual things people do when they trust each other."

The Mirror

"What if she never trusts me?"

"Cross that bridge when you get to it, Mr. Caman. As for now, I think I am going to go to bed." He yawned and stretched his arms.

I was still sitting alone in the kitchen as the sun began to rise. It was Saturday, and I should be going to work. Sarah could use the help. My knees were week when I stood, and I had to grab the table so as not to fall. When my legs had quit shaking, I gulped back my cold coffee and made my way out the door.

Sarah had not won. I was not leaving, and I was more determined than ever that she trust me. I was sure it would happen. It must, or I might be the one to go crazy.

※

I was in the kitchen peeling potatoes when Sarah found me. I was ready to beg her to stay and listen, to let me explain, to talk things out. She didn't give me the chance. After glancing my way, she went to the stove and acted as if I weren't there.

"Good morning," I said. She dropped a pan onto the stove with a clank. Measuring some flour into a bowl, she then cracked an egg and let the yoke splat on top. "Did you have a good evening?"

She glowered at me, and by the bags under her eyes, I could tell her night had been as sleepless as my own. Her words ticked through my head. *I don't trust you.* But what did she mean by that?

"Sarah." I hesitated, not sure I wanted to ask so early in the morning. "Why don't you trust me?"

Her shoulders straightened and her incessant beating of the batter stopped. "How can I, Mr. Caman?" Her voice was cold, and I prepared myself for the blow that was sure to come. "You represent everything a woman should fear in a man. You drink. You philander. You cause havoc on the streets. How am I to trust you?"

The words were rehearsed, calculated. Each was meant to send its own message. Each was meant to send me running. I didn't move.

"The past is a terrible thing, but we can't live in the past. I've made my share of mistakes, but surely you don't expect me to slip back into those patterns of living."

"I don't know, Mr. Caman. I don't know a thing about you. I don't know your mother's name. I don't know your home town. I don't know if you ever went to school or if you were ever an apprentice. I don't know a thing about you, and yet you expect me to trust you."

"My mother's name is Maybelle Lupul. I grew up in the town of Emriville. My father deserted us when I was fourteen, and I have three sisters and one older brother whom I haven't spoken to in about twelve years. I attended school until I was seventeen, and I was well on my way to becoming a rector when... when..."

"When what?"

Scenes from the past flashed through my mind, and I bit hard on my tongue. I couldn't tell her this. No one had the right to know this about me.

"I can't say this," I muttered.

"Because you don't trust me either. Let's face it, Mr. Caman, neither of us trusts the other because we have too much history to know how to trust anyone. So we will both end up alone. I've accepted it. It is time you did as well."

The Mirror

She continued to make her batter, and I continued to peel my potatoes. The past was hanging over my shoulders creating a certain misery I was not sure anyone could understand except one who had had a terrible past. The silence was tedious, allowing the word 'lonely' to dribble around the back of my mind like the incessant dripping of a leaky roof.

Lonely, lonely, lonely. Sarah was right. I would never find someone to care for. Unless...

"I was eighteen when I met Isabelle Higgins," I began. "I have told you much of this already, but there are some things I left out, so please listen. I was working under the good Curate Ingels in order to raise funds to go to seminary and become a curate myself."

"Don't tell me this."

I shook my head and continued. "I thought I had found the love of my life. She was smart, and very pretty. People liked her, and she had the makings for the perfect curate's wife. Almost. You see, I had never really faced any sort of temptation in my life. Everything was very simple. There was the right thing to do, and there was the wrong thing to do. It always made sense to me to choose the right. It wasn't this way with Isabelle.

"She was tempting, to say the least, and many times I was struggling to find the right thing to do. Isabelle was hardly any help, as she herself didn't seem to find anything wrong with any of the things we did. When I would tell her my doubts, she would laugh and say, 'It is not like I will get pregnant. You just keep working and once I'm eighteen we'll marry. You'll see.'

"So I kept working. It was only a couple of months before Isabelle turned eighteen when Curate Ingels died. I was beside myself. Ever since my father had left, the curate had been my mentor. I had even on occasion spoken to him about my struggles with Isabelle. Then just like that, he was gone.

"Isabelle was most upset that I no longer had a job. Without a curate, the town was uncertain what to do with a curate's assistant, so I was left jobless and hurting. But Isabelle was determined that I work. She is the one who signed me up for the army. I hadn't wanted to, but what choice did I have. I was commissioned to leave two weeks after Isabelle's birthday. So the wedding was planned as well as my future career."

"I don't like this Isabelle. She should have never signed you up for the army without your consent. I didn't even know that was possible."

"She said she was my wife and that she would sign the papers as proxy and I would be in later to make sure I was fit for service. Emriville is a military town. Things like that go unquestioned—in fact, they are expected."

"That is not right. I think you should have contested what she did. I am sure someone would have listened."

"I did, and someone did listen. I was set for going to seminary, and I was told I could enter the army as a clergyman after that. I thought this would suit me, and I was excited to tell Isabelle the news. I was sure she was happy for me. She laughed and said it was silly of her to think that I would ever give up my dreams to be a curate.

The Mirror

"The wedding was a week later. I stood in front of the church waiting for her. We had asked the curate from the next town to come and officiate. I remember his cheery smile and rosy cheeks like it was yesterday. It was such a mockery, for Isabelle never showed up, and neither did my brother.

"They had left a note for us saying they were moving away. Isabelle was with child, and it was not mine. She—she said she hated me, and how could I ever think someone like her would marry a boring old preacher like me."

Sarah let out a gasp and I turned to look at her. "That is terrible," she whispered. I ignored her comment, wanting to finish my story, not dwell in her pity.

"I joined the army after, because my entrance into seminary was denied. I lacked any references. The only one I did have had died. I was so angry at God that I denied everything I knew about him. I couldn't believe it anymore, and if that wasn't true, there was nothing stopping me from the things that before were so horrible to me."

"So you became a drunken womanizer who hardly ever considered the consequences of his actions. You were a part of the army the entire ten years that the war continued?"

"Eh, it had just begun when I entered. My regiment was at every major battle. But near the end, it was more a matter of making faces at the enemy than actually fighting. No one really had the heart for it anymore. We all just wanted it to end because nothing was being accomplished."

"It appears the king thought the same. My question is, why you did not return to Emriville once the war was over? You are a man of many trades. You could have easily picked up a job there and continued your womanizing in peace, or did you manage to get yourself kicked out of your home town?"

"That I did, but not in the way you would expect."

"So you weren't caught philandering by an angry father and sent away with the threat of death?"

"Well, not exactly."

"Then what?"

"You won't believe me."

Sarah let out an unladylike snort. "Caman, I have told you often enough for you to know, that I will never trust you. But you have told me this much, you might as well finish your story so I can make my final decision on your character."

"I was beaten in a duel of sorts."

"Well that doesn't seem that unlikely, but how come you're not dead?"

I cleared my throat and tried to think of the least embarrassing way of explaining my old predicament. "My opponent was female, and she didn't like the idea of facing the gallows for an illegal duel."

It was out before I could even ask her not too laugh. The chortle filled the room with mirth, and I felt as if I should sink into the floor. "You were beat by a girl! How bad are you, Caman? You were in the army, were you not? Oh my, I believe I have tears in my eyes."

"Well she was a very talented girl, and I will let you know that she had likely beaten many other men at duels, though those were not such ominous ones."

The Mirror

"And who is this talented girl who beat you in a duel and has beaten other men in duels?"

"Rose Wooden," I muttered.

"What was that?"

"I said, Rose Wooden."

"You mean *the* Rose Wooden who is now *the* Rose Arden, *the* Queen of Samaya?"

"Yes."

"Well Caman, I would have believed you, perhaps I might have been tempted to trust you, but that is the most ridiculous claim in the world. What connection would you ever have with Rose Wooden? I am sure she has nothing to do with the likes of you. I wouldn't be the least bit surprised if she were actually very snobbish."

"Not exactly. She is actually very pretty with a lot of spirit. I was just unfortunate enough to have heard some nasty rumours about her and acted on them. In my lustful, philandering mind, it only made sense."

"Now that I can believe about you, but the rest is foolishness. Who would ever believe that you once wanted to be a curate?"

"Yes, and who would believe that at the same time I was considered devilishly handsome?" My droll remark was not intended to make her laugh. It had just slipped off my tongue in an attempt to make light of the fact that she could not believe me, but she laughed. Sarah laughed so much that I had to find a chair for her to sit in, and she went on until her laughter became gasping breaths that resembled sobs. The gasping continued for so long I began to wonder if she really was sobbing, but it just didn't make sense.

I waited. Sarah caught her breath and wiped the last of her tears—whether from pleasure or pain I was not sure—and looked at me. "You know, Jeremy, I wish I could believe you. I wish that somehow I could just let go of the past to throw it in some dirty trash bin and let it rot. But as much as I try, it is still there. Staring at me like some phantom demon that no one else can understand or see."

She let out a heavy sigh, and this time I understood the tears that tinged the corner of her eyes. "I am so tired. I am so tired of all this mess. But I can't let go. I can't let you get too close. Because if I do, if for one moment I let my guard down, I might find that you are just like he was. And I can't risk that. Not ever again."

I nodded. I knew what she meant. I knew because of Isabelle. And because of Isabelle, I knew that I would never trust Sarah either. Never fully, because she might end up just like Isabelle had.

I left the kitchen. The room was suffocating me with the reality of my life. I broke out the back door and began to run. Pangs entered my chest, but I kept running. I was nearly at the curate's house when I stopped. She was standing outside the house on the street. She seemed to be waiting. She smirked at me, and a hint of recognition flooded my brain, but I wasn't sure.

I couldn't quite place her. She waved slightly, then turned away. The blooming red of her skirts caught my eye. Scarlet. That was her name. Her name was Scarlet. She was the prostitute from Mick's saloon.

A shiver ran up my spine. What did the likes of her want with me? Uneasiness crept into my belly. I wasn't sure what to do. I felt as if I should tell someone. But this was foolishness. I couldn't expect that prostitutes spent their entire day inside. She was likely just out for a walk.

Still the threat of her appearance loomed over me. Pushing it aside, I made my way across the street into the parsonage. The reminder of my shameless beating at the hands of a girl had given me an idea. I only hoped that Stuart wasn't so much of a pacifist that he didn't own a sword.

TWENTY-FOUR

IT WAS SIMPLE, REALLY. The choice was easy. There was nothing stopping me. But I couldn't move. I stared down the long road in front of me and wondered what it would be like to start walking and to keep walking until memories of Owzan and Sarah were long behind me. It was simple. I just needed to start walking.

I stood there for another five minutes before a curse escaped my mouth and I turned around. Leaving would have to wait for another day.

Thoughts collided in my head, bounced off the walls of my skull, and created a great humdrum as I made my way toward the inn. By the time I had reached the front door, my temples were pounding and I considered turning around once more to ponder the road out of town. Instead, I heaved open the back door.

"You stupid child! How dare you go meddling in my things? What, did you think you'd find a candy to scarper down to your chubby little stomach?"

The Mirror

"I was just cleaning. I wasn't anywhere near your or Billy's room. I was in the back rooms!"

The sound of a sharp slap sent shivers down my back. Quickening my pace, I pushed through the door into the hall. Sam stood holding her cheek, bright tears glistening in her eyes. Martha, more vibrant in her anger than I had seen her in months, raised her hand ready to take another swing. I grabbed her wrist before she could harm Sam further.

Martha paled. Her lips thinned and her body shook with the force of her rage. "Unhand me."

I ignored her.

"Sam, why don't you go and see if your mother needs any help. I haven't been around all morning, so I'm sure there is a lot she would like done."

Sam wiped her eyes and pushed her way through the door into the old kitchen. When she was gone, I dropped Martha's hand.

She raised it again to slap me.

There are many things I would have liked to have said. Instead, I clenched my teeth and glowered at the woman. "If it weren't for the fact that you are Billy's wife, and a grown woman, I would wallop your bottom like an impertinent child's."

"You wouldn't dare!" she gasped.

"Don't tempt me. If I ever see you laying a hand on Sam like that again, I will personally make sure you receive the thrashing you deserve."

"I'll tell Billy you have spoken to me like this. He won't tolerate it. I'm telling you. I won't have the likes of you around my inn."

"Good, maybe you'll make my life a whole lot easier," I muttered to myself as she walked away. Sam was hiding behind the first door I opened. She stared up at me, her arms crossed defiantly.

"You didn't go to your mother like I asked you to." She shook her head. "Why didn't you listen, Sam?"

"Because Mom would ask me why I wasn't cleaning the back rooms like she asked. Then I would have to explain, and I don't want to do that."

"Then I will have to be the one to tell her —"

"No! You can't!"

"Sam, she hit you, for crying out loud. That woman has no right to hit you, and your mother will tolerate it about as much as I will."

"Please don't tell her, it will only make things worse."

"How so?"

Sam tapped her foot nervously and played with the ends of her dress's sash. "It just will."

I lifted her chin and made her look me in the eye. "Darling girl, you need to explain more than that, or I will have to march over to your mother and let her know what's going on. Okay? You can trust me with whatever is bothering you."

With a heavy sigh, Sam dropped her dress sash and pushed back the few strands of hair that had come out of her braids. "Well, it's just that Martha and Billy own the inn, and Mom and I are only workers. That is fine and all because Billy is really nice, but Martha is different. She doesn't like Mom and me, and she would look for any reason to get rid of us."

"That doesn't mean she can hit you, Sam."

The Mirror

"I know," she whispered. "But if I told Mom, Mom would likely want to up and leave, and I can't let her do that. Not now. I don't want to leave you and Jace behind. I just can't do that." A tear trickled down Sam's cheek. I wiped it away with my thumb.

"Alright, let's make a deal."

"What kind of a deal?"

"You don't want me to tell your mother about today, and I want to keep you safe. So I propose a deal that if you agree to tell me every time you have a run-in with Martha or you are uncomfortable around her or anything like that, then I will agree not to speak to your mother about this one incident."

"That's not fair."

"How so?"

"Well if I tell you about any other times I have a run-in with Martha, you might tell Mom about them. You are only promising not to tell about this one."

"Well aren't you a young little whippersnapper. You're right, I am not agreeing to keep everything you tell me to myself. But I guess you'll just have to trust me to hold my tongue when necessary. Agreed?"

Sam paused. "Fine. May I go now?"

"Nope, now we must shake on it. I can't hold you to your word unless we shake on it." I held out my hand, and Sam put her small one in mine. "Now remember you gave me your word, and to go back on your word is a serious thing, okay?"

Sam nodded then turned and ran down the hall.

"I thought you had left," Sarah said when I walked into the new kitchen.

"I considered it."

"What stopped you?" She remained busy at the counter and didn't turn to look at me.

"I decided I didn't actually want to leave yet."

Sarah sighed and her shoulders drooped, but still she did not look at me. "I am sure it gets tiring moving from one town to the next. You must be ready to find a place of your own."

"Yes, something like that. I would love to have a permanent residence, but I am sure that will not happen anytime soon."

"No, I'm sure you are right." It was a whisper, almost a desperate plea. "I need to go check on, Sam," she said as she turned and hurried from the room. But no matter how quickly she walked, or how desperately she tried to cover the tears, she did not hide them from me, and as she left the room, I felt a little hope ease through.

***

Mrs. Morgan sat at the kitchen table waiting for me. I pretended not to notice her as I made myself a cup of coffee and stoked the stove to reheat the dinner I had brought home from the inn. I heaped my plate and considered walking to my room, but the table and chairs seemed rather inviting, and I had never been overly bothered by what Mrs. Morgan had to say before. So, I took a seat.

She didn't speak right away. It was her way. She allowed me to take a few bites, savour them, and enjoy the sensation of good food filling my belly. "You had a guest come by the house." The fourth bite soured in my mouth. Guest? Who would possibly want to come see me?

"She said her name was Scarlet."

The Mirror

My stomach went cold and the food tasted like bile in my mouth. I worked my way through a swallow. Pushing my plate away, I asked, "What did she want?"

"Well, she didn't really say. She just asked for you, which I thought very odd considering she didn't seem the respectable type, and I wasn't certain that you would actually know who she was."

I shrugged and pushed my fork around my plate. "I, unfortunately, had an encounter with her about a week ago. I don't think she wants to let me forget."

"Well, you should be a little more careful whom you have encounters with, Mr. Caman. A woman like that is better avoided."

"Isn't that what many people say about you, Mrs. Morgan?" I hadn't meant the words as an insult, but the tense expression on her face made me realize I had overstepped a boundary. "Forgive me," I muttered. "It just seems that you are setting a double standard."

"I know what I used to be, Mr. Caman, and I also know I am not the most respectable woman, but I do not warn you away from Scarlet because she is a lady of the night." I raised my brow, unbelieving. "A woman like Scarlet can eat a man. She's the type who will use you for what you can give her, whether money or pleasure, and when you can't give her enough, she'll spit you out and leave you wondering what happened to the man you used to be."

Mrs. Morgan's words sent a shiver down my back. A woman who could eat a man. These words could only be spoken by a woman who had lived with the likes of Scarlet, a woman once depraved, and a woman—could it be—redeemed?

"Every woman who has found herself in that circumstance feels so lost and empty inside that it seems impossible, irrational, to think there could be a way out. But you have to understand, Jeremy. These are the days of grace. These are the days when there is a way out. Not just for the prostitute. Oh and believe me, they do need a way out. But these are the days for you and me, Jeremy, for Sarah and for Sam."

"I don't need a way out, thank you very much." I pushed away from the table. Picking up my plate, I carried it over to the counter. The dishwater was still in the tub so I dunked my dishes in and began to scrub.

"Did I not see you, then, this morning at the outskirts of town? It was as if you were chomping on an unseen bit that bid you to stay back from the road ahead."

"I can leave when I want to." I dropped the dishes onto the counter and made to hurry out of the room.

"Just remember, Jeremy," called Mrs. Morgan from her serene sitting spot, "these days, while you are yet living, these are the days of grace, but they won't last. Soon death will come, and the door of grace will be shut. Your chances are running out."

Early Sunday morning I woke with a feeling of dread filling my belly like the leaden sick of indigestion. My dreams had been filled with images of a seething Martha slapping Sam, and Mrs. Morgan's voice ringing in my ears. 'These are the days of grace... your days are numbered... these are the days... precious few...' The taunt had continued on and on.

The Mirror

I slapped my cheeks, hoping to bring some clarity to my morning thoughts. Then, pulling on my cleanest garments, I made my way over to the inn. I had promised Sam I would not speak to Sarah about the previous day's incident, but perhaps I could speak with Billy. He would know what to do.

I found the man in the stable milking a tender-eyed, brown cow. He turned and smiled with similar mannerisms as the beast he tended and then turned back to his work. I took my seat and watched for a while as I tried to collect my thoughts.

"A barn is a nice place to sit," Billy said. "Animals have a way of keeping secrets and encouraging more quieting thoughts than the ones that roam human minds."

"The dumb beasts have less to set their minds on edge than humans. Sometimes I envy them that."

"By the grace of God, humans have the means of communicating the terrors that haunt the mind. The relief a listening friend can bring is phenomenal. Perhaps you should unload your burden."

"My words could bring great pain to my friend. Would it not then be better to avoid the damage?"

"The damage is already done. Only honesty can bring a balm now." Billy's tone remained even and warm, but his frame had collapsed slowly upon itself while our conversation continued. I began to think he knew what I wished to speak to him about.

"Martha slapped Sam yesterday. I agreed not to bring this information to Sarah, but I thought it best that you know."

The gentle *pht pht* of the cow's milk streaming into the pail continued, but Billy did not speak. His shoulders shook, but I could not see his face hidden within the cow's flanks. I stood and turned to leave, but Billy's words stopped me.

"The love of a woman can cause all sorts of pain. I have learned too late that I am most responsible to my wife. I should not have put another before her as I have."

"I don't understand."

"If I had loved my wife as I should, perhaps she would not hurt as she does."

"I don't think you should blame yourself."

"No, perhaps not. Well, I better keep working. The pigs still need their slops and it is nearly time for church."

Billy picked up the bucket of milk and left me standing in the barn. With a heavy sigh, I made my way back to the inn to find Sam.

The crowd around the church was teaming with happy faces and the sound of cheerful laughter. It was hard to believe that just two weeks previous, that same crowd had been peevish and tumultuous, discussing the demise of a man once respected. I wondered at the fickleness of human beings and rubbed my cheek where a gash still resided.

The Callaways pulled into the church lot, and Sam sauntered over to their buggy. I took my seat in my regular pew in the back corner. The building held a peaceful hush, as no one dared to be too rambunctious in the sanctuary.

I closed my eyes, hoping to absorb some of the peace of the building, but my thoughts taunted me. 'Lonely, lonely,' she had said. 'These are the days of grace... don't let them run out... These are the days... Lonely,

lonely... they're running out...' I opened my eyes with a start. The church was filling up and I had run out of time for quieting thoughts.

I rubbed my eyes and ran a hand through my hair. A hand on my shoulder nearly caused me to fall out of my seat. Mr. Mitchel pulled his hand away quickly, and a red tinge crawled up his neck and left his cheeks blotchy. I pulled myself into a more presentable position and straightened my jacket.

"I—I," started Mitchel with a stutter. "I wanted to apologize, for that—" he pointed to my cheek, "and I wanted to thank you. I have my life back again, and it is because of you."

"Don't mention it," I muttered, feeling uncomfortable with the man's gratitude.

He shook his head, denying me the ability to shrug away his comment of appreciation. "It is like the preacher said, these are the days of grace, and I almost missed them. I almost missed it all."

I feared he would start to cry. The quaver in his voice told me he was about to lose control. I cringed, waiting for the uncomfortable onslaught of emotion. But it didn't come. Mitchel cleared his throat and slapped me roughly on the shoulder. "Well, just remember, time can run out on you." And then he was gone, sitting with his wife and child quietly in their pew.

I glowered at their backs and tried to get comfortable in the hard wooden seat. The church was beginning to swarm with worshipers, and I felt slightly claustrophobic, but Sam took her seat beside me, the music began, and I was able to blend into the many faces of the congregation.

Stuart Morgan took his place behind the pulpit and I waited for the sermon to begin. "Brothers and sisters, who among you is without sin? Who among you can claim to be perfectly holy?" People squirmed in their seats. My own insides ached with the longing to be rid of the reminder of unrighteousness.

"Let me tell you a story." At these words I rolled my eyes, recalling many stories I had heard since living with the Morgans. "Not long ago, there was a man who owed the king money. It was such a debt, in fact, that there was no possible way of paying it off. One day the king looked in his accounts and demanded that this man be brought before him to pay his debt. So, the man was dragged before his king where he fell face down and begged to be forgiven his debt.

"The king looked on him and had compassion for him. By law, this man could have been thrown into prison. His wife and children could have been made slaves, and he could have been tortured until his debt was covered. But instead, the king declared his debt pardoned.

"The man could not believe his good fortune. He celebrated with his wife and children. There was joy in the household, but there still wasn't any money. The lack of money tainted the man's happiness, and he soon grew bitter. He remembered a friend who owed him a small amount, and he demanded this amount of the friend.

"The friend begged the man, 'Have compassion!' But the man could not. His resentment of his friend and his thirst for the money blinded him. Instead of showing mercy, the man called the guard and had his friend thrown in prison until the debt could be paid.

"The members of the guard did as they were told, but they were confused. Had not this man just been forgiven a large debt by the king? What was this money from a friend that he could not forgive it? So the guard found the king and told him what had happened.

The Mirror

"The king was enraged by the news and called the man back into his presence. The man, believing himself in the good favour of the king, simpered his way in and bowed politely. 'Where is your friend?' the king demanded. 'Have you not brought him with you?' The man was astonished. What could the king care about his friend?

"'He is in prison, sir,' the man replied, 'until he pays his debt.' The king was not pleased with this answer. 'And to whom does your friend owe a debt? Should not it have been pardoned?' The man was displeased with the answer. 'My friend owes me. I have need of the money. How could I forgive such a debt?'

"The king no longer looked down with compassion. Instead, the man's debt was brought back. The pardon was abandoned, and he was thrown in prison where he was tortured. The friend's debt, however, was absolved by the king. He was released, and he lived contentedly with the king's blessing."

My gut wrenched. The story was familiar. I had read it many times. The last time was the day of my wedding. I could still feel the sting of those contemptible words as they had been thrown in my face.

"People of God," declared Stuart. "We all have sinned, and as a result we are in debt to our King in heaven. We cannot pay this debt. We are incapable. The funds are not there. The ability is lacking. But our King is a merciful king. He looks down on us with compassion and has forgiven us our debt."

There were murmurs of assent. People could agree to this part of the sermon. It was easy to see why a good and loving God would forgive good churchgoers like those in the pew. I could not agree with them. God could not be all he claimed to be when there were people like Isabelle around.

"But," continued the curate, "how many of us are like the man in the story who is forgiven much but cannot forgive little? How many of us realize that we are like filthy rags? We are wretches who have been shown mercy by the king. All of us." Stuart looked out across the congregation, waiting for someone to object. Daring all of us to claim our innocence. Not one person stood. I clung to my pew, my rage hardly contained. Forgive little? It was no small thing that Isabelle had done to me, and to my brother.

"Now, we are left with a choice. We can forgive those who have hurt us. We can forgive the man who stole our business. We can forgive the woman who spread a malicious rumour. We can forgive the child who ruined our flower gardens. This is our choice. And what small debts these are compared to what God has done for us. Or, we can hold onto our hurt. We can demand that we are paid for the loss we have suffered. It seems as if life would be so much sweeter with that little extra bit. But is it, really?

"Hear these words, people of God, 'In anger, his master turned him over to the jailers to be tortured, until he should pay back all he owed. This is how my heavenly Father will treat each of you unless you forgive your brother from your heart.'

"These are the days of grace. Don't forget. Your time is running out. The choice is yours. Do you want to live a lonely, unforgiving life, or are you going to forgive and accept the forgiveness of the King?"

TWENTY-FIVE

"OF ALL THE RIDICULOUS WASTES of times there could be. That woman. What did she think she was doing?"

I walked into the kitchen after the service to find Sarah covered from head to toe in flour dust and most of the kitchen not looking much better. I held back a snicker, wondering what type of cooking disaster could have had such results.

Sarah turned in my direction, her finger pointing threateningly before I could defend myself. "Don't you dare laugh. Don't even think of it. That blasted woman came in here and tore a hole in the side of the flour bag and then started spinning around like a senseless child. I came in to make lunch only to get doused by flour."

My belly turned to ice. "Who was that?"

"Martha! I'm telling you, that woman gets stranger and stranger with every passing day. The next thing you know, we'll be sending her to an asylum."

There was a clattering outside the door, and our conversation ended. I peeked around the doorframe, but there was no one there. "We must be imagining things," I muttered, and turned back to Sarah. "How about you get changed while I clean this up?"

"That would be useless. I am covered in flour now. I might as well help clean up before I drag more throughout the entire inn."

"Fair enough. I'll go get the broom."

Sarah rolled her eyes. "Sam put it in the parlour closet. You might as well get the mop while you're at it. This is going to take forever to clean up."

I turned to leave once more and was nearly barrelled over by Sam. Tears streaked her face and loud hiccups escaped from her mouth. "She's at it again. She's done kicked me in the butt like I was a dog. She can't do that. She can't."

"Of course not, darling," I said as I pulled Sam into a hug and then passed her on to her mother, who stood with a stricken look on her face.

I considered whether I should first confront Martha or find a broom, when the back door to the kitchen opened and Billy peeked in.

"Ah Billy, can I have a word with you?"

"Well sure thing. I —" What he was about to say ended with a clatter. Being unaware of the flour, and not as fleet-footed as Sam, Billy went crashing to the floor when he first stepped on the slippery, floured surface.

The Mirror

"What in blazes?" Billy hollered as he tried to regain his feet. Sam made to assist him, but she was no match for his lumbering frame, and it was no surprise when both man and child when tumbling to the ground sending up puffs of flour.

The door behind me thudded with a bang, telling me that another person was about to enter the fray. I turned to warn the newest addition to our muddle, but at the sight of her, my anger flared.

"What is going on here?" Martha shrieked. "Are you being a little snitch? Do you think you can get off without a thrashing when I caught you red-handed?" She was staring at Sam, her cheeks pale and drawn, eyebrows raised to severe points.

"I won't be tormented by your wretched little filth any longer!"

"Don't you dare talk to my daughter that way." Sarah stepped forward to her daughter's defence, her face flushed beneath the coating of flour.

"What do you think everyone says about you when you're not around? A useless harlot. That's what they say. And Samantha, she is the daughter of a whore."

Spittle flew from Martha's mouth onto Sarah's face. I expected her to retaliate, to react, to strike out. But Sarah stood there, stoic and pale.

"Have you said everything you wanted to say?" Sarah asked, her back straight and her poise intact.

"No. I am not done with that little brat." She moved forward with such haste that I almost did not react in time. With a mighty leap, I wrapped my arms around Martha's midsection and brought her tumbling to the ground.

"You witch. You witch! I'll kill you. I'll kill you and your daughter both!" Her hollering continued as I dragged her to the nearest empty guest room and forced her in. She collapsed into a dramatic heap on the bed, and I slammed the door.

Billy stared at me, tight-jawed and trembling. "She doesn't mean it. I swear she doesn't mean it. Most often she adores Sam. I just…"

"Something has to be done, Billy. The next time we might not be around, and Sam might get hurt worse than a slap on the cheek or a kick in the pants."

"I can't send her away."

"Billy, what else are we going to do?"

Billy scratched his neck, his face drawn with a pain I could never imagine. "Can you go get Mr. Nelson?"

"The apothecary?"

"He has aided Martha in the past when she has gone through fits. He will have something to calm her."

I shrugged, not confident that a calming medicine was all Martha needed. But it was a start. "I suppose I could. Will you be able to handle everything here?"

The lines around Billy's mouth tightened in what could only be indignation. "Mr. Caman, I dare say that I love each member of this household more dearly than you do. Because of that, I am far more capable of handling things here than you are."

I nodded meekly and turned to leave. I found Sarah with Sam in the kitchen. They both trembled as they mopped and swept the floor, ridding it of all the flour. Their faces carried a look of surprised shock, and with their floured clothes and pale features, they looked like ghosts.

The Mirror

"Where are you going?" Sarah gasped as I walked past.

"I am to get the apothecary. Billy believes he will be useful to us."

"You will be back?"

"Of course." I stepped out the back door.

The streets were quiet. Everyone was enjoying their day of solitude and rest. I scurried past hollow storefronts, disliking the sense of foreboding they proclaimed. Thankfully it did not take long to reach Mr. Nelson's house. I knocked on the large wooden door, but no one answered. I tested the knob and found it unlocked, so I allowed myself entrance into the man's house.

"Hello?" I called. There was no response.

"Hello?"

"Well you blasted mangy pest of a creature." The muffled cry came from upstairs. I began cautiously up the stairwell but began to run when there was a large clatter followed by what sounded like shattering glass.

"I never in all my years... but I will get you yet... you—you rana catesbeiana."

I pushed open a door at the end of the hall and met a rather curious sight. Mr. Nelson was crawling on his hands and knees, scouring the floor with his eyes. His once white pants were covered in green and brown gunk and looked rather soggy, and he was attempting to drag around with him a rather large and precarious net. In the corner of the room, a table covered in glass apparatuses looked like it had been badly shaken, as many of the items on its top appeared to have been cracked or broken in two.

"Ahha!"

Mr. Nelson sprang from his place on the ground, waving his net about wildly. It came down suddenly, trapping a round, lethargic-looking toad. A delighted titter escaped the apothecary's mouth as he daintily picked up the creature and plopped it into a glass tank and covered the opening with several heavy books.

I cleared my throat. He turned and looked me over from head to toe. "Well yes, Mr. Caman, I can see you have a problem. He licked a finger and dabbed my cheek with its wet tip. I cringed, wondering what type of toad filth had entered his mouth. Seeming ignorant of the possible dirtiness, the apothecary once more stuck his finger in his mouth.

"Hmm, flour. Don't worry, it's not lethal. I am sure you'll be fine after a nice refreshing bath. Perhaps even a dip in the creek. The weather is still fine enough for it, and believe you me the water is still delightfully warm. I had to wade in quite a ways to get that little blighter over there. A marvellous specimen if I do say so myself. I can't wait to see what the inside of him looks like."

"Mr. Nelson, I'm not sick. It's Martha." The apothecary's busyness stopped. His knuckles whitened around the top of the toad's cage, and the deep bellows of the toad were all that were to be heard.

"How ill?"

"I am afraid for Sarah and Sam's lives."

There was a long pause before he spoke again. With a heavy sigh, he let go of the frog cage and moved toward the door. "Let me gather my things. I don't know if I will be able to do anything, but perhaps a good sleep will give us time to think."

"Mr. Nelson, I am not sure what you mean."

The Mirror

"I have a draught of laudanum. While Martha sleeps, we will discuss our next step."

I waited for him to explain more. Instead, I was left standing next to the toad that appeared just as bewildered by his predicament as I was of my own.

The walk back to the inn was silent. It was getting cool out, and the damp wind caused the flour to make my face itch. The thought of a bath was becoming more and more appealing. Mr. Nelson stopped at the front door of the inn, took a deep breath, and stepped inside. The place was eerily quiet.

We made our way past the few guests toward the room where I had earlier made Martha a captive. Billy sat in the hall with his hands balled and his flour-white face looking like that of a melancholy ghost.

"How is she, Billy?" Mr. Nelson asked.

Billy shrugged. "She just kept screaming. 'I won't,' she would scream. 'I won't go to an asylum. You can't make me.' I don't know where she got the notion. I asked her to let me in, but she wouldn't, and she has barricaded the door. I tried speaking some soothing words to her, and that seemed to calm her down because she quit screaming, but now she won't speak at all."

"You did well, Billy. I'm sure that we'll be able to get this all sorted. It should not be that big an ordeal once we get the door open and Martha has calmed down."

I had my doubts, but Mr. Nelson's words seemed to calm Billy, so I forced myself to agree with a nod.

Mr. Nelson gave Billy a reassuring pat and then stood and contemplated the door. With a resounding knock, he banged on the door. "Martha, this is Mr. Nelson. It is time you open the door. I think we should move back up to your bedroom where you will be much more comfortable."

There was no answer and the apothecary's jaw tensed.

"Martha, I do not want to break down this door. That would not be fair to Billy. He will be forced to replace it, and you know what a challenge it is to replace these doors. Not to mention the expense. Be reasonable, Martha."

Still there was no response. Fear was becoming evident in Mr. Nelson's eyes. "Mr. Caman. Were you ever taught to kick down a door?"

"Yes sir."

"Then be quick about it." Mr. Nelson did not give me time to insert my excuses. So with a leery look at the solid oak door, I took a deep breath and gave a mighty kick near the handle. The shock of the force through my leg was enough to make me bite my tongue, but the frame cracked and the door flew open. I turned to hide my pain, but it was nothing compared to the wailing that escaped Billy's lips.

"Caman, come quick."

I turned quickly, and met the ghastly sight of Martha's purple lips and contorted face hanging from a bed sheet tied to the rafter.

"Catch her!"

I only had enough time to respond before Martha's body came crashing into my arms. I heard the whistling sound of her breath. She was still alive. I placed her gently on the floor. Mr. Nelson nearly shoved me out of the way as he tenderly touched her throat and listened to her breathing, desperate fear on his face. "Father please," he murmured. His fingers traced up her throat and then they stopped.

The Mirror

"Billy," he whispered. "I'm too late. I can't do anything for her. Her throat—well, her trachea that is, has been crushed. She can't get air to her lungs, and I have no way of getting it there."

Halting gasps were Billy's only response. Then, with a look of such love and affection, he crawled over to sit at Martha's head. Lifting her gently, he cradled her in his arms. "How long?"

Mr. Nelson shrugged.

"You do not need to stay."

Mr. Nelson picked up his bag and squeezed my arm, informing me it was time to leave. I walked through the broken doorframe, but I turned back, drawn to glance one last time at the morbid tableau.

Billy sat with his wife held close. His eyes were closed and he rocked gently. "I love you, my dearest," he murmured. Tenderly he placed a kiss on her forehead. Then, with a whistling gasp, she breathed her last.

"Mr. Nelson?" I knocked softly on the door down the hall where I had seen the apothecary disappear. There was no answer. A jolt went through my stomach. Recent events had made silence very foreboding. I pushed open the door and to my relief found the apothecary sitting dejectedly at the end of one of the bunks.

I scowled at the apothecary. "You didn't answer my knock."

Mr. Nelson shook his head as if to rid himself of the remainder of his daze.

"Forgive me, Mr. Caman. I shouldn't have been so unthinking, so unkind."

"Are you okay, Mr. Nelson?"

"Oh well enough, I suppose. I had just so hoped to be able to help."

"What was wrong with her?"

"Martha, dear, dear Martha was in a lot of pain."

"Pain?" I asked as I slouched down onto the bed next to the apothecary. "I would have never guessed anything like that."

"That is because I do not speak of physical pain." A heavy sigh. "Life here wasn't always as it is now. When Billy and Martha were first married, it was quite a happy place. They had been given the property for the inn as a gift, and they were determined to make it prosper so that their children and their children's children would be able to make a living from it."

"But they don't have any children."

"Exactly, and that is where the pain comes from. After the first miscarriage, I informed them it was normal, and that Martha would likely rebound and soon they would have a whole passel of little ones running about. But after the fourth and fifth miscarriage I was beginning to grow concerned. Not only was Martha's physical health faltering, she needed time to heal emotionally before they should even consider children. I warned Billy and Martha, but they didn't listen. It wasn't until Martha almost died after the sixth miscarriage that Billy refused to continue like that."

"So what did he do?"

"Mr. Caman, I am sure that you know how children are conceived and the only way of truly refraining from conceiving. Because of that, I am sure you know exactly what Billy did."

The Mirror

I shook my head, trying to make sense of the impossible truth. "How could he?"

"How could he? Mr. Caman, if you knew that giving up one thing, even if that one thing was very desirable to you, would save the life of a person who was very precious to you, would you not give it up?"

"Well I—I don't know. Perhaps. But there is no saying she would have died or even have conceived again."

"Ah yes, well you think as Martha had thought, and because Martha thought that way, she was very bitter. When all her attempts to seduce her own husband failed, she fell into deep mental agony. I can't say I blame her. She had a lot to be miserable about, but it does not excuse her actions. She was very wrong in what she did with her pain."

"How long ago did this all happen, Mr. Nelson?"

"Fifteen years. I had just begun my practice here in Owzan, and boyo, I was not expecting to meet such challenges so early. You see, Billy came to me for help when Martha started to refuse to eat or to leave her bed. I dosed her lightly with an opiate and she seemed to come out of her stupor. She was cured, we thought. I left and was not called back for aid for some time."

"And they never again tried to have children?"

"Well I don't think they very well could. You see, two or maybe it was three years later, I cannot recall, Billy called me again. Instead of taking me to Martha, we went into a back room. Now I must say I was dearly shaking at that moment, because Billy was not the kindhearted man he is now. I thought he was sure to wring my neck and well let's just say I kept my hands tight around my physician's bag as my only defence.

"Once we were safely away from earshot, Billy just let it out and started bawling like a kicked hound dog. I was so frightened and my nerves were so on edge, I swung my bag around and knocked him hard on the head. I am terribly ashamed of myself for acting so rashly, but consider Billy. He is a terrifying man when in a miserable mood."

I would have laughed at this point in Mr. Nelson's story, but the thought of Billy—calm, peaceful, lighthearted Billy—wailing as the apothecary described, portrayed to me a pain I could only begin to imagine. I didn't understand how the two men could be the same person.

"When I had come to my senses and Billy had shaken off the dazed expression, he was finally able to tell me what the problem was. And what a shock I received. Martha, whom I had dosed once very slightly with an opiate, was now heavily using opiates just to make it through the day. She would not let Billy near her unless she was under the influence of the drug, and she was daily more publicly showing signs of being dependent on a substance.

"I was flabbergasted. I had been warned about drug dependency and the care that must be taken with opiates while I was in school, but just one dosage, and so light a dosage as well..."

"I don't think you can be blamed, Mr. Nelson," I said when he slipped out of focus. "When I was in the army, many of the men became addicted to opiates. They were taken to ward off nightmares. Unfortunately, addiction led to rash behaviour and I believe many of them were killed or left the army and became beggars or thieves or other unsavoury sorts in order to support their habit. I saw too much of the terrors of the drug to ever want to take it unless in dire need."

The Mirror

"Yes, well, Martha did not see the danger and it took us, Billy and me that is, quite some time to break her of the habit, and even then we were never quite sure if she was not taking it secretly. Even now, Billy is not sure where all the money from the inn is going. He is sure that Martha was using some of it to support a secret addiction. Anyhow, eventually Sarah showed up and Sam was born. Billy was ecstatic. To him it was like having a child of his own, or a grandchild, as by that time he was old enough to have grandchildren running around. He and Martha were married later in life—one of the reasons they had problems having children, I believe.

"Martha was not so happy. She began taking to her room again, but every time Billy thought she might truly be ill or needing me to come for a visit, she would magically spring back to health and begin helping around the inn. Once, when I came for a surprise visit, I found her, not in her bed as everyone thought she would be, but in the baby Samantha's room cradling the child and crooning to it. When she saw me, she placed the child back in the cradle, and I can still recall her words—they were so potent with rage. She said, 'It is too bad the mother wants to keep her bastard. I would be more than willing to pretend the child was my own. If only she had not survived the labour.'"

Anger was once more searing my gut. How could Martha? How could she even consider that of Sarah, a woman who had never done her any harm, who had helped her in so many ways? But then I remembered... how could Martha, a woman who had so much, kill herself rather than face a woman who had the one thing she could never obtain? Confusion pervaded my anger. I wasn't sure how to think of Martha, the dead woman.

"There's no use in trying to understand or explain Martha. There is too much about the human mind, the human will, the human soul that I fear a doctor will never understand. Perhaps it would be better for you to speak with your preacher friend about what you have seen. I am sure Stuart and God know of the pain and misery that can cause a man to reach for faith or for the devil himself."

Mr. Nelson stood and squeezed my shoulder. "I must go and inform the proper authorities of the death, and then I must speak with Billy about funeral arrangements. Perhaps you would be so kind as to go and find Stuart. I am sure Billy would appreciate the help. I will be back within the hour, and I don't think it wise to leave Billy alone for much of that time. Well, I'm sure that you can see to that?"

I nodded and followed Mr. Nelson to the door. It was time I found Sarah and let her know what had happened. Sam would need to be talked to as well. I felt my heart sink as the weight of everything that had happened pulled upon me. I wasn't sure that Mr. Nelson was right. Misery, I was sure, could only lead to one thing. How else could the devil have such a grasp upon my soul?

TWENTY-SIX

MORE TIME HAD PASSED than I had reckoned. Stuart was no longer at home when I went to find him, and it took Mrs. Morgan's reminder for me to realize he would be at the church as the second service had begun nearly fifteen minutes earlier. I clattered down the dull Sunday streets, passing by the bleak, closed up storefronts and lonely houses. The stark white church doors stood out among the gloom, austere and condemning.

Pushing open those same doors, I was engulfed by the sound of a familiar hymn, but the words were meaningless and slurred, fading as I walked down the aisle. Finally only the organ played as I bent over and whispered in Stuart's ear. "You must come with me. It's urgent."

Stuart's head jerked back in surprise. "Goodness Caman, what happened to you? You look a disaster," he whispered. I was thankful the nearest pew occupant was a few feet away and could not hear my words above the organist, who determinedly played on despite the lack of enthusiasm from the congregation.

"Why don't you take a seat, Caman? The service is going to start soon."

"Stuart, you must come with me now."

"I can't, Caman. Who would give the sermon?"

"Martha's dead."

Stuart paled.

"You need to come for Billy. Billy needs you right now, and Mr. Nelson said it was necessary for you to come. Do you not have notes you could give to an elder?"

Stuart stood and the organist played all the louder. "Do you see Mr. Jameson?"

I pointed the man out.

"Good. I will meet you outside in just a moment, Caman. I just need to tell Jameson that he will be leading the service. It won't take long."

He was right. I had hardly sat down on the top step when he was coming out the door, and we were walking toward the inn. "What happened, Caman?" Stuart asked. "Why are you so filthy? And what happened to Martha?"

"She's dead. I don't know that there is much else to say on the matter. She decided she did not want to live anymore and so she is dead. Dead by her own hand."

Cold. I decided the air felt cold, despite the blazing sun, when Stuart failed to respond to what I had said. It is difficult to respond temperately to death, but it is nearly impossible to respond without the least bit of desperation when someone has taken their own life. For,

The Mirror

how can one hate oneself enough to end their life? But how can one love oneself enough to keep living? I saw these insane thoughts blinking in Stuart's teary eyes. I felt them grappling in the pit of my stomach. 'Too much,' I wanted to yell. It was too much for one person to handle.

"We'd better hurry," Stuart rasped.

It did not take long to reach the inn. The front parlour was empty, but when we reached the back hall, the place began to buzz. The apothecary was speaking with the patrolman, who was trying to shake off the councilman. Billy was weeping beside Sarah, who tried to hold up under the man's bulk. Sam was nowhere to be seen, and the door to the room containing Martha's body was shut fast.

"Where is Sam?" I whispered to Sarah when Stuart had taken a trembling Billy from her hands.

"I—I sent her with the Callaways. I saw them pass and I thought... I thought she would be safer there for the evening." Her hands shook and there was a quiver in her lip.

"Let's go, Sarah. We should get out of here and let the men do their work. Perhaps we should visit the Callaways as well. I'm sure Hope will have a nice cup of tea."

Sarah was shaking her head before I could finish. "I have to sweep the floor in the kitchen, and I should start preparing for tomorrow. It would do no good to tarry in my duties now. The men will still want their breakfast."

"I am sure they will understand, Sarah. Let's just leave." I went to take her hand but she pulled away.

"Please, Jeremy," she whispered. "I just need something normal to do."

It was ludicrous to stay while the place bustled with the many different faces of death, but I couldn't deny Sarah. "Go get the broom, and I'll sweep while you do what you need to for tomorrow. Once things are cleaned up, will you promise to come with me to the Callaways?"

"We'll see," she replied, and tried to slip away. I grasped her arm. "You aren't my keeper, Mr. Caman." Her words were angry, and I turned her loose. With one last venomous look she stalked away.

Working in the kitchen was a silent task. Sarah did not wish to speak to me, and I was in no mood to pick up a one-sided conversation. It wasn't until we were almost finished that one of us broke down and began to speak.

"I'm sorry for my words earlier. They were unkind."

"You were right, though," I replied. "I am not your husband or your brother, so I have no right to order you around."

"Yes, but you were only looking out for my best interest. I should have responded more kindly."

I swept the flour dust into a dustpan and tossed it out the door. There was no use in arguing with Sarah, I would only cause more grief. But Sarah could not let the matter drop.

"It's just that, I don't know, I am so used to... No, it's not that. I just can't... I just can't..."

"Trust me?"

"Of course I trust you," she said as she shoved aside a bowl of dry ingredients. A small cloud puffed from the top of the bowl, but she waved it aside. "What would ever make you think that I don't trust you?"

"You said it yourself," I replied as I took a rag and wiped up the mess on the counter.

The Mirror

"Let me do that," Sarah said as she grabbed the rag from my hand. "When did I ever say I didn't trust you?"

"When I proposed."

Sarah turned scarlet. She hadn't forgotten. I knew she hadn't, but for some reason unbeknownst to me, she had wanted me to forget. I hadn't, and I tried desperately to suppress the tingle of hope that was beginning to rise in my stomach.

"Well, I was probably just scared." She dropped her rag into a bucket and slumped into a chair. I leaned the broom against the wall and followed suit.

Taking her hands in mine, I looked into her eyes and whispered, "I believe you said that people like us had too much history to ever trust again. We are destined to end up alone. Then, that scared me, but now, more and more, I am not sure what scares me more, being alone or trusting someone again. I can't help but think that maybe you might have been right."

"Oh, please don't say that," Sarah whimpered as a tear rolled down her cheek. "I was so wrong. I must have been wrong. If I wasn't, I don't think I can live. I think I would rather be like Martha than live so much longer alone. You know if it weren't for Sam, I would have done it a hundred times over. Oh please tell me I was wrong." She was gasping by the time I was able to bring her into my arms and coo soft words of reassurance that I wasn't even sure I believed.

Sarah's sobs slowed to soft hiccoughs and her breathing began to come at a normal pace. Pushing away from my shoulder, she looked into my eyes, and with a slight shudder, she began to speak. "When I was sixteen years old, I was considered the belle of the town. My father was one of the councillors of Croden, and my mother made the best lemon tarts all the way across the next three counties. Many people agreed on this point, so there was no use arguing about it with her. I lived such an ideal life then. The town was happy, my heart was happy, and I could have any man I wanted to be my husband.

"But I didn't want just any man." Sarah pushed back the curls that had escaped from her braid and tucked them behind her ear. Her hands shook, and I reached to take them but she pulled away. "Don't think I didn't try. I walked many miles with the cooper, and after that, I shared multiple Sunday meals with the baker, the smith, and various suitable farmers, but they were all so unappealing and bland. I—I was a fool at the time, and I thought that love ought to be thrilling. I was so mistaken.

"The town of Croden was for the most part ideal. Were it not for the Heptons, I'm sure many would have settled into our idyllic region. But the Heptons had a way of scaring people off. There were five of them, you see. Mrs. Hepton was alright by herself, and many of the townspeople would try to convince her to leave her good-for-nothing husband when she made a rare solitary journey into town, but she would always reply, 'I ain't leaving my boys no matter how bad it gets. He can beat me dead, but I won't let him hurt my boys.'

"She had three sons. The eldest was Seth. He was said to be as mean as his Pa. All I knew of him was that he frequented the places of less repute and had started many a fight. Bill was the second son. Everybody knew he wasn't much smarter than a brick wall, but he was still smart enough to rile up trouble now and then. He would take on men in the street just to see if he could whup them. Most often he only managed to bang a few heads and split a few lips. Finally, there was Mark.

The Mirror

"I think it was Mark who first intrigued me. He was nothing like his brothers. He was gentle and kind, and often he stood up to his older brothers, taking a beating from them instead of allowing some unknowing farmhand to take the blows. Bill would not have been such a difficult man to stand up to, but Mark stood up to Seth when even the best fighters in town avoided him.

"Mark was courageous and, like him, I wanted to be courageous. So one day, as my friend and I were walking back to my place after a sick visit, we passed by Seth Hepton, and he hollered at us." A sad smile tipped the corners of Sarah's mouth. "I told him if he ever used that language around me again, I would clean his mouth out with soap. He cackled at me. From that day forth, I carried a bar of soap with me wherever I went. It wasn't long before it came in handy.

"I passed by Seth Hepton three days later and he spoke some dirty words. With a courage I can only attest to gaining from Mark, I whirled on the spot and stuffed that soap bar in his mouth and scrubbed as fast and hard as possible before he shoved me away. I had never been so afraid yet so exhilarated in my entire life. I thought he was going to hit me while he stood spluttering and cursing. But when he turned to me, it wasn't anger or loathing in his eyes, it was laughter.

"He clutched his sides in merriment. Not the rude cackle of before, but heartfelt pleasure. Right then and there I was lost. I had thought Seth was, too. We began meeting in secret, and telling each other all about our lives, our wishes, our desires. Seth would tell me these wonderful stories. With his words, he would take me to another world of dreams and fantasies and if-onlys."

"He was a liar, wasn't he?"

Sarah's lip quavered. "To this day I still don't know the truth." I squeezed her fingers gently between my own and waited for her to continue her story.

"I never told my parents about Seth. He was forbidden. He was a man scorned by society and often in trouble with the law. But he was changing. He no longer entered the places of ill repute. He no longer began a fight unless provoked. He was a different person. People noticed, and they started to make a fuss about me spending time with the Heptons. But I didn't listen to them.

"I grew up in a world of innocence. I never believed I could err so much in judging a person. I still can't believe that he didn't at least change a little. In the end it didn't matter. One evening he brought me to his home. His father was there, along with his brothers."

A sob broke past Sarah's composure. "They stood and watched!" she wailed. "I hate them. I hate every last one of them. Because they stood and watched as Seth and his father beat me and raped me. I don't care what Stuart Morgan says. I will never forgive, and as far as I am concerned, Seth can burn in hell."

"And... and Sam?" I had to ask. I needed to know the truth.

"I spent two months in my room healing and never once looking upon the face of another human besides that of my parents and the apothecary. By that time I knew the truth. So I ran away, lest everyone should know my shame."

"And you came to Owzan, where Billy and Martha took you in."

"And here I will stay until I am old and grey, and I am unable to lift the coffee pot anymore. Then I will die, and no one will miss me except perhaps Sam."

"And me. I will miss you."

Sarah shook her head and pushed back her wispy blond hair. "I don't know if I dare hope for that to be true. I—I think that maybe I could love you. If I were given some time..."

Leaning forward, I touched her lips with my fingertip. She looked so innocent and trusting, as if her life had never been torn asunder. I leaned forward and, as gently as I dared, I kissed her lips. That was the first time since Isabelle that I kissed, not a harlot or a woman I wished to use for my own satisfaction, but a woman I longed to cherish and care for, and the knowledge of that left my knees quaking.

TWENTY-SEVEN

COLD. MARTHA'S FUNERAL WAS COLD. Stuart Morgan had fought with the elders and lost. Martha was not to be buried in the church graveyard, but up a hill, and away from those some would deem holy. I gritted my teeth and clenched my jaw as the bitter autumn wind nipped at my nose and tried to make my teeth chatter.

Sarah softly brushed my arm and my fists released their death grip in order to encase her small hand. "Relax, Jeremy," she whispered. "We will make it through this funeral together."

"But why here? Why not in the church graveyard?"

"You know the prejudices, Jeremy. She was a suicide. How can you lay a sinner like that to rest next to one who was a church elder?"

"I wonder then that any should be laid to rest by a church," I replied with a grunt of derision. "Least of all me. They should throw me out and bury me alive here next to Martha."

The Mirror

"They couldn't. Then they themselves would lose their burial plot due to the fact that they were murderers."

"Ah, now I see. I will just have to wait to die, and then they can spit on my grave."

Sarah clasped a hand over her mouth to hold back the chuckle she could not withhold. Sam jumped when she heard the strangled sound, and I realized she had gone quite pale.

"Something wrong?" I asked quietly as Stuart Morgan had begun to eulogize Martha. Sam shook her head, and a slight bit of colour began to bloom back in her cheeks, so I decided not to push for an answer.

I returned my attention to the funeral, and once again my heart was hit by the cold reality of the situation. Billy stood across from me, his pose stoic and unyielding to the tears that Sarah had now succumbed to. Stuart began to pray and when the final amen was spoken, Billy picked up a handful of dirt and dropped it on Martha's grave. "Good bye, my love," he whispered, and a single tear trickled down his pale cheek.

Then he walked away.

The Callaway ladies followed suit, and Sarah and Sam turned to do likewise. "You coming?" Sarah asked.

I shook my head. "I'll be back around dinner time if that is alright with you."

"Of course." A sad smile tipped the corners of her mouth, and she and Sam disappeared down the hill.

When the women were out of sight, Mr. Callaway handed a shovel to me and one to Stuart, and we began the long and arduous task of burying the pine coffin. I had just slumped onto the ground to take a rest when the laboured breathing of the apothecary greeted us as he made his way up the hill.

He stopped with a start. "Oh I—I—oh goodness me. I didn't think anyone would be here still."

"Sit down and join us, Mr. Nelson," I said, patting the ground.

"Well I supposed I could." He sat next to me and looked morosely at the grave. "I thought the funeral was earlier. There was no announcement, you see."

"Yes, well," Stuart started, his voice dripping with bitterness, "the church elders did not think it necessary to speak to the congregation about Martha's death and funeral. It has all been kept quite hush-hush. Which is a shame if you ask me."

"Yes, yes, a mighty shame I agree."

"What brings you here, Mr. Nelson? If you thought the funeral was earlier?" I asked.

Mr. Nelson rubbed a hand roughly across his face but did not answer at first. Shifting uneasily on the ground, he looked at each of our faces before he answered. "To be perfectly honest, part of the reason is tradition. The other part is guilt." He paused as if unsure how to explain further. "I don't know if you could understand the guilt a man learned in medicine feels when he fails to bring healing. I know the faces and names of each person I failed to bring back from the grasp of death. Each person I could not save has a name and a grave that I visit regularly."

"You couldn't have done anything to save Martha," I said, not willing to allow Mr. Nelson to feel guilt over a death that no one could have predicted or prevented.

The Mirror

"No, I supposed you're right. I could not have kept Martha from hanging herself. But there is more. I knew Martha struggled with a mental battle that not even the greatest physician could understand. So I did what a physician must in those circumstances. I prayed to the master physician. But now, when I had ceased my praying, when I had given up the effort as a waste of time..." His lip trembled and his hands shook as he pulled a flower from the lapel of his jacket and placed it atop the freshly turned dirt.

"Oh Father in heaven, have mercy," he rasped. And somewhere deep within my soul that prayer resonated with a power I could not understand.

TWENTY-EIGHT

IT TOOK AN ENTIRE DAY, but at Billy's request, Stuart and I began to go through all of Martha's belongings and sort it into piles to donate to various church organizations. I found it odd rifling through a woman's clothes, but Stuart, who had been asked to do such a task before, hardly hesitated upon opening a drawer of undergarments. Dumping them into a wooden crate, he carried it down the stairs to Sarah, who had promised to help if she was needed.

I smiled and wondered if Sarah would invite me over for supper again this evening. It was because of Sam, I told myself, that I loved being with Sarah so much. But in truth, I knew that my maddening desire to forget everything of the past create my own little heaven in Owzan with Sarah and Sam would soon overcome the last remains of logic clinging to the recesses of my conscious mind. Still, the smile continued to spread across my cheeks.

The Mirror

Stuart soon returned with a small book in his grasp. "Billy won't mind if I keep this," he said, his lips tight and his forehead lined with stress.

"Billy said he didn't want to have any remaining traces of Martha in this room. I think he wants to try to forget the pain. It would likely be best not to mention it to him if you do take it."

"Very well." Stuart tucked the small volume into his coat pocket and we continued with our work.

The room seemed an endless winding trail. Clutter filled the drawers, the closet, and underneath the bed. As we progressed from pile to pile, I wondered at the hurt, the pain, and the hatred that would cause a woman to hoard away sacks of flour and sugar to terrorize a fellow young woman. By the time we reached the shattered mirror, a tear escaped my eye, and with it I mourned a woman lost.

Stuart came up beside me, and together we gazed into the shattered glass. "Where was God, Stuart? Where was God when Martha sought him? Where was he when she needed him?"

"Right beside her. Unfortunately, she could not see him in the mirror."

I shook my head. "That's not an answer."

"'Now we see but a poor reflection as in a mirror; then we shall see face to face. Now I know in part; then I shall know fully, even as I am fully known.'"

"I don't understand."

"Sometimes I don't feel like I do either," Stuart murmured, and we both continued our gazing. With a soft shake of his head, Stuart broke the silence. "It's getting late. Should my wife and I expect you for dinner this evening?"

"Not likely."

"You may want to make an appearance some time. I am told that on occasion you have a visitor come looking for you."

"Everybody knows to find me at the inn."

"Yes well, this ah, visitor, would not feel comfortable making an appearance at such a public place."

I feigned ignorance. "Who is the visitor?" Dread seeped up my legs turning them into leaden stumps.

Stuart cleared his throat, his face now a ruddy shade. "I believe she has dubbed herself Scarlet."

"Send her away. I don't have any affiliation with her, and I never intend to."

"Ah yes, that is what I had thought, so that is what we did, but she still insists upon seeing you."

"Well go to Mick and tell him to keep a better rein in his women. They shouldn't be out harassing common citizens."

"I would, but I believe she has quit her employ with Mick."

I grunted. "A woman of those stripes does not change."

"I beg to differ." My face flamed at Stuart's cold voice, and I recalled his wife's story.

"I'm sorry. Your wife, she is an amazing woman. I meant no slight against her."

"Your apology is accepted. As it is, Scarlet is currently working under the employ of the local seamstress. She says this work more suits her, and I am guardedly optimistic at the warnings of my wife.

The Mirror

But perhaps you should speak with her to find out what she would like. Then you can go your separate ways."

"I won't go out of my way to see her, Stuart. I don't trust the likes of her. If she needs to speak with me so desperately, she can find me at the inn."

"Very well. I will pass on the message."

We continued our work in silence.

༺❦༻

"You're very quiet," Sarah said as we finished our supper later that evening. I nodded, not knowing what to say. "Come, Jeremy, what's bothering you?"

"Did you ever know, or even think, that there was something desperately wrong with Martha?"

Sarah let out a heavy sigh and, stacking our plates to the side, leaned with her elbows on the table and looked at me. "You shouldn't let this bother you so. But no, I never once guessed that Martha was the least bit delirious, just tired and cantankerous."

My fist slammed down on the table before I could control my frustration, and Sarah jumped. "There had to have been some signs. There had to be a way this could have all been prevented. There had to be."

"No there didn't," Sarah replied coldly.

I laid my head in my hands and tried to knead away the headache that had formed. I felt more than heard Sarah come up behind me and begin to rub my shoulders.

"Listen, Jeremy," her voice was much gentler now, "often the matters of the heart are hidden by what we see in the mirror. Even we can confuse ourselves into thinking that what we see in our reflection is what makes up our inner person. But it doesn't, and I am done living like it does."

"'Man looks at the outward appearance, but the Lord looks at the heart,'" I muttered into my hands.

"What was that?"

"Nothing, just an old proverb. I don't know why it even came to mind. Please continue."

"Oh well, I was just thinking, that over the years since—since... well you know what. I have looked in the mirror and every time I have looked, I have seen the scars and the limp, and I thought to myself that that is what I have become. But I am starting to believe I am wrong, and that maybe Martha was the same way. That all Martha could see was herself as unloved, but there has to be more. At least, I want to know that there is more."

"What if you can't find this something more?"

"I'm not sure." Sarah hesitated. "I won't say that I will do as Martha did, but I do not think I will be much better off than she was."

I stood and squared Sarah's face between my hands. "Let me know if you find what you're looking for." Leaning forward, I placed a kiss upon her lips and left. Stuart Morgan would be waiting up for me.

"You know, I have been counting the money since Martha has passed on, and the numbers just don't add up. I mean before we were just making it by, but now, now I don't know what to do with all the money coming in," Sarah said as we worked in the kitchen on Saturday.

The Mirror

"Do you think she was hording some of the money, just as she was doing with the flour and coffee and other things?" I asked.

She shook her head. "I don't know. We didn't find any evidence of that. Perhaps there is another explanation somewhere."

"Perhaps."

The throp throp throp of our knives filled the room. "Well goodness!" Sarah exclaimed as I dropped my pile of chopped vegetables into the pot. "I never thought I would be concerned about too much money."

I smiled at her predicament, and a small giggle escaped past Sarah's lips. I never found out if that giggle would have bloomed into a full-hearted laugh, for at that moment the back door to the kitchen burst open.

"Why hello, Jeremy. I have missed you."

I felt the heat of a flush crawl up my neck. Sarah had turned a very lurid shade of white.

"You don't belong here. If you want your lunch, you will have to wait with the rest until noon. Breakfast has already passed."

Scarlet paid no heed to Sarah's words. With a flick of her wrist as if to shoo away a pesky fly, she turned to me with a beguiling grin. "You know Jeremy, when I saw you the other day, I thought I would be seeing you much more often."

"I don't know what you are talking about."

"You used to be unable to resist my charms, but now you seem so cold."

I felt cold. I felt like I had dipped myself into a basin of icy dread, and now I had only to wait for the worst. "Why don't you go back to Mick? Your speech is addled, and we have no room for drunkenness here."

"My speech is perfectly sensible, as you well know. Besides, I am done with Mick. He didn't pay enough, and his food was atrocious. I can do much better than that if I want."

"Sarah, why don't you leave, and find Sam? I will try to get rid of her."

"Oh please don't send her away," Scarlet said, a feral gleam in her eyes. "I have always wanted to know what it felt like to be the other woman, and I am sure her expression will tell me once we get past all this dimwittedness."

"Get out of here, Scarlet. We don't have time for your games. We have work to do."

"If it must be that way, I guess I shall have to be blunt." Scarlet pulled off her gloves and made herself comfortable in the chair I had abandoned. "I never should have left you for your brother, Jeremy. It turns out he was far more of an idiot than I was counting on, and managed to get himself killed before seeing one battle with the Isbetans. As a result I was left penniless with a child I never wanted."

I was sure I had swallowed some sand or perhaps the remaining flour dust was coating my throat.

"Isabelle?"

It couldn't be her. For the first time I gave her more than a fleeting glance, and my legs turned to jelly. She was older now, but her face, the curve of her lips, the shape of her eyes, they had not changed. A second reality crashed upon me almost immediately after the first. "Rueben is dead?" I croaked.

"Of course the oaf is dead."

I grabbed onto the counter to keep myself from collapsing.

The Mirror

"It worked out for the better in the end. Without Rueben carrying on about keeping the child, I was able to dispose of it and move on with my life."

I heard Sarah stumbling around for a chair, but I couldn't make my legs listen to my command to go help her. I was frozen. Cold. Dead in my grief and shock.

"I—I don't understand."

"Come now, Jeremy, I am sure you are not that dense. It may have been twelve or so years, but surely we could pick up where we left off. Things can't have changed that much."

I felt the blood pounding in my temples, and my tongue seemed twisted in horror as I tried to speak. "You're a—you're a harlot!"

"*Was* a harlot. Past tense is very important. And what does it matter to you? From what I understand, you have not exactly been living the saintly life you once seemed so fond of. In fact, I've heard of many female reputations that you have spoiled. A man such as yourself can't object to a woman having a little fun. Besides, I'm past those days now and ready for a more stable life. What say you?"

"Get out." The hiss came from behind me. Sarah stood shakily pointing at the door. "Get out of my inn."

"Very well." Isabelle flounced out of her chair. "I see I have overstayed my welcome." She busied herself about leaving, but when she reached the door she peered impishly over her shoulder at me. "You know where to find me, darling. Don't be afraid to call. I'm sure we can have a splendid time together."

The door slammed shut. I grasped the counter, waiting for the world to stop shaking, waiting to wake up from this terrible nightmare.

"Well what are you waiting for?" Sarah shrilled at me from her half-collapsed position against the counter. "You going to chase after her?"

"What? No!" I gasped, horrified at the notion.

"Why not? She can give you everything you want!"

"I don't want her. I want you and Sam."

Sarah rolled her eyes and pushed herself into a more formal position. She glared at me. Picking up a rag, she began to vigorously wipe a spot on the counter. "And what will you do when Sam and I are not enough? Hmm? Will you sneak off into the night to have a little escapade with your darling Isabelle, or will you not even have the decency to sneak off?"

"Stop it," I snarled, grabbing the rag from her hand. She spun around and glared at me. "Just because Isabelle is alive, it doesn't change a thing. I still care for you, and I always will. No ifs ands or buts."

She didn't back down. "I know a bluff when I see one, Mr. Caman. Even if you are an experienced liar. You may say now that you will never think of Isabelle again, but when the times get tough, you will begin to wander. What would life be like with no-obligations Isabelle? Wouldn't it be wonderful, just for a day, to live without out any responsibilities?"

"Do you think me so shallow?"

"No man is without faults," she replied matter-of-factly as she took the rag from my hand and began to scrub the counter once more.

"And you? What if Seth were to appear, begging for forgiveness? Would you not run back into his arms ready to listen to all the fairytales about a better life he would paint for you? If men are shallow, then women are fickle!"

The Mirror

"How dare you! I would never—who could ever—" Tears sprang to her eyes, and I began to regret my words.

"I'm sorry, Sarah," I said as I reached out to wipe a tear away. She jerked away. "I was angry, and I said some things I didn't mean."

"But they were true," she said, her voice cracking.

"What?"

Sarah threw the cloth at me and raced toward the door. "I need to go. I just need to go!"

"But lunch!" I hollered after her.

"It can all burn for all I care," was the last thing she said before she disappeared down the hall.

Lunch did indeed burn, along with supper and half of the would-be morning biscuits before Sarah reappeared. She took the dough from my hands, added a handful of flour, and began to mix. I watched in stony silence, not sure if I was ready to forgive her for leaving me all the food preparation. Even Sam appeared to have abandoned me for the day.

I was about to give a sigh of surrender when Sarah spoke. "Sam and I will be leaving on a trip tomorrow. I was hoping you would look after the inn while we are away."

"And where will you go?" I asked, masking the dread that cramped my stomach.

"I think we will start with Croden. It is time that I found my parents, and spoke with them again. Besides, Sam really should meet her grandparents."

"And from Croden?"

"I'm not sure, but I think I just might find some answers about Seth there, and if I don't, I will leave Sam with my parents and go in search of him."

"Don't be ridiculous," I snapped.

Sarah dropped the bowl of batter and glared. "Ridiculous? I have every right to go where I wish, and seeing as you have every capability of taking care of this inn, I have no qualms of leaving it in your hands."

I picked up the balls of dough and slapped them down on a baking stone. "Seth may not have killed you the first time, but given the chance, I am sure he'll make good of his work the second time. What in blazes possessed you to even consider chasing after him?"

"Perhaps it is because I am a fickle woman. I can't stand being in one place for long!"

"Fickle? I think this is far past fickle and ranges in the area of stupidity. Blast, if you have a death wish, make sure no one cares about you before you go and act upon it."

Sarah shoved me away from the mangled biscuits, and began to plump the dough. I attempted to reclaim my spot, but she pounded her fist into my chest, taking me by surprise.

"Don't pretend with me, Jeremy Caman. Don't you dare pretend. If you cared one iota for me, you would have shoved the harlot out the door, but you just stood there and watched. You stood and watched, and I saw for the first time real love in your eyes, but it wasn't for me. It was for that wretch. So don't you lie to me." Tears streamed down her face. The last shreds of gentlemanly behaviour left me, and I could not persuade myself to even offer the hankie in my pocket. Instead, I stepped back and began to stoke the oven fire.

The Mirror

"I have no defence," I said when Sarah did not continue.

"Then do this one thing for me, if you can but still feel pity. Take care of my inn. It is yours now, and if I never return... if I never return, search for Sam in the town of Croden, and bring her back to be raised as your own."

"I will do my best."

Then Sarah left, and I never saw her again.

TWENTY-NINE

"WHY ARE YOU LETTING me read this?" Gustave asked as he flipped to the last page of text in Caman's journal.

Caman pushed aside his empty bowl and shrugged. "If the king was going to release me because I am innocent, he would have done so by now. Would you agree?"

"No. The king doesn't tarry with decisions. If he thought you were guilty, he would have convicted and sentenced you already. The fact that you stay here means there is still a reasonable measure of doubt in the king's mind. He could still release you."

"Well, either way, will you make me a promise?"

Gustave hesitated. "I don't know if I should."

"Please Gustave, if the king decides something against me, would you please take that journal to Sarah? There is enough information, you should be able to find her. Could you, for me?"

"I—well—alright, I will do it."

The Mirror

Caman smiled contentedly. "Thank you, Gustave. I will forever be in your debt."

Gustave squirmed uncomfortably on his side of the prison bars. "Well, you haven't finished yet. You'd better put the rest in words before—well, sooner rather than later."

Caman nodded grimly, taking up the journal.

For two days I managed to get by cooking scant meals for the men, and to my relief they only complained a little after I gave them a discount for as long as Sarah was away. Hope Callaway heard of my predicament, and sent two of her daughters over to help. It wasn't the same without Sarah or Sam, and I felt my mood getting surlier and surlier.

To make matters worse, Scarlet decided to take up walking me home in the evenings. I tried leaving at different times. I tried ignoring her. But like a patient and loyal dog, she waited until I would make an appearance and followed me to the curate's front step.

"Aren't you so pleased I scared that silly female away? Goodness, people were beginning to talk about the two of you as a couple. I knew better, of course. I knew the likes of you could never settle down for a cripple with a child."

"What are you talking about?" I responded to her constant taunts at the end of the first week.

"Oh let's be serious, Jeremy. Even when you were going through for the clergy, you never had any inclination toward children, and the only reason you thought about marriage was because you thought it would secure your position in your chosen profession."

"A man can change," I said, hoping to end the conversation and leave Scarlet once more out in the cold while I retreated to my room in Stuart Morgan's house.

She laughed at me. "A leopard doesn't change his spots. Look at yourself in the mirror, Jeremy. You are just as self-centered as you were before. Even if you did fall for this *Sarah* and her daughter, how long would you be satisfied to live the life of an innkeeper?"

I picked up my pace, and considered plugging my ears. Her words were biting, and the latest nip had gone quite deep.

"Don't forget, my love," she called from where she stood in the street. "I was always yours and will always be. Come away with me. We can live our lives together as two completely selfish beings, and if after a year that doesn't suit you, then run away and be as free as the leopard."

As the next week began, so did the rumours. I was made out to be a mercenary cad who had scared off the delicate Miss Livton. I ground my teeth and served the slop, my latest addition to the inn's menu. Most patrons ate without complaint as long as they got to aim a few well-placed jabs at my moral character while I was still within hearing distance.

In fact, business at the inn picked up, which inevitably was a sign that the gossip was good. Lunch dates were made by the women in order to get the latest news on that Livton woman, who just up and disappeared, and whether that traveling Caman fellow, whom no one ever trusted anyway, had anything to do with it. I was ignored along with the food I painstakingly prepared.

Isabelle gave me some reprieve from her haunting presence, but it only lasted a day or two. I guess she soon decided I needed some more encouragement. She began her taunts again, dripping with seduction and promised relief. I could feel my logic faltering, and the temptation to give in almost undeniable.

Only Stuart Morgan seemed unaware of my plight. He had become more and more introverted over the past weeks, and now was hardly ever to be seen outside his office. I considered demanding some of his time, and venting all my frustrations to him. I even went so far as to stand outside his office door. But I couldn't bring myself to knock.

What could Stuart do? What was the point of even mentioning my problems to him? He had enough struggles of his own. He didn't need to come to my defence every time I felt the least bit annoyed or peeved with those around me. I was a grown man. I could fight my own battles. So I turned and slumped off to my room.

That Friday, I broke.

"Still skulking around that inn, are you Jeremy?" Isabelle asked. "I must admit that you far outlasted my expectations. It must be a dreary life, always working and no one ever paying you any mind. I'm sure I would suffocate from the tedium."

"Well you never were suited to hard work, Isabelle. If I recall correctly, you much preferred tricking someone into doing the difficult things for you."

Isabelle pouted. "Now don't be so mean, Jeremy." She grabbed my arm, and I could not force myself to push her away. Instead, my pace slowed. She leaned in to whisper in my ear. My heart pounded and my feet faltered. "I think you will recall," she whispered, "that I always repaid those who helped me quite handsomely." She kissed my cheek, almost tenderly, then began to walk still clinging to my arm.

I had lost my mind. I was no longer walking toward the curate's house, but senselessly following Isabelle's lead. "The question is," I muttered, not sure what the question was anymore, "how many men benefitted from your repayment?"

"Oh none as much as they wanted, believe me. I was not a harlot by any means."

"You could have fooled me."

She let out a lilting laugh. "Oh don't be so silly, Jeremy. I gave men a taste if it suited my needs, but you, you were always special to me."

We were off the main road and had somehow become lost in a back alley. Isabelle placed her hands on both sides of my face and let me feel the full power of her kiss. My resolve dissipated. I thought only of surrender, of forgetting, of being embraced by someone who loved me.

Isabelle broke free of the kiss and began to toy with the hair at the nape of my neck. "I knew you remembered me, Jeremy dear." There was no denying it. My desire was burning a heated flush across my skin. "So come away with me. We will leave tonight, and never return. There will be no one to miss us, and we won't have to worry about old inns and pesky little children with their mothers."

The Mirror

At the mention of children my stomach squelched. My heart stopped and reality came back to my mind like waking from a comatose slumber. "Children," I rasped.

"We won't need to worry about children, darling," soothed Isabelle, unaware that her charm was breaking.

"You have a child."

"What are you talking about?" Her voice had turned to venom.

"When you came to the inn, you mentioned a child." I felt the strength re-entering my knees. "Where is that child, Isabelle?"

"I don't know what you are talking about."

"Where is that child? My nephew, or niece. Where is he?"

"She's at the orphanage in Emriville, though why you care, I don't know. Now come darling, come..."

She tried to kiss me again. I pulled away. "A girl. What was her name?"

"I never gave her a name. The brat cried all the time. I left her at the orphanage, and that was the end of it. For all I know, she could be dead by now."

"But there was a child."

"Jeremy, you really are going on in the most irrational manner. I must say, have you lost your senses in this cold? Perhaps I can warm you a little." She caressed my cheek tenderly, nuzzling my neck with soft kisses.

"There was a child. You left me at the altar because you were expecting my brother's child."

"That was long ago, darling. Don't you think we can look past my adolescence? I wasn't clever enough then to realize that you were the better man."

"No, no, you weren't clever back then," I said, a hint of understanding just beginning to reveal itself to me. I could feel it building as if I were close to a revelation, but my mind was thick with pain and I couldn't quite grasp the dangling tidbit of truth.

"Yes, dear one, but I am much smarter now."

"And so, am I."

"Oh yes, yes," Isabelle crooned.

"Smart enough to know that if you left me once... if you could leave a child to die in an orphanage... if you could dispel of your grief for my brother... yes, I am smart enough now to realize that you could do the same to me, and feel no sympathy. And, I am smart enough to know that I don't want that. Not anymore."

Her caress stilled and turned to steel. Unsheathed claws etched their way down my face, and I winced as Isabelle pulled away.

"Want! Want! Do you think this is a matter of want, Jeremy? This has far outdone want. It is a matter of duty."

"Duty?" I gasped.

"Do you think that anyone owes you anything? What have you done since you entered Owzan other than cause problems? You would have been expelled from the town months ago were it not for the curate."

"I never did anything wrong. I have worked for my wages and—"

"And left behind enough debts in past cities to cause a stench to be associated with your name. Oh, don't look so shocked, Jeremy. I have been looking for you for a long time. Long enough to know that no one owes you anything, and that if there was anything decent left in you, you would leave with me now and never look back."

"You think I would be better off associating with you?"

"You would only be starting to right the wrongs by marrying me as you should have a long time ago."

"I'm not the one who objected to that."

"But you never came after me."

"I may have been stupid to trust you, but I was never mad enough to chase after the woman who betrayed me. Now unless you have something logical to say to me, I am going to leave, and I never want to see you again."

"I won't become a harlot again! You owe me. You owe me, Caman." She was hysterical. "I won't be a harlot again! I saved you once. You're duty bound to save me. I will die!"

I left her in the street wailing. I kept walking until I was back at the curate's house and in my room. There I stood, and stared at myself in the full-length mirror.

Worthless. Worthless. Worthless. The word was a rhythm pounding in my head destroying any last threads of hope.

"Look at me," I whispered to the gaunt man in the mirror. He stared sightlessly back.

You are duty bound... no one owes you anything...

"Look at me."

Worthless, worthless, worthless.

"Look at me!" I screamed. Grabbing my chair, I smashed the mirror. I swung again and again. "Can't you see, I'm trying? Can't you see? Why can't you just be happy? Look at me!"

I dropped the chair that was now in a sad state of repair. Broken shards of glass still clung to the mirror's frame and my jagged reflection peered out of its depths. "Worthless," I whispered. "Isabelle was right. I should just leave."

"I agree, but I think I have a different destination in mind from what you were intending."

"You are speaking to me again," I intoned dolefully.

Stuart ignored my remark and sat down on my bed. "I see you had a strong desire to redecorate. I can sympathise, but alas, the mirror was a wedding gift, and my wife and I were loath to offend the giver."

"What do you want, Stuart?"

"I thought I might give you some direction."

"I am a grown man. I can make my own decisions."

"Ah yes, I am well aware of that. But you see, I have been doing some thinking, and I think that Sarah may be in more danger than I initially thought."

My chest tightened and I made to leave the room. "Sarah has no need of me. I am no better for her than Seth is."

Stuart stopped my hand on the door handle. "Sarah is going back to Croden, where she grew up. I have been looking through some records from the town, and have discovered that a Sarah Livton was pronounced dead there, some twelve years ago. I am thinking that if our Sarah Livton comes home after these, oh, what was it, twelve years, there just might be some political turmoil and anger that could leave our dear girl very hurt."

"I can't help her. The best thing I can do is leave."

The Mirror

"Go then, and be as worthless as the wretch you tried to destroy in the mirror."

"I—"

"Don't try to deny it, Jeremy. I've watched for days as you have become more and more lost in the image you see staring back at you. Unfortunately, it is all you and this town seem able to see."

"I don't understand."

"I am tired. This town has taxed me to my very soul, and I don't think I can explain tonight. But perhaps this will give you a glimpse of what you are looking for?" Stuart held up a book.

"What is that?"

"It is Martha's diary. I think you will understand it even better than I do. And here, take this as well. It's a journal for you to write in. I find when I can't make sense of a situation, writing it down can help me find perspective. I will be happy to discuss with you what you write later."

I took the two small books and tucked them into my coat pocket, not sure if I was willing to read or to write. "Goodnight, Caman," Stuart whispered. "Perhaps you would be so kind as to sweep up this glass before my wife comes across it. She is very likely to cut herself, and that would not be very healthy for her at the present time."

I stepped aside, and Stuart brushed past, leaving me to dwell in the darkness of my thoughts.

The glass remained. Anger has a way of making a person stubborn and stupid. Giving the mirror one last shove, I watched as it toppled to the ground, a sad remnant of what it was made to be. But there was no satisfaction left to be found there.

I slumped onto the bed, and felt a chill of despair race down my back. I closed my eyes as a hot tear trickled out of the corner of my eye and trailed its way down my cheek. I needed to leave Owzan and everyone there. I needed to move on, as I had far overstayed my welcome. Still I couldn't make myself begin to pack.

Sarah had made me promise to stay. I couldn't leave. She was counting on me to take care of the inn. She was counting on me to take care of Sam if anything happened to her.

Anyone could take care of the inn, and Stuart Morgan would know someone better to take care of Sam. There was no need for me to stick around.

Still I sat on the bed, indecision weighing me down like ten sacks of flour.

There was no point in staying, but leaving seemed too terrible a task to even begin. What spell this town had put on me I couldn't be sure, but it had claimed my very heart's desire.

Heart's desire? Was that what I was seeking. Had I found it in Sarah? How could I be sure?

I fingered the book in my coat, wondering what Stuart had meant about understanding Martha. I pulled it out and flipped to the first page.

I hate you!

Slamming the book shut, I gaped as Martha's first words sank in. But they were not aimed at me, so I opened the journal once more and continue to read.

The Mirror

I hate you! I hate you! OH dear God, I hate you! How many will you take? How many of my children must slip from my womb and into your care before you will allow me to cherish one at my bosom? I don't understand.

All my life I have been taught to fear God above. What I didn't understand was that this fear was to be literal, terrifying, and all encompassing. How wretched a woman I must be if this terrible God will not allow me to have a child. Even Billy must see, for he will not look at me anymore, nor will he touch me.

What hideous sin have I committed? What terrible deed have I done, that I am marked barren among women, a pox to the very sex. I look in the mirror to see my blemish, but all I see is a flat smooth stomach where my womb should be bulging with life.

I know now that I am a carrier of death. God have mercy because I cannot forgive myself.

I felt Martha's pain, and longing. I wondered where God was that he did not see her then. I wondered why he didn't give her the one thing that she longed for. It would have been a simple thing for him to let her bear a child. How often I had heard of it happening. Why did God not do this one thing for Martha?

I flipped through more pages of Martha's pain, intrigued by the cramped script.

I have done a terrible thing. Billy would not touch me, and I was desperate. I coerced a stranger into my bed a month ago. I will feel no guilt over this, for I have conceived. I am certain of it. God has blessed my womb like Tamar...

...Vengeance is mine, says the Lord, and he has had his vengeance. I have lost the child, and Billy will no longer speak to me. He knows what I have done, and the pain is clear on his face. He will never forgive me, but how dare he judge. He is my husband. Why will he not go about his duty as such?

...The witch! She comes into my inn and bears a bastard child, and all Billy can do is ogle. Does he not see me his wife? No. He has not seen me for some years now. At least the woman and her child will leave. I will not be patronized by them in my own home...

He has allowed them to stay, and I wonder if he has grown deaf to my voice as well. Did he not hear me when I spoke of my dislike for the two? Yet he claims they are the help that we need to keep this inn running. We are desperate enough for help, but I wonder how we will feed two more hungry, undeserving mouths. Billy is a fool, and I was the greater fool to have married him so long ago...

The child grows, the inn prospers, and I am forgotten. I begin to wonder if I am invisible. But no, I still appear in the mirror, and harsh is the reality that I see there. My hair is turning grey. There are wrinkles appearing around my eyes. I wonder, if Billy could spare a touch for me, would I even be able to conceive? There is no use in wondering. Billy still has not forgiven me. If he had, he would have long ago given into the temptations of the marriage bed. As it is, he remains chaste as a priest...

There is no more hope. My monthly times have ended. Still Billy will not join me in my bed. I know for certain that any claims to chastity for my safety are a falsehood. I am hated for my wretched sins. I am not worthy of his saintly notice. Then why does he dote on the bastard child?

Her words began to come in shorter segments of anger and pain. At times there appeared to be moments of unconcealed rage, but slowly the emotion dulled to a throbbing, constant ache. Her pain was something she had learned to live with. Questions still tinged the undertone of her journal, but they remained unasked and unanswered. Occasionally the walls of her broken heart would crumble and pain would come rolling off the end of her pen in lines of poetry.

And finally the breaking point came.

The Mirror

I cannot stand to live with them in the house any longer. The pain grows daily. I cannot constrain it to the corners of my heart any longer. They must leave, or I will die. Billy does not see it, so I will have to deal with them myself. I have begun to garnish the money. I have no use for it, but if the inn closes, perhaps then the child will be taken away. I will hide it for now...

That blasted Curate has to come meddling again. We have yet another worker at our inn, and it is making it more difficult to get rid of the brat. I will have to try and scare them off, and perhaps the traveler will leave of his own accord. He does appear to be a rangy sort...

Fie on myself. How could I? I have struck the child. I have showed my true self once more. I have struck the child, and God's curse is once more proved accurate. I was never worthy of having a baby. I was never worthy of marrying the likes of Billy. I was never worthy of running an inn. Oh worthless, worthless wretch. It is time I ended the misery. I am sure someone will find this journal once I have braved this one act of goodness. When they do, they should know that the money is under the floorboard in the second room right next to the large bureau. It belongs to the child. Or the child's mother I suppose...

Can I take my life? I am not sure.
I am hidden in the looking glass
Desperate to escape
But the God who promised to rescue me
Has gone so far away
So I'll wreck this mirror that's captured me
Crush each shard of glass
I'll break down these prison walls
Then be free at last

As each piece of crystal flies recklessly about
My soul begins to shatter some
And I begin to doubt
Now looking at my prison wall, I begin to see
My broken dreams
My torn up soul, and hope's last fading gleam
For looking out the looking glass is still me.

These were her last words. They resonated within my soul like the continual dull drizzle of a dismal spring day. She understood the pain of looking in the mirror and seeing only the blemishes. She understood what it felt like to not add up. To never be good enough. To wonder if there was a reason, a stain, or a sin that made the one you love turn away.

But Isabelle was not running away from me anymore. I had loved her once. Was that not reason enough to try and reconcile with her?

I knew the answer to that already.

Isabelle was just as trapped as me, just as trapped as Martha was, in the mirror. I could not save her and she could not save me.

I closed my eyes and allowed myself to drift into a daze of what-ifs. What if I had never met Isabelle? Could I have been happy as a small-town curate much like Stewart Morgan? I shuddered to think of how many persons I would have hurt had I ever been successful in following my dream career. Even then, when I had looked in the mirror, I had known myself inadequate. Isabelle had been right then. I could have been a curate a year earlier, but I had put it off, for fear of what it would mean to actually take the calling.

The Mirror

What if I had never joined the army? The torments of military life had seemed a good escape. I had justified my sins as an excusable result of all that I saw on the battlefield, but then the war ended, and I went home. The mirror did not lie then, either. I was without excuse for my faults, for many in the army did not do the things the crasser of us did.

What if I had never found Sarah?

The thought brought me up short. Ever since Sarah, I had begun to hope, even to change. For a while I had thought maybe I would be able to become something better. I had become a part of the community. But now Sarah was gone. What would happen to her?

A gut-wrenching fear grabbed hold of me and I began to pace my room, ignoring the glass shards that still sprinkled the wooden floor.

There was nothing I could do, I told myself over and over. How could I stop an angry town from destroying a woman they thought was dead? It was impossible. No one but the king himself could deal with a mess in records like that. It wasn't likely that I would ever get an audience with the king. I was less than the least. I didn't even have money. How could I even get to the king to even try to petition an audience?

I recalled a line in Martha's journal mentioning hidden money, and I wondered how much she had stowed away.

The thought was reckless. Even if there were enough for a horse, the king would never see me. The king had better things to deal with. There was no hope.

The king would not see me, but perhaps the queen...

A spark of hope ignited in my heart. Running to the inn, I found the money Martha had hidden. I cannot say for sure how much there was, but buying a horse did not begin to dent the vast amount of coins and bills that were under the floorboard.

So, with money for a horse, and a little for food, I left Owzan, for Emriville, as I had been told the queen and king were spending some time there. But by the time I reached my home town, they had left, and I was desperate. Turning my steed around, I began to race toward Silidon. With any luck, I would not be too late.

Gustave watched as Caman slept soundly. It had taken a lot out of the man to write the last words in his journal. He had scratched out nearly as many sentences as he had written, and once Gustave had seen him wipe away tears. Now the poor, tormented man slept fitfully.

A war waged in Gustave's mind as he stared at the journal tucked securely against Caman's side. The relief watch would be by soon, and Gustave would be free to do whatever he desired, at least for several hours. There was a clanging as the door above opened, and Gustave knew he had run out of time. Opening Caman's cell door, he grabbed the journal and securely locked the prisoner in once more.

"Been chatting it up with the prisoners again, Gusty?" the relief guard asked as Gustave walked toward the exit. "Best be careful, or you'll lose this job too. And I don't think Shoals will be as forgiving this time."

On most days, the reminder of Shoals would have had Gustave blushing scarlet, but he had too much on his mind to take note of the jibe.

The Mirror

"Hey, make sure you're back in time, Gusty. I won't take too kindly to having to sit in this dank pit more than I have to."

Gustave scurried out of the prison and down the street. It did not take him long to reach the palace gates, but by the time he was facing the guards, his legs were shaking with dread.

"What are you doing here, kid?" the guard asked. "Come on, get moving."

"M–my name is Gustave de Giarden, and I have an urgent message for the king."

"Hmm yes, as if I'm going to believe some Isbetan brat has a message for the king. Go on now, before I decide to press charges."

"I was raised here in Samaya, and I work at the prison just off Main, and I have an urgent message regarding the prisoner Jeremy Caman that I believe the king will want to hear. Please, will you at least request an audience for me?"

The guard looked at him uncertainly. "Alright, you wait here. I'm going to go make that request, but if there is any funny business, my friend over there is going to run you through before he asks any questions. You got it?"

Gustave swallowed the lump in his throat and nodded. He paced back and forth as he waited for the guard to return, and much sooner than he expected the guard was back, a grim look on his face. "It seems the king will honour your request. Follow me."

The gate was opened, and Gustave followed the guard up the palace stairs and into a small parlour.

"What is this important message?" the king asked as Gustave bowed low before him.

"Your Majesty, when I was going through the prisoner Jeremy Caman's things, I came across a diary."

"Did this diary belong to Mr. Caman?"

"No Your Majesty, it belonged to a woman by the name of Martha."

"And what did this diary say?"

"Well, it said some strange things, sir. I brought it for you to look at."

Gustave handed Martha's diary to the king and watched as he read the first entry. "Is this all you have to give me?" the king asked.

"No, Your Majesty. I found another book, a journal, but it was blank. Caman said his curate had given it to him in order to write in it. I–I allowed him to write."

The king raised his brow, and Gustave blushed scarlet. "I did not think it was up to the prison guard to grant those under his care such things as paper and pencil."

"No, and it won't happen again, Your Majesty."

"Let me guess, he wrote something you think I should see?"

"Yes, Your Majesty," Gustave said to his toes. "He asked me to give this journal to Sarah, if anything happens to him. He seems to have given up hope that you will be merciful."

"And after reading this journal, do you think I should be merciful?"

"I have no right to say, Your Majesty."

There was a knock on the door and Shoals entered with a rather bewildered look on his face. Gustave slunk back hoping not to be seen.

"Ah, Shoals, I have been waiting to hear from you," said the king as the knight bowed before him.

"Yes Your Majesty, but please, let me explain."

The Mirror

Henry intimated that Shoals should take a seat. "It's good that you should come now, Shoals. I have just been discussing with this prison guard some things regarding Mr. Caman. Perhaps what you have to say will shed some light on the situation."

Shoals turned and looked at Gustave, and his face turned a putrid shade. "What are you doing in the palace, Giarden? I forbade you to come near the place."

Gustave looked uncomfortably from the king to the knight, neither of whom showed much emotion. "Why have you done this, Shoals?" the king asked quietly.

"He's the adopted son of that traitor Grierson, and he's Isbetan as well. I would have thrown him out of the country, but I couldn't find any evidence against him."

"Is this true?" the king asked Gustave.

"Yes, Your Majesty," Gustave replied.

"And still you came to the palace?"

"Yes, Your Majesty."

"And you did this for Jeremy Caman's sake?"

"Yes, Your Majesty."

There was a pause. "Tell me, Mr. Giarden, did Mr. Caman pay you, or promise you any recompense for bringing me this book?"

"No, Your Majesty. He doesn't even know I have taken it," said Gustave, staring miserably at his feet.

The king glared at him, as if looking for a lie. "Very well, you may stay while Shoals tells us his news. Then you will return to the prison and wait there until I have made my decision about Mr. Caman."

Shoals looked sceptically at Gustave, but began to speak. "I went to the record keeper as you had asked, and soon found a Miss Sarah Livton of Croden deceased some twelve years previously. I then went in search of Owzan's records, but you must understand the difference between the two towns. Croden is an old town of old families that has not changed much over the past hundred or so years, but Owzan is young, and the town is constantly changing. As a result, its records are in total disarray. It took me a better part of the day to determine that I could not find a single Sarah Livton in residence in Owzan, and I was about to report this to you, when I came across a Miss Samantha Livton born in Owzan a little over eleven years ago. So I began my search again.

"I was just about to give up and send a page to you with my findings when a judge by the name of Bartholomew Gales came into the record house seeking to amend the records from Croden. Of course I was curious, and when I asked him what he knew of Croden, he told me a most fantastic tale."

"Has he seen Sarah?" the king asked.

"Something to that like."

"Tell us what wild tale this judge told you, and perhaps Mr. Giarden and his journals will be able to fill in the missing pieces of this curious story."

THIRTY

(Four weeks earlier)

"**A**REN'T YOU EXCITED to be going on a holiday?" Sam ignored her mother's words and turned toward the wall of the coach. Sarah let out a heavy sigh and quit trying to engage her daughter. They would have an entire week in the mail coach. Sam would have to speak to her eventually.

One week. It was hard to believe that after so many years, it would only be seven days before she would see her parents again. It seemed impossible, but slowly, steadily the coach pulled away from Owzan and moved closer and closer to Croden.

Sarah clenched her fists, fighting the urge to jump out of the moving vehicle. Bile rose in her throat, threatening to choke her. Inhaling a deep breath, she looked out the window and tried to consider this trip a holiday as she had told Sam it was. With time, her heartbeat slowed and her courage returned. Plastering a smile on her face, Sarah settled further into her seat and hoped her gumption would not fail her before she reached Croden.

The day passed by in miserable silence. Sarah took out a basket of food when she thought it was about noon, but Sam refused to eat. At dinnertime, they stopped at an inn. "Eat, Samantha," Sarah demanded when she saw her daughter balking at the food. "You may be angry at me, but starving yourself is not going to change the situation. We are going to Croden whether you like it or not."

Sam glowered at her mother, but obediently picked up her spoon and began to eat with loud slurps and smacks of her lips. Lifting her own spoon, Sarah ignored her daughter and did her best to enjoy her supper.

The stew sat like a leaden clump in the pit of her stomach. She longed to go back home. Jeremy would be waiting, her daughter would be happy with her, and she would not have to face whatever waited in Croden. But she couldn't back down. There was too much at stake, and she would always regret her actions if she turned back now. Forcing another smile to her lips, she took a sip of water and pushed away the rest of her stew. Sam followed her cue, dropping her spoon with a splattering clatter into her bowl and pushing it away.

The second day in the coach passed nearly as silently as the first. Sarah almost wished it had remained just as silent when Sam decided to speak to her at noon.

"You didn't let me say goodbye."

"I'm sorry, darling. There wasn't time to say goodbye. We would have missed the coach. Besides we will be back within the month, and we will be so busy you will hardly have time to miss anyone."

The Mirror

"I miss Mr. Caman already, and he might not be there when we get back. For all we know it will just be Billy taking care of the inn, and everyone will have left because we aren't there to feed them. We need to go back now."

"Well we can't go back now, Sam, so you'll just have to get used to the idea that we are going on a trip, and we won't be going home until our trip is over."

Again the coach fell into silence.

Day three was an agony Sarah had not anticipated. Her longing to return to Owzan filled her like a fever, causing cold sweats to trickle down her back and a booming drum to resound behind her ears. But she resisted the urge, and the day passed.

On the fourth day, Sam forgave her.

"So where are we going?" Sam asked as she stared curiously out the window.

"We are going to Croden."

"Where is that?"

"It's in the south of Samaya, while Owzan is closer to the north, though not quite the furthest point north."

"Will we get to see some Isbetans?" Sam had perked up at the notion of seeing one or some of the notorious enemy of Samaya.

"I am sorry, child, but we would have to be travelling a little further east to be near the Isbetan border. As it is, the most notorious person we might encounter will be the town drunk, but we see lots of that in Owzan."

Sam's lips puckered into a pretty pout. "Well then, why are we bothering to go to Croden? It sounds as if it's just like Owzan."

"They are a lot alike, but Croden is where I grew up."

"Oh," Sam said, then fell silent.

Sarah could see the enormity of her words working through Sam's mind, but she did not volunteer any more information. Never before had she mentioned anything about her past life to Sam. She had said someday she would know the truth. Someday when she was older. But perhaps the time had finally come to let her know. She would wait, for now. Maybe when they were in Croden she would have the strength for that conversation.

It was several hours later when Sam spoke again. "Will I meet my dad in Croden?"

Sarah closed her eyes, fighting back the tears that threatened. Would they see Seth? Would he have dared to remain in Croden? What if he had? Would she have the strength to face him, to accuse him, to change the way her life had been going for so many years? "I doubt your father will be there."

Sam's brow furrowed. "Then why are we going?"

"Because… because it is a place to start. That's all I am going to say for now, Sam," Sarah said when Sam made to ask another question. "I am not sure I can answer all your questions right now. There will be a time when I give you all the answers you want. But not now."

"Well when will you tell me?" Sam shouted.

"Samantha Joy! That is no way to talk to your mother."

"But I want to know." Tears of frustration and anger glistened in the corners of her eyes. "Please, Mom. Can't you just tell me my dad's name?"

The Mirror

Sarah glared out the window, trying to ignore the pleading tones of her child. Her child. Not Seth's child. Seth had no right to share in her joy, or to take away from it. This was her child, not his.

"Mom, just a name. Please."

"Seth Hepton. His name is Seth Hepton."

"And—and was he handsome?"

Sarah let out a heavy breath. "It doesn't matter anymore, Sam. Whether he was handsome or not. It doesn't change what happened."

"Okay Mom, thank you."

Sam spent the rest of the day making silly comments about the scenery and asking trivial questions about what they could expect for the rest of the journey.

And so the rest of the journey passed. Sam kept up a constant chatter, and Sarah did her best to answer her questions and to keep the mood light and happy. But nothing could lift the dark mood on the last day as the carriage rolled ever nearer to Croden and Sarah began to pick out familiar landmarks.

Sam peered out of the window as Sarah made comments about passing buildings and long stretches of woodland or open fields. "I fell out of that tree when I was eleven. My parents and I were on our way back from our uncles, and we had stopped for a picnic. I ran off to play, and was scolded when I returned muddy after falling." The trees passed by.

"That house belongs to the Mordens. At least it did." The house fell away as they continued along the road.

"The farmer who worked that field, his wife made the best jam in all of Croden and the surrounding area."

Eventually they came to the hill overlooking the small town. The sky was ablaze with fiery reds and oranges as the sun set on the horizon. A flush of dread seared Sarah's cheeks as she looked upon the once familiar town and contemplated what it would mean to continue their journey into the valley where it lay. Clenching her jaw against the urge to shout, Sarah waited and the coach rolled on down the hill.

Minutes after her struggle began, it was over. The coach halted in front of the inn, and the door opened. Taking a deep breath, Sarah stepped out of the coach and turned to help Sam down. The child looked about with wide eyes. "Are we here?"

"Yes," Sarah replied a bit roughly. "Now help me grab our bags so we can go get our rooms and some dinner. We'll—we'll start to explore in the morning."

Sam nodded and went to grab her small valise.

"Well lookie here, Gertrude, we have company," the innkeeper greeted as they walked through the door. A stout and round-faced woman stepped out of the door in the back and smiled broadly at them.

"I dare say you're right, Jed. Two lovely ladies to join us this evening. My, it has been a while since we've had strangers stay at our place. Welcome, welcome." She bustled around the counter and began sweeping them toward the seats at the bar. Sarah almost tripped over the heavy bag she was carrying as they were very nearly pushed into the seats.

"My name is Gertrude Fink, and that there is my husband Jedidiah. We's the innkeepers here ever since the last lot hit the kipper. Bought the place for a song off the bank. Only problem is, there ain't many visitors to keep us in business. So's Jed does a bit of work on the side, and I keep the place running, we make it by."

"I see," Sarah said, trying to be polite.

"We run an inn back in Owzan, but it is always loads busy," Sam said.

"Hush now, Samantha. You mustn't—" but Sarah's rebuke was interrupted by Mrs. Fink.

"Owzan, you say? I've heard of the place. It must be fairly busy, being a day's ride from Nevensburg. It is the second biggest city in Samaya, next to Silidon of course."

"Yes we do have a few passers-by coming from or going to Nevensburg, but our biggest customer base is local, as we serve dinner to thirty or more persons every night," Sarah said.

"But—"

"Speaking of which," Sarah cut in before the innkeeper could express her shock, "my daughter and I are very hungry after our day out in the coach. Is there any way we could get some dinner?"

"Well right away, of course." Gertrude Fink disappeared through the door behind the bar, but returned quite suddenly, cheeks flushed with apparent embarrassment. "Supper will only be a moment. I forgot that there was nothing yet prepared, but in the meantime, Jed... Jed? Why, wake up man, we can't be dozing off while there are guests to be seen to."

Jed startled awake and jumped out of the chair he had fallen asleep in next to the fire. "Yes'm hmm um right. You were saying, Gertrude sweet?" Settling himself back down into the chair, he smiled placidly at his wife, then stretched and covered his yawning mouth.

"Well, I was saying you should show our guests their room while I fix them up some eats. Then after they're all good and settled, I'll have something hot and hearty ready and waiting for them."

"Right you are, Gertrude. Now ladies," he said, picking up their bags and walking toward the rooms, "if you don't mind following me, I will show you a fine place to lay your heads."

Sarah and Sam settled into their room then returned to the dining area for potatoes and ham and gravy. It would have been a pleasant enough meal if not for Mrs. Fink's persistent chatter. Sarah had no interest in engaging the woman. But soon enough they were able to make their excuses and retire to their room for the evening.

"She talks a lot," Sam muttered as she cuddled under the blankets.

Sarah let out a huff as she settled next to her daughter. "Sounds like somebody else I know."

"Yeah," replied Sam sleepily, "Stuart Morgan does like to talk a lot too, doesn't he."

For the first time in a week, Sarah let out a real and hearty laugh.

Sarah stole out of the bedroom early the next morning, trying her best not to wake Sam. She made her way toward the dining room and hoped there would be breakfast ready. Doubt clung about her as she opened the door and stepped inside.

Much to her surprise Mrs. Fink was already awake and bustling about the room.

The Mirror

"Oh my, you are up already. Well I have some porridge ready if you would like to start with that. I thought to leave the eggs and bacon till later, but I'll rustle you up some real quick if you'd like."

Sarah took a seat by the bar. "Porridge will suffice for now."

"It's the darndest thing," Mrs. Fink said as she came back into the room laden with a bowl each of porridge, cream, sugar, and raisins. "I can't remember the last time we were so busy. Two more guests came in last evening. Can you believe that? We have a grand total of four new guests. Though mind you, the other lot likely won't stay long. They were here just for a night they said. Transporting a prisoner. I can't say as I know anything about the fellow they were talking about. Seems he murdered a girl before my time at the inn. But they caught him. Came all the way from Emriville they did. I hadn't even heard of the place, well, that was until the king and queen decided to have a visit there."

Sarah's palms began to sweat. "Who's the man they brought here? Do you remember his name?"

"Oh now, what did they say his name was. Let me think. Tyler? No, that isn't right. His last name was something like that. His first name was from the Bible, I think. Oh goodness, what was his name?" She paused and closed her eyes. It was the stillest Sarah had ever seen her. Suddenly her eyes popped wide open. "Caleb Taylor. That was what the new lot called the fellow. His name was Caleb Taylor."

Sarah relaxed against the back of her chair. It was not Seth. She shook her head. What would it matter if it were Seth? Didn't she want to see him hang? Yes, of course that is what she wanted. But she wanted a chance to speak to him, to accuse him first.

"I need to ask you a favour," said Sarah, interrupting Mrs. Fink who had begun to ramble again. "I was hoping you would look after Samantha this morning. I have some business in town, and I can't take her along. I promise she won't be any harm. I just don't want her wandering away from the inn."

"Why of course. I wouldn't mind that one whit. Mind you, I would avoid the market square if you can, as there are bound to be a whole lot of gawkers trying to find out what's to be done with that criminal."

"Of course. I will avoid it at all costs."

Pushing away from the bar, she thanked Mrs. Fink for the meal and went to speak with Sam.

"Wake up sleepy girl," she whispered as she gently shook Sam awake. "I need to talk to you."

Sam opened bleary eyes and looked up at her mother. "What time is it?" She yawned.

"I think a little past seven. I'm having a hard time believing you can actually sleep this long when at home you're up at the crack of dawn."

"You leave the curtains open at home."

"Ah, well." Sarah smiled at her sleepy daughter. "I have to go for a little while. I want to try and find some people I used to know."

Sam started to push up off her pillow. "I'll get dressed right away."

"No, no, darling. I want you to stay here for now. Mrs. Fink knows you will be hanging around, and she has an excellent breakfast ready. Enjoy your breakfast, and then see if there's any way you can help out. I'll try to be back for lunch, but it really depends. A lot has changed since I lived here."

"I want to come with you," Sam whined.

The Mirror

"Not this time, child. I will tell you all about what I was doing when I come back, but I really must do this on my own. I can't be sure that everybody will be happy to see me, and I don't want them to hurt you by accident. Okay, darling?"

Sam looked ready to argue, but with a sigh of resignation, she agreed.

"Good girl. I'll be back." With one last kiss to Sam's forehead, Sarah left.

The morning was cool with the crisp scent of a new autumn. Taking a fortifying breath, she made her way toward a once very familiar house.

It took her longer to reach the house than she had expected. She had gone the long way around to avoid the central square, but she didn't recall it ever taking so long to reach home when she was younger. But time had a way of making a person forget. Soon enough the front door came into view. Clenching her fist, she walked up the front stoop and knocked.

No response.

She knocked again, harder, but there still was no response.

"I don't think you will find anyone home, dearie," said a quiet voice from the neighbour's yard.

When Sarah looked over, she was surprised to see a much older Mrs. Engelton sitting on her front porch. She wondered if the woman would recognize her. It did not matter if she did. Sarah needed some answers.

"Do the Livtons still live here?"

Mrs. Engelton shrugged. "I don't think anyone could ever persuade Ezra Livton to leave that house. He always did dote on that building."

Sarah smiled. She had forgotten that about her father. "You said that I wouldn't find anyone home. Do you know where I might find them?"

"Well," replied Mrs. Engelton as she got up from her rocking chair and went to stand at the short fence that separated the two yards. "I do believe that Ezra is at the town square. Goodness knows he will want to have a say in all the goings-on."

"Oh, well I was hoping to avoid the town square. Would Mrs. Livton be around?"

"You will have to look in the church yard for Mrs. Livton."

"Excuse me?" Sarah shook her head, not sure she understood what Mrs. Engelton was saying.

"Hannah Livton died not long after her daughter did."

"Her daughter? Sarah? Sarah is dead?"

"Goodness child, where have you been? This all happened twelve years ago."

Sarah grabbed hold of the door handle in order to keep standing. She wasn't sure how she was supposed to take the news. Her mother was dead, and Mrs. Engelton thought she was dead. Sarah heard her breaths coming in shallow rasps.

"Are you all right, dearie?"

"I think I might faint," Sarah gasped as the front door began to spin.

The older woman was soon at her side lending her an arm to lean on. "You come with me. You look as though you've been hit by a plague. We'll make you a nice cup of chamomile to calm you down, and then you can be on your way."

The Mirror

Mrs. Engelton led Sarah into her kitchen and helped her sit in a chair. Sarah laid her head on the table in front of her and willed the room to come back into focus. She felt a warm cloth being placed on the back of her neck, and she closed her eyes to enjoy the soothing comfort.

Taking a deep breath, Sarah finally opened her eyes and sat up. The cool cloth fell to the table, and Sarah crumpled it in her hands. Turning, she looked to find Mrs. Engelton staring at her.

"You look familiar. Do I know you?"

Sarah considered telling her the truth, but she still wasn't sure what it all meant. "I was a friend of the Livtons," she said instead. "Sarah and I knew each other quite well, but we lost touch a little over twelve years ago."

"Well then, my news must have come as a bit of a shock to you. No wonder you were about to faint." Mrs. Engelton shook her head. "Well, I should be ashamed of myself for the way I told you. But there is nothing to be done about that. Now take your tea and we'll visit awhile."

Sarah sipped her chamomile and let the herbal tea relax her tensed nerves. "What happened to Sarah and Mrs. Livton?"

Mrs. Engelton took a seat across from Sarah and sipped her own tea. "It really was quite the tragedy. You heard about the Heptons? You know, the family of scalawags that lived in the wood?"

"Yes, I recall them."

"Well, Sarah was spending quite a bit of time with that Seth fellow, the oldest of the Hepton boys. She really was causing quite the scandal, but some of us were hoping she would work a change in the boy, and for a while it looked like she might. But then one day it just went bad. Nobody knows what caused the change. I guess a bad apple is always a bad apple. Anyway, Seth, he hurt her, in the worst way. He stole her innocence without her consent."

Sarah shuddered. Yes, that is what Seth had done. He hadn't raped her. He had stolen from her. He had stolen what was most precious to her, and she had not consented. No, she had not consented in any way at all.

"Yes, yes, it is really dreadful. I remember the day after. You see, after Seth had done that awful thing, he left Sarah on her doorstep bloodied and pretty near dead. Ezra hardly let anyone come near her, but the apothecary did go in a few times, and he let us all know that it looked like Sarah was on the mend. We all rejoiced at that news, but then even the apothecary hushed up about how Sarah was doing. Finally, two months after that awful night, they took her body out of the house in a wooden box. It was rumoured that she died of complications, but truth be told, I think she died of a broken heart."

Sarah felt a tear roll down her cheek. Nearly two months after Seth had hurt her, the apothecary had suggested it was possible she was pregnant. A week later she had been sure of it, and she had run away. So they had decided it was best to say she was dead rather than admit the truth to the rest of the community. She understood. Wasn't that the reason she had run away? She couldn't admit to everyone that she was pregnant with Seth's child.

"What happened to Mrs. Livton?"

Mrs. Engelton shook her head. "Her story just adds to the tragedy. After her daughter died, she seemed to lose her purpose in life. She became surly and angry. She would scream at her husband a lot. Not everyone knew that, but Hannah screamed at her husband most nights, and I heard some of it. Then one day she stopped leaving the house. Then the apothecary started visiting again. Then a month or so later, they were taking her out in a second wooden box. Some suggested she might have committed suicide. I don't agree. Hannah was always too strong for that. I think it was as the apothecary said. Scarlet fever at her age would do anyone in, let alone someone who is mourning the loss of a daughter."

"Yes, scarlet fever is deadly. You said that Mr. Livton was in the town square?"

"Aye." Mrs. Engelton shook her head as if to clear it of the remaining reminiscence. "Yes it is a wonder that you come asking about Sarah today of all days."

"Why is that?"

"Her murderer has just been caught. He's the man that they are likely going to hang in the town square today."

The room was spinning again. It couldn't be. The innkeeper had said the man was called Caleb Taylor. It couldn't be Seth.

"They say they are not going to announce the verdict till nine, but the gallows have already been put up. To me that means the verdict is clear, they just have to pass it by the council."

"They're going to hang him? Are you sure?"

"Yes, of course. I like to think that if Sarah were alive she would save him, what with the marriage clause, but seeing as the poor girl died, well, that is murder, sure and certain, and the only punishment for murder is death by hanging."

"I need to go," Sarah rasped. "Thank you for the tea, but I really must find Mr. Livton."

"Wait," called Mrs. Engelton as Sarah made her way toward the door. "Why don't you wait, dear girl. If you wait but fifteen minutes, the hanging will be over and they will have the body away by the time you get into town. You really don't want to see the hanging. It's a ghastly sight, really not suited for a woman."

"I'm sorry, but I must hurry."

Sarah raced toward the town square. She must stop them. They couldn't hang Seth. They couldn't hang Seth for murder when she wasn't dead. It wasn't right.

The crowd was massive. Sarah pushed her way through until she could finally see the centre. Her heart pounded.

There he was. Seth Hepton. Even bruised and bloodied she could still recognize the blond boy she had thought she had fallen in love with.

They kicked the chair and she screamed. But no one heard her above the jeering of the crowd. She watched his face twist into a contorted blue death mask. Then her world went black.

THIRTY-ONE

"TAKE IT EASY THERE," crooned a soft male voice as Sarah's world began to come back in focus. "Now don't rush things. People always only manage to hurt themselves when they rush things. There you are, there you are."

Sarah opened her eyes, then hurriedly blinked them shut again. A confused mess of images played in her mind's eye as she tried to remember what had happened. Placing her hand on her forehead, she groaned.

"Let me get you a cool cloth," the voice soothed.

"No, wait. I'm alright." She pushed herself up only to be overwhelmed by blackness once more.

"As I have said, you must take it easy, or you will only cause yourself more harm. But do people ever listen? Well of course not. So listen now. I am going to get you a cool cloth, then I will help you sit up, and then we shall talk. Until then, rest your head down, and relax. You will do yourself no favours by stressing over things that you cannot change."

The voice disappeared, and Sarah felt her body slump back into whatever it was she was lying on. She tried to think what had happened. She had seen Seth. She had seen Seth, and they were hanging him. They hanged him because they said he had killed her. But how could they believe she was dead? She had left, yes, but she was not dead. She was alive. She was alive and had a daughter. Seth had hanged for the one crime he had failed to commit.

Pain tore through her chest as if she had taken the lashing, not Seth. How could this have happened? How could things have gone so terribly wrong?

Sarah felt the damp cloth being placed on her forehead, but she ignored the tender touch, not knowing now if she did want to talk.

"So some time has passed and now you wish to ignore me. That will not do. It is time for you to get up and for us to talk. I do not demand you open your eyes, but here is my hand. You may grasp it. No, child you must not ignore me. For your own benefit, grasp my hand, and we shall sit you up."

After only a few more moments' delay, Sarah acquiesced and grasped the man's hand firmly. Quite suddenly, she found herself sitting with a bundle of soft cushions behind her back. She opened her eyes in shock.

An elderly man with pale grey eyes looked into her face. "Ah, well, it is lovely to see that you have decided to join the land of the living again."

"I—well," Sarah paused. "I never left... did I?"

"No, no, of course not," laughed the man, "but you have been unconscious for the past hour or so. Why, it is almost eleven o'clock." He

The Mirror

pulled out a pocket watch and tut-tutted. "Dearie me, only five minutes to the hour."

"Well then, I really must go. I have somewhere else to be at eleven, and I shouldn't be late."

"Really?"

"Yes," replied Sarah, doing her best to cover the blush that would reveal her lie.

"Well then, let me escort you."

"That won't be necessary." Sarah looked around frantically trying to find the door, or any exit for that matter.

"I insist."

"No, I—goodness!" she finally exclaimed when she could not seem to find her bearings. "Where am I?"

"My dear lady, you are at the parsonage. I am Curate Eli Yates, the man who caught you when you fainted. I brought you to my house so my wife Mae could tend you, and when you started to stir I came in order to speak with you. Does that answer all your questions?"

"Not nearly," Sarah muttered in frustration.

"Well then, stay for tea and we can talk. Perhaps we can answer more of your questions."

"Very well, but I really must be back at the inn by one. My—there is someone waiting for me there, and she will be distressed if I do not appear by then."

"Then we'd best get started. I'll go put the tea on. While I'm away, you may decide the best question to ask first."

Sarah pondered Curate Eli's words and began to think about the many things that haunted her heart. There was an ache there, and she could not quite decide what caused it. Had seeing Seth opened the wound she thought had healed long ago? Was it anger that made her dizzy and turned her gut into a turbulent and icy sea, or was it grief?

How she longed for time to think! But time was not granted to her. Curate Eli walked in with a tray set for tea.

He prepared her a cup, and set it on a nightstand by the bed she lay in, then he prepared his own before he spoke. "You have had a few moments, now let us begin answering your questions."

Sarah's mouth went dry. She took a sip of tea to gain more time to think.

"Whatever happened to Curate Wellhousen?" It was a safe question. One whose answer would take time and give her a chance to think.

"The good curate was strongly encouraged to retire after he shouted down a young girl, calling her, if I recall correctly, a hellish, gold-digging daughter of the devil."

"Goodness, what had the girl done?"

Curate Eli smiled. "I believe it was really the curate's son, Avery, who was the problem. You see, he had proposed marriage to the girl, and she had accepted. Curate Wellhousen did not approve of the match."

"Why ever not?"

"This particular young woman had a very severe flaw in the curate's eyes. You see, she was a widow with a young son. This son, whom most of the town adored, and still quite admires, had the audacity to make quite the display of himself when the curate was giving a sermon. This would not be so unforgivable had it not been that the dean of the Seminary in Silidon was present for this particular sermon.

The Mirror

"Pride wounded, Wellhousen wanted nothing to do with the boy or his mother. So, when his son came home declaring his passionate love for that exact same woman, Wellhousen over-reacted a little. That was about four years ago. Since then, there has been some reconciliation between the young lady and the old curate, and it is not often Wellhousen is seen without his grandson."

Sarah nodded. She could remember Avery as a boy. He had been kind and sweet-tempered, much like his mother. His father, the curate, had been stern. A very strict man who painted a picture of a life that was black and white.

"But I am sure you did not come to Croden seeking out news about Curate Wellhousen. Please, let's delay no longer. What do you long to ask?"

"How do you know I didn't come to Croden for the sake of visiting Croden? I could just be passing through."

"Someone who is just passing through does not ask about the old curate, nor do they attend a hanging. Which leads me to believe that you know something about this Seth Hepton who was hanged today."

"I—well, I... Curate Yates, what do you know of the Livtons?"

"Very little. Mr. Livton is an old and bitter man, but he attends church faithfully and lives a relatively quiet life. I believe his wife and daughter died in the same year about a decade ago, maybe longer. I can't remember for sure. All I do know about their deaths, I heard just recently."

"Because of Seth Hepton?"

"Yes, because of Seth Hepton."

There was a long pause. Sarah sipped her tea and wondered how to continue. "Sir, are you on the council?"

Curate Yates offered a sad smile. "Yes, I am, as the curate almost always is."

"Can you tell me some things about Seth Hepton that I just can't quite figure out? Some things that you as a member of the council will likely know?"

"I can try. But as you know, many of the councillors' deliberations are to remain confidential. Our meetings are not open to the public in order to protect the privacy and the rights of the people who are falsely accused, as well as the respectability of the councillors who might say things a little too quickly when under the pressure of passing judgement."

"Yes of course, but I just wanted to know, how is it that you caught Seth Hepton?"

Curate Eli shook his head. "We never caught him. Most people had forgotten about him. He could have lived out the rest of his life, but he turned himself in."

Sarah's hands shook. She placed her cup and saucer down lest she spill her tea. "Why? Why did he turn himself in? Did he think he would receive mercy and be able to walk away unharmed? Was he delusional, or drunk?"

"No, no, he was quite sane. In fact, I would go so far as to say he was respectable."

"Then it doesn't make sense. Why would he turn himself in?" Sarah was biting her cheek trying to keep herself from shouting. She wanted to understand. She needed to understand.

The Mirror

"I believe the answer you are looking for is God."

"God?"

"Yes, God. I believe Seth Hepton found God, and I think he was convicted."

"So you are saying that Seth found God, and God spit in his face and told him to go hang. I thought God was supposed to be merciful."

"God is merciful, but he does not promise an easy life. I believe that when Mr. Hepton found God, he longed to seek restitution. Yes, he knew that might mean he would hang, but hanging and being at peace with God is far better than living a lie and being hounded by guilt daily."

"I don't agree."

"I never asked for you to agree. I was only giving an opinion."

"Very well, I have another question. Why was Seth beaten before they hanged him?"

"There are multiple reasons for that, and here is where confidentiality constrains me. I will tell you only the basic facts, and you must decide for yourself what they mean. When Seth Hepton arrived in Croden, he went first to Mr. Livton's house. Mr. Livton, believing himself threatened, dealt the man some blows. In his fear, he may have gotten carried away. He and two other men took Mr. Hepton to the mayor's house. At that point he appeared to make a run for it. He was dealt a few more blows in the recapture. After some discussion with two gentlemen from Emriville, it was discovered that Mr. Hepton had assumed the name Caleb Taylor, either legally or illegally, we are not certain. What we are certain of is that he has been acting as the curate of Emriville for the past six years. He did have a legal certificate to do so, but many on the council still deemed it necessary to give him the customary lashes as an example to all others who might take the office of curate so lightly."

"So you think Seth should have received all those beatings? You believe that anyone who becomes a curate and isn't all ribbons and bows should be punished for his audacity?"

"I believe that all have sinned and fallen short of the glory of God. And I believe that God is far more merciful than I or any man will ever be."

"That is not a good answer."

"Neither was your question one that I can give any more credence to."

Sarah scowled at the curate. He was not being as helpful as she had hoped, and she considered leaving without finishing the conversation, but there was a question niggling out of the recesses of her mind that would not be ignored. "Fine. I still have another question."

"Very well, what would you like to know?"

She hesitated. Could she trust this man that she had just met? "I—I want to know. Did Seth have to hang?"

"Well according to the law, anyone who murders shall be put to death by hanging. We had no other choice."

Sarah was shaking her head. "What I mean is, if the girl had not died, if he had just violated her, would he have been hanged?"

Curate Eli paused and looked at his hands. His thumb massaged a circle in the palm of his other hand as if he could read the what-ifs of the world by the lines found there. "If," he began slowly, "the girl were still living, there are many possibilities. Often the case is dragged out

The Mirror

for many, many weeks. The girl must be summoned to testify, and she is often given a choice in the verdict."

"What are her choices?"

"I don't see how this really matters in regards to Seth's case, as the girl is dead."

"Please sir, just humour me for now."

The curate swallowed. "The girl would have three options. Either the criminal could hang, or be imprisoned for life, or they could be married. You must understand, though, these cases are so rare and most often they end in a hanging."

"But not all of them."

"No, not all of them. Before I came to Croden, I was the head of a congregation in Silidon. There was a case where a young woman was raped. There was no doubt about it. The man who had done it had grown up an orphan and was at that time apprenticed as a wheelwright. No one would have said he was an evil man, but he did have some bad habits, such as excessive drinking. Well the how and the why don't really matter all that much. All that really matters is that he did it, and instead of asking for him to hang, that girl took a chance. She married him. She wasn't daft enough to go and live with him right away, but she married him, and they each went their separate ways until he could no longer live with the weight of the mercy she had shown him."

"What happened to him?"

"He started going to church. He built a home for his wife. He wooed her until she was convinced to come and live with him as man and wife. And to this day, they are happily married with several children. But what does it matter?"

"Just one more question."

"Very well."

"If there is a child, what happens?"

The curate gasped and covered his mouth. "The person you are to meet..."

Sarah's lip trembled. The curate had already guessed. "Curate Eli, what happens if there is a child?"

The curate was trembling. "If there is a child, the couple is forced to marry. The theory is that if there is even the slightest chance of forming a happy home with two parents for a child, that is preferable to a child living with the knowledge that their father was hanged for making them come into being."

"What if the theory is wrong?"

"Then we pray upon God's mercy to rectify the mistakes that we as earthly lawmakers are prone to make. But you said only one more question. It is my turn. Why does all this matter?"

Sarah put down her empty cup and saucer. Her hands no longer shook, and her voice had a strength that she was not sure belonged to her. "I would have married him, Curate Eli. I would have married Seth Hepton despite what he did to me. I would have married him for my daughter's sake. His daughter's sake. I would have married him because that would be the only way I would have been able to forgive myself."

"Then you are, as I thought..."

"My name is Sarah Livton. I ran away from home twelve years ago after Seth Hepton raped me, and I discovered I was pregnant with his child. I ran away because I couldn't bear the looks of pity and shock, or the condescending glances of those who believed I deserved what I got. Because deep down inside, I knew I deserved what I got. I lied to my parents. I lied and I went to the Heptons' that night knowing full well what could happen. But I was too proud. I was too proud of my own self-righteousness that I could not understand why God allowed it to happen. But now I see that God was only putting me in my place. And when I look in the mirror, I see just how much I fall short, and I know that God could never heal the brokenness inside of me."

"Oh God, what have we done?" whispered the curate. "His blood, shall it be on our hands!"

Sarah pushed herself out of the bed and made her way toward the bedroom door. "I need to go find my daughter. She will be wondering where I am."

"Wait." Curate Eli stopped her before she could reach the door. "I have never been in a situation like this before, but it reeks of danger for you and your daughter. Do you think anyone will recognize you?"

"They haven't yet."

"Good. Good. It is best it stays that way until we can work out what to do."

"What to do?" Sarah shook her head. "There is only one thing to do. I will take my daughter, and we will go back to where we came from. I am dead to these people. It is best if the dead remain dead."

"So you would leave justice undone?"

"There can be no justice in this situation, Curate. What do you think will happen should the people in this town find out I'm alive? Some will say what's done is done and leave it at that, but that group will be in the minority. Some will say that Seth got what he deserved and that my father was a hero for declaring me dead and making sure

Seth Hepton got hanged. But there will be another group that will be embarrassed that they were taken in by the ruse. They will want justice again, and by the end of the week, there will be another grave in the churchyard. This will only add to the uproar, and soon my daughter and I will be caught in the midst of a bloody battle of what is just and what is not and how the situation can be rectified. I will not do that to her. It isn't fair. Sam needs to be back safe and sound in our home."

Sarah continued to walk. She was just about out the door when the curate spoke again. "Tell me this. When Samantha asks you someday about her father and what happened to him, what will you tell her?"

"I will tell her the truth. Her father is dead, and there is nothing we can do about it."

"No, there is nothing you can do about the wellbeing of his life, but you can still do him the justice of making sure people remember him, not as a murderer, but as a man fallen, and a man redeemed."

Sarah hesitated. "I can't change the way people think."

"No, that is true. But you can give them a chance to change themselves by letting them know the truth."

"I will think about it."

"Then I will meet you at the inn later on this evening to discuss it some more. The longer we let this matter lie, the bigger the confrontation we will face when the truth comes out."

"Very well. Until this evening, then."

"Until this evening, Miss Livton."

THIRTY-TWO

SARAH FOUND SAM helping Mrs. Fink in the kitchen. Her daughter appeared to be completely unimpressed. Sarah thanked the older woman for watching her daughter, then the two of them made their way outside to go for a walk.

"It was so boring this morning, Mom. I asked if I could help make some lunch, but Mrs. Fink thought I was too young to be able to use a knife. Can you believe that, Mom? I've been using a knife since I was five, and I have only cut myself once. I told her this, but she didn't believe me. I even showed her my scar, and she said that was the reason why I should not be using a knife. So she had me mixing the batter while she measured out the ingredients. Can you believe it, Mom? I know how to make bread already, but she wouldn't let me measure out the ingredients!"

Sarah allowed Sam to chatter as her mind wandered through the day's events. So much had happened since they had arrived at Croden, it felt as if her heart had gone through a wringer and come out bleeding and broken. She had left Owzan in search of answers. Now she had more questions than when she had started out.

"Mom, what happened here?"

Sarah startled out of her reverie and looked around. They were in the town square. She had meant to avoid the place, but it seemed that her feet had led her there of their own accord. "Oh, goodness, Sam. I am sorry. I didn't mean to lead us here. This is the town square, and there was a hanging here this morning. We should leave. There are some shops down the road—perhaps we can explore those for a while."

"Really? An actual hanging?"

"That's what I said."

"Did you go and watch it?"

"Not intentionally."

"I want to watch a hanging someday."

Sarah stopped. Sam stumbled as she tried to match her mother's motions. "What would ever make you say such a thing, child?"

"Jace said that a hanging was a wonderful thing. He said when a person gets hanged it's because they deserved it, and we should be happy, not sad. So I figured if I saw a hanging for myself, I would be able to know whether Jace was right."

Sarah swallowed the lump in her throat. Did everyone automatically believe a person who was hanged got what they deserved? Was there no notion that justice could have been thwarted, that an ill-advised council could have made a mistake? Would everybody believe Seth to be a murderer? Of course they would. There was no reason they shouldn't. Her grave, after all, was already in the Croden churchyard.

The Mirror

"Sam," Sarah croaked past a dry throat, "I need to show you something, and I need to tell you a story."

"Okay, where are we going?"

"You will see."

They walked silently toward the church. Curate Eli was out in his yard with his wife Mae, but he acted as if he did not know her as she walked past and entered the churchyard. She paced up and down the rows of tombs, searching out the names. Occasionally she was caught off-guard by a new tombstone that had not been there before she had left. There were so many familiar names, but none were the one she was looking for until the very last row.

She had been preparing herself for it, but that did not lessen the shock when Sarah came upon her tombstone. The plain script stated her name, birth date, and apparent date of death. No other words were scripted, as if there was nothing else to be said about this person laid to rest in the churchyard.

Sarah sat in front of the tombstone and Sam took a seat beside her. "Was that your mom?" Sam asked, pointing to the grave next to the one Sarah stared at. Sarah fought back the tears as she glanced at her mother's grave. How she longed to see her again. But she was twelve years too late.

Sarah managed to speak. "I need to tell you a story, Sam."

"Okay."

"I'm going to try my best to make it make sense, but I am not sure that it will."

Sam shrugged, as if it didn't matter to her, but Sarah saw the hunger in her eyes as she stared at the grave with Sarah's name on it.

Taking a deep breath, Sarah began. "A long time ago, when I lived in Croden, there was a family that everybody knew was no good. They were a mother and father with three boys and though they mostly kept to themselves, the boys were known to come into town to get drunk, pick fights, and visit places much like Mick's at home, but far worse.

"I was very foolish back then and decided I would try to change them. So I started talking with the oldest of the boys, but what I soon discovered was that under all that meanness there was a heart. There was a kind man who longed to escape his life, but couldn't see past the father who beat him every night.

"So we became friends. But like I said, it was very foolish of me, and... and..." Sarah paused. "Before I go on, Sam, I want to make sure you know that I love you. You know that I love you with all my heart, no matter what?"

"Yeah, Mom, I know, and I love you too."

Sarah nodded and tried to collect herself. "When this young man invited me to come to his house, I thought it was a chance to make a difference. I was wrong. Now, do you remember when you asked me what the word rape meant, but I wasn't going to tell you until you said you were going to go ask Mr. Caman?"

"Yes."

"Well that is what happened to me. I went to the Heptons' house, and Seth Hepton took a very special thing from me and left me bleeding and near death on my parents' front porch. When I found out a little while later that I was pregnant, I ran away from home, and went to Owzan where I had you. But when I ran away, my father had me declared dead. So everybody in Croden thinks I am dead."

The Mirror

Sam's brow was furrowed as she worked through what her mother had told her. "So my father is a really bad man." Sam spoke with so much pain in her voice that Sarah wondered if she should have told her this story at all.

"He did a bad thing, but I am not so sure that he was really the evil man that everyone seems to think he was."

"Why?" Sam whispered.

"Because I knew him. I heard the stories he told, and I fell in love with the man he could possibly become. Only I don't know if he ever became that man because I ran away, and so did he."

"Do you hate him?"

Sarah thought about the question. It was filled with the innocence of a child trying to understand the pains of a shattered world. It was the question from her child, whose dreams were breaking with the reality of who her father really was.

"I hated him once, but that was a long time ago. I have tried to hate him since then, but I have come to the realization that Seth is not the only one to blame for what happened that night. I was the one who went. Seth tried to tell me it would be a bad idea, that his father was worse than any of his brothers. But I didn't listen to him. I went because I was proud, and I wanted to change them all. I thought I was a good enough person, a good enough Christian, that God wouldn't let anything bad happen to me."

"But he did," whispered Sam. "Why did God let it happen?"

Sarah pulled up some of the grass as she thought about the question. "At first I thought it was because God hated me, and I still haven't ruled that out. But more and more I think it is because God lets us feel the consequences of our sins. Don't ask me why. You will have to ask Stuart Morgan that question."

Sam nodded and began looking at the gravestones. "Are we going to try and find him?"

"Who?"

"My dad. Are we going to try to find him to see if he has changed?"

Sarah shook her head as a single tear rolled down her cheek. "I'm sorry, Sam. We're too late."

"What do you mean?"

"The man who was hanged today, there was a reason I ended up watching it happen. The man was Seth Hepton. He was your father, and now he is dead."

Sam jumped to her feet. "No! You're lying." Angry tears poured down her cheeks, and a few stray blond hairs wisped about in the cool autumn breeze, making her look like a fragile porcelain doll.

"Sam, please sit down and we will talk."

"No, I don't want to talk!" Picking up her skirts, she turned and ran.

"Sam!" Sarah rose, reaching for her daughter, and stumbled. "Samantha, wait!" Sarah spit grass from her mouth and lifted her head, looking around frantically. Her daughter was long gone.

Picking herself up off the ground, Sarah began to make her way back to the inn. She passed by the parsonage, where the curate was still working in the front yard with his wife.

"Curate Eli," Sarah called, her voice shaking.

He came over to his fence and leaned over it conversationally. "How may I help you, Miss Livton?"

The Mirror

Sarah pressed her palms to her eyes to stem the tears before she spoke. "I need to speak with you tonight, privately. What happened to Seth, it was wrong, and it needs to be fixed. I—I think I am willing to do something about it."

"Very well. How about we meet around eight. I will come to the inn, and I am sure that Mrs. Fink will be more than willing to provide us with a private room to speak. In the meantime, I believe your daughter would love some of your time."

At the mention of Sam, Sarah's eyes filled with tears again. "She has spent her whole life wanting a father, and now we come back to Croden to discover that we are just a day too late. I don't know what to tell her."

"I always find that the best place to start is to tell her that you love her."

Sarah nodded. "I'd better go." She waved and continued to walk back to the inn.

Upon entering the inn, Sarah was met by Mrs. Fink. "Well I was just coming to find you. That little girl of yours came racing in here in the middle of a fit, and I wasn't sure what to do. So I put the kettle on, thinking maybe some tea would calm her down, but now she won't open the door, and I didn't want to intrude."

The poor woman looked flustered. "Thank you for your kindness," Sarah said in as happy a tone as she could muster. "If you don't mind, I will take the tea tray in to my daughter. We have just received some shocking news, and I am sure it will take a while for Samantha to calm down."

"Well then, I will leave you to it. A girl always needs her mother in these situations, not some strange lady she doesn't know from Eve. I'll go fetch that tray."

"Samantha, dear," Sarah whispered as she pushed open their bedroom door. Sam had burrowed under the blankets right to the centre of the bed. Sarah wondered if she was sleeping, but could still make out Sam's quivering form and knew she was working hard at suppressing her sobs.

Walking over to the bed, she placed the tea tray on the side table and sat next to Sam. She took a breath. "A long time ago, I was much like you. I loved going to church, singing silly songs, swimming in the creek, and cooking in the kitchen with my mother. I was very happy, and many people said I had a bright future. But I was not a very good person inside, and I made some very bad choices that meant I got hurt really badly. I was hurt so badly that I almost died, and for a while I wished I had. Out of all that, you know what made me want to live?"

Sarah paused and waited.

"What made you want to live?" Sam finally whispered from under the covers.

Sarah smiled and pulled up the sheets so she could see her daughter's face. "You did, my little girl. When you were born, I loved you so much, you made me want to live. I wanted to live and give you the life I had thrown away. I wanted you to be happy and healthy and strong. And I think I have done alright. I know sometimes I do things that hurt you. But I try every day to let you know that I love you."

Sam crawled out from under the covers and wrapped her arms around her mother. "I love you too, Mom, and I am happy. I just so wanted to know my dad. I wanted to see what he looked like, to give him a hug, to be hugged back." Sam's words ended in a whimper.

"I know, darling, I know," Sarah whispered as she stroked Sam's hair. They sat like that for some time, rocking back and forth.

Finally, Sam broke away and pushed the hair out of her face. Her eyes were red and swollen, and her nose was streaming. Sarah pulled out a handkerchief and handed it to Sam, who wiped her nose. "Thanks." Sam noticed the teapot. "Do you think that's still hot?"

"Let's give it a try." Sarah poured out two cups and tested her own with a small sip. "Hmm, warm but not hot. It will have to do."

Sam took her cup and added two spoonfuls of sugar. Sarah cringed but did not object.

"So, are we going home now?" Sam asked.

Sarah sighed. "Unfortunately, no. We have to stick around a while longer because some laws were broken when they hanged Seth Hepton. The main one being that they said he murdered me when here I am."

Sam bit her lip, and Sarah wondered if she would ask the question that she dreaded. But Sam just shook her head. "How long do we have to stay?"

Sarah breathed a little easier. Sam had not asked whether Seth could have or should have lived. She just wanted to go home. "I'll meet with the curate of Croden this evening, and he will be able to tell me how long it will take. But I don't think it will be too long. We can go home soon, okay?"

"Okay," Sam agreed, and Sarah breathed one more sigh of relief.

Curate Eli showed up at precisely eight o'clock and was escorted to a private room where Sarah waited. Her mood had grown steadily darker with the day until she was left with nothing but a fierce determination to deal with the problem and then get out of Croden as fast as possible.

"How do we deal with this problem, Curate?" Sarah asked as he took his seat.

"Good evening. How are you fairing, Miss Livton?"

Sarah blushed. "I am well, thank you. How are you?"

"Very well, all things considered, but that is another matter. I believe you would like to get right down to the business at hand. Quite understandably. So, I will tell you what I believe should be done."

"Good."

"I am planning to call the council together tomorrow for an emergency meeting. We will discuss for a while, and then I will call you in to the meeting to testify that you are indeed living and that you have borne a daughter as a result of Seth's crime."

Sarah held up a hand. "They will not ask to speak to Sam, will they? I can't make her speak to them when she has only just learned about her father."

The curate studied her worried face for a moment. "I believe I can convince them that they do not need to speak to your daughter. But I warn you, they may want some proof that Sam was conceived on that evening."

"Speak to the apothecary. He can attest to the fact that it appeared I was with child after the attack."

The Mirror

"Yes," replied the curate, "but unfortunately, the apothecary also affirmed your death for your father. I doubt he would be likely to confirm your information in that case, and were that not so, it would still be a useless attempt, as the apothecary died over a year ago."

"Oh," Sarah whispered. "Then they will just have to deal with Sam's birth date. If not, they will have to wait until Billy can come from Owzan to testify when I came to the inn and what condition I was in. He would do it, but it would be a real bother for all of us. And take up a lot of time."

"I doubt that will be necessary. As it is, after you have spoken your piece, the council will decide if a crime has been committed. If so, one person will be sent to collect a judge, and the rest of us will go to arrest your father."

Again Sarah stopped the curate. "I want to make one request of you."

"What is that?"

"I want to be able to speak to my father before the council does. I want to have a chance to understand why he did what he did."

Curate Eli hesitated. "I don't know if that is a good idea. Your father may try to run or do something rash. You may also be in danger if you go to visit him alone."

Sarah shook her head. "I doubt that. My father is a proud, stubborn man, but I doubt he could physically reach out his hand and hurt me."

"Very well, I will grant your request. You will have the morning to speak to your father, and in the afternoon the council will meet."

"And eventually the judge will come and there will be a trial, but why do we need a judge?"

"At this point we are beyond our council. Obviously our council was duped once in this case. We want to make sure it does not happen again. An outside judge will ensure the trial is fair."

"What will my father be charged with?"

"Seth was hanged very possibly illegally, and it was your father's testimony that put the noose around Seth's neck. Your father will be tried for murder."

Sarah's throat was so dry she could hardly speak. "And if he is found guilty?" She looked into the curate's eyes, bracing herself. "What will be his punishment?"

The curate paused. "His punishment will be death by hanging."

Sarah nodded, picked up her skirts, and left the room.

THIRTY-THREE

"**Y**OU'RE LEAVING AGAIN?" Sam murmured sleepily as Sarah opened the door to their rented bedroom.

"Hush little one, I won't be out long," Sarah replied, hoping Sam would go back to sleep.

"Can I come with you?" her daughter asked as she pushed herself up from the bed.

"No, Sam. I'm sorry, but I need you to stay here again. I'll be back before you know it. But it is best that you don't come with me."

"And you aren't going to tell me where you are going."

"Not right now."

"Fine," Sam huffed and burrowed back under the covers.

Sarah left with a sigh and made her way toward the one house she least wanted to visit. This time the trip seemed far too short, and she faced the front door. It felt odd, but she knocked. A low grumbling moved steadily toward the door until it opened with a "What do you want?"

Sarah stared at her father, not sure what to say. It had been so long, and he had become so old. In the twelve years she'd been gone, his forehead had become lined with bitterness, and the scowl on his face had caused his cheeks to sag. She once had thought her father handsome, but little remained of that man.

"H–hello, Father."

Her father pushed up his glasses and looked a little closer at her. Turning away, he grumbled something about seeing things and was about to close the door on her.

"Wait." Sarah grabbed the door. Her father pulled harder, but Sarah wouldn't let it go.

He relented. "Well, what do you want?"

"Are you going to invite me in?"

"Do what you like. What do I care?" he grumbled as he walked in, leaving the door open. Sarah followed.

Taking a seat in the parlour, her father picked up a paper and began to read.

"I sent you letters," Sarah said, not sure what she wanted to say to her father now that she was there.

"You can have them back." He pointed to a drawer. Sarah opened the drawer to find a stack of letters. All of them were unopened.

Sarah fought back the angry tears. She had written every week until Sam was born, and when the letter that she'd had a daughter

The Mirror

went unanswered, she had given up. "Didn't you care what happened to your daughter?"

"My daughter died, twelve years ago. Seth Hepton killed her."

"Is that what you tell yourself so you can sleep at night?"

He didn't answer her.

"Look at me, Father. Am I not your daughter? Am I not alive and well?"

He didn't look up from his paper. "I don't know who you are."

"Well then, we will have to see what the council has to say. If they think I am your daughter, you will be tried for murder. But I guess if I'm not your daughter, you will have no concerns."

Her father's face paled, and his mouth tightened. "You wouldn't go to the council. What would be the point? Seth is dead. Nothing can be done about that now."

"So you don't think Seth deserves justice?"

"Justice?" Sarah had finally hit her mark. Her father threw aside the newspaper and jumped to his feet, hands clenched. "Look what he did to you. Don't you see every time you look in the mirror, the scar down your face? Don't you remember his cruelty every time your leg cramps and you limp? Don't talk to me about justice, daughter. Seth Hepton got his justice."

"So, I am your daughter now?"

"I'm not sure. My daughter would never want me to hang."

"Well, my father never would have wanted me dead so much that he made a false grave. Honestly father, why couldn't you just answer my letters?"

"Why did you have to leave?"

"You know why I left." Sarah sighed and collapsed to the couch. "I have a daughter, Father, but I guess you don't really care about that either."

Her father sat down and rubbed a hand roughly down his face. "You could have come home."

"To what? I could have come home to find out that you had me killed while I was gone? And what would you have done then if I decided to go looking for Seth? Would you have tied me to my bed? Held me captive in my own home?"

"You wouldn't have been so rash as to go searching for Seth."

"Then why? Why did you do it? Why did you say I died?"

He picked up his paper again and began to flip through the pages. "My daughter did die all those years ago. You aren't my daughter. Not really. Seth Hepton killed you when he violated you."

"No, Father. Seth stole from me. He hurt me, yes, and I may have changed a little, but you are the one who killed me."

Sarah picked up her skirts and made to leave. Just shy of the door, she turned. "Just so you know, the council will be by later on this afternoon to arrest you. Perhaps you should think on what you have done in the meantime."

Her father didn't reply. Instead, he flipped another page in his newspaper. With angry tears in her eyes, Sarah left.

Sam was waiting for her at the entrance to the inn. "So where'd you go?"

"I went to my father's house," Sarah said, not caring any more if Sam found out the truth.

"Why couldn't I come with?"

The Mirror

"Because my father is the one who told everyone I was dead, so I didn't know how well I would be received when I arrived, and I didn't want to put you in danger."

Sam didn't respond right away. Instead, she followed Sarah into the inn, through the parlour and to their bedroom. "Was he happy to see you?" she asked when they were alone.

"No," Sarah said with a heavy sigh. "He was far from happy to see me."

"Oh." Sam began to pick at the sleeve of her dress.

Sarah sighed again. "Come here, little girl." Sam ran to her mother and Sarah wrapped her arms around her. "It's okay. I never really expected that my father would welcome us back."

"Why doesn't he want us, Mom?" Sam whimpered into Sarah's shoulder.

Sarah stroked her hair as she thought about what to say. "I think it's because he was hurt when I left. He was so hurt, and he couldn't forgive Seth for what happened. So instead of dealing with the pain, he buried it deep down inside, and it began to grow like a disease, and it made him very unhappy."

"But, wouldn't seeing you again make him happy again?"

Sarah shook her head. "Because his anger is like a disease, it keeps getting worse, and what do I do if you are really sick?"

Sam made a face. "You make me eat some ginger or drink some chamomile."

"I make you take something that will help your body get rid of the disease. What my father needs to get rid of his anger is a good dose of medicine, but unfortunately, I don't think there is a medicine strong enough in this world to heal him."

Sam snuggled a little more against her shoulder, and they sat together awhile.

"I think we should go for a walk," Sarah said. "I'm going to have to leave you for a while again this afternoon, so I think it is best that we get some fresh air while we still can."

"Okay," sighed Sam. "Where are you going this time?"

"I have to talk with the town council so they can fix the mistake that was made."

"Are they going to raise you from the dead?"

Sarah laughed at her daughter's innocent question. "Sorry darling, but only God can raise the dead. They are just going to make sure that the truth is told."

Sarah and Sam began to stroll through the stores in the town square, but it didn't take long for Sarah to feel like people were staring. Not everyone seemed to notice them, but the mercantile owner followed them through the store at a distance, quickly turning away when Sarah looked. The confectioner whispered with a customer while she and Sam perused his candy choices, and a lady stopped her on the street, seemed about to say something, then ran away. Sarah thought the lady's name was Mrs. Nordam, but so much time had passed, and she couldn't be sure.

"I think I want to go back to the inn," Sam whispered.

"Okay," Sarah whispered back.

The Mirror

Mrs. Fink had lunch waiting for them when they walked through the door. They ate in silence. It wasn't until Sam pushed her bowl away that she spoke. "So, when do you have to go?"

"I have to wait until Curate Eli comes to get me."

As if her words had summoned him, the curate walked through the door.

The curate nodded to Sarah and offered Sam a weak smile. "Miss Livton, are you ready?"

Sarah turned to Sam and squeezed her hand. "Be good, little girl. I'll be back soon."

Sam sighed and laid her head on the countertop. "I'll be waiting," she said a little too dramatically. Sarah smiled and turned to follow the curate.

The meeting was to be held at the parsonage, so Curate Yates took her back to his place and offered her a comfortable chair in the sitting room. "The other councillors should be coming soon. There have been some rumblings around town about your appearance, so I have rethought the itinerary for our meeting. I would like it very much if you would be present from the beginning. That way we save some time that would normally be wasted on pointless arguing over who you are."

Sarah nodded mutely.

"Would you like some tea while you wait?"

Sarah shook her head. She wasn't sure her trembling hands would be able to hold a cup.

"Very well." The curate turned to make himself comfortable in a large rocking chair by the fireplace.

Sarah heard the front door being opened by Mrs. Yates, and the stamping feet of several men as they filed into the house.

"Rumours, rumours, rumours," muttered one man as he entered into the sitting room. Three others followed after him.

"What is the rumour, Avery?"

Sarah bit back a gasp when she recognized the first man to enter the room as Avery Wellhousen.

"There is talk all over town about Sarah Livton. Some people say she is walking among the people because she really loved Seth and thought he deserved better than what he was given. But it is all nonsense. Sarah Livton is dead."

Two more men entered. Sarah recognized them as Joseph Mendelson and Gregory Bishon.

Mr. Bishon took his seat and groaned loudly. Sarah guessed he would be nearly seventy now, but he was obviously well enough to continue on the council. "Nordam is coming, but he was going to stop by Dalton's house so we wouldn't have to wait a half hour for him to arrive." He noticed Sarah and stopped. "Who are you?"

Both Mendelson and Avery spluttered at the sudden jump in the conversation, but both turned to where Bishon pointed.

"H–hello, Mr. Bishon."

"My goodness," gasped Avery, his face going pale. "It can't be."

Sarah squirmed uncomfortably as the men continued to gape. "Gentlemen," Curate Eli interrupted, "we all know it is rather impolite to stare. How about we all take our seats."

Avery promptly sat, but almost missed his seat. Catching himself, he sat erect and continued to stare.

The Mirror

The door opened again and Mr. Nordam walked in along with Dalton McGuire. "Eli," Nordam stormed, "are you calling this meeting because of the rumours? I can't believe it. My wife comes to me and tells me she ran into Sarah Livton today. If you hadn't called the meeting, I would have. These rumours need to stop. Avery, what is your problem?"

Avery's mouth was still gaping but he managed to point. Sarah blushed when Mr. Nordam's penetrating eyes came to rest on her.

"Well, I see that there is some credit to these rumours." With a heavy sigh, he settled himself into a rocking chair similar to the curate's on the opposite side of the fire.

"You can stop gaping, Avery," Dalton intoned. "It is obvious she is not a ghost. You are only going to make yourself look like a fool."

Avery blushed. It was obvious he was the youngest member on the council, and Sarah wondered how he had managed to obtain such a prestigious position.

"Gentlemen," Curate Eli called, bringing the room to attention. "I called this meeting because of a rather interesting occurrence. After the hanging yesterday, I came across this young lady in the crowd. After we had talked for some time, it came to my attention that her name was Sarah Livton."

A nervous intake of breath and a slight grumbling passed through the men, and Sarah wished she could disappear into her seat.

"Ah yes," continued the curate, "I can tell you all see the problem. Sarah Livton is supposed to be dead, and the man we just hanged died for her murder."

"The question," said Dalton with a sneer, "is whether this is the Sarah Livton that we all thought dead?"

Sarah frowned. She had never liked the McGuire family, and she wondered now if Mr. McGuire would cause trouble. She steeled herself. "My name is Sarah Livton. I am daughter of Ezra and Hannah Livton. I ran away twelve years ago after being raped by Seth Hepton. I came back now because I wanted to find Seth."

"Why?" Avery asked, a look of horror on his face. "Why would you want to find him?"

Sarah was about to answer when Curate Eli cut in. "I believe we can all say with certainty that this is Sarah Livton, which means we have a problem on our hands. It means that someone faked her death, and it means that Seth Hepton was hanged with an improper trial."

"It is not so horrible," stated Nordam. "Rape is also punishable by death, and there is no doubt that the man committed that crime. So I elect that we only address the fact that someone faked Miss Livton's death. Unless, of course, there are extenuating circumstances."

"There are," replied the Curate.

"Oh please, do tell," said Dalton as if hearing a good joke.

"There is a child."

"Oh goodness," Mendelson blurted out, but his sentiment was mirrored on the faces of all but Dalton.

"A child, a child, that means nothing. How do we know whose the child is?" stated Dalton coldly. "Miss Livton has not been in our community for twelve years. A lot can happen in that time."

Sarah met Dalton's gaze. "Her birth date lines up—"

"You could make that up."

The Mirror

The men in the room began to grumble. Sarah felt the tension rising, but she wasn't sure what to do. "I–I..."

"There is no proof, and there is no way of knowing if the child belongs to Seth Hepton!" shouted Dalton above the rising tumult in the room. Each of the men had decided they needed to speak their mind, and the ensuing uproar was enough to make Sarah tremble. She sank back into her chair as accusations were cast and the shouts grew louder and louder.

Only Avery sat unmoved amidst the chaos. He looked at her, his eyes searching, then, with a voice that bespoke authority, he called out, "Silence!" The gentlemen hushed, and those that were standing took their seats once more.

"Thank you, gentlemen," he said. "Now, there have been many accusations thrown about and many valid questions raised."

Dalton made as if to say something, but Avery cut him off. "Yes, Mr. McGuire, I recognize there is no proof of these claims, and that needs to be considered, but please, let me finish. First, let us speak of what we can be sure of. We condemned Seth Hepton as a murderer, not as a rapist. A murderer. It was agreed just the other evening that more would be needed to condemn Seth if he was guilty of rape alone, especially considering the remorse he showed."

Again Dalton stirred, but Avery held up his hand. "The second thing we can be sure of is that this young lady is indeed the Sarah Livton that we all assumed dead at the hands of Seth Hepton. The third fact we must deal with is the presence of the child. I know we are all certain there is a child and that it is Sarah's, as the rumours around town all speak of the ghost of Sarah walking about with a child that looks exactly like her.

"Now, these facts present a couple of problems. First, no matter how easy it would be to say that Seth got what he deserved, he did not get a fair trial. He was, therefore, not given justice, which our country says every man will be served whether to his detriment or his benefit.

"Secondly, there has been a crime committed that must be addressed. We hanged Seth Hepton at the witness of Ezra Livton. He testified that his daughter died as a result of the wounds inflicted by Seth. This was evidently a lie. We must, therefore, address this new crime and hopefully by doing so we can rectify the wrong done with Seth's hanging."

Silence fell as Avery finished his speech. Sarah no longer had any questions as to how he had made it onto the council. Each member seemed to contemplate his words, but it was Bishon who finally spoke.

"I think we all know what needs to be done. Dalton, I believe you will have the easiest time accessing a judge. I think it best that you leave today so we can have the trial as soon as possible."

"Oh, I suppose, but that will mean at least a week away from my shop."

"We will make sure it gets taken care of. You have never had to worry about that, Dalton," Bishon replied sternly, and Dalton acquiesced. "Nordam," Bishon continued, "I believe you will be able to make a formal arrest, and I will notify Mayor Clark. We likely should have included him in this meeting." The men cringed at the mention of including the mayor. "But, unfortunately, the mayor always seems to have more important things to do. Perhaps we will have to let him announce the upcoming trial. I am sure he would like such a public task."

The Mirror

The men all stood to leave. Each took the time to shake hands with the curate, but many averted their eyes as they passed by Sarah. Avery was the last to leave. He held out his hand to Curate Eli, then turned to Sarah.

"I think," he said softly, "that my wife would like it very much if you would come and visit. How about you bring your daughter by for dinner this evening?"

"That would be very nice."

"Good. I will come by the inn around six to pick you up."

"Thank you," Sarah murmured, then watched as Avery, too, disappeared out the door.

THIRTY-FOUR

SARAH AND SAM SPENT that evening at the Wellhousen's house, talking about old times. Sam was ecstatic to hear stories about her mother when she was younger, though Sarah wasn't so keen for her daughter to hear all the stories that Avery and his wife Melanie remembered. But it was with a sigh that Sarah left later that evening, thinking that the coming week would be quite boring as they waited for the trial.

She couldn't have been more wrong. When the word got out that Sarah Livton was back, alive and well, many visitors came to the inn, some to catch up while others had more sinister intentions. After a yelling match between Sarah and old Mrs. Mandin left Sam in tears and the Finks down the hall pretending they couldn't hear the horrible things Mrs. Mandin was saying, Sarah asked Mr. Fink to monitor the visitors that he allowed in. With a frown Mr. Fink agreed, though he loudly bemoaned the potential loss of customers.

The Mirror

And so the week passed quickly, and Dalton McGuire returned to town with the judge.

No one had dared mention the arrest of Ezra Livton in front of Sarah, so it was quite eerie to see the morose-faced judge take up residence in the room down the hall from them at the inn.

"What's he here for?" Sam whispered to Sarah as they watched him discreetly from a crack in their door.

"For the trial," Sarah whispered back breathlessly.

"The trial?" Sam replied a little too loudly. "What trial?"

"Goodness, haven't I told you the reason we haven't left Croden?"

"I thought it was because you wanted to see all those people."

Sarah shook her head. "No, Sam. We would have left a week ago, but we have to stay for the trial of my father."

Sam's eyes went wide. "Why is he going on trial?"

"Because his lie meant that Seth was hanged. If my father had not lied about me dying, Seth would still likely be alive today."

"Oh." Sam moved away from the door toward the bed. "May I come to the trial, or do I have to stay at the inn again?"

"I think you can come to the trial. Actually, I think it best. It would be good for the judge to be able to see you."

"Because I am Seth Hepton's daughter?"

"Yes. Yes, because you are Seth Hepton's daughter, and you deserve to have a father."

They both slept feverishly that night, and the next day it was announced that the trial was to be delayed until the following day, as the judge wanted some time to collect himself and rest from the journey.

The town spent the day in tense silence waiting for the hour when a verdict would be announced.

Sarah woke on the day of the trial feeling nauseated and weak. She forced herself to eat breakfast and to tie Sam's hair back in braids. Together they made their way toward the small courthouse and took a seat in the front row. The rest of the building filled quickly, and soon the jailer walked in with her father, whose hands were tied in front of him.

Sarah heard the harsh whispers as she waited for the judge to appear. "Hussy" and "slut" were the kindest words thrown in her direction from many of the more outspoken in the crowd. But everyone was too curious about the outcome of the trial to do anything more than speak threatening words.

At last the judge walked in. "Please be seated," he said in a monotonous voice when he got to the desk at the front of the room. "My name is Judge Bartholomew Gales, and I will be presiding over this trial. All my decisions are final and will be carried out under the supervision of the council and the mayor. If there are any objections as to how this trial is to take place, I would like them made clear now." He paused to allow time. "As no objections are presented, let us begin. Would the council please present the accused and the charges."

Nordam stepped forward and outlined the charges, and the long and tedious trial began. Each member of the council was called forward to speak about the hanging, the events beforehand, and the ones that followed. Sam began to nod off as the hours ticked by until finally the judge had finished speaking to the last of the council members. With a look at his pocket watch, the judge stood and dismissed the crowd for lunch.

The Mirror

The rumblings of the crowd were giving Sarah the jitters, and it was with great relief that she saw Avery and his wife walking toward her and Sam. "We thought you might like to sit with us," Melanie said quietly, throwing a dirty look at Mr. Janson, who had been approaching Sarah with an ominous look. Mr. Janson turned aside, his fists clenched at his sides.

"Yes—yes, that would be wonderful."

When they returned from their lunch break, the judge called Sarah's father to the stand.

"Tell me, Mr. Livton, is this woman your daughter?" Judge Gales asked.

Mr. Livton turned and looked at Sarah. "I have no daughter. My daughter was killed by Seth Hepton."

"When did your daughter die, Mr. Livton? Do you think you can describe the occurrence of this death?"

Mr. Livton's eyes never left Sarah's face as he spoke. "Twelve years ago. It was June, and Seth Hepton dropped her off on our doorstep bloody and near death. Sarah came to for a while and told us what Seth had done to her. We called the apothecary, and he said it was amazing she was still alive. She improved physically for some time, but then everything seemed to turn. She became morose and sickly. One of her wounds became infected, and two months after being dropped on our doorstep, she was gone."

"Please clarify, Mr. Livton, what do you mean by gone?" Judge Gales asked.

Mr. Livton looked at the judge. "She was dead."

"And who was witness to her death?"

"The apothecary at that time, Harper Thomson, and my wife Hannah."

"And are either of these persons available to attest to Miss Livton's death?"

"No, they are both dead."

"And there are no other witnesses?"

"We had closed the coffin before it left the house, as the sight of my daughter's mangled body would have been quite frightening for many people."

"Very well, Mr. Livton. I would like you to take one last look at this young lady and tell me if she is your daughter."

Sarah saw no feeling in her father's eyes as he turned to her. "My daughter is dead."

"Thank you, Mr. Livton, you may step down." Her father rose and stepped back to his seat next to the jailer. "Miss Livton, please take the stand."

Sarah took a deep breath and stepped forward. The judge swore her in, and she took an unsteady seat on the stool set up in front of the audience.

"Well, Miss Livton, as you can see, we have a bit of a problem."

"Yes, sir," Sarah said, her mouth dry.

"You claim to be Sarah Livton, but Ezra Livton claims his daughter is dead. It is my job today to decide who is telling the truth. So tell me, Miss Livton, what happened twelve years ago?"

"I ran away, sir."

"Yes, I have heard that, but my question is why? Why did you run away, Miss Livton?"

The Mirror

"Because of Seth," Sarah replied, a little uncertain where the line of questioning was going.

"Were you afraid that Seth was going to come back? Did you think you would be safer away from Croden?"

"No, of course not. I wasn't afraid of Seth."

Judge Gales raised his brows. "You weren't afraid of Seth after what he did to you?"

Sarah shook her head. "Seth only did what he did because of his father. Seth—Seth was different. At least, I think he was. I have to believe he was."

"Why is that?"

"Because if Seth did it of his own accord, then I was completely blind, not just partially blind, and then all of it was my own fault."

Judge Gales rested his chin in his hand and gave her a long, searching look. "A man should never treat a girl in that manner, no matter the provocation. You should not blame yourself. But if you were not afraid of Seth, then why did you run away?"

"I wasn't going to. I was going to stay and heal, but then... then— you have to understand, I just wanted to forget it all."

"Of course."

"Well, I found out I was pregnant. I was pregnant with Seth's baby, and I would have a daily reminder of what happened because everyone would know, and they would stare. They would look at my child and shun her, and I couldn't bear that. So I ran away to a place where no one would know about me and Seth."

"I see. If that was the case, why did you come back?"

"Because it has been twelve years, and despite my best efforts, I cannot forget Seth. Sometimes I remember the awful thing he did, and the way my life changed, and I hate him for it. But other times I remember his stories, his gentleness, his passion, and I wonder if I will ever finish with this foolishness and stop loving him."

A silence thick with conviction hung over the courtroom. "You didn't know Seth," Sarah whispered.

"He hurt you," Judge Gales reminded gently.

"But he didn't kill me."

"You may step down."

The silence in the courtroom broke, and the buzz of whispers that ensued was enough for the judge to call for order before a reluctant hush fell over the crowd.

"Samantha Livton, please step forward."

Sarah paled. Sam wasn't supposed to be called. She never would have brought her. But Sam stood, legs shaking, and made her way to the front stool and sat down.

Judge Gales offered her daughter a reassuring smile that did nothing for Sarah's roiling stomach. "Now, Miss Samantha, I need you to promise that you are going to tell the absolute truth."

"Sir, Stuart Morgan told me lying is a sin, so I already promised him I would do my best to tell the truth."

Judge Gales smiled and nodded. "Very good." The judge paused and Sam began to squirm on the hard wooden seat. "Miss Samantha, do you know why I called you up?"

Sam nodded. "You want to know if Mom is really who she says she is or if the person she says she is, is really dead."

The Mirror

"That's right. Do you know why it is so important that we find out the truth?"

Sam screwed up her face as if piecing together a very complicated puzzle. "I don't know, sir. I just don't understand why anyone would ever lie about who they are. I mean, who would want to come all the way to Croden for a lie like that, especially when they have a nice home in Owzan with friends, and Mr. Caman, and Stuart Morgan? That just doesn't make sense to me."

"You're right, it doesn't make sense. But I want you to know that if your mom was lying, we could all leave and go back to our homes, but if that man over there is lying, I will have no choice but to condemn him to death."

Sam paled and clamped her jaw shut.

"Is there something you would like to say, Miss Samantha?"

Sam nodded.

"Then why don't you say it. You are safe here."

Sam's eyes widened and Sarah saw the tears of frustration gathering. "I can't," she whispered.

"Why not?"

"Because I promised not to lie."

"Then how about you tell me the truth?"

"I don't want Mr. Livton to die, sir. I thought once that I wanted to see a hanging, but my dad was hung last week, and I never got a chance to meet him. Well, that man there is my granddad, and I know that he doesn't want me, but I still don't want him dead."

"Thank you, Miss Samantha. You can go sit with your mother now."

There was no one else. It was time for the judge to make his verdict. Sarah held her breath. There was so much evidence, she was certain her father would be convicted, and with a jolt, she wondered how she would feel when the words were spoken that sentenced him to death.

Judge Gales had the attention of everyone gathered. "It is easy for me to see what has happened here. The difficult part in this case is to decide what to do. Ezra Livton, you have been given the chance to gain your daughter back, along with a beautiful and intelligent granddaughter. Instead, you obstinately hold onto your anger and refuse to accept the woman who stands before you.

"According to the law, I have every right to condemn you to death, and don't think that I'm not tempted. But I think what we all need to understand is that this case is much bigger than just a simple lie. It was not just this man's testimony that condemned Seth Hepton to death." Judge Gales roved his eyes over the crowd. "If you believe you are innocent, remember the testimonies given, and ask yourself if you were among the ones calling for Seth Hepton's death. Then remember, that man's death was not the result of one man's testimony, but the result of a community's anger at an entire family and the pain that a man now dead inflicted upon his sons and wife.

"Here is where I agree with Miss Samantha. It is time for the death to stop. It is time to end this anger and this hurt. Therefore, Mr. Livton, I am requiring that you dig up the grave that is evidently not your daughter's. In this way, any who have doubts can see that Sarah is not dead. Curate Eli Yates, I trust you will be able to correct the formal records.

The Mirror

"As for the rest of this community, I want you to think long and hard on what happened here. Did Seth Hepton do a horrible thing and deserve to die? Very possibly, but not one of you stopped to listen to his story. No one cared enough to look past their own supposedly righteous anger to ask one simple question. Why?

"Why would Seth Hepton do such a horrible thing? Why would he return this woman to her father's doorstep? Why, after so many years, would he return and turn himself in? These are not the signs of a murderous man, but of a man convicted of wrong. One who sought forgiveness, yet he was shown no mercy.

"All of you, leave this courtroom today, and remember that there are no longer any more fingers to point, or blame to be had. The truth is out, and now we must all deal with our own convictions in regard to what happened in this place." With his final words spoken, Judge Bartholomew Gales stood and left the courtroom.

Silently, row after row, each person filed out of the courtroom till only Sarah remained with her daughter and, much to her surprise, Avery Wellhousen.

Avery twisted his hands nervously as he approached Sarah. "I want to ask your forgiveness," he said quietly.

Sarah's surprise grew. "What for, Avery?"

"The judge was right. We all did want Seth dead. As much as we may have spoken about justice and keeping him alive, we still all knew the outcome even before we came to a conclusion. We wanted him to pay so much that not one of us questioned him." Avery looked disgusted with himself. "I have never seen a greater breach in justice, and to think I was one of the ones who committed it."

"Don't blame yourself, Avery. It wouldn't have happened if the truth had been known."

"I'm not so sure about that, but I would like to make amends as best I can anyway."

Sarah nodded, hoping that if she acquiesced, she would be able to ease Avery's conscience.

"Seth's body was taken to Emriville. I believe you will find people there who know what he all did these past twelve years. I thought maybe you would find it comforting to go there and find him. I've arranged for a coach to take you and your daughter there. It will be around this evening to pick you up."

Sarah felt a slight blush crawl up her cheeks. "Thank you, Avery. I would like that."

Sarah waited for Avery to leave, but he continued to stand there looking nervous. "Look," he said in a whisper as the back door opened and a curious boy peeked around the corner. "I don't know if you have heard some of the talk around town, but some people aren't too pleased you are back. Despite what the judge said, I think there is going to be trouble, so the faster you leave, the safer you will be."

Sarah tensed and glanced to Sam. "What do you mean, Avery?"

"I mean don't open your door to anyone but the Finks tonight. In fact, stay in your room if you can until you get onto the coach."

"I'll heed your words," Sarah replied in a whisper when she realized Sam was listening.

Together the small group walked to the door, and Avery escorted the two girls all the way to their room, giving strict instructions to the

The Mirror

Finks about visitors and when to summon Sarah and Sam to get on the coach.

The few remaining hours until six passed by tediously as Sam and Sarah paced about their room. Sarah was beginning to think all their precautions were for naught when she heard shouting from the parlour.

"I don't care what you think, Fink! She should have stayed dead!" There was a rumbled response and some scuffling. Sarah heard the click of a door opening down the hall and peeked out of her own door to watch as Judge Gales strode down the hall, a look of purpose upon his face.

She watched from a crack in her door as the Judge sized up the man in the parlour and began to speak calmly but firmly. "If you have a problem with my ruling, you will speak to me, and me alone. If you or anyone else lays a hand upon Miss Livton, I will personally make sure that you are punished to the full extent for your crime. Now go home before I have you convicted for disorderly behaviour."

With a dark scowl, the man left, and Judge Gales turned back up the hall. Sarah jumped back from the door, hoping he didn't catch her spying. But the judge walked directly toward her room, and knocked politely on the door.

Hesitantly, Sarah opened the door the rest of the way and looked out. "Miss Livton, I believe there is a coach waiting for you and your daughter. Would you allow me the honour of escorting you?"

Sarah nodded and hurriedly she and Sam gathered their luggage and followed the judge as he marched them quickly toward a waiting coach.

THIRTY-FIVE

SARAH AND SAM STEPPED out of the coach in Emriville and looked around. "Did you know this is where Mr. Caman grew up?" Sam whispered as she stared at the nondescript city square.

"Yes," replied Sarah, "I seem to recall that." She pointed down the street. "The inn is likely down that way. How about we go see about a room?"

They found the inn, but it was with some frustration that Sarah realized that there was a huge and bustling crowd around the front door. "Wait here," she told Sam. Pushing her way through the crowd, she found the innkeeper, and immediately left the building fuming.

"What's the matter, Mom?"

"We won't be staying here, Sam. Outlandish, who could ever— who would ever... Common thievery, that is what it is. The king and queen... well good for him," Sarah grumbled as they walked away from the inn.

The Mirror

She was so caught up in her fuming that she did not notice Sam tugging on her arm until it was too late. Ploughing into the street, she ran into a lady walking peaceably by the crowd at the inn. With a startled yelp, the young lady dropped her basket and stumbled back a few paces.

"Oh, I'm dreadfully sorry. I..." Sarah spluttered.

The young lady brushed off her skirts and smiled. "You just came from the inn where that fool of a man tried to charge you an arm and a leg just to sit down?"

"Well, yes."

"He's been at it for the past few weeks. Ever since the king and queen left. He seems to think he has a right to charge extra because the prince and princess were born in his rooms. He's plum out of his mind is what I think, but that doesn't change the fact that he's still charging far more than what most people can afford."

"Exactly what I was thinking."

"Which means you probably need a place to stay."

"Indeed. Is there another inn around here somewhere? Or perhaps a pastor's family that will take us in for a few nights?"

"Emriville is too small for another inn, and unfortunately, our minister just died, but you are more than welcome to come home with me. My husband and I have a house that is much too big for the two of us, and we are more than happy to have guests."

Sarah paused. Sam had just dropped one of their cases down beside her and let out an exhausted huff. "I don't know who you are," she blurted out a little impolitely.

The girl laughed. "My name is Katy Deplin, and I live just outside of town with my husband Josh Deplin, the town blacksmith. Now that you know who I am, how about you tell me your name."

"My name is Sarah Livton, and this is my daughter Samantha."

Katy paled slightly, but soon recovered herself. "You know Miss Livton, I think that God intended for you to bump into me today. Now that I know who you are, I am certain that you and your daughter are to stay at my place."

"But how do you know that?" Sarah asked.

"I knew Seth, and he is the one you are looking for, is he not?"

Sarah nodded mutely.

"Then the two of you come with me. We will have a nice hot meal and then we shall talk."

THIRTY-SIX

ELIZABETH THE NURSERY MAID carried her bag down the palace stairs. Servants stared at her, questioning her every step. Yesterday some had dared to smile at her, but now, bags in hand, she received only glowering stares and judgmental glares. She sighed as she heaved her travel bag out of the way of a large decorative vase at the foot of the stairs.

"Elizabeth!"

Elizabeth swung to see who was speaking. Her bag moved with her, crashing into the vase and sending it tumbling to the floor. The elegant piece clanged when it made contact with the marble, and Elizabeth sighed with relief when she realized it was not made of glass.

"Sir Borden, you scared me."

"Back to those antics, are we?" Sir Borden said as he stooped to pick up the vase. Setting it back in place, he smiled at her. "It is John.

You called me John in Emriville, and you will call me John here in Silidon as well."

Elizabeth ignored the man and turned to walk toward the front doors. "Not so fast, you minx," chimed John as he came up beside her. "Let me take this for you." Grabbing her bag, he lifted it out of her hands and swung it lithely at his side.

Scowling at him, Elizabeth stopped in her tracks. "Sir Borden, I am perfectly capable of carrying my own bag. As for you calling me a minx, that is completely unacceptable. I will not take such derogatory language from you."

"Well, I'll be," muttered John from where he had stopped a couple of steps in front of her. Turning on the spot, he paced slowly back and sauntered in a circle around her.

Elizabeth tensed at his scrutiny. "What are you doing?"

"I am trying to figure out what you could have done with one Elizabeth Mede I used to know. The one that would have put up with any bad behaviour from a person because she thought that was all she deserved. Now I can make speculations as to where that person is, but it would be completely inappropriate."

Elizabeth blushed. "Well," she said breathily. "I might speculate as well as to where the Sir Borden went that blushed any time he mentioned something that had the remotest chance of being inappropriate."

"Ah," replied John as he finally came face to face with her once more. "That is an easy thing to answer. I am not the same John. I am the John who fell in love with a young lass who I am going to marry someday. And there is no shame in that, so the old John had to disappear."

The Mirror

"And who is this lucky young lass that you will marry? I had not heard of an engagement. Her majesty is usually on top of those things. I am surprised she has not mentioned it to me."

A glint entered John's eyes. "Her majesty wouldn't know because the young lass has not said yes yet. But perhaps you could take pity on a fellow and give him a kiss of luck so he can be sure of the answer his lady dear will give him."

Elizabeth stepped toward him. He reached out a hand and caressed her cheek. Taking heed of his momentary distraction, Elizabeth took hold of her bag and pushed past him. "I am sorry Sir John, but I wouldn't want to make your lady love jealous. Then you would be most certainly sure of your answer."

John raced to catch up to her. Elizabeth couldn't keep the smile from blooming across her face when he once more grabbed the bag from her hand and matched his pace to hers. "Any lady love would have the right to be jealous of such a winsome lady as you. But my woman has more sense than to be jealous. She is the most intelligent woman I know."

"Intelligent or not, every woman deals with feelings of jealousy. It is something we must all deal with at some point in our lifetime. But with the help of God we can overcome it."

"Very wise indeed, but what sorts of things would make a woman such as yourself jealous?" They were walking down the steps to the carriage and John held up a hand to assist Elizabeth.

Elizabeth was about to answer when a young lady raced across the courtyard. "John," she squealed. "You have not been around for ever so long. What has the king had you up to now? Or was it the queen? She does make such demands of you."

John smiled and gently removed the lady's hand from where it had a vicelike grip on his arm and, placing it in the crook of his arm, he swung Elizabeth's bag on top of the carriage where the driver would secure it. "Yes, Miss Beton, I have been away, but it has been pure pleasure. I was in the town of Emriville, making acquaintances there. It was a real adventure for such a small town."

"Well," said Miss Beton, "you must certainly come to dinner tonight. You can tell Father, Mother, and me all about your adventures."

Elizabeth, feeling like an intruder standing on the steps, made to leave, but John took hold of her arm with his free hand and tugged her gently toward the conversation. "I am sorry to say that is an impossibility. You see, Miss Mede and I leave this very day on business of the king."

Elizabeth curtsied, trying not to step over her station. Miss Beton lifted her nose in acknowledgement. "I see," she said, obviously unhappy with the delay in her plans. "Well, you must promise me that once you return, you will come directly to our home for dinner. You know you are always welcome."

"Thank you, but I fear I must be about business now. Have a good day, Miss Beton."

Miss Beton gave a slight curtsy and strode away.

When she was some way off, John turned on Elizabeth. Leaning in close, John pointed a finger in her face. "Understand me, Elizabeth," he stated hoarsely. "Never, ever, curtsy to a lady such as her. You are now her superior. She will curtsy to you, and she will be made known of her true class."

The Mirror

"What class is that?" Elizabeth asked. "I am a servant. If she were to be less than me she would be one of the poor. It is very obvious she is not that."

"Nay, you are right. She is worse than that. She is the type that grovels at men's feet and then ensnares them. Her boasts make her think she is better than those who have greater morals than she."

Elizabeth watched as the woman of their discussion walked about the courtyard. "And yet," Elizabeth murmured to herself, "you ask what I am jealous of."

John took hold of her shoulders and leaned even closer.

"This is inappropriate, Sir Borden," Elizabeth murmured. "You will catch people's attention and your lady love may have reason to be jealous."

"You have nothing to be jealous of. You are beautiful, Elizabeth," John whispered, despite her objections to his nearness.

"Thank you, Sir Borden," Elizabeth whispered. "But right now my discomfort is outweighing my jealousy. Do you think that perhaps you could release me?"

A grin split John's face. "I would, but that would provide me great discomfort. And I must look out for my own best interests, you know. Besides, my pain would be so much greater if we separated, than yours if we did not."

"Oh bother." Elizabeth sighed. "Is this what I am going to have to put up with the entire way to Emriville?"

"Perhaps longer," teased John. "But perhaps you will learn that you actually don't mind. Can you imagine that?"

"No. I think I will always find you intolerable. I've felt that about you since the day you stepped into the post office. You were a nuisance then as well."

"I am wounded."

"Well you might not feel the pain so much if you stepped away somewhat."

"You are once again mistaken, but I have already gone over my argument on that part, so let's not repeat it."

Elizabeth sighed and tried to shrug away from the pesky courtier. Just as she pushed, he took a step back, causing her to stumble into his arms. A mischievous grin lit John's face. "I always knew it would be painful for you to separate yourself from me, Elizabeth, but we must remember that we are in a public place."

A red flush crept up Elizabeth's face as John restored her to her feet a couple of steps away from himself. "We'd best be going," she said.

"Oh yes." Pulling out his pocket watch, he made a face. "We're running late. You should have mentioned something earlier. Oh well, we'll just have to make up time." John held up a hand to help Elizabeth into the waiting carriage.

"Sir Borden, I think you have forgotten something." John cringed and turned to see Sir Shoals standing behind him.

"Is that so, Sir Shoals? What is it that I have forgotten?"

Shoals moved toward the carriage and stepped into it. Settling himself into the corner nearest the door, he looked out at John. "A chaperone, of course. I can't have you gallivanting around the country with my daughter in tow without a proper chaperone. It would be entirely inappropriate."

The Mirror

"Killjoy," muttered John as he stepped into the carriage and took his seat. Elizabeth smirked at his remark.

"What is that you said?" asked Shoals.

"Oh, I was just commenting on your wisdom. I only hope that I shall be able to protect my daughter so thoroughly if I am ever so blessed with one."

Elizabeth coughed back a laugh and Shoals gave her a concerned look. "Are you okay, daughter of mine? If you are ill, you may return to the palace. I'm sure her majesty will understand completely. It is never convenient to travel when one is ill."

Clearing her throat delicately, Elizabeth replied, "No Father, I am quite well. It was merely a tickle in my throat."

Shoals let out a slight humph and turned on John. "Well young sir, are we going to get this expedition on the way or not? Or is there some reason we are waiting? I am quite impatient to get going."

Rising slightly, John shut the carriage door and tapped the roof. There was a slight jerk, then the carriage took off down the streets of Silidon.

"Well, it is done," said Rose as she walked into the library toward her husband. "Elizabeth, John, and Shoals are all on their way to Emriville. Now, will you explain to me all that's going on and why I need to find another nursery maid?"

Henry set aside his book and held out his hands to his wife, who took a seat next to him. "Do you have your letter from Katy?"

"Yes, and she mentions Sarah Livton staying with her, but Henry, I don't understand, is Caman telling the truth then? Is Sarah alive and well, and if so, who is this Samantha?"

"Samantha is Seth's daughter. It's all here in Caman's journal." Henry held up the book he had been reading. "I was sceptical as well," Henry added when he saw the look on his wife's face. "That was until I heard Shoals' report about a recent trial in Croden. Sarah is alive, Rose, and Seth never should have been hanged." Henry could not hide the bitterness in words.

"So what do we do now?"

Henry sighed heavily. "Sarah is in Emriville, we know that from Katy's letter. She is safe, but I thought Elizabeth might be able to help her settle her feelings toward Seth. Judge Gales has promised to follow up on the situation in Croden to make sure things there settle down, and I have an appointment with Jeremy Caman in..." Henry pulled out his pocket watch. "Well, I'm already late."

Picking up the journal, Henry kissed his wife. "Would you like me to send Caman to the library to speak to you after we have concluded our appointment? I'm sure he'll be more than happy to tell you all about Sarah and Samantha."

"Yes, I would like that. Have Samuel summon me when you are finished."

"Very well. Until later, my love."

The Mirror

"Where's Gustave?" Caman asked when he woke the next morning to a new guard's glaring face. The guard's scowl lines deepened and he turned away.

"The little git is late, and I have to wait for him to show up before I can leave this pit," he said as he walked away.

There was a creaking and a bustling from up above and Gustave scurried into the room. "You can leave, Ryans," he said between gasps. Taking the key off the hook on the wall, he made his way toward Caman's cell.

"Now what are you doing?" the guard named Ryans asked as he watched Gustave begin to open the cell door. "You can't do that."

"King's orders," Gustave replied and hastily handed Ryans a sealed letter.

"Well then, I will take him." Ryans pushed his way toward Caman's cell.

"Read the letter, Ryans. I'm to take him. No one else. Now if you wish to disobey a direct order from the king, be my guest, but don't complain when you're punished."

Ryans blushed scarlet as he ripped open the letter and began to read. "Well," was his only reply as he dropped the letter and disappeared up the stairs.

"Where are we going, Gustave?" Caman asked as his cell door finally opened.

"You have another audience with the king," Gustave replied as he shunted Caman toward the door.

"Wait. Where is my journal? Gustave, what happened to my journal?"

"You will see. Hurry, before we are late."

"What do you think of our room of mirrors?"

Caman jumped to attention when he heard the king's voice, and moved away from the ornate mirror he'd been staring at. "Your Majesty," Caman said as he bowed. "I was told to wait in this room. I hope I have not intruded in any way."

Henry ignored his comment. "Gustave," he said to the guard at the door, "you will find Colonel Jasper at the training grounds. Report to him there, and he will give you further instructions on your new assignment." Gustave bowed and left Caman and the king quite alone.

"I have some news that you may appreciate, Caman. Your lady, Sarah Livton, is quite safe and currently in Emriville staying with a close friend of the queen's. It seems that a very wise judge sorted everything out in Croden, but I am sure the entire story can wait till later. For now, let us talk."

Caman didn't know what to say. "Very well, Your Majesty."

"Do you know the story behind this mirror?"

Caman shook his head. "It is very beautiful. That is why I was admiring it so, but I was rather puzzled by the phrase carved above it. 'Now we see but a poor reflection as in a mirror.' I remember Stuart Morgan saying something to the like, but not understanding what he meant."

The king nodded slowly. "The story goes that my great-great grandmother was a very vain and ostentatious woman who continually sought out remedies for aging and elixirs to re-establish youth. She was so vain that she hired a very talented man to make this mirror. He was

The Mirror

a celebrated craftsman, so she gave him free rein to design the mirror as he would.

"On the day the mirror was revealed, the queen was enamoured by its dazzling beauty, but the words above puzzled her. So she went about seeking their meaning. Many of her advisors attempted to flatter her, saying that the craftsman wished for the queen to realize that the mirror could only give a poor account of the queen's beauty. Others were not so generous and claimed that the mirror maker was insulting the queen, saying her vanity was unwarranted and that he truly found her hideous. Even when the church men of the time did their best to explain the biblical phrase, they were unable to comprehend the craftsman's intent, and the queen was left unsatisfied.

"Finally, after days of watching the queen brood over the phrase on the mirror, the chief advisor suggested that the mirror maker himself come and explain. So the man was called to the palace to stand before the queen. The man was said to be hideous, with large teeth and a beak-like nose. So hideous was his appearance, the queen could almost not bear to have him in her presence, but her desire to know the answer to the riddle was so great that she allowed him to stay.

"When asked what the words meant, the mirror maker was astonished and said, 'Oh my queen, I beg you not to take insult at the challenging words written on your mirror. The words were meant only as a reminder so that when one looks in a mirror, they may know that they do not always see the whole story. Yes they may see a beautiful face, but when they examine their heart as they have just done with their countenance, will they find the same beauty within?'"

Caman waited for the king to continue with his story, but he seemed lost to some kind of reverie. "What happened to the mirror maker after this encounter?" Caman asked when his curiosity got the better of him.

"Finding the man brash and ugly, the queen kicked him out, only to call him back a few days later to further explain the mirror. This happened multiple times before the queen admitted the man's wisdom and decided it would be more convenient to spend long hours talking with him if they were married. So the two were married, and are said to have made a very splendid royal couple."

"Did this really happen?" Caman asked, a little perplexed.

"Well, it's hard to say." The king turned away from the mirror and took a nearby seat. "The history of that time is a little muddled, but it does make an excellent story, and it is one that generations of kings now have used to teach their sons."

Caman stared into the mirror. "I don't think I understand it." He read the inscription again. "I'm not sure I understand yet what the phrase means."

"It took me a long time to understand as well, but I think that is because there are so many layers to its meaning. There is the first layer which was explained in the story, about outer beauty being a poor reflection of our heart, which is far more important."

"And what of the other meanings?"

A small smile crossed the king's face and he rose to stand just behind Caman's shoulder so they both could look into the mirror. "What do you see when you look in the mirror, Caman?"

"I see myself."

"Yes? Is that all you see?"

The Mirror

"Well, I see you, sir... and... and I see the room behind."

"Hmm. Very limited."

"What else am I supposed to see, sir?" Caman asked, exasperated.

"Look once more and see if you can look a little deeper."

Caman leaned closer, his green eyes staring back at him from the mirror. "Look at me," he whispered, a jumble of thoughts beginning to coalesce in his mind. "I was once told a story about a man hidden away because his appearance was so wretched. When I look in the mirror, I feel like that man, but instead of hidden away because of my appearance, I feel hidden behind my appearance, lost in the looking glass." Caman's reflection frowned back at him. "I wish someone would look past my appearance and the things that I have done and see all that I want, all my desires, all my pain, and be able to heal me. But no one does. They just see me, and want to be done with the horrible man that I am."

"The phrase above the mirror is a part of a whole. The whole verse says, 'Now we see but a poor reflection as in a mirror; then we shall see face to face. Now I know in part; then I shall know fully, even as I am fully known.'"

"A verse from Corinthians, the chapter on God's love."

"Yes," replied Henry, "but I would think that would be a comfort rather than something to scoff at."

"I'm sorry, Your Majesty, but this is hardly a comfort when for the past twelve years I have had nothing to do with God."

"Yes, I can see then how the prospect of speaking to God would be terrifying."

"It's not the fact that God is terrifying that causes this verse to lack comfort for me. It's just that it doesn't seem real or possible. So many things have happened in my life."

"I have read your journal."

"Then you know what happened between Isabelle and me. You know what happened to Martha. If God knows me fully, and if God is all-powerful, why did he allow it? Why didn't he keep me safe, or provide what Martha needed? I can't trust that God. I can't forgive that God for all that he did. Especially if what this verse says is true."

The king tapped his chin in thought. "Caman, when you are looking in the mirror, and I am standing here, can you tell exactly what I am doing behind you, or do you just have a hint?"

"Well, I have a hint." Caman spun as the king raised his hand as if to strike him.

"Ah, only a hint. Because now that you face me, you can tell that I meant not to strike you, but to clasp your shoulder."

Caman shied away as the king placed his hand on his shoulder, but was forced to follow his gentle prodding toward some chairs. "Have a seat, Caman," the king insisted as he took his own seat.

Choosing a plump armchair, Caman settled into the seat and waited for the king to speak.

"Consider this, Caman. We cannot see our future. We can hardly even guess at what the weather will be like tomorrow. But God holds the future in his hands. He sees it all clearly, just as he sees us more clearly than we do ourselves. Do you think, therefore, that God maybe knows what he is doing in our lives? Do you think that maybe when things happen and we think that God is striking us, and that he is unfair or unjust, that he is really embracing us and protecting us from an even greater harm?"

"But why does it have to hurt so much?" Caman moaned. "Why couldn't he make it easy? Why does everything have to be so difficult, and the road so hard to follow?"

"I don't know for sure. But I do know that God is good. I know that he is faithful and will never leave us nor forsake us."

"How can you know?"

"Because I trust him."

Caman leaned forward and placed his head in his hands. "Trust is hard to come by in my life. I have too often been betrayed."

"Never by God, Caman. You just need to be brave enough to accept his love, and I am sure that even if you may not understand everything that happens in your life, you will have the strength to face each new day with courage."

"I don't know if I am that brave, sir."

"Do you at least have the courage to try?"

Caman nodded, and the king gave his shoulder an encouraging grasp. "I will give you some time to pray about it. When you feel you have had enough time to think, ask one of the servants to help you find the queen. She has not had the privilege of reading your journal, and she would like to know more about Sarah and Samantha. I am also sure she can tell you some things about Seth that you do not know. In the morning, there will be a carriage waiting to take you to Sarah. If I don't see you before then, God go with you, Caman, and I pray you will find the courage you need to trust in him."

THIRTY-SEVEN

"WHAT HAPPENED TO YOU, Seth? How did you end up in Emriville of all places? And a preacher? Why didn't you just keep on living? Take a wife, start a family. Why did you have to go back to Croden?"

"Because living a lie is a worse death than dying because of the truth."

Sarah spun. When she saw the newcomer, she scrambled to her feet from the foot of the grave and hastily brushed off her skirts.

"I'm sorry. I didn't think anyone would come this way," Sarah said.

The lady smiled and moved toward the two grave markers. "Hello Mark. Hello Seth," she said, as if very familiar with the persons buried there and comfortable visiting their graves. She took a seat amidst the dirt and grass and continued to look contentedly at the tombstones.

"Please join me," she said when Sarah did not resume her seat. There was a shy innocence about the woman that made Sarah want

The Mirror

to trust her. She sat back down and continued to stare at Seth's grave, wondering if the desperate longing to see him face to face again would ever go away.

"You know," said the woman softly, "Seth was quite the gentleman, with his pale eyes and golden hair. Most of the ladies of the town longed to be the one lucky enough to win his regard. For a long time I thought he considered all the females too inferior to be his wife, or at least too sinful. I almost never got the chance to learn that it was not the women he thought too sinful, but himself."

"Why are you telling me this?" Sarah asked, but her question was ignored.

"You see, Seth lived with the ghosts of his past, the guilt of the old man that he couldn't seem to shake. Try as he might, he could not make amends for all the awful things he had done. Try as he might, he could not forget the girl he had loved so much but had hurt even more severely. He could never forgive himself, so he continued on miserably."

"Who are you?" Sarah prodded, not sure anymore that she trusted the woman beside her.

The woman sighed and turned away from the graves to face Sarah. "My name is Elizabeth Mede. I have lived in this town for most of my life, but it was only in the past year that Seth became one of my dearest friends."

"Did you think to marry him?" scoffed Sarah.

"No, Miss Livton, I sought only a friend when none other would even deem to look at me." There was a slight blush on Elizabeth's cheeks, and Sarah felt ashamed of her harsh words, but she could not bring herself to apologize.

"How do you know who I am?" she asked instead.

"Katy told me where I could find you, and as my entire intent in returning to Emriville was to speak to you, I thought I should seek you out right away."

Sarah felt suspicion continue to rise inside of her, and she jumped to her feet, not sure if she should stay or run. Considering the woman, she guessed that she was safe for the present and decided to remain standing, though wary.

Elizabeth blushed. "Oh goodness, I really am botching this. Let me explain. When the queen and king visited Emriville, it was to re-acquaint themselves with persons they had met before under much different circumstances. As Katy had lived with the queen before she had become queen, they continued in correspondences. I, on the other hand, had entered the queen's employ while she stayed in Emriville and continued in her employ when she left. Am I beginning to make any sense at all?"

Sarah nodded tentatively, but her crossed arms suggested that she was nowhere near trusting this woman who seemed to know far too much.

"When the queen returned home after Seth was buried, it was to find a Jeremy Caman waiting to seek an audience with her."

"Jeremy was in Silidon?" Sarah asked, her hostility melting at the mention of Caman.

"Well, yes. He was very concerned about you. At least he must have been, because he and the queen were not on good terms, so he risked a lot going to speak to her."

The Mirror

Sarah felt herself collapsing to an unladylike seat on the ground. Jeremy had gone to Silidon for her. *Why?*

"After Caman told the queen and king about his concern for you, they both were quite troubled, because just weeks earlier, Seth had been hanged for killing you, who were now possibly alive. She and the king wondered how best to deal with the situation when a letter arrived from Katy saying that you were in Emriville, and a Judge Bartholomew Gales reported a curious trial that had taken place in Croden to a knight very near to the king. There was also supposedly a journal found in Mr. Caman's possession that explained some things. After that, it was easy for the king and queen to decide that the only thing left to do was to send me to Emriville to speak to you about Seth."

The soft chirping of birds filled the meadow as Sarah sat head-in-hands trying to process all that Elizabeth had said. She felt herself grasping at straws trying to put all the pieces in order, yet amidst the chaos in her mind, one fact stood firm. "What more is there to know about Seth? My father had him killed and made sure everybody thought I was dead as well."

Elizabeth shook her head slowly. "That is only the beginning of the picture. I don't think it fair, though, to blame your father for everything that happened to Seth."

Anger rose like a beast inside of Sarah. "Fair, fair?" she shouted at the splendidly dressed woman still sitting on the ground. "What would you know of it? You've probably been coddled all your life with a father who adored you and gave you everything your pretty little heart desired. You don't know what it is like to scrape your way through life doing your best to be ignored by everyone because you have a child without a husband, and then when you try to go home, no one answers your letters. You don't know what that is like."

An unexpected fire blazed in Elizabeth's eyes, and when Sarah thought she would back down, she stood serenely, her face cold and emotionless as she replied in a calm voice. "I don't understand, do I? Tell me, Sarah Livton, what do you know of my life? Do you know that in Emriville, most people would have me hide my face and blush when passing by? They think I should be ashamed to be alive because everybody knows I am a bastard child. I saw my mother hang herself because she was unwilling to live with the reputation she had made for herself so that I was left to care for a man whom many considered stricken by God after he suffered multiple spells that left him more dead than alive. Yet, I cared for him because he was the closest thing to a father I had.

"Don't think I don't understand, Sarah. I have spent many years with the scars of one man's mistake, but I am learning more and more that I cannot blame him for all the hurt I have suffered. I can't blame my true father for the cruelty that other people have inflicted. I cannot blame him for the hurt that still resides in my heart, and I can't blame him for the unhappiness I have built up in my heart all on my own. He is just one man, and he made a mistake, but that does not mean he is the creator of all my woes."

It was Sarah's turn to blush once more. "I didn't know," she whispered.

"No you didn't," Elizabeth replied with a softness in her voice that let Sarah know she was forgiven for her ignorance. "You also didn't know that Seth went to Croden assuming he had murdered you. He

The Mirror

knew that he was going to die, and it didn't matter that your father faked your death. Seth admitted to murdering you."

"Still," Sarah said, tears forcing their way down her face, "my father could have told the truth. He could have let Seth know the truth. He could have let the entire community know the truth."

"So could you have. What kept you away from home for twelve long years?" she asked gently.

"Fear, shame," Sarah replied with a shrug. "I didn't think I could bear to see their pity, and I wasn't sure if my father would ever let me back in his home."

"But you could have come back and found out."

"I didn't want to find out. I didn't want to know what they had said about me while I was gone. I didn't want to know what they all thought of me now."

"Why? What could they possibly think about you that would be so horrible?"

"That I got what I deserved."

"Is that what you believe? Do you believe you go what you deserved?"

"Every time I look in the mirror, I see the scars. I see my limp, and I know that it was all my fault. I was too vain and too proud, and I caused the pain that both Seth and I experienced."

Again silence fell. There seemed little left to say, and Sarah was certain there was nothing Elizabeth could say to appease the ache in heart.

"Just as you can't blame your father entirely for Seth's death, neither can you blame yourself entirely for the pain in your life. Seth made his own choices, and I don't think he ever would have put any blame on you. He knew he could have protected you from his father. But I think this is enough talk of blame. We can't live our lives trying to blame someone for every little fault in this world, or there won't be a single person whose head isn't hung in shame."

"Easy for you to say. You don't have to be reminded every time you look in the mirror."

"Don't I? The only reason people were certain that I was an illegitimate child was because my hair was black rather than fair. I was tempted to cut off my hair when I was younger because I thought it would be better to be bald than to have this reminder every time I looked in the mirror."

"Then how do you ever look in the mirror now?"

"I'm learning that when I look in the mirror, I only see part of the story. I'm starting to see when I look in the mirror that even though I have dark hair and even though my past has been broken, God sees a much bigger picture than what I can see in the reflection, and that in his picture I am a child he loves even when others don't. I am a child he has washed of all shame and that no one can hold me to that shame anymore because Christ died to take it far away."

Sarah wiped at the tears on her face. "I've been angry at God a very long time," she whispered. "I have a hard time believing he could just forgive me now that I see I need his forgiveness."

"It took Seth a long time as well. He wanted to pay for his own salvation."

"Did he ever find forgiveness?"

Elizabeth smiled. "He did. He found God's forgiveness, and then he went to Croden to try and find forgiveness from your family. He would have sought you out directly, but he thought you dead."

The Mirror

"Nobody forgave him."

"We humans are really good at holding grudges, and seldom are we as gracious as we should be, considering the grace that has been shown us."

"Then why did Seth bother looking for forgiveness? He knew it wasn't likely to be given. He could have kept living in Emriville. He could have done a lot of good here. Katy told me what a marvellous minister he was. He could have kept being a minister and changed a lot of lives."

Elizabeth was shaking her head. "I can't say for sure what good there was in his death, but I know asking for forgiveness was the right thing for him to do. It would have been dishonest and, therefore, sinful for him to continue as a preacher. I can also tell you that I feel such pain from his death that sometimes I still get angry with God, but then I am reminded that it is just like looking in the mirror. I only see a poor portion of all that God is doing. If I could see everything he was doing, then I would understand why he let Seth die."

Sarah pushed herself up off the ground and began to pace. "I thought the only reason why I wanted to see Seth was because I wanted to talk to him." Elizabeth waited for Sarah to continue her thought. It was a few tearful minutes later before she finally said, "In truth, I wanted to see him again so I could unload some of the guilt I was carrying onto his shoulders. I thought that maybe if I could yell at him, if I could scream and see him cower under the same guilt that I have been living with for over twelve years, that maybe I would feel better. When I got to Croden and discovered he had been killed, I felt cheated, and I needed someone else to unload my guilt on. So, I tried to unload it all on my father, but it didn't make me feel any better."

"What do you want now, Sarah?"

"I just want to be done with all of it. I want to be able to live without the weight of my past. I want to look in the mirror and be content knowing that the past is done and that I don't have to live in guilt any more. I want to be happy again."

"No human can take your guilt away. I tried and tried to find a person to take away my shame, but only God can do that."

Sarah nodded slowly. "I think I've known that for a long time, but I've been too afraid to go to him."

"Just remember that he is far more merciful than we will ever be."

"Can you tell me more about what Seth was like in the end?"

Elizabeth grinned. "I think you would have loved him more than ever if you had seen him. He was incredibly handsome, with such a passionate way of speaking that it was easy to be persuaded by any one of his sermons."

"Was that my dad?"

Both Elizabeth and Sarah turned at the unexpected voice. "Come here, Samantha," Sarah called.

Sam ran to her mother, who wrapped her in her arms. "So, were you talking about my dad?"

"Yes, I was," replied Elizabeth. "Did you know you have his eyes?"

"I don't know if I want to have his eyes. My dad was a bad man."

"Your dad did a bad thing, but he also did a lot of good things. I don't think you should be upset that your dad did a bad thing when a lot of dads do bad things, my dad included."

"What did your dad do?" Sam asked.

The Mirror

"My dad left me and my mom when we needed him very much, and he never came back for me for a very long time, even when people said all sorts of bad things about me."

"Did you forgive him?"

"I'm working on it."

"I don't know if I can forgive my dad. I never even got a chance to meet him."

"Maybe your mom can tell you all about him, and then maybe it will be a little bit easier to forgive him."

"I could do that," whispered Sarah. "I'll do that for you, Sam. You should know all about what a great man he was. You should know how you are so much like him, yet so different at the same time."

"I think I would like that, but I still don't know if I will be able to forgive him."

"Well, maybe we can work on that together. Okay little girl?"

"I'll try."

Sarah turned to Elizabeth. "Thank you, for—for talking. It helped a lot."

"You are very welcome, but I must tell you yet that her majesty requested that you stay in Emriville, as Jeremy Caman is sure to join you here soon."

A faint blush crept up Sarah's neck. "Oh," she almost sighed. "I guess then we'll have to impose upon Mrs. Deplin's hospitality a little while longer."

"I am certain that she won't mind."

"Then perhaps we will see you around town?"

"Perhaps." Elizabeth waved as both Sam and Sarah moved away down the path leading from the meadow.

With a heavy sigh, Elizabeth leaned a little more heavily onto Seth's grave. "How I miss our early morning talks, Seth. There is so much going on right now that I wish I had someone to share it with. Someone who could help me make sense of it all."

"Perhaps you would be willing to talk to me about some of these things."

Elizabeth sighed heavily. "Sir Borden, I thought gentlemen didn't eavesdrop."

"I think that depends entirely on the gentleman," replied John. "Personally, I have found eavesdropping a very effective means of learning things that I have needed to know. Mind you, Rose has scolded me many times, saying I am rude to do such a thing."

"What have you been up to other than eavesdropping, Sir Borden?"

"Your father and I have spent the better part of the morning haggling with the innkeeper, explaining to him that indeed the king and queen required him to lower his outlandish prices as he would soon find himself without business if he did not. The bloke is a little bit thick, though, so it took us quite a while to get the message through. Your father is there still helping the poor fellow re-establish some order in his place."

"That does seem like a dilemma. I hope he hasn't caused too many problems."

"Nothing that can't be fixed. But speaking of problems, tell me what's on your mind."

The Mirror

"You don't want to hear my worries, Sir Borden. I am certain you have better things to do with your time."

"You are to call me John, and as of now, I have nothing to do. Besides, I am always very concerned if you have a problem."

"Perhaps that is my problem."

"Please do explain."

Elizabeth buried her face in her hands. "You don't understand, John. I've lived for years with no one caring what I did with my life. No one caring whether I had enough food or a warm place to sleep or someone to ask me how I was doing. Now it seems as if in a blink of the eye, I have a father, and I work for the queen. I wear expensive clothes that I feel just might make me trip and have so much food that I don't even prepare because there is some fancy cook somewhere preparing it for me. If that weren't enough, I have people asking me how I do every other minute in Silidon as if it is the most important question in the world."

John took a seat and began to pull at a patch of late-blooming dandelions. "I will be sure to tell Shoals that you wish to have less spoiling."

"Yes, and no. My father has been wonderful, but the change is just so overwhelming, and I feel so... so unworthy. I mean, I hardly have to work anymore, and the work I do is pure pleasure. I just feel there has to be something else. There has to be something I should do, or there should be some catch about it all."

"Elizabeth," John said, all hint of teasing out of his voice. "The problem is that none of us deserve the blessings we receive. That is part of what makes them gifts, but where I think you are wrong is that you believe you are somehow inferior to all the others at Silidon."

Elizabeth raised her hand as if to protest, but John hushed her. "Don't argue. I know you, and I know you have lived your life believing you weren't one iota to anybody. But now that has changed. And, do you want to know what the catch is?"

"Yes," sighed Elizabeth, relieved that just maybe there was something in all of this that made sense to her.

"The catch is, you have to give it all back. I don't mean that every time you receive a dress you should go give it to the poorhouse. What I mean is that it all belongs to God, so you should use what you have been given to honour him. Be generous with your money. Be kind to those who serve you and serve others as best you can. Do not look down on others because they are in a lower station. Those types of things."

"That doesn't sound too hard," whispered Elizabeth, and John laughed.

Reaching out a hand, John caressed Elizabeth's cheek. "Not to you, not yet. But someday, when you get used to having a father and wealth and important friends, it will start to get a little harder. The challenge will then be to continue with your generosity and not cling to earthly things, because they all eventually fade."

Elizabeth nodded. A blush crept up her neck. "There is still something else that confuses me."

"What's that?" John asked kindly, dropping his hand to his side.

"It's just that sometimes I think that maybe, by the things you say, that you want to be more than friends, but other times I'm not so sure, and I feel so confused inside. Sometimes I think that what I feel is... is maybe love, but then I get so scared. And I don't know if that is what you meant and... and..." Elizabeth stilted to an embarrassed stop.

The Mirror

"I shouldn't have said anything," she whispered when John didn't respond, and she stood to leave.

John stood as Elizabeth turned. "Did I ever tell you," he said before she could get very far, "that I love you?"

Elizabeth turned back to face him with an uncertain smile. "What do you mean by that, John? I thought you were going back to Silidon to propose to some high-class lady."

Taking a step forward, John took Elizabeth's hands. "I do want to propose. I have for some time now, but the girl's father asked for that time. He asked some time to get to know his daughter. I told him I would give him the amount of time it took me to woo my love."

"And what did this father say to your impertinent speech?"

"I didn't give him a chance to respond."

Elizabeth laughed. "Well then, how has wooing your lady love been going?"

"I'm about to find out." Keeping hold of Elizabeth's hands, John knelt down on one knee. "Elizabeth, I had so many notions of taking you for carriage rides and expensive dinners. I want to give you so much, and I wanted to propose to you in a much more romantic way, but I can no longer wait to hear your answer. I wish to marry you, if you will have me."

A large smile bloomed on Elizabeth's face as her uncertainty vanished. "Yes, John. I would love to marry you."

John pulled Elizabeth into a tight embrace. "I love you so much, my dearest Elizabeth."

"I love you too, John."

"Oh goodness," said John as he pulled out of the embrace, his cheeks flushing crimson. "I almost forgot." He started patting his pockets. "It is here. I've been carrying it around for so long." With a sigh of relief, John reached into his pocket and pulled out a ring.

It was Elizabeth's turn to blush. "Oh my. You can't mean that for me."

"You don't like it?"

"It's beautiful, John. But it must have cost you far too much."

Taking Elizabeth's left hand, John slipped the ring on her finger and pulled her close again. "It is worth it, for you."

Gently, softly, they shared their first kiss.

THIRTY-EIGHT

Caman tried to be patient as the carriage plodded slowly into Emriville. It all looked so familiar yet so foreign. He wondered if anyone would recognize him. He cringed at the thought of certain women remembering him. He had whispered many false promises the last time he was in town, and even if he wanted to, he could no longer fulfill them. The truth was, he had told them what they wanted to hear in order to get what he wanted.

"Did you see me then, Lord?" Caman whispered. "Did you see me, and still do you offer forgiveness?" He wasn't sure that God answered, but still the king's words haunted him.

"We'll be there in about five minutes," the driver told Caman as he urged the horse a little faster.

They passed out of the town and moved a little into the country before they came to a large house and barn that both looked freshly erected. The driver turned down the lane and stopped in front of the house. Opening the door, the driver bowed. "I will be at your disposal until the lady is back at her inn at Owzan."

"Thank you. I would offer you the use of the barn, but as this is not my place and I do not know the residents here..." Caman shrugged. "Perhaps they will be the generous sort."

The driver laughed. "Don't you worry any. The king has already made preparations for me. If you don't mind, I will take my horses and yours to the stables next to the inn. We will be just a short walk away, and well cared for."

Caman reached into his pocket and pulled out some coins. "Take these. I'm sure that should cover the cost of the horses at least."

Again the driver was laughing. "You've not spent enough time around the king. He has more than provided for the horses. Come claim your horse when you are ready, but you shall not be paying me anything."

Caman's mouth stood agape as the driver took the carriage and horses back toward town. The king's generosity was astounding, and Caman was sure he couldn't account for it.

The front door behind him burst open, startling him from his reverie.

"Jeremy, is that you?" Sarah was standing in the door, an apron over her dress as if she had just come from the kitchen at the inn. Caman smiled at her, liking the way her eyes danced in the sunlight.

"Hello Sarah," he said.

"Oh goodness," she whispered as she ran out into his embrace. "It is good to see you again. It has been far too long."

Caman closed his eyes and relished the feel of her in his arms. "I've missed you terribly," he whispered into her hair.

The Mirror

"Have you really?" she asked with a teasing look. "Come now, haven't you had your hands full with Isabelle and the inn?"

"I haven't been at the inn for over two weeks," Caman replied, taking Sarah's hand and walking toward the house, "and Isabelle is no longer in my life. I finally realized how much she was deceiving me into thinking she could give me what I wanted."

"Two weeks, Jeremy!" Sarah nearly shrieked. "Who's taking care of the inn?"

"Is that really all you think about, dearest Sarah? I am trying to pour out my heart to you, and you ask about the inn?"

A look of concern wrinkled her brow. "But my inn, Jeremy?"

A small smile crept onto his face. "You are so concerned about your inn, yet you left it in my hands when I can't even make a decent bowl of porridge."

Sarah giggled, then grabbed her mouth as if to hold back a more robust laugh. "What was I thinking?" She finally allowed herself to laugh. "You must have scared everyone away."

"If only," Caman grumbled. "Your leaving was good enough gossip to bring all the biddies in to buy at least a little gruel so they could chat about the horrible Mr. Caman."

"Well, they were right. Such a horrible man to leave an inn that was bequeathed to him. He should have been ashamed of himself."

"Ashamed to admit defeat as a cook and leave your inn in the capable hands of the young Callaway ladies?"

"But how did you ever convince them?"

"They enjoyed their work the last time, and I said we would pay them wages."

"Jeremy, I can hardly pay you wages."

Caman let out a heavy sigh. "Do you think that I can wait to explain how you are now a wealthy woman until after we have talked about much more important things?"

Sarah's mouth formed a small 'o' before she regained her thoughts and pushed open the door to allow them into the front room.

"The Deplins have been very generous with their time and their home. Sam and I have been enjoying our time here, and I believe there is someone here as well whom you will recognize. Her name is Elizabeth Mede. Apparently she works for the queen. There is also the queen's cousin, Sir John Borden, and a Sir Shoals. We really have been enjoying ourselves. I have been helping Katy in the kitchen, as she has never had to serve so many."

Caman clung to Sarah's hand as she led him through the house, and for the first time in a long time, he prayed for wisdom, for strength, for forgiveness, and most of all for Sarah. He wasn't sure if his prayer was heard, but still he smiled as Sarah kept rambling on their way to the kitchen.

It wasn't until much later that he had a chance to speak privately with Sarah again.

"So," Sarah said, "you say I am rich and that I own a horse. Sam is very excited about that, but I would like to see this horse that I supposedly own."

Caman held out his hand. "Why don't you come for a walk with me, and I will show you."

"That sounds lovely. I'll go get Sam. She will want to see the horse."

The Mirror

"Not this time. I will show Sam tomorrow. For now, there are things we need to talk about. Things that Sam does not need to be around to hear. At least, not for now."

"I'll go get my wrap."

The two walked silently toward the town. "Much has happened over the past few weeks," Caman said. Sarah only nodded, allowing Caman to continue at his own pace. "You're different than when you left. Happier."

"I have more to make me happy now."

"Is that because Seth is dead?"

Sarah shook her head. "No, I would rather he wasn't. I think I would like to see him again, but I am told that he was a believer in the end."

"Is that so?"

"Mm-hm."

"Sarah," Caman began, not sure how to continue. He stopped walking, took her hand, and placed it in the crook of his arm. "I—I'm not sure how to explain it all, but Isabelle is no longer in my life. I thought for a while that she could make me feel whole inside. Especially after you left."

Sarah squeezed his arm gently and pulled him forward. Caman sighed heavily and used his free hand to rub absentmindedly at his jaw.

"What happened?" Sarah asked.

"She has a daughter. I have a niece that she just left at an orphanage, and I couldn't bear the thought of that."

"So what did you do?"

"I ran away from her."

Sarah laughed, and Caman frowned at her. "I'm sorry," she gasped. "I can just imagine you running from her, she being so tiny, and you so big." Sarah chortled once more before she grabbed her mouth to hold back her laughter.

Caman smiled as the picture she painted came before his mind. She was right. It was ridiculous.

"Then what did you do?"

"Well, I gave up trying to run the inn. And I already told you about Martha's diary and going to the king and queen. I was so desperate and miserable there. Both my attempts at being happy and whole again had seemed to disappear, and the monarchs didn't seem to promise that I would find you again."

Caman turned to Sarah and, brushing a hand down the side of her face, he smiled sadly. "I still thought that if I found you, and if you agreed to marry me, I would be whole again."

"Do you still believe that?" Sarah asked, a little breathless.

"No," Caman replied, and a smile bloomed across Sarah's face.

"I am glad to hear that. Because if you only knew how broken I am, you would be running the other way."

Taking Sarah's hand once more, Caman continued to walk. "The king showed me that the only one who can make me whole is God."

"And do you believe that?"

"I am trying to."

"Me too," Sarah whispered.

Caman stopped suddenly and stared.

"What?" Sarah asked.

The Mirror

Caman's mouth gaped for some time before a laugh made its way right from the pit of his stomach. "Oh Sarah, I do believe that God is telling me 'I told you so.'"

"What on earth are you talking about, Jeremy?"

"I was so afraid that you would be annoyed with me for talking about God. I thought I would lose you for sure. But the king said to trust God, and well, goodness. I believe I am being shown."

"Me angry with you for talking about God? Don't be silly, Jeremy. I would have been furious with you. But it seems we were both meant to be convicted by God."

"Is that why you are happy now?"

"Incredibly, immensely, wonderfully so."

The two walked on slowly. They came to the stable, and Caman showed off the horse he had bought for Sarah. Then it was time to walk home.

"You know what it feels like?" Sarah asked as she brushed shoulders with Caman. "It feels like I have been sick for a very long time. Like the flu, or something more sinister that was eating away at me. Like I was slowly dying inside, just looking for one more reason to get through the day."

"Mmm. I think I considered myself, ah, let me think, how did the one man phrase it to me? Ah yes, he called me a poisoned apple."

"Really? Why did he call you that?"

Caman cleared his throat and looked away. "Let's just say he found me and his daughter in a compromising situation."

"Oh." Sarah blushed. "Well then, I suppose he was being very polite."

"Indeed, I thought he was being very kind, but the picture stuck with me. A poisoned apple, ruined for all time."

"Then I would be, hmm. I suppose I would be the blemished peach, the one no one wants to pick because there is something wrong. My stain of guilt."

"So we were both rotting away."

Sarah was laughing again. "Sam would have a fit if she heard us comparing ourselves to fruit."

"Then I would have to tell her that just because she's a nut, it doesn't mean she can't be a part of our fruit family."

"Oh goodness," Sarah laughed. "I haven't heard a joke like that since... since I lived with my father." A dark shadow fell across her face. "My... my father," she whispered again, more sadly. A tear slid down her face. "I may never speak to my father again, and I never got a chance to say goodbye to my mother."

Caman pulled Sarah close, and she cried softly into his shoulder. "I'm sorry," she whispered when her tears had passed. "But with everything that has been going on, it just hadn't sunk in yet."

"Don't be sorry. I was once told that there's a time for mourning."

"And after that time?"

"I think, after that time, there is a time for healing."

"I like that. Though right now it is hard sometimes to see past this hurt."

"Now we see but a poor reflection as in a mirror."

"What was that, Jeremy?"

Caman smiled and pulled Sarah into a tight hug. "Something I learned at the palace."

The Mirror

"Will you tell me about it?" Sarah asked.

"Someday," replied Caman. "Someday."

EPILOGUE

"WHY THE SOMBRE FACE, my love?"

"Oh Henry," Rose sighed. "I'm trying to find someone to replace Elizabeth. Now that she and John are getting married, I can't very well expect her to stay on as a nursery maid. It really is a bother to find someone."

"Aren't you happy that John and Elizabeth are getting married?" Henry asked as he took a seat next to his wife.

"Thrilled," replied Rose as she flipped through the pages in front of her. "I just never thought there would be so many people who I would need to interview for a nursery maid."

Henry took the papers from Rose and placed them into a neat pile at the side of the writing desk. "Let my mother take care of that," Henry said. "Or at least let her help," he added when Rose glowered at him. "She loves this sort of work, and she is bored."

The Mirror

"Very well." Rose stretched as she leaned back in her chair. "What have you got there?" she asked when she turned to look at her husband.

"Ah. This is something that is sure to make your day a little better."

Rose held out her hand to take the envelope, but he withheld it. "Not so fast, my lady love. I think I deserve a reward for delivering this letter so rapidly."

"Oh, and what type of reward would a king wish for?"

"A kiss from my queen, of course."

Rose gave him an assessing look, then leaned forward and gave him a kiss on the forehead.

"Hardly a kiss."

"Well, your task is hardly completed. If you wish to collect the rest of your reward, I would think it necessary for you to deliver to me the letter."

Henry laughed and handed it over.

"It is from Jeremy Caman," Rose said. Henry nodded. "Let's see what he has to say."

My Dearest Monarchs,

"Henry why didn't you open this letter? It is addressed to you as well."

"I thought you might like to read it first, my love."

"Yes I would. Thank you, dearest."

Henry smiled and leaned back in his chair with a lazy smile. "Please continue, my queen. Your king is waiting anxiously for his reward."

Rose smiled and continued to read.

Cassandra Nywening

I pray you do not find me impertinent for writing. Sarah and I wished only to thank you for all you have done for us, and I thought perhaps you would like to hear the end of my story.

Sarah and I met up in Emriville, where we spent a few days in the house of Katy and Josh Deplin. Their hospitality was a blessing from the Lord, as it allowed me the time to reacquaint and make peace with my mother before leaving for Owzan once more. Once we reached Owzan, I am relieved to say that Sarah agreed to become my wife. Stuart Morgan promised to perform the wedding ceremony.

This is where I must relate some sorry news. Mrs. Morgan, who for some years has been battling illness, finally succumbed. It is funny. I never knew her name until the day of her funeral, and when I learned it I couldn't help but wonder at the irony. Her name was Ruth, meaning friend. It seemed odd to me that the friendless one would be named friend. Yet the more I think of the great services she did for this community in the quiet of her own home without anyone knowing, the more I realize, she is the greatest friend this community had, and she will be sorely missed.

Stuart Morgan mourns in his own manner. He has become more solemn and his smile is less forthcoming. But, he carries on, day by day. Sarah and I wished to give him some time before he was to marry us, but he insists that he would love it if we would have the wedding within the next few weeks. So our planning commences.

The Mirror

    There is one more matter which may be of some interest to you. Isabelle was still in Owzan when we returned. The Callaways said she had been haunting the inn while we were away. Her presence reminded me of something I had pushed to the back of my mind. With Sarah's approval, I approached Isabelle and discovered the date of birth of her daughter, my niece.

    Isabelle did not like my questions and when she realized I was not going to give in to her temptations any longer, she disappeared. I don't know where she went. Mr. Mitchel informed me that she had appeared at his place but was promptly told to leave. She has not been seen since.

    The information I have gleaned from her has been most helpful. I have contacted the orphanage in Emriville, and a child there matches the description I have provided. Her name is Anna. By the time you receive this letter, she will be on our doorstep as the newest member of our family.

    We are all nervous, to say the least. We do not know what it will be like to have another child in the house, but we could not leave her once we knew of her existence. We can only trust now that God will provide.

    This is the end of my story, and the beginning of my new life. I will forever be grateful to your majesties for the part you played in bringing Sarah and me together. As it is, I remain your humble servant.

    Jeremy Caman

"Well," sighed Rose. "I am happy for him."

"Good, but I wonder, now that you have read your letter, do I get my reward?" Henry teased.

"I don't know," Rose teased back. "I believe I have already given you satisfactory payment."

"Hardly." Getting up from his chair, Henry leaned over his seated wife and gave her a kiss full of promises for the happy years to come.

Also in the Hidden Grace Trilogy:

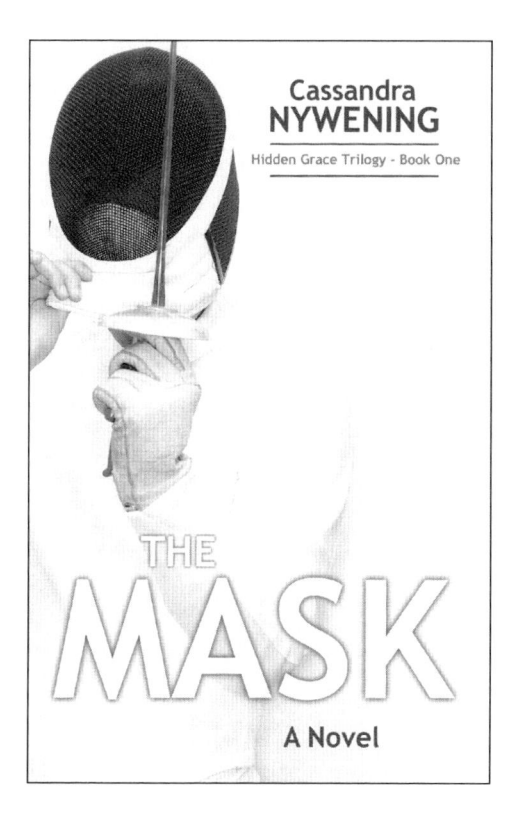

Book One: *The Mask*

Rose Wooden is only seventeen years old and not ready for marriage! Forced into choosing a spouse within the year, she is torn between the curate, Caleb Taylor, who seems perfect; and the mysterious stranger, James Hyden.

Meanwhile, Prince Henry Arden is searching for a bride who will love him for who he is and not his money. Rose is the strangest lady he has ever met, and he finds it refreshing. He only wonders what she will think when she finds out his secret.

Also in the Hidden Grace Trilogy:

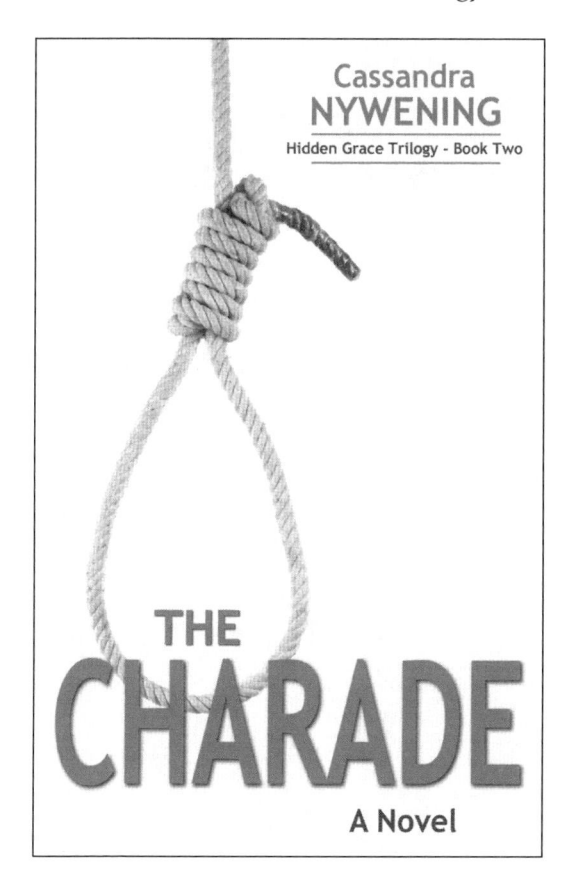

> Cassandra
> **NYWENING**
> Hidden Grace Trilogy - Book Two
>
> **THE CHARADE**
> A Novel

Book Two: *The Charade*

The upcoming visit of the King and Queen has the town abuzz. But not everyone is so happy. Caleb Taylor sits in agony wondering if he will be able to keep the secret from the Queen he had once professed to love, and Elizabeth Mede tries to fade into the background even as she is constantly pursued by the Queen's cousin. Caleb and Elizabeth begin to find solace in each other's company. However, time passes, secrets surface, and not a single person is left untouched or unchanged.